"[*The Gun*] offers an addictive—one might even say compulsive—night's worth of chillingly unnerving entertainment."   —*The Richmond Times-Dispatch*

"[Nakamura] straddles the crime-literary fiction boundary like few others. It gives a new twist to Chekhov's rule: a gun mentioned in the first act—or here, a gun found by a dead body in the opening pages—must eventually be fired."   —*Maclean's*

"[A] powerful existential thriller."   —*The Sunday Times* (UK)

"The psychological downward spiral into obsession is what drives this book, and during my reading, I couldn't help but think that Alfred Hitchcock could have created a brilliant film adaptation."   —*BookPage*

Praise for *Last Winter, We Parted*

"Crime fiction that pushes past the bounds of genre, occupying its own nightmare realm . . . For Nakamura, like [Seichō] Matsumoto, guilt or innocence is not the issue; we are corrupted, complicit, just by living in society. The ties that bind, in other words, are rules beyond our making, rules that distance us not only from each other but also from ourselves."   —*Los Angeles Times*

"This slim, icy, outstanding thriller, reminiscent of Muriel Spark and Patricia Highsmith, should establish Fuminori Nakamura as one of the most interesting Japanese crime novelists at work today."   —*USA Today*

"Some of the darkest noir fiction to come out of Japan—or any country—in recent years . . . Nakamura's stories, however labeled, are memorable forays into uncomfortable terrain."   —*Mystery Scene*

"A tense, layered story . . . [Nakamura's] stripped-down prose and direct style drop the reader straight into his nightmare."   —*The Japan Times*

"A coldly sophisticated, darkly disturbing logic puzzle written in the style of the great ice queen of the genre, Patricia Highsmith."   —*Richmond Times-Dispatch*

"Deeply erotic and haunting . . . climaxes with a shocking twist."
    —*Ellery Queen Mystery Magazine*

"Extremely dark and certainly twisted."   —*Suspense Magazine*

Praise for *The Kingdom*

"Nakamura has described *The Kingdom* as a sister novel to *The Thief* . . . But the new novel bests its companion."   —*The New York Times Book Review*

"Few protagonists in modern crime fiction are as alienated as those in the challenging, violent, grotesque tales of Japanese author Fuminori Nakamura . . . Yurika's struggle to escape her vexed fate elevates this shocker well above the lurid."
    —*The Wall Street Journal*

"Multilayered and intense . . . [The] monstrous crime lord 'Kizaki' is a formidable nemesis." —*The Independent* (UK)

"Dark and strangely seductive . . . A recommended read for fans of noir as well as for anyone looking to be mesmerized by a masterful storyteller."—*Pank Magazine*

"A face-paced, dark novel of psychological suspense, told in a succinctly poetic style." —*Ellery Queen Mystery Magazine*

Praise for *Evil and the Mask*

"Karma runs thicker than blood in *Evil and the Mask*, the thought-provoking and unpredictable new novel by the Japanese zen-noir master Fuminori Nakamura." —*The Wall Street Journal*

"A brilliant novel from one of Japan's most current authors . . . If you love Patricia Highsmith, you'll love Nakamura." —*Globe and Mail*

"A hard-to-put-down novel of ideas and a savage comment on nihilism, both Japanese and global . . . Shouldn't be missed." —*Booklist*, Starred Review

"A twisted tale of revenge . . . mixing noir and the existential question of free will." —*The Japan Times*

"Full of themes that everyone can appreciate . . . Nakamura blurs the line between light and dark, good and evil. He illustrates that nothing in life is completely black and white." —*Tulsa Books Examiner*

Praise for *The Boy in the Earth*

"Absorbing . . . Just what abuse the narrator suffered as a youth is one of the puzzles to be solved (in horrific detail) by *The Boy in the Earth*. Another mystery is whether he will find a nonfatal way to break out of his Kafkaesque memory palace. By the book's end, the reader comes to care about the second answer as much as the first." —*The Wall Street Journal*

"Although many orders of magnitude darker, Nakamura may be the spiritual heir to Kenzaburō Ōe. This is existential literature at its compelling and nauseating best . . . His work isn't merely noir as titillation; it's the hideous truth below the surface, and he is one of the most vital writers at work today in Japan." —*The Japan Times*

"[Nakamura] has demonstrated time and again, and does so again here, that he is one of the best crime novelist working today." —*Pank Magazine*

"*The Boy in the Earth* offers readers a darkly philosophic musing on violence, history, purpose and what it means to be alive, told in elegant prose." —Shelf Awareness

CULT
X

FUMINORI NAKAMURA

Translated from the Japanese by Kalau Almony

SOHO
CRIME

Original Japanese edition published in 2014 by Shueisha Inc., Tokyo.
This English edition published by arrangement with Tuttle-Mori Agency, Inc.,
Tokyo, on behalf of Shueisha Inc., Tokyo.

First published in English in 2018 by
Soho Press
853 Broadway
New York, NY 10003

Library of Congress Cataloging-in-Publication Data
Nakamura, Fuminori, 1977–author. Almony, Kalau, translator.
Title: Cult X / Fuminori Nakamura ; translated by Kalau Almony.

ISBN978-1-61695-786-5
eISBN 978-1-61695-787-2

1. Cults—Japan—Fiction. 2. Terrorism—Japan—Fiction. 3. Criminals—Japan—
Fiction. 4. Suspense fiction. 5. Mystery fiction. I. Title.
PL873.5.A339 C8513 2018   895.63'6—dc23 2017043255

Interior design by Janine Agro, Soho Press, Inc.
Case design concept by Jeff Wong

Printed in Canada

10 9 8 7 6 5 4 3 2 1

CULT
X

O Varuna, what has been my greatest transgression?—*Rigveda*

"She's alive."

The bar's blue lights faintly illuminated Narazaki's face. Their malicious glow seemed to bleach the color from his body. *Has his face always looked like that?* Kobayashi wondered. He looked like he'd lost something he needed to go on living. Yet his gaze was terribly powerful, and had a strange radiance.

"She's really alive?" Narazaki's voice was rough.

"I wouldn't lie, and it's no mistake. Ryoko Tachibana is alive." The woman who had vanished from Narazaki's life, who had hinted at suicide and then disappeared.

Kobayashi realized quite a bit of his whiskey was gone. His hand was moving his glass to his lips automatically. He was almost unsure he was in control of it.

"Okay, look." Kobayashi hesitated. "I don't think you should get involved."

"Why?"

"Well . . ."

To Kobayashi, Narazaki's relationship with Ryoko Tachibana had always seemed a bit off. When Kobayashi had happened to see her last month, he hadn't had the courage to speak to her, but—maybe it was because of the work he did—he'd decided to tail her. She'd gone into an old apartment building. Without a doubt, it had been her.

"You looked into it for me, right? Tell me what you found."

"Well . . ."

Kobayashi could hear shouting coming from a table at the far side of the room. The voices gradually lost strength and vanished, as if dissolving into the darkness.

A few weeks ago, when Kobayashi had told him he'd seen Ryoko Tachibana, Narazaki had looked surprised, but also seemed to have already known. Like it somehow made sense to him. Kobayashi had given Narazaki the address of the apartment building, but for some strange reason Narazaki had insisted Kobayashi investigate instead. It was true, Kobayashi did work at a P.I.'s office, but he hadn't even been there six months. So far he'd mostly just assisted the other investigators, and had never worked a case alone. He'd felt a case like this would be too much for him. But he'd taken the job, if reluctantly, and he had actually discovered quite a lot in a short time. There was something odd about that, he thought. *How could someone like me, someone still training, find so much out so easily?*

"Is there some big secret? Something that would hurt me?"

"Not exactly . . ."

A peal of laughter from another distant table. In the dim light of the restaurant, Kobayashi could only make out the outlines of the people laughing. He caught himself drinking again. He was trying to get drunk. Why?

Should I tell Narazaki what I'm worried about? Kobayashi wondered. He had all the material he'd collected about Ryoko Tachibana in his bag. She'd been born in Nagasaki Prefecture, had attended elementary through high school there, and then moved to Tokyo to enroll in Rikkyo University. But she'd withdrawn, and that trail of information ended. She next surfaced at a meeting held at the facility of a certain small religious organization in Tokyo—the kind of organization people didn't hear many good things about. But eventually she'd vanished again. She reappeared last year, and that was when she met Narazaki. There were no traces of her life between the time she left that religious organization and when she met him. She'd just somehow appeared before Narazaki, then vanished again.

This religious group also bothered Kobayashi. It was the sort of thing one just shouldn't get involved in.

And now she had already moved out of the apartment he'd seen her enter.

Kobayashi stared listlessly at the counter. The three bartenders looked like triplets. They moved slowly and emotionlessly. Kobayashi shook his head slightly.

"I understand you're puzzled. But, in any case, she's not dead. That I confirmed. And given that . . . Look, what's clear is that she left you. She probably had her reasons. I understand that's not enough to satisfy you, but she left you."

Kobayashi's whole investigation of this woman had felt strange. As he traced her history, it was as if a single line had been prepared for him to follow. Like she was somewhere in the distance, beckoning him. Kobayashi took another sip of whiskey. She should have known he worked at an investigator's office. Had she shown herself to him that first time on purpose? But why? Why would she do that?

"Listen." Kobayashi turned to face Narazaki. "Let me say this clearly. I've got a bad feeling about this. You shouldn't try to find her. There's no need for you to get dragged into whatever this is."

"Why?"

"You have your life."

"My life?"

"You could get hurt."

"That doesn't matter."

Kobayashi would remember, for the rest of his life, Narazaki's next words.

"The life I lived . . . That life has no value at all."

Kobayashi stared for a second at Narazaki's face. In the end, he handed him the envelope filled with everything he'd found about Ryoko Tachibana. There was a small commotion at the table next to them. Kobayashi sipped his whiskey. As he drank, he realized he was getting drunk so he would be able to give the envelope to Narazaki.

He watched Narazaki open the envelope, wondering what his role was. If this were a novel, he probably wouldn't be anything more than a side character. Whatever happened to whom, it would have nothing to do with him. He'd just be the cog that happened to set things in motion.

The other customers gradually headed home. Eventually, only Narazaki and Kobayashi were left in the dim bar. The blue lights illuminated only Narazaki.

Though there was no longer any need for him to drink,

Kobayashi ordered another whiskey. His life had no value—that's what Narazaki said. *That may be true*, Kobayashi thought. Even to Kobayashi, Narazaki's life did not seem like a fulfilled one. Certainly, his life was not something anyone would be jealous of. Just like Kobayashi's.

PART 1

In front of Narazaki was a gate.

It was an old, enormous wooden gate. There was something written on it, but the characters had faded and Narazaki
couldn't make them out. *Should I go straight in?* Narazaki was
unsure. *There's something strange about this place. But isn't it
just a normal house? It seems more like a house than a church
or temple.*

The gate cut through the frigid air and towered over Narazaki. It seemed like it was looking down on him, testing him,
about to pass down some sort of judgment. Looking up at
the gate, Narazaki was made aware of the smallness of his
own body. He wasn't ready to go in, so he walked past. The
building was surrounded by tall brick-and-clay walls, and
Narazaki couldn't see inside.

He recalled Kobayashi's report. Ryoko Tachibana
had certainly belonged to this group. The founder was

named Shotaro Matsuo, a man who called himself an amateur intellectual. The group seemed to be some sort of religious organization, but they didn't have a proper name, they weren't registered as a religion, and the whole concept of "believing in" their faith seemed foreign to them. They didn't worship a particular god—in fact, the group's focus seemed to be pondering the question, "Is there a god?"

What were they? Narazaki didn't understand.

As he passed the gate, Narazaki thought to himself, *I always do this. I always hesitate.* It was as though he wanted to spend the rest of his life stuck, the days sinking away heavily. Though they were unhappy, he wanted to savor that unhappiness. The languor seemed to be his very flesh, and he could never leave it. But he had decided to stop living that way. He would follow the pull of the gravity he had begun to feel within himself. He would give himself up to whatever came. He didn't care what would come of it.

He made one loop around the building. *I am walking now,* Narazaki thought. *Walking, without paying attention to anything. How can I walk this way? Like my heart and other organs just keep moving on their own. Like they're strangers wriggling in my body.* Narazaki took a deep breath. *What am I thinking? It's because of that gate—it's messed up my mind.*

He was here to find out what he could about Ryoko Tachibana.

He was back in front of the gate. It was still too big. Just as he was about to open it, he noticed the intercom. His finger reached toward the button. He wasn't ready. *What will happen if this is a cult? Maybe they'll lock me up.* His pulse quickened. *Maybe I'll be brainwashed and go mad. Maybe I'll wind up one of those paranoid nut jobs without even realizing I've been brainwashed into acting that way.* Narazaki pressed the button. He heard a dull chime. *I pushed it. It's too late now.*

"Yes?" It was the voice of a middle-aged woman. Not what Narazaki had expected.

"Is Shotaro Matsuo in?"

"To whom am I speaking?"

Narazaki's body tensed up. *No going back now.*

"My name's Toru Narazaki. I'm . . . I'm not really anyone."

If I ask where Ryoko Tachibana is right away, they probably won't tell me. I'll just pretend I'm interested in their group, and ask about her a little at a time. I'm not going to join them or anything. Narazaki realized he was smiling.

"Not anyone?"

"Yeah."

"So you're not with the media?"

"No. If you want, you can look through my things."

"You need to see the old man—I mean, Matsuo-san—about something?"

"Yes."

There was a pause, and then the gate finally opened from the inside. Three people came to meet Narazaki: a middle-aged man and woman and a younger woman. Narazaki had imagined they'd all be dressed in white shrouds or something, but all three were wearing normal clothes. The middle-aged woman had on an apron printed with Rilakkuma, the brown cartoon bear. Narazaki was a bit surprised.

"Please, come in."

Narazaki entered. On the other side of the gate was a large open space. Faintly blue gravel covered the ground, which was scattered with stepping stones. *It looks like a Shinto shrine*, Narazaki thought. But there were no torii gates. There was also a large pond, but there didn't seem to be any koi.

The middle-aged woman in the Rilakkuma apron said, "I'm sorry for asking, but you really aren't with the media?"

"No. I'm just curious about your religion."

"Religion?" asked the middle-aged man. There was a little white in his short-cropped hair, but the expression on his face was youthful. "Well, we don't practice any religion here."

"You don't?"

"It's hard to explain," the younger woman said. "Do you want to learn about healing power?"

"Healing power?" Narazaki asked. He was a bit surprised.

"You're not interested in that? Well then, we should start with his talks."

"Yeah, that's a good idea." The middle-aged man laughed at Narazaki's confusion. "We can let him inside the house, can't we? He doesn't look like he'll cause any harm."

Several people were sitting on the wooden veranda that ringed the mansion. Narazaki felt their stares as he was led from the gate into the house. *Is this okay?* Narazaki wondered. *How are they letting me through so easily?* He had no choice but to follow.

The mansion was large but old, and, compared to the exterior, the inside was unimpressive. Narazaki was taken to a spacious tatami sitting room at least forty square meters in size. Its stillness seemed to be in direct proportion to its size. He took a seat on a cushion.

"Your name was Toru Narazaki, right? I'm Yoshida," said the middle-aged man.

"My name is Mineno, and the woman in the apron is Tanaka-san," the young woman added. Mineno had thin eyes. She was beautiful.

"Where did you hear about us?"

"From a friend."

"A friend? Ah, I see."

What did she see? He had hoped they would press him further. He had answers prepared for them.

The young woman spoke again. "I know you went out of your way to come here, but I'm sorry to say Matsuo-san isn't in."

"He's not here?"

"No. He's been sick."

Yoshida laughed. "It's funny, right? The man heals others, but then goes and gets sick! And on top of that, he can't use his healing powers on himself, so he winds up in a university hospital, getting treated with Western medicine!"

"Shut up!" Mineno told Yoshida. But she was holding back her laughter, too.

What was going on? They were laughing at their leader getting sick?

"We should explain," Mineno said. "Healing power is mostly just a joke. Matsuo-san doesn't really think he can heal people." She smiled. "And it's a bit strange for us to let you in even though he's in the hospital, but we have a rule to not send anyone away."

"How much do you know about this place?" asked

Yoshida, as the woman with the Rilakkuma apron came in, carrying tea.

Narazaki thanked her. He still didn't have the courage to say what he wanted. "Honestly, I don't know much."

"That's impressive, showing up without knowing anything," Yoshida said, laughing. "So, shall we tell you a little about this place? Don't get your hopes up. We're not a religion, so we can't be sure we'll meet your expectations. The people who've shown up lately have come expecting too much. We have to make sure they don't get disappointed and cause any trouble."

HERE WAS what they told him.

Shotaro Matsuo, the owner of the mansion, often meditated alone in his garden.

Long ago, there were no walls, and passersby could see him meditating. He was known in the neighborhood as a weird old man. No one knew about his past, or even if he'd always lived there. It seemed he had just appeared one day in this old mansion that everyone had assumed was abandoned.

One day, an old woman suffering from an inexplicable pain in her legs stopped by. She asked Matsuo to pray over her. Even doctors couldn't figure out what was causing the pain, so she visited every faith healer she could, but she saw no improvement. "You're always sitting here, meditating," she said. "You might have some kind of power. Won't you pray for my legs, just to see?"

Matsuo was surprised, and said he didn't have that sort of power, but he invited the old woman into his mansion for tea. Matsuo lived with his wife, Yoshiko. The three of them talked about many things. Both Matsuo and his wife, Yoshiko, sympathized with the woman's pain. Matsuo tried rubbing the woman's legs, but nothing happened.

"Thank you anyway," the woman said. "Can I come again?"

The Matsuos nodded. She visited for several weeks, and the woman's legs began to get better.

"BUT, LIKE I told you, don't get your hopes up. The cause of that woman's pain was stress," Yoshida said. "That's how religious healers have been treating illnesses forever. Sure, there may be some people who have actual powers, but I can tell you that Matsuo-san isn't one of them. Like Jesus said, faith will save you. That's at least partially true. There are legends that when Jesus Christ first appeared, he cured tons of sick people. It's probably true. If you really believed from the bottom of your heart that this man had the power to cure, that he really was the son of God—well. The human body's ability to cure itself is truly amazing, and stress causes so many ailments. If you're overcome by emotion from seeing God right in front of you, that emotion may activate something amazing inside you."

Yoshida smiled.

"And I think exorcisms are the same sort of thing. Some exorcists may actually drive out evil spirits, but some just *convince* the subject that all the stress inside their body is a single spirit that they can banish. Look, I'm not criticizing anyone for their beliefs. As human civilization has progressed, we've given up on those methods of healing. We no longer recognize gods and spirits as causes of illness, so we don't try to activate the body's own immune system by invoking those things. I'm sure before modern medicine this was an incredibly important form of healing for people."

THE WOMAN whose legs healed spread Matsuo's praise through the town. Gradually, people started visiting, then claiming their mysterious heart palpitations and their stiff necks got better. Matsuo continued to tell everyone that he didn't have any special power, but his insistence began to offend the people who believed in him. Matsuo truly wanted everyone to get better, so he found himself in a dilemma. He was being made a religious figure against his will.

Of course, many people didn't get better. Those who didn't began to censure Matsuo. It must be awful to not be healed when others are. Matsuo didn't take money or anything, so there wasn't too much of a problem. But little by little this organization began to change.

"DON'T YOU feel calm here?" Mineno asked.

Looking at their smiling faces, Narazaki found it more and more difficult to breathe.

"There are plenty of trees," Mineno went on, "and with the gravel garden, all the sound gets sucked up. It's so peaceful, like being at a shrine."

"That's very true," Narazaki said, his voice emotionless.

"More and more people started saying that just being here makes them feel good. They said maybe instead of healing power, there's just something about being here . . . Maybe this place is what they call a power spot. People have even come from other prefectures. They never seem particularly religious. They're just like, 'We heard there's something here.' Matsuo-san and everyone opened up the garden, and people would say, 'If you got a torii, it would be just like a shrine.' Matsuo-san has always had something about him that attracts people. We started holding an event once a month. We set up a bunch of folding chairs and everyone listens to Matsuo-san speak. It's almost like a natural phenomenon. We've been doing it since the end of the bubble, when society seemed so uneasy."

Narazaki nodded, although he didn't really want to hear more about Matsuo.

Yoshida began speaking again. "Whether you find Matsuo-san's talks interesting or not, they're unique. He never says, 'Believe in this god.' It's more like, 'I wonder if this god's out there.' Even young people like the talks, since he's always questioning. It doesn't cost anything to attend our gatherings, so it's rather low pressure."

Narazaki nodded again. *What should I do?* he thought. *Why is Ryoko Tachibana involved with this kind of group?* He couldn't see why she had to vanish. He had no interest in the history of this group. It was not the religious fringe organization Narazaki had imagined. He'd hoped to stumble into something wilder, something that would change him completely. Something that would make him lose all concern for morals and ethics and the confused human condition. Something that would obliterate him and the life he had lived until now.

Narazaki had no business with these kind people. There was no need to listen to these boring stories. There was no need to hesitate anymore. He spoke up. "There's a woman, Ryoko Tachibana, who I think came here."

They all looked at him.

"What? You're looking for someone? You didn't come to hear about Matsuo-san?"

"Well, that, too. But I'm also looking for this woman."

"We wouldn't know her by that name," Yoshida said. "There's no membership or registration system here. And people also use fake names."

"This is her," Narazaki said, taking out a photo. Everyone in the room looked at the picture. It was just a few seconds, but it felt infinitely long to Narazaki. The uneasy silence seemed to make the room grow even larger.

"This woman?" Yoshida stared at Narazaki. He was no longer smiling. "How do you know this woman?"

"Wait," Mineno said, as if to stop Yoshida. But she was clearly unsettled. "I'm sorry, but—are you involved with this woman?"

What happened? They're all looking at me. Narazaki took a mindful breath. "It's a bit difficult to explain our relationship. But I'm looking for her."

"Why?" Yoshida asked quietly.

Should I tell them everything? Will I get tangled up in something strange? Narazaki caught himself smiling. "She ran away."

"Ran away? Do you know what kind of person you're looking for?"

"What kind of person? What do you mean?"

"He doesn't know," Mineno said to Yoshida. "If he knew about her, he'd know he wouldn't find her here."

"You're right."

The room grew quiet again. The woman in the apron stared at the floor, unsure of what to do.

"Whatever happens, you should probably listen to what

we have to say," Mineno said. "It's probably easiest to understand if we explain from the beginning . . . About what happened to Matsuo-san, and the people who came here. I think that will be the easiest way to explain who this woman is . . . And I think you'll want to hear this."

The wind began to blow gently, causing the windows of the sitting room to rattle as if in pain. *The air is dry*, Narazaki thought. *If I lit a fire, I wonder if it would all burn. The pillars, the ceiling, everything holding this mansion together.*

"Yeah, we should start from the beginning," Mineno said. "It's pretty complicated . . . You were very serious when you showed us this picture. So we should be serious, too, and explain everything thoroughly."

ALL SORTS of people would gather to hear Matsuo-san speak on the second Saturday of every month. Some people were drawn to his personality, but others saw something sacred in him. Most of those people had been involved with some other religion but had lost hope in their various faiths. There were also suffering youths. People who had been failed by their friends, or lovers, or the companies they worked for, or maybe even another religion. There weren't many, but a few came to study—study how to start their own religion. To use Matsuo's talks as references for their own sermons. Anyone who had been attending the talks for a long time could spot those types immediately. They were always focused on results, and they had voices that cut right through you. They left unpleasant impressions.

There was one man who appeared to be in his fifties who called himself Sawatari, but that may not have been his real name. Five years ago, there was an incident at one of Matsuo's regular Saturday talks. The talks were the most popular they'd ever been. About two hundred people were gathered in the garden. In the middle of speaking, Matsuo suddenly collapsed. Later we learned he'd had a stroke. The moment he fell over, Mineno and the other long-time attendees panicked and rushed to the stage. But from the audience a voice declared that Matsuo had been possessed by god. I've seen this before, the voice said. A god has descended upon him.

Everyone grew frantic. The person who said they'd "seen this before" revealed they meant they'd seen it at a service at another church. Others who were new to the talks misunderstood, and assumed the person meant Matsuo had collapsed before. When some people tried to help Matsu, others shouted, "Don't get in the way!" and, "If you interrupt he may die." Some attendees thought the collapse was part of a staged act, that this was proof that we were some shady cult, and they were shouting out of anger and disillusionment. There was total chaos.

"IT WAS something of a blind spot we had," Mineno said quietly. She seemed scared. "Since we didn't get too involved with the participants and simply gathered instead, no one really knew anyone else . . . If we'd had officers to manage the group, it probably would have been easier to handle the situation. And at the time, Matsuo-san's wife, Yo-chan-san, was out . . ."

THOSE WHO tried to rush to Matsuo were stopped by force. Folding chairs collapsed and confusion spread. Thanks to Yoshida, who called an ambulance, medics soon arrived, but some of the audience members tried to stop them from coming in. Fights broke out. The paramedics must have been confused. There was screaming and weeping. But gradually attitudes changed as people realized the old man really had collapsed. Eventually, they managed to get Matsuo on a stretcher.

Matsuo's life was saved, but he could no longer move his left arm. If he had made it to the hospital a little sooner, they might have been able to prevent that. But Matsuo didn't blame anyone. No one had done anything wrong. Those who'd mistaken what was happening for a spiritual phenomenon— those people who had experienced so much unhappiness and hoped to be saved—they only wished it could be the truth. They saw things the way they did because of their pure desire to be saved by something great. One could even say that Matsuo's paralyzed left arm was born out of their suffering. "This isn't enough," Matsuo later said. "One left arm can't take on all their suffering. Not that I have the right to do that, anyway."

Since that incident five years ago, the talks had changed. Many people were disappointed that Matsuo was not holy, and others put distance between themselves and the group after experiencing that strange disturbance.

While Matsuo was in the hospital, people still assembled every second Saturday, hung around for a while even though there were no lectures. That's when Sawatari showed up. He'd watched the uproar when Matsuo collapsed, unmoved. He saw that those frantic people who believed Matsuo had actually been possessed would be easy to manipulate. Yoshida watched from afar as Sawatari made his way among the gathered crowd, talking to people. In less than a half hour, he had collected a group of people who were crying in front of him. That day, Sawatari took about fifty participants with him and vanished. Many of the people who followed him were highly educated. Later they would realize they still had more to learn about him.

"MATSUO-SAN WAS scammed," Mineno said quietly. "Someone asked him to donate part of the land he owned for a charity hospital, and without thinking much about it, he handed it over. But that land was never used for a hospital. Before he knew it, it was sold and resold, and was eventually used to build a highway. But that's not all. We don't know the details, but the contract he'd signed had a stipulation sneaked in that required him to give up more and more, and he suffered a pretty big loss. The scam was carried out by a sham investment firm Sawatari was involved with. Matsuo-san doesn't like to talk about it—really, none of us know anything about Matsuo-san's life before he showed up at the mansion—but it seems Matsuo-san and Sawatari have a long history together. Anyway, Sawatari took a chunk of Matsuo-san's property and a bunch of the people who used to come here and vanished. And . . ." Mineno suddenly went quiet.

Yoshida finished the story. "That woman you're looking for,

she was involved with that investment firm. She's one of the people who scammed Matsuo-san. She vanished with Sawatari—or maybe it's more accurate to say they returned to their own cult."

"Their own cult?" Narazaki repeated.

"Yes. She's not here. They're part of a nameless cult. They came to the attention of the Public Security Bureau once, and after that they went underground. It seems the Bureau just calls them X, since they have no name. It's a pretty frightening name. Maybe there's some other reason they use it, but I'm not sure. The woman you're searching for, and we're searching for, is there."

THIS DARK room. How much longer will I be here? One week? One month? This tiny room. Walls all around me. My head hurts. No, maybe it doesn't. I saw it a second ago—ah, a door. There's a door. Mom? If I just close the door, it'll be okay? It's not okay. Not at all. It's not okay because there's a hole in that door. Because I used the drill from the woodshop to make a little hole.

I don't feel hungry any more. There's no strength left in my body. When was the last time I ate something? When was the last time I drank something? A sound. I heard a sound. There's a warmth rising up from deep within my body. It's a happy warmth. A sound. I heard a sound. Just now, I heard someone knocking. But from where? From the other side of these walls? That sound, it's telling me I haven't been forgotten. Knocking. They remember me. Thank you! Thank you so much! Even though it hurts so much, even though there's nothing left for me to throw up, I feel myself far more clearly than when I was working at that company. What should I say? If I just close the door it'll be okay? Do you think so, Mom? Myself, much *clearer—I exist. That should be obvious. But it's not. Now I know I exist. Now I am here, full of pain. No, I exist in this space as pain. I've become pain, and am here, in this world. My arms and legs. My organs, my genitals, my body can't move anymore, but my mind feels like it's boiling over. A flood of consciousness. I'm so aware, I want to vomit . . . Where is that woman? Or was that just a dream? If I just close the door, it'll be okay? Do you really think so, Mom? The second floor of that run-down hostess club. The scary second floor, where the windows rattled on windy days. I knew I shouldn't do it. I knew I shouldn't look. But even though I was just in elementary school, I couldn't help it. I wanted to see. I wanted to watch and play with myself. You, taking that strange man in so beautifully with your sturdy hips. You, taking him in so beautifully, and liking it. If I just close the door, it'll be okay? I was jealous of those men. If I paid twenty thousand yen, could I do that to you? Should I say more? I wasn't just jealous of those men holding you. I can't stop the words from pouring out. I don't feel like I need to stop them. I was jealous of you, too! Those men, those men filled with lust, they didn't care about me in the next room. They didn't care about me. They just wanted you. Those men, with those strong bodies, their violent passions, you took them in with your sturdy hips. You're amazing, Mom. You could just keep taking everything those big men had. All of it, all of it, with a face that looked so, so, so happy it made me burn. I wanted to be like you. I wanted to be wanted like that. No one would ignore me. They'd want me too much. And then, and then after. And then I began to empathize with girls when I had sex. I didn't worry just about my pleasure. I imagined the woman's pleasure, pleasure that would burn her up . . . That's why I can drive women wild. So intense, so*

intense. Ahh! I thought I was good. I thought I was a coward.
But just that part of me—just that part was strong enough to
ruin my life. What is this music? Oh, I know. I know this song.
I've heard it so many times in this room. It's Bach. Bach. "I
call to you, Lord Jesus Christ." But why? Why this song with
those images? Men gathering around my mother and this song?
There's no way. Could Jesus Christ have been there? When I
got on all fours and brought my eye up to the hole and wat-
ched you in the throes of pleasure, I felt like I was being called
by something. I was being led by something. Could that have
been Jesus Christ? Was he there? Was he there somewhere? No,
was he the place itself? Savior? No. Not savior. Not savior, fear.
It was fear. Why did Jesus Christ show me fear? Because it's my
true being? Is that my true being? Did Jesus Christ show me
my true being? Why? To lead me somewhere? To what sort of
abyss? Why? Why would he be so cruel?

Knocking. Thank you. I haven't been forgotten. But my vision
is getting cloudy. The door? If I just close the door, it'll be okay?
My true self. My vision . . . I feel like I'm going to vomit. Nothing
comes out. My throat spasms a little. I can't tell if it hurts, or if it
feels good . . . What? The door? The door is opening?

"CONGRATULATIONS."

Light streamed in from the other side of the door.

Collapsed on the floor, the skinny man looked up toward
that light. It wasn't strong, but he had been in the darkness
so long it was bright to him. *Is that light?* the skinny man
wondered. *Ah, there are people. There are people.*

"Are you all right? Congratulations! You did well. You did
very well."

The long-haired believer helped the skinny man up and

led him from the small room. There was light everywhere. The long-haired believer was crying. The skinny man felt his body grow warmer. *For me? Are they crying for me?*

"Ohhh . . ."

"Don't worry. You don't have to speak. Congratulations. The leader will meet you."

The leader? Really? The skinny man's body began to tremble. *For me? Oh, there are so many people. They are all smiling at me. Some are crying for me. For me? Thank you. You were the ones who knocked for me, right? You were the ones who kept knocking for me, to let me know I hadn't been forgotten, right?* A warmth spread through the skinny man's body. *Have I ever felt this much, this much joy?*

"Congratulations!"

"Congratulations!"

"Congratulations!"

The skinny man was led by the long-haired believer up the stairs. To the twenty-first floor. The twenty-first floor, where only the chosen can enter. *I get to go to the twenty-first floor! Me . . .* At the edge of his blurred vision, he saw a door. Their steps rang out on the hard stone tile covering the expansive floor. His consciousness faded, but all the sounds resonated through his body. There was a massive door. All he could see was that tremendous door.

The long-haired believer spoke again. "I cannot go any farther. Congratulations. The leader will meet with you shortly. You must be so moved. You must be so happy."

The door opened. It was dark inside. The leader was sitting in a chair. He could tell from just one look—that was the leader. *I came here to meet you. I came here to meet you. To meet you. To meet you. I was born to meet you.*

"You have overcome. You are wonderful."

The leader's voice was low but strong. The skinny man collapsed in tears.

"Your life of suffering, your unrewarded life will end today."

". . . Yes." The skinny man stared up at the man speaking, tears streaming down his face.

"No one will hurt you here."

". . . Yes."

"There are no idiots here, no one who will fail to recognize your strength."

". . . Yes."

"There is no one here who will interfere with your life."

". . . Yes."

"You are my disciple. My irreplaceable disciple. To us, to me, you are an irreplaceable friend."

The skinny man continued to cry, unable to stand.

"Your life is here. All your reasons for living are here. I plan to change this world. I want your help."

"Yes."

The skinny man rose to his knees, and joined his hands together as if praying to the leader. His tears would not stop flowing. They were so violent and warm he didn't know what to do.

"Leader." *What in this life has meaning? My comforts, dreams, pride?* "I give you my life, leader." *I give it all to you.* "I am yours."

"SINCE THEY have no name, we have nothing else to call them," Yoshida said under his breath. "Cult X."

3

". . . Cult X?"

What a strange name, Narazaki thought. Like the name of some trashy TV show.

"Have you told the police about this scam?"

"Matsuo-san didn't want to," Yoshida said, looking fed up. "Because of whatever that old connection is between Matsuo-san and Sawatari. I don't know the details."

It began to grow dark outside. Narazaki felt as though the lights inside were growing stronger—manmade lights stretching out everyone's shadows.

"And what about you? Can we hear your story?" Yoshida asked. "I'm sorry we can't be of much help to you, but we're also looking for this woman. Well, we're looking for Sawatari, at least—without Matsuo-san knowing, of course. Maybe there will be a hint in your story."

"Honestly, I don't know much," Narazaki said.

"What do you mean?"

How much can I tell them? Narazaki wondered. *But I haven't lied. I really don't know much about her.* "Well, she just vanished. That's it."

"So . . . were you lovers?"

"It's hard to say."

In the silence that followed, Narazaki noticed Yoshida staring at him. The woman in the Rilakkuma apron was still staring at the ground. The clock's second hand moved slowly.

"Well, thank you for coming. I think you'll be back," Mineno said softly, as if exhaling. "This is probably a difficult topic for you, so talk to us when you feel ready. Would you like to watch a DVD before you leave tonight? We have recordings of Matsuo-san's talks. When Matsuo-san's not here, the people who come to visit always watch them."

"But—" Yoshida interrupted.

"What? You think we should try to force him to talk? Do you think Matsuo-san would want that?"

Yoshida looked at Mineno, a perturbed expression on his face. Mineno ignored him and gave Narazaki a cautious look. "I'm sure Tachibana-san is also in the video." Mineno stood, and Yoshida reluctantly followed suit. Narazaki followed them out of the room and down the old hallway. The floor was worn but well polished.

"It looks nice in here," Narazaki said. He felt he had to make up for not speaking earlier.

"Oh, we're cleaning. Matsuo-san's coming back."

"Coming back? So he's not that sick?"

"It's just hemorrhoids," Yoshida said.

Mineno couldn't help but laugh. "Hemorrhoids. Really

bad hemorrhoids that required surgery. Unbelievable, right? A religious leader with hemorrhoids?"

They led Narazaki to a tatami room with a TV and an ashtray. It was smaller than the previous room, and for some reason the heater was already on. He could hardly believe it as they said goodbye, leaving him all alone in the room. *Do they trust me?* he wondered. *And it doesn't look like they can lock that sliding wooden door from the outside.*

Narazaki stared blankly at a cardboard box filled with DVDs. He had expected them to be lined up more showily, as might befit videos of the group's leader. He picked one up and lit a cigarette. He had started smoking again a month ago.

On the cover was a picture of a thin old man. Was he in his seventies? Narazaki couldn't tell. His eyes were large, and his short hair had a lot of white in it, but he had a good-looking face for an old man. His left arm was moving, so this must have been from before he collapsed. He was wearing a gray sweater and beige chino pants. He really didn't seem like a religious leader. He was sitting on the wooden veranda of the mansion, and fifty or sixty people sat in folding chairs in the garden.

Since he'd pretended he was interested in their faith, Narazaki felt he had no choice but to watch the video.

MATSUO-SAN'S LECTURES, 1, PART 1

Well, today I'd like to talk about something rather serious. Everyone, you all know about the Buddha, right? The Buddha. The man who's said to have founded Buddhism. Buddhism is what they practice in temples, not shrines—shrines are for Shinto rites, and they have their own gods. We're talking about the religion where people ring bells on New Year's Eve. Temples. Temples are for Buddhism.

You know about the Daibutsu, right? Those big statues of the Buddha. What do you imagine when you think of the Buddha? You probably at least think he was a good guy, right? [Light laughter.] He did good things, was filled with compassion, and tried to lead even sinners to heaven . . . But was he really like that? Was Buddha really a "good guy"? That's what I'd like to talk about today. That and the most recent theories of neuroscience. These two topics are connected very closely.

The Buddha's real name was Siddhārtha Gautama. Some say he was born in India in 624 BC. Others say it was 463 BC. No one's really sure. Regardless, he was born between four hundred and six hundred years before Jesus Christ. He was born into royalty, but when he was twenty-nine he abandoned his wife and children, left the palace, and wandered the world. It's said that when he was thirty-five or -six he reached enlightenment. His teachings—what became Buddhism—spread not just through India, but also reached China and Japan. There are plenty of temples in Japan, too, right? Much is said about how the Buddha led his life. Some stories are so fantastic one can only assume they're legends—like the ones that say he flew through the sky without a ship.

People later expanded on the early ideas of Buddhism, and there are a vast number of writings from later periods. Of course, all of those books are worthwhile.

But, in truth, I have no interest in the teachings of Buddhism. I'm interested in the Buddha himself. What kind of person was he, and what did he teach? Unfortunately, none of the Buddha's original teachings survive. The same is true of Jesus Christ. It was his disciples, the people who followed him, who passed his words on to later generations.

There is one collection of teachings called the *Sutta Nipata*, it is the oldest extant Buddhist teachings. I was surprised when I read this work. It was rather far removed from the image of Buddhism I'd had until then. This work had already been mostly lost by the time Buddhism was passed from India to China and then Japan. In other words, it didn't have much impact on Buddhism in East Asia. But this is the oldest of the Buddhist scriptures, and as such may be the one that best captures the Buddha's true voice.

It is said that of the books in the *Sutta Nipata* the oldest are the fourth and the final fifth book. How these later books wound up being the oldest is thought to be a matter of the editing style. In the case of Islam's Quran and Hinduism's Rigveda, the older parts come first. There are all sorts of editing styles.

Now, let me read a few sections.

One must sever oneself from the root of delusion, the thought that thinking brings wisdom.

The philosopher Descartes was born in 1596. His famous phrase, "I think, therefore I am," was contradicted by the Buddha here in the *Sutta Nipata* about two thousand years before Descartes was even born. Western philosophers continue to argue over this or that point in Descartes, never even realizing that the Buddha contested his claims millennia before they were made.

For whom there is no desire, for the monk who has cut off the stream (of existence) and abandoned all kinds of works both good and bad, there is no pain.

In other words, they don't do bad things, or good things. Religious doesn't mean good! They don't worry about good and bad at all.

Under all circumstances the independent holy man neither loves nor hates anyone; sorrow and avarice do not stick to him, as water does not stick to leaves.

A holy man loves no one. Of course, there's no romantic love either—this text says you must abandon all your romantic desires as well as all other desires. Women are humans. They've got organs, and they get runny noses, and take shits. It makes you want to ask, "Are you serious, Buddha?" There really is also a section that says we all shit, so don't act high and mighty.

An accomplished man is not led by holy works, nor by tradition.

Let a monk not depend upon what is seen, heard, or thought, or upon virtue and holy works.

As Bhadrāvudha and Alavi-Gotama have left their fate, so, too, shall you.

. . . How about that? It doesn't sound like a religion at all, does it? To quote Hajime Nakamura, a world expert on ancient Buddhism, "Buddhism itself exists in the rejection of teachings." How cool! "In the beginning, Buddhism did not preach saddhā, or the belief in teachings, but rather pasāda, or the idea that through listening to teachings one could purify one's heart." In

other words, there's a possibility that Buddhism wasn't
a religion at all. The Buddha "did not believe himself to
be the special founder of a religion," writes Nakamura.
And he goes on to claim, "If one doesn't abandon 'Buddhist Studies,' one cannot understand the *Sutta Nipata*."

So what about the Buddha's enlightenment? While
it's quite difficult to understand, let's turn again to the
Sutta Nipata.

*For him who both inwardly and outwardly does not
delight in sensation, consciousness ceases.*

*Name and shape are totally stopped by the cessation
of consciousness.*

Name and shape are, in brief, the body and spirit that
give shape to individual humans.

In other words, the Buddha rid himself of all desires.
There was no comfort or discomfort; he did not gain
pleasure from any sensation; and he stopped himself
from distinguishing things, thinking "this is that," and
"that is this." He achieved a state of nothingness. A state
where one does not even think to desire, or think to give
up a desire. A state of nothingness where even thinking
about such things was unnecessary. In the West they'd
call it an absolute nothingness, more absolute than
emptiness. One is not attached to anything. Those who
achieve that state do not return to the endless cycle of
death and rebirth. They are outside the process of samsara. They live in a state of nothingness far removed
from comfort or discomfort. To rephrase this, they can
find no need to be reborn. They have achieved salvation, or a state of nirvana. Nirvana is the absolute state
one achieves after abandoning all desires, eradicating

sensation, and not distinguishing between things. It is nothing. It is also a final state where one does not even recognize oneself as nothing. How terrifying! And what comes after salvation? That's what I start to wonder. But maybe not thinking is itself "salvation." Buddha was not conscious of becoming a god after escaping samsara, and one gets the impression that he never even considered that possibility. All that's left is a state of ease. How about that? Would that make him the world's strongest man, or what? He was freed from the burdens of the world, and no longer even cared about the gods. In a sense, he surpassed the gods, didn't he? He was free from their demands, their claiming things should be this way or that way. Buddha was totally free. *A human had, on a spiritual level, surpassed the gods.* At least I think one could say that.

This is what one man thought almost twenty-five hundred years ago. Of course the teachings of Christ are amazing, but the Buddha was also quite the man.

Let one not be with a natural consciousness, nor with a mad consciousness, nor without consciousness, nor with consciousness gone; for him who is thus constituted form ceases to exist.

"Nor without consciousness, nor with consciousness gone." These words can be written down easily enough, but they are difficult to comprehend, right? How does one interpret them? Maybe one could say that nirvana is also a state that surpasses the logic of written words. Or one could say that when one reaches nirvana, only then can they understand these words.

These words may make one think of Uchoten, the

Heaven of Nothingness. Some say the Buddha flew off to a different world. But at this time, the buds of the "Middle Path" had sprouted, but had not risen to the foreground. Many teachings, like that of the "Three Worlds," had not appeared yet either. Those thoughts stem from the Buddhism of later ages.

You have all already started to wonder, I suspect—in the end, how could this 'religion' grow?

Exactly. In this form, it would be difficult. Everyone would have to live without romantic love. No one would have children. Humanity would go extinct. One can't imagine a world where normal people strive to reach Nirvana. Thus, Buddhism was transformed. But I don't mean to say that Buddhism now has completely strayed from the Buddha's teachings. I'll touch on that again at the end.

Do you remember the words of the Buddha that I mentioned at the beginning of this talk?

One must sever oneself from the root of delusion, the thought that thinking brings wisdom.

Those words that contradicted Descartes's famous claim two thousand years before he made it. I'm an amateur intellectual, and recently I've been researching the brain. The brain and consciousness. What is this thing called consciousness that we've come to use to think about ourselves? During my research I realized that the Buddha's words closely resemble some of the most recent theories of neuroscience.

MATSUO-SAN'S LECTURES, I, PART 2

Our brains are composed of over one hundred billion neurons and the synapses that connect them all. It is amazing to even imagine. Over a hundred billion! That's an absurd number.

The human body is made up of countless atoms. Another tremendous number.

Let's look at proteins, for example. They play an incredibly important role in building the human body.

It's said that the fifteen or sixteen million kinds of proteins in the human body are made by the combination of just twenty-four different kinds of amino acids. Amino acids make proteins, which in turn serve as the building blocks of the human body. If we look at just one of those amino acids, alanine, we see it's made up of H_3C, NH_2, OH, and O. It's a chemical compound comprised of different atoms. And of course the brain is also comprised of countless atoms on the micro level. Atoms are made up of even smaller parts: protons, neutrons, and electrons. And protons and neutrons are in turn made up of quarks, which are even smaller. The smallest object the average scientist currently believes to exist is the quark. When we measure the size of an atom, we use angstroms (Å), and one angstrom measures one ten millionth of a millimeter. You can see that they are extremely small. All of the human body is comprised of chemical compounds. And every time I repeat this it amazes me, but the hundred million neurons in our brains are likewise made up of these chemical compounds. Neurons are made up of atoms, and function through micro-level chemical activities and the firing of countless electric signals. This is amazing to think about. But it's really how the brain works.

So how is consciousness born out of all these chemical reactions? It's quite strange, isn't it? What is consciousness in the first place? It's the "me" that thinks this or that. But what is this "me?" "We" think on our own, and act on our own, right? I'm talking now because I am willing myself to talk. But, in actuality, there has been some startling research.

A scientist by the name of Benjamin Libet conducted a famous experiment. According to his results, before humans are conscious of trying to do something, the parts of their brains responsible for those actions are already activated without their even noticing. What does this mean? Basically, before you are conscious of trying to move your finger, the neural circuitry in charge of moving that finger has already been activated.

According to the results of Libet's experiment, .35 seconds after your brain tries to move your finger, your consciousness—in other words, "you"—become aware that you are trying to move it. Point two seconds after your consciousness, or "you" becomes aware of trying to move it, it actually moves.

And plenty of neuroscientists agree this is correct.

There is no one part of the brain that controls consciousness, or "me."

Consciousness and "I" are born out of the broader work of the brain.

Without brains, consciousness and "I" would not exist.

The activity of the brain reflects consciousness and "me."

But consciousness and "I" have no causal effect on the actions of the brain.

What does all this mean? Of course there is the possibility that consciousness and "I" have no agency at all, and my existence is merely a "mirror" reflecting the activity of my brain. When "I" and my consciousness are thinking this or that, I am not actually deciding what I will do or what I am thinking about. I am just convinced that it is me deciding those things. In actuality, our brains are working in some realm we can't sense, and we are simply following behind, tracing our brains' decisions. This is the true nature of consciousness and "me." It's as if "we" are all just sitting in seats called the "self," watching our own lives pass by.

Huh. The crowd's gotten a little noisy. You must be thinking, How ridiculous! Yes, it really is ridiculous. We'll come back to this once more at the end, but first, let's go on.

Now, I want you to remember the Buddha's words.

One must cut oneself from the root of delusion, the thought that thinking brings wisdom.

This may mean that without doing any science experiments or dissecting anyone's brain, just by staring at his own consciousness and meditating, the Buddha discovered that his consciousness, his "I," didn't have any true form. And that'd be truly impressive. He might have discovered that what's working is not "me," but these chemical compounds that comprise my brain. What starts any activity is not "I," but a "brain" made of "chemical compounds," which "I" cannot even see. "I" simply follow along. But how did the Buddha observe this?

I mentioned earlier that the human body is composed of countless atoms. And since we eat food, and then relieve ourselves, within a year the atoms that make up our bodies are completely replaced. In other words, the atoms that make up this finger of mine will all be replaced. My finger maintains the same shape and qualities because of DNA, and because the atoms are made to recreate the same specifications. The atoms must be replaced because all materials, and this includes those that make up humans, must obey the second law of thermodynamics. To put it very simply, on the atomic level, if you just leave something alone, it will grow disordered. Even solid objects eventually break down. To prevent that, living organisms must continually replace the atoms that make up their bodies with fresh ones. If they didn't, their atoms would move toward disorder and their bodies would fail. So eating serves another necessary role besides nutrition. DNA, deoxyribonucleic acid, is also a chemical compound. It's kind of scary, right? To think the Buddha might have seen the world that way.

Even looking at people, maybe he could see them not as "humans," but rather as "loose collections of atoms that are constantly changing but maintain a solid form." Or maybe even as "bodies that are constantly changing, yet somehow convince themselves that there's such a thing as the 'self.'" Maybe when he saw someone bump into someone else, he saw nothing more than one loose collection of atoms bumping into another loose collection of atoms. Because he did not find pleasure in sensation, he didn't feel anything when his brain showed him the world "the way people see the world." Of course he wouldn't consider the meaning or value of it. He would just remain in a calm state where countless atoms moved through space, flittering all around.

To tell the truth, when I meditate in this garden, that is the state of mind that I try to achieve. Well, that's a lie. In truth, I want to achieve a state of selflessness while maintaining my interest in women. [Laughter.] Don't you agree? Women are just so wonderful! [Laughter.] But there's a contradiction between trying to abandon all desires and wanting to hold on to my desire for women. In a sense, that would be a harder state to achieve than the one Buddha did. [Laughter.]

Well, that's it for the major points today, but let's talk about the brain again for a moment.

Earlier I said that when "I" and my consciousness are thinking this or that, I am not actually deciding what I will do or what I am thinking about. That I am just convinced that I am deciding those things, and in actuality, my brain is working in some space I can't sense and I am simply following behind, tracing my brain's decisions. So, then, why does this thing called consciousness appear in our minds? Do we need it?

This has something to do with evolution. According to one explanation, lower-level consciousness without the conception of self, a proto-consciousness, was born somewhere along the evolutionary path from reptiles to birds, and also from reptiles to mammals.

At this stage of the evolutionary process, a complex two-way circuit between the part of the brain called the thalamus and the part called the cortical layer was formed, leading to proto-consciousness. Why? It seems that consciousness allows response to all sorts of situations, and is thus beneficial for living things. The brain is reflected in the mirror of consciousness, and it becomes easier for the activity of the brain to understand itself.

Furthermore, it is said that the reason "I" came to be is because this system grew even more complex. High-level consciousness arose at a more advanced stage of the evolutionary process. It is said that humans and maybe orangutans have "higher consciousness." I think dolphins and chimpanzees may have it as well.

Apparently, the reason consciousness becomes an "I" at higher levels is deeply related to memory.

To maintain a large memory, it is necessary to have a sense of unity, an idea that one being experienced all these remembered things. Without that, there'd be confusion. That's why this being called "me" was born of the "loose collection of constantly changing atoms that maintains a solid form."

The brain decides all, and my consciousness and I just follow along. However, one mustn't think, "Well, if it's all just my brain, it doesn't matter what I think. I might as well just destroy myself." This is no good because if you think that way, your brain will come to think that way as well. (Properly speaking, you are your brain, after all). So it does matter if you try to destroy yourself. I will say it again, if you think you should just destroy yourself, your brain will become self-destructive as well.

Of course what I am saying now is not verifiable neuroscientific "truth." But there is an argument that the brain is the device that runs things, but our consciousness has veto power. It's convincing, but it's not one of the leading theories. There's also an old explanation that our consciousness can alter the state of our brains. Consciousness is agency. We cannot say for sure if either theory is true. So just remember that there are several arguments for why you shouldn't think negative thoughts.

There's no need to worry about this in your day-to-day

life. Besides, it might all just be erroneous scientific con-
clusions. However, if you ever find yourself questioning
your consciousness, thinking, "Maybe I'm not actually
deciding anything," or "Maybe I'm really just a spectator," then the clashes within your ego, the fights and
wars, appear truly hilarious. You may be able to see your
wallowing (and don't worry, wallowing itself is a good
thing!) from a different perspective. You could think to
yourself, "Ah, my brain is upset again! This collection
of atoms is such a pain!" And then one thing becomes
clear: how unbelievably incredible the system of the
brain that produces "consciousness" is. One hundred
something million neurons working nonstop at unbelievable speeds and intensities. Any being with that
sort of system of consciousness within itself is truly
incredible. Without consciousness and "me," the brain
wouldn't be able to grasp its own functioning. In other
words, it's the same as saying you are your brain. And
when I say "you are your brain," both "you" and "your
brain" are unique. I'll talk about this again later.

However . . . If this is true, it leads to a terrifying
conclusion. Souls may not exist.

That is, if one defines a soul as the way your consciousness goes on existing after you die, that wispy
thing that climbs its way up to some heaven . . . If consciousness is just the product of the mechanisms of the
brain—simply a mirror that reflects the functioning
of the brain—then there's a good chance souls don't
exist. Without the systems in the brain, consciousness
wouldn't exist. When the brain dies, consciousness also
vanishes.

In physics, the existence of the soul is generally rejected. But . . . I think they exist. Souls. And I think they exist without contradicting physics. I will discuss this some other time.

Finally, I'd like to mention the Buddha one last time. Obviously, I cannot know if the Buddha I've described here actually existed. I'm just an amateur intellectual, and I've just put together lots of different information and facts. I don't care if you think I'm trying to start a new sort of Buddhist sect or cult, some sort of religion. But, as I said before, what I've mentioned about the brain does not contradict Buddhism. I'd like to end by quoting Hajime Nakamura again.

"I find the fact that the content of Shakyamuni's (the Buddha's) enlightenment, the starting point of Buddhism, has been *passed down differently in different traditions* to be both a serious problem and one of the defining qualities of Buddhism.

"First of all, *there is no singular teaching in Buddhism*. Gautama himself (the Buddha) did not want the content of his enlightenment to be explained formulaically. He explained it differently depending on the circumstances and whom he was speaking to. <redacted> He did not rely on established principles or religions, but rather *considered actual people as they were* and attempted to help them achieve a state of contentment. <redacted> This position, which could be viewed as a practical philosophy, *allowed for the creative construction of countless starting points*. I consider this to be the reason for the proliferation of so many different kinds of Buddhism in later days."

In other words, the Buddha said many different things depending on whom he was teaching. To quote further:

"With his gracious and calm attitude, the Buddha managed to include even heretics in his teachings. I think part of the reason Buddhism was able to spread so widely in later years and provide that warm light to human hearts was because of these aspects of the personality of the founder Gautama (the Buddha)."

What a beautiful way of thought Buddhism is! The Buddha may have been quite eccentric, but he was a good guy.

Well, this talk went all over the place. Let's end here.

MINENO WENT out to the porch.

It was already dark outside, and a gentle breeze stirred the trees. *So calm,* Mineno thought. *When I'm here, time passes slowly. Even though my consciousness pains me so much. Even though my consciousness shows me all these things.*

Had he finished watching the DVD? The talks were complicated. She didn't always get them.

She heard the sound of footsteps behind her, and felt herself automatically tense up.

"Why didn't you want to press him?" Yoshida asked from behind Mineno.

She didn't have the energy to turn around. "It seemed hard for him to talk about. We only had to talk about the group's history. He would have had to tell us about himself."

"I guess you're right."

"Even if we'd asked, he wouldn't have opened up right now. I also figured this is how Matsuo-san would handle him."

"I see."

Mineno's heart fluttered. Even though the garden was so still, the trees, the gravel, and the gentle wind seemed to have wills of their own. They seemed to be waiting, menacingly, for something to happen.

"Hey, Yoshida-san. What did you think of him?"

"Actually, that's what I wanted to ask you."

They could hear the wind. It was getting cold.

"He doesn't seem like a bad person."

"But he has a nervous face. If we introduce him to Matsuo-san, I don't know what would happen. He seems proud, and like he's easily hurt, so it'll probably take some effort before he opens up. But . . ."

"But what?"

"I've got a bad feeling about him. I can't quite put it into words, and I don't think it's his fault, but just the fact that he came here now . . ."

". . . I thought the same thing."

Like he'd destroy something. Without meaning to, just by being here. But to fix the current situation, something had to be destroyed. *It would be fine if it was me,* Mineno thought. *If it benefits everyone else, I don't mind being destroyed . . . Or do I?* Mineno clenched her jaw and scratched her cheek. *That's not true, is it? You want to be destroyed, don't you? Look, look at you!* Mineno shook her head. *It hurts.*

"Hey," Yoshida said. Mineno caught herself recoiling at the kindness in his voice. "I'm sure you can talk to Matsuo-san, even about the things you can't tell us."

"What?"

"Don't hold it in. If you hold it in . . . you'll die."

Mineno didn't have the courage to turn around. She

wasn't sure what kind of face she was making. She breathed in deeply and made herself speak, just like she'd been doing since she was small. "What are you talking about? You idiot! Quit goofing off and start cleaning."

Not everyone can become happy by coming to this sort of place. Mineno stared blankly at the garden as she listened to Yoshida's footsteps recede. She noticed herself clenching her jaw again. *I'm so far from Matsuo-san's ideals.*

"What if we could start our lives over?" Ryoko Tachibana had asked. "Would you be content to live the life you lived and become the person you are now again?"

What did I tell her then? Narazaki wondered. *Did I lie, and tell her, Of course? No. I must have answered honestly.*

"IT'S JUST as if 'we' are all sitting in seats called 'the self,' watching our own lives pass by."

That was what Shotaro Matsuo had said on the DVD. *If that's true*, Narazaki thought, *then the show in front of me is truly boring. I paid attention to what was going on around me and lived carefully. I took no risks. Even though there was nothing for me to protect. That's why I cracked like that.*

Narazaki caught himself staring listlessly at all the empty cans on his table, each with just a little something left inside. The smooth aluminum of all those countless surfaces sent a sudden chill across Narazaki's skin. *I should just throw them out. Maybe if I clean my room I'll feel a little better. But I have no energy. I'm drunk.*

He looked up at the ceiling, at the curtain hiding his window, at his dim bedside light. *I'm looking at my room,* he thought. *If I put it in Shotaro Matsuo's words, my room is being shown to my consciousness, which is me. I'm drunk with nowhere to go. Because I felt like there was nothing to do but get drunk. What a boring brain I've got.*

It was strange that he'd even met Ryoko Tachibana in the first place.

It was a few weeks after quitting his job, when he was on his way home from the library. In the midst of his feverish lethargy, Narazaki had decided to start reading again. He used to read a lot. If he just turned the pages, the words would take him far away from this tiresome world. Now no new books really jumped out at him, so he went to the library to get some he'd read a long time ago. He could think of a few books where the main character was unemployed. He checked out some of them and bought a can of coffee. As he took a seat at a bench in a nearby park, someone called out to him. When he thought about it now, that's where the strangeness had started.

"You have lots of books."

What an odd way to approach someone. At the time he'd been tired. He liked being alone, but part of him wanted someone's company. Maybe it was because Ryoko Tachibana was beautiful. Maybe it was because she knew about Sartre. How many people his age in Japan knew that much about Sartre? How many people had read *Nausea*?

Her appearance was strange as well. There was no sense

of "nowness" in her clothes or hairstyle. Her straight black hair was slightly too long. And her clothes looked less like fashion choices than like things she wore just to cover her skin. As if she were embarrassed to dress herself up—or maybe as if she had no concept of dressing up. Not the kind of woman who approached strangers. But Narazaki understood now, after hearing Yoshida's story. She dressed like someone far removed from this world. He had seen that sort of plainly dressed woman back when the new religions were causing a stir.

They parted that day, but when he went to return his books, she was at the library again.

Was it a coincidence? Or was she just at the library every day? She had several books by contemporary writers he didn't know, and a copy of the Bhagavad Gita, which she held as if she were trying to hide it. When he looked it up online he'd found it was a Hindu story. *A young Hindu woman?* he'd thought. Maybe she was just interested in India. Regardless, in the midst of his loneliness, he'd found himself strangely attracted to her. *Was it because I'd quit my job?* Narazaki wondered. *It felt like my life had hit an air pocket. Back when I was going to work every day, I wouldn't have felt so upended.*

They'd gone to a café and exchanged phone numbers and email addresses. They ate together several times. It had been years since Narazaki had slept with a woman, and he wanted to sleep with her as soon as he could. When they held hands on the way back from the restaurant, her palm had been strangely sweaty. *She must not be comfortable around men,* he thought. But he didn't feel the need to hold back. They stopped in the dark and he tried to kiss her. Her body grew stiff, but she tried to accept his kiss. In the end she turned her face away and said, "I'm sorry."

"No, I'm sorry," Narazaki responded reflexively. He didn't know what to do.

"It's . . . Just give me a little time."

Was she that inexperienced with men? Narazaki was confused. But he'd seen the lines. When she moved suddenly to avoid Narazaki's kiss, her long sleeve fell back. Under the strap of her wristwatch, which was thick for a woman's, he could see the thin lines. Narazaki stopped himself from trying to pull her in again.

Ryoko averted her eyes and spoke softly. "I'm sorry . . . Will you see me again?"

Maybe she was trying to get over something. Narazaki forced a smile.

"Yeah, I want to see you again. As long as it's all right with you, that is . . . I won't do that again."

They met once a week after that. *What a strange relationship.* They'd hold hands, but they wouldn't kiss. There were times when Narazaki would notice she was crying as they walked together. When that happened, he'd ask her questions, but she'd remain silent and shake her head.

Two months passed, then three. She came to his room and Narazaki tried to pull her body to his. She went stiff. When Narazaki stepped away from her, she cried.

"Did something happen to you before?" Narazaki asked quietly.

She shook her head. "I'm sorry . . . I . . ."

"Don't worry. We can sleep together like this, holding hands."

Narazaki offered his hand. She just stared at it.

"I'm no good . . . I'm not good for anything. I . . . I should just die already. Maybe . . . Maybe if I died . . ."

"What are you talking about?"

"No. Don't worry. I can't die. I'm sure I still can't die. And I . . . I . . ."

"Tachibana-san?"

All the while, Narazaki continued to offer her his hand. She stared at him like he was a dead man, like he was burned into her retina. Like she was looking at a dog she was about to abandon. She cried and stared, and then turned suddenly and left the room, taking her plain clothes and her too-long hair. Narazaki didn't have the energy to follow her.

The next day, Narazaki was unsure of what to do, but he called her. Her phone number had been changed. He remembered the strange things she'd said about death. *Should I go to the police?* Yet he was overcome by listlessness. *Come to think of it, I don't know where she lives. I don't know anything about her. What would I even tell the police? "She went missing, and she may try to kill herself." "Where does she live?" "I don't know." "How can we contact her?" "I'm not sure."*

Narazaki took a coin from the drawer in his desk. EXE had been carved into it. He'd found it on the counter of his bathroom sink. The only people who had been in this room in the past few years were Kobayashi and Ryoko Tachibana. He had asked Kobayashi about it, but he said he'd never seen it. So it must have been hers. Now for some reason it began to bother him. *What is this? Some sort of commemorative token?* It was too poor in quality to be foreign currency. Maybe it was a decorative button from a bag or something?

A month after Ryoko Tachibana left, Kobayashi told

Narazaki he had spotted her. Narazaki felt relieved to know that she was still alive, but he didn't have the courage to go see her. So he asked Kobayashi to investigate her. Part of him was still clinging to something. But to what? To her? What could it be?

Cult X. The coin said EXE. *This is too suspicious. Why did she talk to me in the first place?* Come to think of it, he had sensed someone watching him before she'd approached him that day as he was leaving the library.

The people at Shotaro Matsuo's mansion had told him Cult X had lured away educated people. *But I'm not educated. They wouldn't scout someone useless like me.*

Narazaki didn't know what to make of it all.

Because of his headache, Takahara couldn't focus on the words. He put the book he was trying to read down on his desk, placed a cigarette in his mouth, and lit it.

He looked at the cell phone he had left on his bed. He thought about picking up the book again, but did not. He couldn't calm himself down. He'd promised himself that no matter what life threw at him, he'd remain calm. But here he was, unable even to read because he was waiting on a call. Takahara got up from his chair and turned on the radio. Shostakovich's String Quartet No. 1. He tried to give himself up to the melody, but his head continued to throb. He looked at his phone again. It was already fifteen minutes past the time they'd agreed on.

It's disgustingly quiet, Takahara thought. *The adherents all lead quiet lives. Who would imagine that one of these apartment buildings is actually a compound operated by a religious group? Who would imagine that there was an organization hiding from the Public Security Bureau here?*

Takahara began to write aimlessly. He heard a knock. Upset with himself for being surprised, he crumpled up the paper and put it in his drawer. A woman entered. She was thin, young, and had short brown hair. Takahara had talked to her two or three times before. She was one of the Cupro girls, the sex workers who had been recruited by believers. The Cupro girls were here as professionals, not initiates.

"Excuse me. I brought you coffee."

"Thank you," Takahara replied. Did his words sound gentle, as he intended? "But you don't need to do that, you know. You're not a maid. I can make my own coffee."

"I'm sorry."

"No, don't worry. I'm not mad. Thank you. I appreciate it."

The woman placed the coffee cup on the table. There was no sign she was going to leave.

"Where's *your* cup?"

"My cup?"

"Since you went to the trouble of bringing this to me, let's have a cup of coffee together. I'll make you one."

"No, really, I don't need any."

"It's no problem." Takahara forced a smile. She probably didn't drink coffee. He took a bag of black tea from his shelf. "Is it okay for you to be here?" he asked. "It is Monday."

"Yeah, I took a day off today. What about you, Takahara-san? Since it's Monday . . ."

"Ha ha ha." Takahara forced a laugh. "I don't go. If an officer were there, it would be hard for everyone to do what they wanted."

"I guess you're right."

Takahara looked at the phone on his bed. Still no call. What would he do when the phone rang? He'd have to send the woman outside.

"How much longer are you with us?" Takahara asked as he placed the tea in front of her.

"Two more months."

"That's great. Congratulations."

"Yes . . . Thank you . . ."

"Is something wrong?"

"It's just . . ."

Is something wrong? What am I saying? Takahara thought. *I shouldn't let myself act so superficially. All of my words are hollow. My whole life is hollow.*

"It's . . . It's scary."

"Going out into the world?"

"Yes . . ."

Takahara turned off the music. Everything was ready. He better hurry to the main act.

"I just think that when I leave, it'll start all over again. I think I'll fall for some strange man again. I'll suffer and go broke again . . ."

"I see."

At times like this one must not say, "It will be okay." After all, things aren't okay.

"I know it'll happen again. That's how it always was. I know in my head . . . But . . ."

"You don't know anything about what's going to happen. All you know is how it was before."

She looked like she was thinking. Takahara took a breath.

"In the end, you wound up that way because it's what you wanted. That pain . . . Pain has its own gravity. Even though it's so awful you don't know what to do, you want to stay in that pain."

"That may be true."

Instinctively, Takahara faced the woman. He had expected her to disagree.

"But why?" she asked.

"It may be because you hate both yourself and your partner. And being in that painful situation feels real—it has a certain pull. It's like a bad habit." Takahara stopped speaking. He wouldn't tell her she reveled in her pain because it made the sex better. He wouldn't suggest she did this to make herself feel alive despite her vain existence, which she hated so much she wanted to end herself. He wouldn't say sleeping with a man she didn't love was too great a pleasure, or that sex tinged with hate and love and unhappiness was a wonderful thing.

"I'm scared . . . I might have to stay here a little longer."

"So you want to go to the twenty-first floor?"

"Would I have to?"

"Not necessarily. But probably."

Takahara lit another cigarette. His phone still hadn't rung. It was an important call. It was so important it might decide everything . . . His head began to hurt again.

"Of course, the leader is an amazing person . . . He's amazing, but . . . there's something about him. I can't quite put it into words, but . . ."

"Don't worry. What you say will stay between us."

"I feel like . . . I'd lose myself. If I was with him. And I'm scared of that."

She's smarter than I realized, Takahara thought. Which would mean the scouts had failed.

"I see . . . But it's not hard, is it? Being here?"

"No, everyone treats me well, and there aren't any dirty people. And it's just once a week . . . And I can have time off like this. It's so different. From the places I've been before here."

"Really?"

Then what kind of happiness are you hoping for? But Takahara didn't say that. Nor did he ask if she'd be satisfied to give herself over to passion. *And after that, why not move on, do drugs, and chase the very limits of pleasure until you turn to ash? Or compromise a bit and marry some dull man?* Words kept racing through Takahara's mind. *Then you could have a child, and live your life saying, "I've found fulfillment in the home!" You could stick your kid's picture on your New Year's card and make a point of sending it to as many people as possible. What about the happiness that comes from your child leaving your side while you try not to let them, continuing to cling to them? What about doing a great job at work, being praised by everyone, and getting interviewed by a magazine, even though secretly you might still be insecure? Or what about giving yourself up entirely to religion? What about the pleasure that comes from despising the external world, and believing that god will protect you, and that when you die you'll go to heaven, and then actually dying and becoming nothing more than space dust, but since you're dead at that point, not feeling any unhappiness? What about the joy of believing in that hackneyed message that you must love your everyday life, forgetting about dissatisfactions and material wants, and actually going through with it and loving what you do every day? So, what's it going to be? There are other kinds of happiness, too. In this life, there are many things that bring people happiness. You can knock down others to achieve your own happiness. Your happiness brings unhappiness to others. Your unhappiness was probably the result of someone else's happiness. Our happiness exists in a space created by ignoring the world's starving people. What do you think about that? Would you like to become a monk in India and transcend everything?* Takahara smiled. He wouldn't say any of that.

"Takahara-san, I think you'll never be satisfied," she said suddenly.

She is, Takahara thought. *She really is smarter than I thought.*

"I think that no matter what kind of happiness you find, no matter what kind of counseling you do, you'll never be saved. I just get that feeling."

Takahara's heart began to race. He smiled. "Ha ha, how rude! I *am* happy."

"I'm sorry . . . I just get that feeling." She took a breath. "I want to make you just a little more at ease. I can't save you. I know that. And I'm sorry, but Rina-san can't save you either."

What was happening all of a sudden? Takahara looked at her. Her eyes were moist, and her voice had grown louder. *What a joke! All she's done is move from the filth of the outside world to the filth here.*

"Why do women always think, 'I can change this man, I can save him'?" he asked.

"Some do, but not all women are like that. You seem to like to categorize everything to make yourself feel better."

She's smart, Takahara thought. *She says the most irritating things to me, like she's trying to get a rise. This scout really did fail.*

"But. But I think I can save you. But just for three seconds."

"What?"

"Takahara-san, even if you don't like my body, when you come inside me, for that three seconds it takes you to come inside me, I think I can . . ."

Takahara stared at her. Her eyes and lips were wet. *I see,* Takahara thought. *She's even more of a handful than I imagined. Just like the leader said. Women are the only thing we'll never understand.* Her white blouse was open at the chest, her left shoulder exposed. Her smooth, white shoulder. Her skirt revealed an expanse of thigh. *Three seconds,* Takahara thought. *Three seconds of happiness.*

"I appreciate your intentions, but you know that personal advances are forbidden, right?"

"But, Rina-san—"

"She's different. She has permission."

"Then I want permission, too."

"Please, calm down. You're just anxious about leaving here."

But what about those three seconds of pleasure? Takahara wouldn't ask that either. Why give that to someone like Takahara, who was already imagining the laziness he'd feel after ejaculating?

Takahara smiled as kindly as he could. "Calm down and think about this. Look, look at how you're acting right now. This is why you've been unhappy. This is why."

How fake. My words are so fake. There's no way she can calm down. What good would it do her to calm down? Life's boring if you're calm. Why should she want that? As long as you're just trying to grab at the happiness right in front of you it doesn't matter if that leads you to hell.

Takahara stared at her again. He imagined her when she

was innocent. Maybe when she was in middle school she liked a lot of boys. There were probably lots of classmates who lusted after her, too. *I haven't had sex with that many women, but that's not what she thinks. If I did break the rules and responded to her advances, all it would lead to is an hour of distraction. Should I make her scream, telling her the whole time, Don't make any noise, we can't get found out?* Takahara smiled. But pleasure didn't fit into his plan. It would only get in the way.

"Takahara-san, I . . ."

She stood up, moved closer to him, offering her hand. Suddenly his phone rang. Takahara's heart began to race.

"I'm sorry. My phone. We'll talk about this later."

Her hand fell. It had no place to go. Takahara ushered the confused girl out of his room. He'd have to send her to counseling.

Takahara answered his phone. This was the call that would decide everything. He spoke as quietly as he could.

MATSUO-SAN'S LECTURES, II, PART 1

Everyone, today I'd like to talk about the universe. The beginning of the universe. And what is said to be the oldest of Indian scriptures, the Rigveda.

What really is this universe we all live in? How was it formed in the first place?

The planet we live on exists in a space we call the solar system. The collection of countless groups of stars and planets like our solar system is called a galaxy. From far away, the galaxy we live in looks like a disk. The radius of that disk is approximately fifty thousand light-years. It's so large that it would take fifty thousand years to traverse, flying at the speed of light. In this universe, we can currently see about one hundred billion galaxies. There are one hundred billion galaxies, each with a radius of about fifty thousand light-years. This is a tremendous number. Our universe is shockingly large.

One of those hundred billion galaxies, ours, is called the Milky Way. And our solar system is about twenty-eight thousand light-years from the center of our galaxy, out toward the edge. In other words, even in just the Milky Way, our solar system is way out in the boonies.

So, how was the universe created? I'm not sure if this is true, of course, but I will tell you about one theory that is currently quite influential. This theory claims that our universe was formed about thirteen billion seven hundred million years ago.

First, everyone, please imagine a vacuum. There's no air, nothing. Just space. Of course, there's no such thing as a complete vacuum. If you look closely at that vacuum, there are microparticles even tinier than atoms suddenly popping up and then vanishing in the next instant. This happens constantly. It's quite strange to think about, isn't it? In other words, even a vacuum is not truly nothing. It's constantly fluctuating between something and nothing. It exists as both nothing and something. This is quite difficult to wrap our heads around. [Laughter.] But, for a moment, let's abandon common sense. In what appears to be nothingness, in that vacuum, there are particles popping in and out of existence. Please, just accept that that's how it is. In that space, the usually contradictory concepts of something and nothing coexist.

Further, it is said that the universe did not start in

a particular instant. It did not start at a given temporal point.

Back then, time as we experience it, as one continuous line where past leads to present, didn't exist. There was no past or present—just "imaginary time." Our minds cannot comprehend how time worked then. Our brains were built to sense time as if it flows from past to present. But in this "imaginary time," there is no discernable "beginning." Our universe suddenly appeared as something incredibly small.

How did it appear? This phenomenon is called quantum tunneling. It seems microparticles are able to borrow energy from elsewhere for just an instant. This strange quantum tunneling happened, and the particles that had been popping in and out of existence *came to exist*. In that instant, imaginary time transformed into time as we know it, and just one second after one thousand and thirty-four minutes, really just one instant after that, the Big Bang happened and the universe expanded explosively. Just point one seconds after the birth of the universe, the temperature rose to one trillion degrees. It's said that the nuclei of elements like helium were formed within three minutes of the Big Bang.

But this leads us to a question.

If this is true, what was there before?

Since there was only "imaginary time," one could simply answer that there was no such thing as "before." However, there is another theory that there must have been another, different universe, some sort of "mother universe." Our universe may have been tied to this other universe through the effects of quantum tunneling, and the moment they connected, our universe was born. There are still others who think our universe began at this limitless moment, which is called "the singularity." In physics nothing can be limitless, so this "singularity" would break the rules of physics. However, after that, the laws of physics kicked in and the universe expanded accordingly. This "singularity" explanation is generally rejected these days, but I find it to be quite appealing.

Now, let's talk about the Rigveda.

The Rigveda was created sometime between twelve hundred and one thousand BC and is the oldest Indian scripture. It came before the scriptures of Judaism were written down, and is much older than either Buddhism or Christianity. It is the oldest Hindu text. Isn't that exciting? A text that's now more than three thousand years old? In it is the following passage about the birth of the universe.

There was not nonexistent nor existent: there was no realm of air, no sky beyond it. What covered it, and where? And what gave shelter? Was water there, unfathomed depth of water? / Death was not then, nor was there aught immortal: no sign was there, the day and night's divider. That One Thing, breathless, breathed by its own nature: apart from it was nothing whatsoever. / Darkness there was: at first concealed in darkness this All was indiscriminate chaos. All that existed then was void and formless: by the great power of Warmth was born that Unit. / Thereafter rose Desire in the beginning, Desire the primal seed and germ of Spirit. Sages who searched with their heart's thought discovered the existent's kinship in the nonexistent. / Transversely were their ropes extended: what was above it then, and what below it? There were begetters, there were mighty forces, free action here and energy up yonder. / Who verily knows and who can here declare it, whence it was born and whence comes this creation? The gods are later than this world's production. Who knows then whence it first came into being?

How about that? This three-thousand-year-old text is in keeping with our most advanced physics. I first picked up the Rigveda to research legends, but I was truly surprised when I happened to find this passage. I could write a book about just this coincidence! [Laughter.] One can understand desire as the first particles' desire to be born and to expand. The sages or wise men are a mystery, but I believe they can be understood as some sort of metaphor. You could also imagine they actually existed (maybe in the mother universe). Even the claim that "Gods came after the expansion of the universe" is pretty amazing. That means the growth of the universe was not the work of the gods.

The most recent particle theory says the following. The smallest elements that make up the world are not particles, not those little dots, but rather incredibly tiny strings. These strings vibrate, and changes in their vibrations alter the fifty or sixty particles we now recognize. This is called Superstring theory.

Transversely were their ropes extended: what was above it then, and what below it?

That quote is from the Rigveda. There are "strings" here as well. In this passage, this word "ropes" appears so suddenly, the timing seems almost unnatural. The

Rigveda's cosmology foresaw our most modern theories of the universe. How is such a thing possible? There are probably people who think it's a coincidence. They probably assume that the person who wrote this passage, whose name we no longer know, was just hallucinating or something. Actually, I think that myself. So why did his fantasy hit on the truth of the universe? Why did people so long ago have such extremely abstract ideas like "there was neither nothing nor anything"? I believe that the people who wrote this text knew about the structure of the universe.

Atoms know about atoms. If the word "know" as we usually think of it doesn't fit here, we could also say that atoms embody atoms themselves. I believe the writer of the Rigveda was a human, so his brain, too, must have been made of countless atoms. Atoms know about atoms. Atoms contain the secrets of atoms. Could that collection of countless atoms have shown the writer and their consciousness the true nature of this world? People three thousand years ago had never experienced the overabundance of useless information we all live with now. Could the structure of our brains be completely different from theirs?

The people who wrote this passage likely meditated and arrived at a "certain state," then saw these images. The truth contained within atoms. Just as the Buddha would do several hundred years later to come to understand the true nature of consciousness. In other words, I wonder if the truth of the world is not already contained within our brains. I can't help but think it is.

Let's move on. I'd like to talk about how the more

you research the universe, the more you find yourself feeling that this universe is just too perfect for humans and other life.

First of all, if not for three-dimensional space, humans would never have come to be. And if the dynamics of the universe had not been as they are now, and the earth did not circle the sun in the fortuitous way it does now, it would have crashed into something. On a smaller level, if the fundamental charge, which determines the strength of electromagnetism, or the coupling constant of protons and neutrons, which determines the strength of the strong nuclear forces, had been even just slightly different from what they are now, carbon, the element that makes up biological life, would have never been formed. Of course, without carbon there would be no living things. Without protein, we couldn't have DNA, and without DNA we could never produce proteins. That means that at the origin of human life, both proteins and DNA must have existed. I can give many more examples like these. It's almost like you can say *this universe was created to produce life*.

Of course, you could also disagree. You could say, "It's because humans exist that we can look back and think everything was made for us. Of course the universe humans came from is good for humans!" Or, "There are lots of universes besides ours, and it's because this one is good for humans that we were born here. There are countless other universes where we failed, where we were born but then quickly vanished."

Of course. But I'd still like to stress that this universe is just too perfect for humans. There must be some meaning behind that. Physicists for whatever reason reject the human-centered perspective. And they reject spirits and other worlds and gods. However, can they really say such things definitively? To expand on this, I'd like to talk about some of the mysterious points in modern astrophysics.

In 2003 NASA reported that ninety-six percent of the universe was made up of unknown substances and energy. According to the most recent numbers, it's actually about ninety-five. The things that make up our bodies, the air, stars and planets, those compounds and energies we understand—atoms, fundamental particles—make up just five percent of the universe.

Well, what is the remaining ninety-five percent? About twenty-three percent is said to be "dark matter." While its true form is still a mystery and no one seems to understand it completely, dark matter has mass, but does not react to other materials. It passes right through other materials, like ghost particles. Does dark matter only exist at the edge of the universe? Apparently not. It seems it's all around us. It's passing through our bodies right now. It's everywhere. Some claim that dark matter can pass through different dimensions. Different dimensions? It sounds like fiction, but the universe itself is as strange as most of our fantasies.

For example, there's Einstein's theory of relativity. According to this theory, space bends. Gravity is produced through these bends in space. To sum up Einstein's theory quite briefly, those eternal constants, time and space, are actually relative. They expand and shrink. That's the theory of relativity in a nutshell.

And this has been confirmed through experiments. It is also thought that gravity has an effect on other dimensions as well.

The remaining unknown seventy-two percent of the universe is said to be "dark energy." It has the opposite effect of gravity on its surroundings, and is said to be involved in the constant expansion of the universe. This energy also holds the key to the end of the universe. If we could understand this energy, we'd know what the future has in store. But let's talk about that later.

Let's discuss one more mysterious point. There's a theory called Brane theory in contemporary astrophysics. It claims that our universe is just a thin film floating in a larger, ten-dimensional universe. This isn't science fiction. It's something that famous contemporary physicists around the world are actually researching. One dimension is a line, two is a plane, three is space as we know it. But what about the other dimensions? Some say that the fourth dimension is time, but if there are ten dimensions, what are the rest of them? There's still no answer to that question.

We can see that astrophysics and physics aren't perfect. On the contrary, physicists still have not integrated particle theory (which we so often see in science fiction) with Einstein's theory of relativity. They say that when the two are integrated, we will have a super theory that can perfectly explain the structure of our universe. But that still seems quite far off.

Well, we'll discuss the fact that this super theory is still incomplete when I talk about how I imagine the world.

MATSUO-SAN'S LECTURES, II, PART 2

First, let's talk about the smallest compounds that make up this world.

I've discussed this before. The atoms that make up these compounds are made of protons, neutrons and electrons, and protons and neutrons are made up of even smaller things called quarks. Assuming there are even smaller particles, let's imagine there's a smallest unit. What's happening inside those smallest units? It seems to me that there are two possibilities.

First, possibility one.

If we assume that the world is not closed, that is to say, that there are other dimensions, I believe the insides of those particles would be something like caves. Properly speaking, we would only be able to see the entrance to those caves, but beyond that would be what we call in human terms alternate dimensions. But there is actually no clear boundary we can point to and say, "Here's another dimension." I believe it's more like a gradation. In other words, while we usually refer to our world as three-dimensional, it exists somewhere in a reality that includes other dimensions. At least that's what I think. These alternate dimensions are not separate worlds, but areas where light and electrons, even time, cannot be differentiated. There may not even be time there. Things are born and disappear. The concept of existence may not even exist there. Many other worlds are layered on top of this one. That's what I think.

Then there's possibility two.

In this case, there are no alternate dimensions. Which means if humans were to look inside the smallest unit (which would be impossible, but let's imagine they did anyway) all they'd see is a black expanse. If they looked harder, they'd see something that looked a bit like light. What I'm saying is, I wonder if they wouldn't see something that looks exactly like this universe. It sounds quite a bit like a fairy tale, doesn't it? When they looked inside this miniature world, they'd see their own universe. How would they react? They would probably be moved by the weirdness of this world. Or maybe they'd tremble in fear.

Another reason I believe the universe is too perfect for humans is that there are these two possibilities.

Possibility one.

Unfortunately, in this case there's a chance that everything's a coincidence.

If we looked at our world on the atomic level,
even our sophisticated human society would look like
nothing more than atoms clumping together and separating. Everything would amount to nothing more than
the continuous chemical reactions of atoms. In that
case, even what we call life would be nothing more
than these reactions, and one could go so far as to say
it has no meaning.

Then there's possibility two.

In this case there's a chance that the combination of
atoms in this world connects back to "a certain state."

If we trace it all the way back to the beginning of
the beginning of the beginning, both life and society,
just as I said before, would still be nothing more than
the chemical reactions of atoms. But there would be
meaning behind that.

I said before that our brains, which produce our consciousness, are made of collections of atoms. This is
what I think that would mean.

When atoms arrange themselves in certain ways,
they produce consciousness.

And, *atoms have always had the power to produce
consciousness*.

I think this is the truth. Our brains, these collections
of atoms, do produce consciousness. And how strange
is that! So why wouldn't other atoms have the power to
produce consciousness by joining together?

Of course, consciousness is a human concept, and
some would say it's nothing more than an illusion. But
if that were true, one could also say this: atoms always
had the power to produce the illusion of consciousness.

And that's the same thing as producing consciousness itself. Isn't illusion also nothing more than a human concept?

Now I want you to remember something I mentioned before. Human consciousness cannot affect the brain. In other words, human consciousness, which is an abstract thing produced by a collection of atoms, cannot affect the body, a material thing, which is that collection of atoms. Why? Maybe this is one possibility. Consciousness belongs to a different space than the three-dimensional world of our bodies.

In other words, I wonder if consciousness exists as part of some other dimension sticking out into our own. The most recent science says that dark matter may be made up of particles able to move between different dimensions. Of course, I don't mean to say that consciousness is dark matter. I said before that maybe many other dimensions are layered across this one, forming a gradation. So some of the tendencies of atoms come from those other dimensions. Maybe they tend to head toward, to overlay themselves on, other dimensions when they combine. These dimensions are not far away, and there aren't any clear borders between them. Instead they're something like the front and back sides of this world. I think they're laid on top of each other. I also think maybe those things we call ghosts are fragments of consciousness that make up part of this gradation.

Life is born from connected atoms, which are made from the collection of many kinds of particles. I believe the evolutionary path that led us from the wavering between something and nothing to the existence of humans was taken in order for consciousness to be born. Atoms naturally want to connect to other dimensions. That's why they try to create consciousness. In other words, they are drawn to that space, to other dimensions. Maybe what we see from an evolutionary perspective, or the perspective of natural selection, as living beings' progress toward consciousness is, on an atomic level, nothing more than atoms being pulled to other dimensions. Maybe we came to be like this because we are being drawn in to somewhere else.

In which case, our consciousness, and our existence, has meaning. It may not be what we humans usually think of as meaning, but if nothing else, it is more than coincidence. After all, atoms always contained the ability to produce consciousness through their joining together. This would also explain why the universe is so perfect for life and humans.

So, what are these other dimensions? I'm not sure. It's easy to imagine they're heaven and hell. And if consciousness is just a channel to those places, the level of consciousness achieved is not likely to matter. The consciousness of ancient animals and the high-level consciousness of humans would differ in type, but their value would likely be the same in such a world. In fact, there may not even be a concept of value. Such a world would resemble something like a thoughtform, a tulpa. A reality supported by our shared thoughts.

Many physicists and neuroscientists say there's no such thing as a soul. But, as I said before, science is not all-knowing. Quantum theory and the theory of relativity have still not been consolidated. While some say that alternate dimensions are just too small and simply cannot be seen by humans, I wonder if it's not the entrances to those alternate dimensions that are too small to be seen. If there are alternate dimensions and dark matter all around us, no one can say confidently that there are no entrances we just can't see within these collections of countless atoms that make up our brains. When humans die, that collection of atoms breaks down. However, our consciousness may just slip through one of those entrances into another world. When we enter that thoughtform, we may learn the whole truth of this world. Or we may not. We may just be absorbed like some sort of nutrient. Either way, that's something to look forward to when we die. There's still much I want to say about the universe and humans.

Well, finally I'd like to talk a little bit more about the universe itself.

I've said that there are a trillion galaxies. When we look at them all from far, far away, we know they look something like a beehive.

But it looks like there's nothing in the cells of that hive. Basically, those membrane-like lines that demarcate the hexagons, those lines themselves are packed densely with galaxies—collections of stars—and seem to shine. And when we look at this structure, it also resembles the neurons of the brain.

This is quite extraordinary. I'd like to end today's talk here.

NARAZAKI RETURNED the DVD to its original place and left the room.

Mineno and the others had greeted Narazaki warmly when he returned to the mansion. Yoshida looked like he wanted to say something, but he didn't press Narazaki, and Narazaki did not say a word about Ryoko Tachibana. Tanaka, the woman who had been wearing the Rilakkuma apron, was wearing an apron with a kettle printed on it today. The kettle had a face, and there was a speech bubble that said, "You ready to boil?" *Did she make that herself?* Narazaki wondered. *What is she trying to accomplish, wearing something like that?*

As he walked down the hallway now, Mineno approached him. "What did you think of Matsuo-san's talk? Was it interesting?"

There was a large man next to her. It was the first time Narazaki had seen him.

Narazaki smiled. "There's a lot I don't get . . . Are his talks always like this?"

Mineno laughed softly. "No, there are all sorts. Lots of his talks are hard to understand, though . . . But he also does things like read his story, 'The Last Cholesterol.'"

"'The Last Cholesterol'?"

"Yeah . . . It's a short story about old folks whose doctors told them they couldn't eat any more cholesterol. They really enjoy eating their last raw egg over rice."

"How . . . surreal."

"There are other types of lectures, too," the large man next to her added, smiling. "There's also one called 'The Adult Video Revolution.' Matsuo-san is apparently always unsatisfied with the way pornos are shot. I guess he hates extreme close-ups and low angles. He said that the actresses work so hard, but the directors have no talent . . . Anyway, in his talk he said he came to realize that instead of focusing on them, he could change himself."

"Change himself?"

"Yeah. If you just focus on pretending that the women are old girlfriends or women who stabbed you in the back when you watch them . . ."

"I see." Narazaki managed to laugh ambiguously.

"If you're unhappy with the world you can either change the world, or change the way you see it. He thought he'd talk about that by focusing on adult videos. The talk was a spectacular failure, though. The crowd booed, and Matsuo-san got mad . . . Anyway, he's finally coming back, so next time you can watch him in person."

"He's coming back?"

"Yeah, he'll get out of the hospital tomorrow," Mineno said. Why hadn't she said that first thing? Her long, thin eyes looked slightly moist. She was beautiful today, too.

"We'll introduce you to him as well. I'm sure he'll be pleased to know you've been watching his DVDs."

NARAZAKI LEFT through the front gate.

Shotaro Matsuo is getting out of the hospital, Narazaki thought. *Will I meet him?* He had an inexplicable interest in the man. *But what will I do? Will I learn how he sees life, be moved, and return to work? Can I even go back to work? Can I go back, even though I've never once thought I wanted to go back at all?*

Narazaki kept walking. He felt comfortable in the mansion. He wasn't sure why, but Mineno said the same thing.

There was something there that calmed people down. *Mineno*, he thought. *She's beautiful. What am I doing? What do I want? I guess I should just meet Shotaro Matsuo first. I won't worry about why I'm doing it. I'll just meet him.*

"You're Toru Narazaki, right?"

He turned around and saw a young woman behind him. As soon as he saw her, he knew she wasn't from the mansion. But why did he know that? His heart began to race.

"You've been searching for Ryoko Tachibana, right?"

"What?" Narazaki looked at the woman blankly. She had brown hair and large eyes. She reminded him of someone. But who?

"I'll take you to her."

"Where?" When Narazaki asked, the woman smiled. For some reason, her smile struck Narazaki as familiar. Several cars passed. The wind was freezing.

The woman answered him softly. "To our faith."

9

The woman smiled and stepped in front of Narazaki.

What am I doing? Narazaki tried to get his thoughts straight, but found himself following this woman. His heartbeat quickened. She'd clearly said Ryoko Tachibana's name. *But does that mean Ryoko's called for me? What for? How could she know I was here?*

The woman's legs, sheathed in black stockings, moved beneath her black skirt as he followed her. She didn't turn around. *I could run away.* There was a station wagon in the distance. A man was standing next to it. *Is she going to tell me to get into that car?* It was all too suspicious.

He thought about asking, *Why'd you choose me?* And, *Why'd you scam Shotaro Matsuo?* But he could ask those questions whenever he wanted. *Should I ask before I get into the car? Maybe she is listening to my footsteps to make sure I'm following.* Narazaki hoped she was. She stepped into the car.

The man waiting next to the car sat down in the driver's seat. Narazaki stopped in front of the station wagon. The woman looked at him, smiled, and offered him her hand from the car. To help him into the car. To help him make a decision.

Narazaki stared blankly at that hand. He'd seen this happen many times before. Before she'd left, he'd offered his own hand to Ryoko Tachibana from the edge of his bed. His whole life he'd been offering his hand to the world, but hadn't been able to hold on to anything. He had been waiting with his hand stretched out, but nothing had grabbed onto it. Of course no one had offered a hand to him before. He heard a siren in the distance. Narazaki took her outstretched hand. It was warm. He got into the car, putting his weight into his own knees so as not to burden the woman.

The sliding door clicked shut. It was too late.

The faint smell of the woman's perfume permeated the car.

There were sheets spread across the windows so he couldn't see outside. The front and back seats were divided by a curtain. Even if Mineno or Yoshida or Kobayashi were right in front of him, he wouldn't be able to see them. The engine revved. The car began to move. Narazaki was transported away from the places he knew. His own life was growing distant.

No. Narazaki immediately corrected his thinking. There was a strange feeling of elation within him. It was as if the further the car went, the realer his life became. This moment was different from what he experienced every day. He felt like he was truly living. He felt the air brushing his fingertips, the position of his hips where he sat, and even the clothes he was wearing. He could feel clearly the progression of time. *This moment passes, then it comes again, then again, and again it will pass.* He noticed the texture of the leather upholstery of the car. It looked too raw to be artificial. Was it some kind of animal's skin? Could an animal's skin be cut into such a shape? The car slowed down, and he felt other cars overtaking them. His ears caught the strain of a jangling tune, then it faded into the distance. Then a siren flared up, but that sound, too, vanished quickly.

"Where are we going?" Narazaki asked the obvious question.

The woman turned and looked at him. Just that slight movement caused her faint perfume to ripple through the air. The smell filled his mouth. It filled his body.

"You don't need to worry."

She smiled again. His eyes dropped to her soft chest. Her stockinged legs were crossed as if they were squeezing something. *I really don't have anything to worry about. I have nothing to lose. There is nothing in my life I need to protect.*

The faint light passing through the curtains vanished, and the car finally came to a stop. He wasn't sure how far they had gone. Narazaki opened the sliding door solicitously, as if to save the woman the trouble.

The concrete beneath his feet was rough. They were in an underground parking lot. The man opened what looked like the building's service entrance, and Narazaki followed the woman inside. The man stayed behind. The woman led Narazaki down a dim hallway and opened a door on their left. In the dim light stood a woman wearing a surgical mask. He couldn't see her face.

She sat Narazaki down, and rolled up his sleeve. The room smelled of disinfectant. When he saw the needle, he tried to speak up.

"Don't worry," said the masked woman. Her voice was soft, as if to let the frightened Narazaki know she thought kindly of him. "Look. There's nothing in this needle. Look very closely."

There really was nothing there.

"We're going to draw a little blood. And we'll need a little urine. Just a little ceremony to celebrate you joining us."

Could he fail this kind of blood test? *It's better than them putting something in me*, Narazaki thought. He let them take his blood, and walked to the bathroom with a paper cup.

Afterward, he continued down the dark hallway with the woman. They waited for an elevator. The sound of it rattling down the shaft rang through the silence, and then came a soft chime. The doors opened as if the elevator were inviting him in with a will of its own.

The woman said nothing, but she continued to smile. *Does she think it's too late for me to run?* Narazaki stopped the thought. *She's right, I'm not going to run.* She pressed the button for the eighteenth floor. *This building is so quiet. It's like there's no one here.*

The elevator doors opened, disgorging them reluctantly, and they walked down another dark hallway. On the left side of the hallway were many doors, like the rows of doors in an apartment building. He felt like they had walked quite far. The woman stopped and opened a door. *Room 1807.* He followed her into the room.

The woman spoke suddenly. "Please turn around for a second."

The room was filled with a dim red light. Narazaki turned around and faced the door he had just stepped through. It looked like the entryway to an apartment. His mouth was dry, but still he somehow swallowed. His heart was racing. The air was damp. Narazaki was sweating.

"You can turn around now."

When he did, the woman was wrapped in just a bath towel. Her body was illuminated by the faint red light, and her posture seemed shy. Behind her was a bed. A large bed—a bed where you could do anything. Narazaki was breathless.

"Tell me whatever comes into your mind."

"What?"

"Whatever you're thinking."

Narazaki couldn't take his eyes off her body. "I don't understand what you mean."

"Just say whatever you think—just say it. Don't hesitate. Don't lie to yourself . . . No matter how embarrassing. Even if you can't say it to anyone else. Your secrets. Your ugliness. Your past. Everything . . . Tell me everything you think."

"You're beautiful." Narazaki finally managed to say. His throat was dry.

"What else?"

"I want to . . . No, but . . . No, there's no but. I haven't, for five years."

She smiled and grabbed both of Narazaki's arms. She pressed her chest against him. Narazaki felt the softness of her body. He tried not to move his hands, but it was hard to resist. She was soft and warm. The scent of her perfume sank into his body.

". . . Music. Music."

"Music?"

"Yes, music."

Words bubbled up in his mind and spread like molten

lead. The woman wrapped her arms around Narazaki's neck.
He hugged her.

"Music—it would block their voices. Angry voices." The
words flowed from his mouth. "My parents—always yelling
. . . Anger is scary for a little kid, isn't it? It's—it's not a big
deal. I don't have any special tragedy worth talking about . . .
It's just . . . I was so weak."

The woman ran her lips along his ear.

"When I could hear them fighting in the living room, I
put on music. Japanese music. Foreign music. Any kind of
music . . . Music blocks fighting voices. It replaced them
with happy sounds. Sometimes I'd also think about passages
I like from books. I like books. Then I'd be okay."

Why was he saying this? His body grew weak.

She nodded, as if trying to encourage him.

"I was weak. I couldn't really accept my parents' fighting.
I was so weak, I needed music and novels to save me. Children are all weak. And when you're weak, you're forced to
recognize your weakness. Those angry voices make you
uneasy inside. When you're exposed to that every day, even
little things scare you. It becomes a conditioned reflex.
When you hear yelling, you can't help but grow uneasy. I
was relieved when my parents got divorced. I didn't have to
hear them shouting. I knew that my existence was a burden
for them. My first memory is of trying to walk. I reached out
to my mother but she didn't take my hand. Our eyes met.
I could see in her eyes that I was a bother. When I heard
them yelling, I'd picture those eyes, and I kept thinking they
were telling me to disappear. I didn't care about my parents'
love. If only their shouting voices would go away. At some
point, I grew obsessed with rationality. I used logic to protect

myself, like a suit of armor. It was like seeing the world
through a semitransparent film. I reasoned that there was
nothing I could do. Because we're all just human, there
was no point in having high hopes for those around me.
I just kept trying to not make anyone mad. I wasn't ambi-
tious. I went to college out in the boonies and then got
a job. It was the middle of the hiring freeze. There were
no good companies taking on new employees. I did stupid
work with absolutely stupid people. Even that I did because
it seemed like the logical choice. I thought there was no
helping it. Humans made our society, so there was no way
society could be good. My boss kept yelling at me. I tried
not to get him mad, but it didn't work. When my boss yelled,
I played music in my mind—Bill Evans's "Waltz for Debby."
And I also thought about Dostoevsky's *The Idiot*. That beautiful last scene with Prince Myshkin. I was okay as long as
I did that. I did so much overtime. Lots of my coworkers
developed neuroses and stopped coming to work. Everyone
around me was useless, and since they were useless they
wound up at a company like that one. And since my boss
was just a useless idiot who took his own frustrations out on
his subordinates, there was no reason to be bothered by his
yelling. I played music in my head. But one day the music
stopped. I thought it was strange. Prince Myshkin vanished.
I wondered what had happened, and suddenly my boss's
lips—his lips suddenly looked disgusting to me. Yes, even
now I remember it clearly. It's his lips, I thought. His teeth.
They were disgusting. He's talking, he's talking, I thought.
He's so disgusting, he should just die. He's so disgusting, he
should just die. And I—I shoved his face as hard as I could
with the palm of my hand. And he fell over, and hit his desk

hard. There was this loud noise. Do you think I felt better? If I'd felt better, maybe things would have been different. But when I came back to my senses, after I had shoved his face, I worried about what I'd done. No, actually, right when I shoved him, I had already come to my senses. I thought what I'd done was mean. *How awful. What should I do,* I thought. I was right back in my everyday life. Shouldn't I have stopped myself? Why had I done it? No, *why had my brain done it?* And *why did my brain come back to its senses right then?* It would be so much simpler if I had just gone crazy."

The woman cradled Narazaki's head against her chest. Narazaki was short of breath, and realized he was about to fall asleep. But he wouldn't sleep. He had no sense of reason, and there was no music.

"Why did you come here?"

"What?"

"Why did you come here?"

"I came for Tachibana."

No. That's not it. Narazaki caressed the woman's breasts with his fingers. The bath towel had fallen, and her breasts were right before his eyes. Narazaki buried his face in her chest. He put her nipple in his mouth and sucked. He sucked loudly. He heard himself lick that nipple. She allowed it.

"I hate myself. I don't matter. I hate myself and my life."

"Yes," she answered. She was panting, exhaling heavily, but she spoke in a whisper.

Narazaki couldn't take it anymore. "I came here to reject my life—by joining a group everyone thinks is weird. I came here to reject my life, and everyone who talks so high and mighty about everything . . ."

The woman gestured for Narazaki to come to the bed. She kissed him. Their tongues touched. Narazaki took her tongue into his mouth greedily. He took off his clothes. He felt her suppleness and warmth with his whole body. She was already quite wet.

"Ah . . . Ah!" She closed her eyes and moved her hips. She took Narazaki's finger into her body and shivered. He could feel the insides of her body reacting violently. "Your finger . . . How embarrassing! With just your finger." She moved her hips as if she were convulsing, stroking Narazaki's penis and trying to draw him into her body.

"Condom . . ."

"Don't worry, no one here has any sexually transmitted diseases . . . You remember those tests you just did? You passed."

Narazaki's penis entered her. It was enveloped in softness. It was as if it were being sucked into her. Narazaki thrust violently. She had become wet again.

"I'm on the pill—you can come in me as much as you want. Ah, ah! Use me as much as you want."

She wrapped her long legs around Narazaki's hips. He couldn't separate his body from hers. He had no desire to. His chest and belly were covered in sweat. She looked at Narazaki with shy eyes, and exhaled into his ear. She clung to every part of his body. They couldn't even change positions. She kissed him, leaving his lips wet.

"I remember," Narazaki said, breathing heavily. "You look like the first girl I loved . . . You're not her, but you look kind of the same . . . That first moment I wanted someone . . ."

Was she still smiling? Narazaki couldn't make himself look.

Narazaki woke up bathed in dim red light. He was in the same room.

He sensed someone else in the room, and saw the back of a woman in the darkness. He didn't remember falling asleep. Had he fallen asleep while they were having sex? Had they just kept going until they'd wound up like this?

Narazaki felt uneasy without her right beside him. *I didn't do anything rude to her yesterday, did I? Did I behave properly?* These things started to bother him. This was a constant habit of his. "Hey," Narazaki called out. The woman turned around, and he let out a surprised, "What?"

"The woman you were with yesterday has already left. Today I'll be here for you."

She smiled. She was wearing nothing but a bath towel. *Today I'll be here? What does she mean? What is this place?*

"I thought I'd make breakfast," she said. *She's beautiful.*

I wanted that girl so badly yesterday. But I'm already thinking how beautiful this new girl is. Narazaki wanted to laugh out of hopelessness. *I'm the worst. But this is me.* The woman opened the front of her towel. Narazaki was breathless.

"Look. You're already so hard."

The woman caressed Narazaki's penis. Narazaki kissed her. He buried his face in her chest. He sucked on her nipples. Just like he had yesterday.

"Mm . . . You're like a baby."

Narazaki began to move his tongue. He touched the nipple he wasn't sucking with his fingertips.

"Mm . . . Babies don't do that."

Narazaki ran his tongue over the woman's sweaty body. She giggled invitingly. *I'm becoming a pervert,* he thought. *But—is that wrong? What's wrong with what I'm doing?*

NARAZAKI HAD just woken up when the door opened and a man with long hair entered. Where had that last woman gone? Even though a man had just walked in, Narazaki didn't feel embarrassed. Was it because his lower half was covered with a blanket? No, that wasn't it. It was because the man was smiling. And his smile showed he had no desire to punish Narazaki. No. More than anything, his smile showed that they were the same.

"You are going to meet the leader," the long-haired man said quietly.

The leader. I wonder if that's Sawatari? The man who scammed Shotaro Matsuo.

"Please get dressed. Your clothes have been cleaned. I'll wait outside."

He had been wearing this black tracksuit for a long time.

He should have been used to seeing his own clothes, but for some reason they looked like someone else's abandoned shell. *How long have I been here?* Women didn't come every day. They came for about four days in a row, then no one came for two, and then they'd start coming again for another four days. Was that about right? It was slightly off from a weekly cycle. *I've really lost track of myself,* Narazaki thought. *But could I be satisfied just losing myself in women? After one night's sleep, part of me already wants a woman again. It's like an addiction, a bad habit.*

Have I already been brainwashed? Narazaki wasn't sure. But he couldn't imagine that all the sex was just some sort of free service. *Is this normal here? Maybe this is just the way things are here?*

Narazaki got dressed and opened the door. The long-haired man was waiting outside. Narazaki followed him down the hallway. It was quiet. It was like the building was alive, but the people inside it simply sat silently.

The long-haired man opened a door. There were stairs on the other side. It seemed they wouldn't take the elevator. His shoes made a hard clicking noise.

The man turned around. "I can't go past this point. But you will meet the leader."

It was too dim for Narazaki to see the expression on the man's face. Narazaki walked past him and opened the door in front of him. A man sat in the dark. *So this is the leader.* Narazaki couldn't make out his face, but he was certain. This man was different from other people. He was older, but his facial features were sharp. *How old is he? This is Sawatari. There's no mistaking it.*

"To reject life," the man whispered suddenly.

Narazaki stared at him. "What?"

"Isn't that what you said? When you first got here?"

Should I nod? I'm not sure.

"You are great. That's all we need."

Narazaki thought the man was smiling. *Why?* His eyes wouldn't quite adjust to the dim light. His heart was racing.

"Why me?" Narazaki finally managed to ask. His voice was hoarse.

"Why? What do you mean?"

"I'm not good at anything."

The room was too quiet.

"Good? You think there are good and bad humans? You're still worried about things like that?"

The man leaned forward low in his chair, turning his face to look up at Narazaki. He was expressionless. *What is this man?* Narazaki's throat went dry.

"What is this place?"

"Does it bother you?" The man leaned back again deep into his chair. "That's strange. Most people live without knowing what the world they live in is, or what their fate has in store for them."

"That's true." *Why am I agreeing? I don't mean to say I'm satisfied not knowing anything about this place. Or maybe I do? Is there any reason for me to learn more?*

"Will you choose to go on suffocating in this country of asphalt and exhaust fumes, worrying about what other people think? Or will you join us?"

Narazaki couldn't take his eyes off the man.

"It's not up to you to choose. You are my disciple. I need you."

He's trying to act like a father. In that room I was just in, they sent those women to try to act like mothers. They are infiltrating the empty spaces in people's lives. That's how they do it, Narazaki thought. But he felt there was something deeper to this than what one could find in a manual on brainwashing. *The world is mysterious. And this cult is no different.* Narazaki realized he was kneeling. *When did I do that?*

"People pray," the man said. "In the West they lock their fingers, and in the East they put together the flat palms of their hands. This difference represents the difference in their feelings toward god. To lock your fingers represents the strength of your plea to a god who controls your fate. In the East we are more reserved. It's as if we're saying, 'If it's possible, I'd like you to consider me as well.' Now your hands are on your lap. That's good. Go back to Matsuo."

"What?"

"Infiltrate Matsuo's group. I will send you orders later."

"Why?"

"Why?" Narazaki thought he sensed some emotion in the man's empty face, but he wasn't sure what it was. *"That's how life is.* No one can know why they are doing what they do. But there is one difference between me and the rest of the world. I need you."

There's no way I can agree to this. But Narazaki got up. He was already convincing himself to do as he was told.

"We will call you back from time to time," the man said. Like a father teaching his son a warm life lesson. The women rose up in the back of Narazaki's mind. "A little decadence is good for you."

11

Narazaki looked again at the screen of his cell phone, which had been confiscated and then returned to him. More than a month had passed. He'd thought it had been about three weeks. His sense of time was off.

He left the cult in that same station wagon, its windows sealed off with sheets. That way he couldn't tell where they were.

The world inside the cult had seemed like fiction. Narazaki had focused too hard there, and his enervation seemed to warp space. Maybe life in most cults felt like that. Narazaki recalled the crazy terror attack from when he was in high school, when they'd released sarin gas in several subway cars at the same time. The terrorists had been cult members. That day everyone's lives had felt like fiction—everyday reality was powerless in the face of that sort of dramatic plot twist. But everyday reality is vast and subdued. Eventually, it dismantles the drama, sentences to death those who enacted it, and returns everything to normal. The dead are forgotten, and the living begin to prepare again for the next work of fiction to appear.

Narazaki entered through the open gate. Was it because Sawatari had told him to? Even he wasn't sure. Narazaki could think of nothing except meeting Matsuo. The truth was he wanted to return to that dim compound—to stay in that tight space, inside those women. He heard a voice say: *pitiful*. It might have been his loneliness speaking to him.

He could see Mineno from across the large garden. She noticed him, too. She was wearing a long beige coat. *It's good that I ran into her first*, Narazaki thought. But he could see the unease on her face.

"Are you okay?" she asked. "You've lost a lot of weight."

Narazaki had a hard time speaking. Looking at Mineno, he thought how beautiful she was. As she approached him, he imagined having sex with her. He didn't have the strength to smile. He was useless.

"I had the flu."

"For a whole month?"

"No, but it took forever to get my strength back. I'm finally feeling better," Narazaki said. Mineno did not seem to feel sorry for him. Maybe they knew already. Or maybe they'd thought from the beginning that he was from the cult.

"Matsuo-san is here. When we told him about you, he said he wanted to meet you. Come this way."

He could sense reluctance in her movement. Maybe she could smell all those disgusting women on his body.

He walked down the hallway of the mansion and stopped

in front of the sliding fusuma doors. He didn't see Yoshida. Mineno opened the door.

"Matsuo-san, this is Narazaki-san."

There was an old man sitting on a cushion. He looked smaller than he did on the DVDs. He was very skinny. His left arm hung limp. From the videos, Narazaki had thought Matsuo was in his seventies, but now he realized he was much older. He was wearing a black sweater and green pants, sitting with his legs crossed. His eyes and ears were huge. He looked at Narazaki.

"What did you think of my DVDs?"

Do his eyes look big because he's so skinny? Narazaki won dered. His pure white hair wasn't long, but it was so thick it seemed to be overflowing. His chin was narrow, his nose finely shaped. Though it was covered in wrinkles, his face was well put together. He was clean-shaven.

"Oh, they were wonderful," Narazaki managed to say.

"What did you watch? Did you see 'The Last Choles terol'?" The old man's voice was thin, but it carried.

"No, not yet."

"Ah, that's too bad."

Matsuo's face went blank, like he had suddenly lost all interest. He grabbed a wood-patterned backscratcher with his right hand and scratched around his feet. His back wasn't particularly hunched.

"Mine-chan," he called out suddenly. "Let me touch your boobs."

Narazaki looked at the old man, shocked. What was he saying?

"No," Mineno said calmly.

"In exchange, I'll let you touch my dick."

"Absolutely not."

Narazaki stared at the two of them, flabbergasted.

"Why not? Isn't that fair?"

"No, it isn't fair."

"Are you saying that men and women aren't equal?"

"That's right. Women are better."

"Narazaki-kun."

"Yes," he answered, startled at being called on.

"Will you ask her?"

"Ask her what?"

"About her boobs."

"What? Really?"

"Really. This is your training."

Training? What is he saying? Has he gone mad?

"I . . . can't."

"I told you. It's training."

"Training . . . ?" Narazaki looked at Mineno. She seemed upset. "Umm, may the leader touch your breasts?"

"No."

"Failure!" The old man was upset.

What is this? Narazaki was getting caught up in something bad, but he wasn't sure what.

"You failed! And I thought I was going to make you a . . . what's it called? Uh, an officer. But if Mine-chan won't let me touch her breasts, you fail. If you change your mind you can come back, Mine-chan."

Mineno left.

What's going on? I thought she was this old man's disciple.

"But, Narazaki-kun, if I did touch Mine-chan's boobs, if she wanted me to, what would I do then?"

"What?"

"I'm asking you what would I do if she changed her mind. I'd have to take a Viagra."

"Oh . . . Really?"

"Really! Well, maybe not. Maybe I could manage without it."

The old man scrunched his eyebrows. One of his sleeves was slightly pushed up; Narazaki noticed he was wearing a Doraemon wristwatch. Unbelievable. This group was in the worst possible state. Their leader was going mad.

"How is Sawatari doing?"

". . . What?"

The old man was looking at him. But he hadn't spoken particularly harshly. His voice remained soft. "Oh, right. You can't tell me about that. But he's probably doing okay, right?"

Narazaki was at a loss for words. He couldn't get his thoughts straight.

". . . Uh."

"Well?"

"How—?" Narazaki blurted. His heart was racing.

"How? Oh, how did I know you were there? Well, you came here looking for Tachibana-chan, right? And then you vanished for a month, and showed up again. So wouldn't it be normal to think that in that time you'd been lured in by them, and they sent you back here again? Also, you look so gaunt."

"I . . ."

"Oh, don't worry, don't worry! You don't have to say anything. If you tell me anything, you'll be betraying them, right? But since I know, you can stay here without feeling guilty. I am the leader of this place, after all."

Narazaki stood stunned. What was this old man? His heart beat even faster.

Come to think of it, he still hadn't introduced himself.

"If—if you assume that's true, would that be all right with you?"

"All right how?"

"Well, I mean, it might be . . . disadvantageous for you to have me around."

The old man stared into Narazaki's face with interested eyes, and then burst into a grin.

"Disadvantageous? There's no helping that. But you came here because you wanted to talk to me about something, right? Why would I turn you away? Even if you hate me, I like you. Isn't that good enough?"

MINENO WASHED Matsuo's dishes.

He seemed to be eating properly. But he was picky. *Soon he'll come saying he wants a snack. I wonder if he'll take a manju. But he must be healthy if he can harass me so much.*

Yoshiko came into the kitchen. Over the past few days Yoshiko had tried to stay near Mineno. But Mineno couldn't talk to her about it.

"Don't worry about the dishes. I'll do them," Yoshiko said.

"I'm almost done."

Every time Mineno saw Yoshiko she thought the same thing, that she must have been very beautiful when she was young. Even now she was rather pretty. She was short, but her back was straight. Yet she must have been well over seventy.

"Don't worry about the snacks. You can leave him."

The back of Mineno's head hurt. Maybe she'd tied her hair too tight.

"No, I'll take them."

"He's going to harass you again."

Mineno smiled slightly. "He doesn't have the courage to actually touch me, so it's fine."

"That's true, but doesn't it bother you? You should just pull out his dentures and shove that manju down his throat."

As Yoshiko opened the refrigerator, she began to sing. It felt like the moment was almost right. *Will she say something, I wonder? But she might think that if she says something, I'll stop coming here. Cowardly humans. Cowardly and kind. She definitely won't say anything. But still . . .*

"You're pregnant, aren't you?"

Mineno looked at Yoshiko, surprised. Yoshiko was smiling.

"You're really stubborn—you really weren't going to say anything. You can't see it in your body yet, but I can see it in your attitude and your face . . . And the aura you're giving off." Her face grew wrinkly when she smiled. Something scratched at the edge of Mineno's memory. Not an image, but an absence. Mineno's mother had never looked at her with a face like that.

"The father's Takahara-kun, right? That would be my guess, anyway."

Mineno couldn't say anything. She was about to cry. Her eyes fixed on Yoshiko's thin hand as it shot out and grabbed the faucet handle, turning off the running water.

"It's hard, isn't it? You know he has another lover, right?"

"Yes."

Mineno noticed that she was responding as if by reflex. *Why does Yo-chan-san even know about Takahara-kun's relationships? Takahara-kun was one of the people who helped scam Matsuo-san.* She couldn't get her thoughts straight.

"Do you know who Takahara-kun's lover is?

"No."

"It's Rina-san."

Mineno couldn't breathe. Her heart began to race.

"Well, she told us her name was Rina, but we all found out that was a fake name when Narazaki showed up. Ryoko Tachibana. He came here to look for her, too, right? . . . How complicated."

When Mineno had first heard the name Ryoko Tachibana from Narazaki, she hadn't recognized it. But then he'd showed her Rina's picture. Even then Mineno hadn't known that this woman was Takahara's lover. She'd known he had someone, but never imagined it was Rina—she'd thought Rina and Takahara were only business partners. *It doesn't matter. I have to apologize.* Mineno had started seeing Takahara after he'd scammed them. *He betrayed us, and I . . .* And it hadn't only been once. *So many times. So many times I could forget who I was.*

"Don't worry. Shotaro knows, too."

"What?"

"We know everything, you know. You haven't done anything wrong."

"But . . ." Mineno's voice cracked. "It was after they tricked Matsuo-san."

"It's fine. There's no problem. That's love for you . . . Shotaro was more disappointed that you obviously like young, cool guys."

Mineno stared at Yoshiko, dazed.

"Don't worry about it. Just take care of your body. I can tell from looking at your face you're going to keep it. Now you can give birth with one less thing to worry about."

Her hand touched Mineno's cheek. Mineno realized she was crying.

"I don't have any children, so I can't give you much advice."

Yoshiko left, singing another song Mineno didn't know. Mineno watched her back as she walked away.

But Matsuo-san and Yo-chan-san don't know, she thought. *They don't know that even though I'm sorry for what I did, I don't regret it.* She really did want to apologize to them, but if Takahara called her now, she'd go running to him. She'd happily give herself to him. If he told her to steal something from Matsuo, she'd cry the whole time, but she'd do it.

She clenched her teeth.

I want to die.

Mineno had gone to the obstetrician twice in the past few days, and twice had been told that she wasn't pregnant. Even though she knew she must be. Takahara's child must be inside her. *It absolutely, absolutely is.*

Mineno placed her hand on her stomach, as she had done many times since her period, which was rarely late, had failed to come.

The doctors don't understand. I must be pregnant. I must be careful. I must protect this child.

MATSUO WAS sitting on the toilet.

He thought to himself that he was preventing the expansion of entropy, and laughed.

Narazaki had looked so young, only a little over thirty. A young man trapped in a tiny hell. But probably surrounded by women—that sort of hell was enviable.

Matsuo coughed, gently at first, but the cough grew

stronger, so he covered his mouth with toilet paper. There was blood.

"I know," he whispered. He tossed the toilet paper away unhappily. "I know," he whispered again. *But let me last just a little bit longer.*

It would be nice if it was painless, he thought listlessly. *How tragic would it be if this long life of mine ended with pain?* Matsuo laughed. How many people really believed it was hemorrhoid surgery?

He left the bathroom as if nothing had happened.

The air was damp. It was like the moisture had failed to become mist and was just clinging to his body instead. *It will probably rain tomorrow.*

The lobby of the Publikum Hotel. A massive chandelier hung from the high ceiling. If there was an earthquake, would it fall? If it did, all the glass would shatter and pierce everyone below. Though it wasn't pleasant work, he had to keep track of these sorts of contingencies.

Takahara passed through the lobby and entered the adjoining café. He was wearing a suit and carrying a newspaper as instructed. He took a seat and ordered an iced coffee. He opened the newspaper like an actor in a play.

A thin waitress brought him his iced coffee. He took it with a smile. Her eyes lingered on Takahara. She's beautiful, he thought.

Before sitting down, Takahara had checked his surroundings. There were no cameras. The other customers had grim looks on their faces. It seemed they were all carrying some private burden. Takahara had been told to sit and read the newspaper, that someone would approach him. He lit a cigarette and scanned the paper. All the articles in the politics section reported the successes of government officials.

The customer next to Takahara was eating pasta. Takahara imagined the shreds of noodles he bit off mixing with the saliva in his mouth and falling back to his plate. He felt the urge to vomit, so he turned back to the newspaper to make himself feel better.

News of starving people in Africa. Lives that could be saved for the cost of one rich person's dessert. People who killed each other in the name of god. The people who used them.

There was a man sitting at a somewhat distant table. He was a Westerner. Takahara's head began to hurt. His pulse sped up. *Is it him? It must be. But I can't get flustered. There is nothing at stake.*

He turned back to the paper. He couldn't read because of his headache. He could process the individual words, but not the overall meaning.

I promised myself to always remain calm no matter what. He lit another cigarette. *My hand isn't shaking, is it?* His headache grew worse. The other tables grew blurry. His vision began to go out of focus at the periphery. With his slightly blurred vision, he noticed that the Westerner was looking at him. The man seemed frozen, like a sticker pressed onto the scene. Was this some sort of signal? *I need to understand what he's saying.* "Outside?" Takahara mouthed the word in Japanese. The man didn't respond. Next, Takahara tried English. "Outside?" Still no response. His hair was long, and his eyes were blue. Just when Takahara thought he must be wrong, a Japanese man at a table even farther away moved his fingers slightly. He was pointing outside. Despite his headache, Takahara stood. He paid. The Westerner showed no signs of moving.

He left the hotel, and after a moment his phone rang. Takahara answered in a serious tone. There was a lot of noise in the background, but it didn't sound like the café he'd just left.

"You're being followed. I'm sure of it." It was a man's voice. Deep.

"By who?"

"I don't know. Probably someone from your cult."

Takahara tried to think. He had come here by taxi. Who would follow him?

"The meeting is canceled."

"Wait!"

"Don't worry. We'll contact you again."

They hung up. Takahara could do nothing but listen to his own heartbeat.

What was happening? Had his subordinates followed him? Takahara considered the possibility. *No, that can't be it. They still don't know that I've been in touch. It couldn't be . . . Has the leader found me out? Did someone confess to him? No. No one I've involved can contact him directly. I can trust them. They have blind faith. They believe in our cult, and the leader, and me. They all believe that this plan is the leader's. They believe themselves to be the best of the best, hand-picked by the leader. They also believe that if they tell anyone else, they'll lose their position. I couldn't have been found out. Everything must be going according to plan.*

I have to find the culprit, Takahara thought. *I have to find the culprit.*

MATSUO-SAN'S LECTURES, III, PART 1

Today I'd like to talk about these beings called humans.

First of all, what do you all think happens to our bodies after we die? If your family's Buddhist, you're cremated, so you'll be taken to the crematorium and burnt, and everything but the bones becomes smoke.

But actually, even when the human body is burnt in a crematorium, it doesn't disappear. As I've told you before, our bodies are made entirely of atoms. When your body is burnt in a crematorium, the bonds between atoms are broken at the molecular level, but the atoms that make up our bodies are not actually destroyed in that process. Of course they don't vanish. The atoms that made up our bodies rise into the sky as smoke and spread everywhere. In other words, we continue existing across the surface of the earth.

And then those molecules may become part of someone else's body. They may bond with other atoms in the air, become molecules again, be taken up inside some other living thing, and if someone eats that living thing, they may become part of a human again. For example, the atoms that made up the body of Himiko, the ancient empress of Japan, may be in your body now. Please look hard at your hand, your fingers. There is a chance that the parts of people who lived long ago, and even those who died just recently, may be in there.

It is thought that since the birth of the planet, none of the atoms here have vanished. To destroy the nucleus of an atom requires certain conditions found in outer space, or special tools like a particle accelerator. So you could also say that *all the components of people's bodies have been being reused since long ago.* Of course, this includes not only humans, but all living things. All things, generally speaking, have been being recycled since long, long ago. Looking at it this way, don't you think it's sort of amazing? There are many pieces that made up many ancient things inside our bodies now. When some living thing is born, it does not just appear here out of nothingness. Materials that already exist in space and on earth come together, and as they fit together, they form something larger. That's all.

Here I'd like you to remember something I've discussed before. Within a year, all the atoms that make up a human body will be replaced completely. The materials that make up our bodies have been being reused since long ago and will continue to be replaced. So what are we?

In this world, individuals may not exist, at least not on a material level. We are constantly changing, and when a human dies, the substances that made up their body are recycled to make something else. It's as if we are *part of some larger, constant flow* that has continued from long ago up to the present. There really is no such thing as the individual here. People say, "We're all one," but that's not just a saying or abstraction. It's actually true on the material level.

So why do we think we exist as individuals? That is the work of the brain.

Our brains make us think humans are all individuals. Our brains produce the concept of the individual (me), and even though all our cells are constantly being replaced, that individual, that me, is passed on from instant to instant. How strange is that! Even though the material that makes up our brains is constantly changing, I continue to exist as I was. How is this possible?

Remember that my consciousness and I cannot act on the collection of atoms that make up my brain. We have been reusing the same materials that built bodies long ago, and even now they are constantly changing. And yet this thing called me continues to exist from one second to the next until I die. This "I" that is passed on from moment to moment, which I recognize as myself, can't act on anything. It is the atoms that make up our bodies that have always had the power to produce this "I" by joining together.

This is too strange.
What does this all mean?
What are we?

We'll think about these questions as I continue my talk. But for now, let's talk about human fate.

Imagine you hit a billiard ball. Once it's hit, we can predict what will happen to it. Of course, we can't do the precise calculations, but logically we could figure it out based on the force and angle with which the ball was hit, the friction of the table, air resistance, and—if an earthquake were to occur right afterward—the tension of the earth's plates, et cetera. Right after the cue ball is hit, the balls it will go on to strike have already been determined, as have the specific pockets they'll fall into.

I've discussed before that the universe began with the Big Bang. A type of explosion. Which means that how the universe developed depended on the amount of energy, its force, the temperature, and what kind of particles were emitted. In other words, if there had been a different amount of energy, one would expect a different universe. Which means one could potentially argue that it was already determined that the universe would take the shape it did right after the Big Bang, as soon as it was born.

I also mentioned before that if the value of the elementary charge that determines the strength of electromagnetism, and the coupling constant that determines the strength of the strong atomic force that holds together protons and neutrons, had been slightly different from what they are now, humans may not have been born. Can't we rephrase that and say that *this world was filled with the possibility of bringing about human life*? This universe was filled with the potential to bring about stars and planets, and the potential to create the sun. If we put it a little more extremely, can't we say that it was decided this would all happen? Was it not determined at the moment of the Big Bang that humans would come into being? I'd like to assume that this is true.

To advance this hypothesis, let's talk a bit about biology. I want to think about the simplest of living things: single-celled organisms. I'd like to get to the root of the problem of free will by looking at these simple organisms.

For example, consider the paramecia. These single-celled creatures are used to living in water at a temperature of twenty-five degrees Celsius, so naturally they gather in areas that are twenty-five degrees. Of course, they all get there by moving this way and that, and only gradually assemble in those twenty-five-degree spots. And in a very animal way, some of them arrive late. If there were some food outside of that twenty-five-degree spot, the latecomers would benefit.

While the paramecia that are already in a spot that's twenty-five degrees tend to stay there, even they constantly leave and return and leave again. And the more parameca there are in one spot, the more their movements seem independent. If there are only a few of them, there's less individuality. The larger their number, the more slow ones there are, and the more they circle around showily. There's more variety.

And the strange part about this is that it holds true even for bacteria with identical genes. Even though these simple creatures have perfectly identical genes, depending on the number in their group, their movements come to be more or less unique. In other words, the more these simple creatures gather together, the more volition they seem to have. And, on top of that, their volition also seems to increase the worse the conditions they live in get.

So what is the origin of these paramecia's volition?

We know that it arises from the electric noise within their cells. When there is a large electric vacillation, their direction changes. And this electric noise comes from heat variation within their molecules. Molecules move because of heat. While these movements seem to be completely random and irregular, changes in the surrounding temperature and many other things cause the electricity to fluctuate, and then the paramecia suddenly start to move. In other words, the origin of their volition is heat variation within molecules. How scientific.

There is a very convincing explanation that we humans, who have advanced from paramecia to reach the peak of evolution, have a volitional process going on within us and cannot halt it. I also believe this is true. We don't just respond to external stimuli by producing electrical noise and then reacting. Even if there is no external stimulus, advanced animals like humans can produce their own electrical noise and move their own bodies. The electrical noise we produce is the origin of consciousness.

Again, please remember that human consciousness cannot affect the brain.

In which case, what is free will? Do we have free will? The answer would be no. The origin of free will is the fluctuation of molecular heat. In other words, everything originates as a chemical reaction on the atomic level. Which means that from the time of the Big Bang, it was already decided that humans would come into existence. And if that's true, our lives, what every human has done in all of our long, long history, all originated with fluctuations of molecular temperature. And if everything is simply the chemical workings of atoms, that would mean everything was already decided at the time of the Big Bang. But this must be wrong. Or, accurately speaking, *it may be wrong*.

Now we will need to talk about quantum mechanics.

MATSUO-SAN'S LECTURES, III, PART 2

Quantum mechanics is, to greatly simplify, a theory that describes an incredibly tiny world that can't be explained by traditional understandings of causality, namely classical physics. If you hit a billiard ball, we know it'll follow a certain trajectory. That's true. However, on the micro level, you often can't simply explain things by saying that happened, so this will happen.

Let's look at an example. Let's say a proton and an atomic nucleus collide with a certain amount of energy. This doesn't always lead to the same result. There is a certain chance that proton and nucleus will wind up in state X, and a certain chance they will wind up in state Z. We cannot find conditions under which the collision will lead only to state X. So we can only discuss the results in terms of probability. This means that we don't always experience the more likely scenario, so adopting quantum theory means everything in this world becomes a matter of chance or probability. The current state of the world is the result of many coincidences.

To see "causality" in the motion of physical objects, first we must observe those objects. Unfortunately, it is incredibly difficult to observe electrons, for example, precisely. Even shining a light on particles as small as electrons causes them to move. Light is both a particle and a wave, and it basically kicks the electron out of place. A detailed explanation would be quite long, so I'll be brief, but if one tries to confirm the position of an electron, its speed becomes unknown, and if one tries to confirm its speed, its position becomes unknown. We call this thing the "uncertainty principle." And in this imprecise microworld, it is only natural that we cannot predict causation. We can say that physics' principles of causality break down. We can only describe the objects of this world in terms of probabilities.

However, this is entirely a matter of human observation, and has nothing to do with the reality of these objects, I think. We need not consider everything based on the limited nature of human perception.

There was a famous debate between Bohr, who was a pioneer in quantum theory, and Einstein. Einstein criticized Bohr, saying something like, "God doesn't play dice with the world. We must be able to explain nature more perfectly than by covering everything up with probabilities and odds. However, at the moment, humans cannot grasp this perfection, and we must use probabilities and statistics, as they are an effective tool to explain the world."

Quantum theory is useful for describing the world, but it is just a tool. It would be silly to make it the foundation of our understanding of the world. Einstein claimed that nature is not controlled by vague sets of probability. There must be a definitive explanation of causation at the root of things. However, these days Einstein is generally considered to have lost this debate.

But who was actually right? The concepts of quantum theory cover a lot. The theory is enormous. According to these concepts, traveling back in time is possible, and—though it seems incredible—humans can even pass through walls. However, the probability of such an occurrence would be one divided by ten to a power so high that if you wrote three zeroes every centimeter, the number would be several hundred thousand light years long. In other words, it's an absurd number. This theory is unmistakably incomplete.

I would like someone to appear and solve these mysteries for us. These problems don't stop with physics. It would be quite interesting to combine them with theories of the brain. The brain is also made up of atoms, and if we could understand how cause and effect work in terms of atoms, we'd be able to understand everything about the brain. It would be the greatest discovery in human history—how everything is decided. In other words, we would have discovered fate. Love, work, even the most trivial-seeming of gestures would all ultimately become just like that billiard ball.

But we cannot make any definitive statements at this point in time. So we can only discuss things in terms of possibility.

First, we have the theory that the fate of everything is predetermined. This is the argument against quantum mechanics, that on the quantum level everything is undecided. In this scenario, we can still imagine a future where we've discovered the cause of everything. That would make us nothing more than the audience in the completely scripted show called *Our Lives*.

The second option we have is to rely completely on quantum theory. Everything in this world would boil down to probability and chance. This would mean believing that humans and this earth came into existence totally by chance. And that there's no such thing as fate. In this second case, we are the audience to an unscripted show that is just a series of coincidences.

No, that is not quite accurate. There are limits to what sort of "coincidences" can come to be. Please remember that the universe was filled with the possibility of producing humans. *Even if we suppose that the origin of human life was chance, the probability of it was not zero.* To give a contrary example, the chance that now all of you listening to me speak will suddenly grow wings on your back is zero. In other words, the possibilities of this world are limited, and there's no such thing as total randomness.

So, we are the audience watching a show called life that is a series of coincidences within certain limits. That would be more accurate.

So, which is correct? I believe that both are correct. In the end, they're the same thing.

Everyone, please think about your past. From the time you were born until now, you've followed a single path here.

Someone with a deep knowledge of quantum theory would probably say that there are versions of you who have chosen each possible life, and you are nothing more than one of the possible yous. This world was created through human choices, and there are as many worlds as there are choices people have made.

But I don't care at all about that sort of stupid argument. Saying that doesn't make anyone feel better. It doesn't change anything. Because the you of this world has followed a single path up to this moment.

And in the same way, I'm sure your future will follow a single path. At some point you will do this, and not do that, become this, and not become that. But those events become one path made up of the succession of choices that you made at those times, in those instants. That path will continue until you die. Nothing will change the fact that no matter what sort of choices you make, no matter what you do, *when you turn around,* those choices will form a single path. You cannot walk two separate paths, and you don't need the burden of imagining you could. You should just follow your path.

Whether that path is already decided or is something you can change, in the end, it's still one path. It's decided. It's fate. In the end, fate is nothing more than a human concept. Chance is also nothing more than a human concept. However, there's no mistake. You are walking down a single path. I gave the example of paramecia before. Like them, we should just live our lives looking for a comfortable twenty-five-degree spot. However, on this path, humans must bear sadness. For we are the only beings that are clearly aware we will eventually die.

In other words, to be human is to be conscious of the fact that we will die, and to know that in this great, unceasing flow of atoms, we continue to travel along our single path for seventy or eighty years, and then vanish. If you believe that consciousness cannot act on the brain, then you are simply being presented with that path, being continually made to see that you will die. Human consciousness has grown highly complex. And because of that our pleasures are immense, as are our sadnesses. Our breadth of emotion is the greatest among all living things because of our high level of consciousness. But in the end we will die. Even though we've known such great pleasures in this world, we will die. Trillions of humans have died. Trillions more will probably die.

This world was always filled with the possibility of humans coming into being. And atoms have always had the power to create consciousness by joining together. This must mean something. As I've said before, I believe we are part of a gradient that includes other dimensions. It would be strange if we weren't. This world is too perfect for it to all be coincidence. The path we walk cannot be unrelated to that gradient. And that gradient must be connected to countless stories.

Since ancient times, humans have had advanced consciousness and have continued to yearn for stories. We don't just create gods; we also always create legends about them. You all watch television dramas and read manga, right? Even gossip about famous people is stories. Humans are the only animals on this earth that desire stories. Our lives are stories, and as we progress through those stories, we seek more stories. *In other words, we exist amid overlapping stories.* I believe the overlapping nature of these stories has something to do with the gradient. What's important to these layers of other dimensions is not the actual movement of our bodies, what we speak, or see. I think what appears in our minds, how our consciousnesses work, is probably more important. Our consciousness is overlaid on those layers. We are staring at ourselves from those layers. And we are experiencing stories.

To rephrase this, humans are just stories that appear in that great, unceasing flow of atoms. And I wonder if we're anything more than just the audience watching those stories from a different layer. I wonder if it is this strange balance between existing in this layer and another—this strange balance itself—which makes the world the way it is. Maybe there is *something* that desires our stories. But we had better live as if at some point there will be meaning. We must strengthen our bodies and pass through this single story, through this flow of atoms. That's what it means to live.

This story is difficult. I don't want to sound like I'm saying anything irresponsible or overly optimistic about life. But no matter what, we must pass through this story.

If we generalize, there are two different attitudes about life: one found in the East and one in the West. In the West many people think of this life as god's test. People there live their lives thinking that when some difficulty arises, that is fate, and it is a test from god. God only gave you such a test because you can pass it. You could also just call it a test of fate, without using the word god. It is beautiful to see people challenge fate. I believe it is, at least.

In the East, people value the impermanence of all things. Everything returns to nothing. Everything eventually disappears, so there's no need to worry about a difficult life. Suffering and sadness will eventually disappear as well. You must swallow your suffering and sadness, and wait for them to vanish into the peace. It is beautiful to see sadness and suffering disappear. I believe it is, at least.

There is no choosing which attitude is right. I feel that the truth is somewhere in between. You could also say that both are true. I think sometimes you must challenge fate, and other times you must wait for everything to vanish. Whether everything is decided or everything can be changed, you must be strong of will and choose the path that appears before you. You need that sort of attitude to keep going.

Everyone, please continue along your path and live through your story. Those countless atoms that have been here since the distant past—this highly refined, massive and complex system—everything is here for your story. The atoms currently giving your body shape will remain after your death. They will be here for someone else's story.

The laws of physics, this system of countless flowing atoms, is an incredibly fertile and extravagant thing.

May you all find your comfortable, twenty-five-degree spot. That's it for today.

15

"Excuse me, leader."

A man in white dragged a cart through the door.

The leader's room on the twenty-first floor was about thirty square meters. The whole space was dimly lit, and in the back was a door that led to his bedroom. The leader watched the man pulling the cart with blank eyes. There was a box on the cart, and in that box, a bound woman.

"Here is the woman from the religious organization I told you about."

The leader looked at the woman in the box expressionlessly. She was bound messily with layers of the kind of plastic rope used for packing. *Is she too scared to scream?* the man in white wondered.

"Mm," the leader murmured nebulously. She was tall and beautiful—was he attracted to her? The man in white wasn't sure. He began to worry.

"The religion this woman practices forbids sex. Also the excessive exposure of skin."

The leader got up from his chair and looked down into the box. The woman was wearing a white blouse and a long black skirt.

"Of course masturbation is also forbidden."

"I see. A cult." The leader's voice was monotone.

A cult? the man in white asked himself. *Isn't this a cult, too? No, we're different. This isn't a cult. This is . . . What is it? I haven't trained enough. Recently, I've been led astray by strange thoughts.* The man in white looked up and found the leader's grave stare resting on him. His heart leaped. *Did he see it? Did he see my doubt?*

"If they have sex, will they die?" the leader asked suddenly. His eyes showed no sign that he cared about the man's doubt.

Confused, the man said, "Yes. Both the women and the men who sleep with them."

"Mm."

"Six of them have actually died . . . We're not sure how."

The leader exhaled. What sort of feeling was he expressing? He didn't seem to be sighing or laughing.

"That's simple. Their god killed them."

The leader approached the woman. The man panicked and forced the woman in the box to stand. She struggled and fell over.

"I'm sorry. I should have put her to sleep."

"What for?" the leader asked.

What for? The man didn't understand. Two men entered the room. *Where did they come from? Was there a door somewhere?* The woman struggled as they carried her to a reclining chair like a dentist's. There were unpleasant-looking pipe stirrups attached to the chair. The men untied her, and then used the rope to bind her to the chair. They tied each leg to a stirrup, forcing her to part her legs. The woman struggled, but the men's expressions did not change at all. When they were done securing her in the chair, the men vanished back into the shadows. It was too dark to see where they went.

"What is the name of your god?" the leader asked the woman. She glared at him, but the leader's expression did not change at all. "What is your god's name?"

She didn't answer. The man answered for her. "He has no name. He simply protects his followers."

"How boring."

The leader laid his hand on the woman's long skirt and pulled it up. For some reason, the man in white felt as if someone were watching him from above. *What if*, he thought. *What if their god really exists? Not only will this woman die, but won't the leader die as well?*

This man used to be in the same cult as this woman. He had since joined this religion and learned that everything he had believed was false. He had had sex and he hadn't been struck down by their god. But deep in his body, a feeling he couldn't completely erase was returning. *What about this woman who still believes? Six believers have died—actually died. Six idiots who had made their vows to their god, but secretly indulged in debauchery. What if?* he kept wondering. *What if? Even people who don't believe in god don't go around kicking over other people's family shrines.*

The woman screamed. She was crying. The leader had

pulled her skirt all the way up. The man could see her white underwear. He looked away.

"No! No!" the woman was yelling. He took off her blouse, revealing her forbidden skin. He touched her underwear and bra. She tried to pull away, but the ropes restrained her. He ripped off her bra and underwear. The lights from the high ceiling lit her sweaty body. Though her cult believed there was no need for them, the woman's breasts were supple, overflowing with life. Her nipples were on the larger side. *What a body*, the man in white thought. *This is what her body looks like under her clothes* . . . He realized he had been watching the whole time.

The leader sucked on her breasts.

"Please stop! We'll . . . We'll . . ."

"You'll what?"

"Oh, god!"

The woman looked up at the lights. Her hair was a mess. It looked lewd. Her thin eyes glistened with tears. From where he was standing, the man in white could see her vulva between her long legs. The leader stuck his finger in her. He moved it gently.

"God . . . god . . ."

"What are you moaning about?"

". . . Why?"

Liquid ran down her legs.

"You," the leader said.

"No."

"I'm right. This is the kind of woman you are. It's been a long time, so you can really feel it now."

The leader bowed over her and stretched his tongue to her genitals, like a bug lapping up its food.

"Ah . . . Ah!"

"Mm?"

"God!"

"Yes, god is watching. Death is near."

The sound of her puddling wetness filled the room. *Can she hear that?* the man in white wondered. *Death, it's in this room.* The leader ran his mouth over the woman as if he was thirsty and wetting his throat with a glass of water.

"Ah! Ah!"

"Are you going to come? You should come."

"No! I . . ."

"Show your god."

"I'm sorry! Please forgive me! Ah . . . Ah . . . Please forgive me!"

"Mm?"

"God! God!"

"Do you like it when god watches?"

She raised her hips. She screamed.

"No! Ahh!"

Her body began shaking violently. But the leader didn't stop. She screamed, "Stop! Stop!" Her body convulsed again. She squirted disgustingly far. Drops of liquid reached the feet of the man in white.

"Ah! Ah! Ahh!"

Her body continued to convulse. She twisted in pain, and her chest heaved wildly. The leader undressed, then put his own genitals inside her writhing wet body.

"No!"

"I think death is supple and round . . . What about you?"

The leader moved his body. Pierced, the woman could only make indistinct noises. *Does she feel it?* the man in white wondered. Mysterious tears fell from his eyes. *How awful,* he thought. It had always been hard for him. They said he'd lost his parents because of his ancestors' desires. He had joined a reclusive group of women and lived for years deep in the mountains in a small hospital-like building. He lived under their strict precepts, and their ban on desire. He had spent his days feeling the presence of god.

The woman clung to the leader as if she didn't know what to do with all the pleasure she was feeling. Her legs were spread awkwardly wide. *You should cling to him,* he thought. *Cling to him. Cry out with your disgusting voice, and cling to him. Nothing we do is forbidden. It doesn't matter what people think. None of it matters.* He felt god watching him. *If you're going to kill me, kill me. We are only human. If you're going to kill me, do it.*

The leader continued to move his hips, and stuck his tongue in the woman's soft mouth. The leader was quite fit for his age. He was beautiful. *As beautiful as water,* the man thought for some reason. *Beautiful liquid.*

"Ah, ahh!"

The woman was licking the leader's tongue.

"Ah, ah, ahhh!"

The woman shook again violently, and the leader's body also trembled slightly. *Existence is trembling,* the man suddenly thought. *The leader is coming inside her.* The man was struck by the look that passed through the leader's eyes. *He should be in the midst of pleasure, but he's distracted by something. What is it? What?*

"You will live on the twenty-first floor," the leader said softly, pulling out of her. The woman nodded. Her cheeks were red and her eyes wet with tears. She was beautiful. *The look of a woman filled with sperm*, the man thought. *Her body is filled with sperm.*

"You do her too," the leader said to the man in white. The man nodded so naturally he surprised himself. *This isn't good,* he thought. *She and I, all we've done is leave one mess for another. But,* he thought, *it's not bad, either. All the leader did was have sex with her.*

The man in white stood before the woman with her legs spread. Their eyes met. At that compound she had been like a sister. *I never thought of her as such a beautiful woman.*

"Excuse me," the woman called to the leader.

"Mm?"

"Please watch. I want you to watch."

The woman looked at the man as if challenging him. She stared straight at him and smiled. Her lips were wet. She was beautiful. She had been set free. This wasn't good or evil. This had nothing to do with good or evil at all. *We've been set free. We . . .*

The man touched the woman's cheek gently.

The room was dark. Another day with no time to spare.

Takahara stared at the believers gathered there. There were sixteen people counting Takahara, in the twenty-five-square-meter space. They were all looking straight ahead. Their eyes were full of dedication and hope as they waited for Takahara's words.

They are happy, Takahara thought. *I want to be like them. But is the one who betrayed me here? I'm not sure. Will the leader see through me?*

"Conditions report. Sasahara?"

"Yes, sir," Sasahara said solemnly. He seemed to be barely suppressing his anticipation. There must have been some progress. "The exchange of the PPSh-41s which I reported on last week will be carried out next Tuesday. The gang members have already received the weapons, so we just need to make the exchange."

"Where will you make the trade?"

"In an apartment. They took out a weekly rental."

"Any possible risks?"

"I cannot say there are none, but I don't see how it would be strategic for them to attack us."

Takahara thought. As if in response to Takahara's silence, Sasahara continued to speak.

"If they were to attack us during the trade, it would either be to take our money without giving us the PPSh-41s, or because they do not have the guns and simply plan on stealing our money. For that reason, five of us will go to the rendezvous. I'm certain that this much money will not be worth the hassle of having to clean up five bodies. Of course, there is the possibility of them stealing the money without killing us, but our associates are well known in the underworld. I assume they wouldn't leave any evidence of making an unfair deal."

Takahara kept thinking. Would they really be okay? That wasn't what Takahara was worried about, though. What if this was a trap set by the police or Public Security? No one could be sure that it wasn't.

"And in the case that this is a Public Security Bureau trap," Sasahara said, ready to address Takahara's concerns, "we plan to say we belong to an extreme leftist group. We will likely be arrested, but that doesn't matter. The other believers will continue our mission."

The five men who were to make the trade looked hard at Takahara. Their expressions were entranced and fulfilled. Takahara couldn't help but be moved by them.

"I see. I won't forget your dedication."

Their eyes shone. A collective noise escaped from the

crowd, as if the joy inside them had leaked out. Their bodies swayed, and their breathing and voices merged in their sense of elation. They were becoming one. Inside they were all screaming in rapture.

"We are the elite."

"Yes."

"We are the chosen ones."

"Yes."

He could feel the heat of their bodies seeping into the air. They were all looking at Takahara. They were lost in their desires, and filled with forceful passion.

"We will need to train to use these PPSh-41s. I'll leave that up to you," Takahara said, looking at Yoshioka.

Yoshioka nodded gravely. He had once been a member of the Self-Defense Forces. "You don't need much skill to use an automatic rifle."

TAKAHARA CLIMBED up the freezing stairs.

The sound of his shoes echoed, making him feel like someone was following him. He stood before the leader's door, the previous elation still lingering in his body. He couldn't imagine that one of them had betrayed him. He couldn't believe that one of those men with such pure faces could be the informant. All he could imagine was that there wasn't an informant, that he had been found out by the leader himself. But how?

Takahara took a deep breath and knocked on the door. An indistinct voice came from inside. When he opened the door, the leader was lying on a couch, sadly petting a woman.

Monster, Takahara thought.

There was a hell inside the leader. But instead of resisting that hell, he let himself sink into it. *How can he hold women like that, with those gloomy eyes? He might as well not sleep with them, but still he reaches out for them as if out of habit. Unmoved. Like an insect licking sap from a tree.*

"Leader, you called?" Takahara asked quietly. *This bastard,* Takahara thought. *Even though he's a bastard, I'm still nervous in front of him. It's because he's a monster. His mind has failed, but his expression doesn't show it.*

"I didn't call you."

The leader wasn't looking at Takahara, but rather at the space between them. Were his eyes even seeing? What could he be looking at?

"I'm sorry to disturb you."

"You're not disturbing me. Oh, you mean her." The leader slowly stretched his neck out toward the woman next to him, and seized her tongue with his fingers. She did not resist. She let him do what he wanted to her. Takahara waited, tense. *There are people who type text messages to one person while talking to someone else. This bastard has sex.* Takahara felt himself about to smile.

"That woman, the Cupro girl . . . she tried to come for confession. She said she had personal contact with you."

The leader spread open the woman's legs and studied her genitals as if he were looking at a stain on her clothing. Takahara let out a small sigh. Was she so jealous that she'd lie like that? Just because he hadn't slept with her?

"I sent her to counseling."

"You aren't going to punish me?"

"Mm?"

Takahara could hear a wet noise coming from between the woman's legs. She started taking heaving, short breaths.

Takahara knew the leader wouldn't punish him for this contact with the Cupro girl. But he wanted to know something else—whether the leader had found out about his plan or not. He looked at the leader's eyes. He couldn't see any indication one way or another there.

"I wouldn't punish you. My successor."

Liar, Takahara said in his head. Why hadn't he ever made this cult an official religion? It wasn't just to hide from the Public Security Bureau, was it? *You're planning something. You must be planning something.*

The leader moved his fingers as if it were a great hassle. Like he was playing with a loose button on his coat. The woman, twisting in pleasure, shot Takahara short glances. Was she embarrassed at the wet sound coming from between her legs?

"I sent her to counseling. I'll try to make her want you more."

"So you won't bring her up here?"

"Mm."

This man could probably even lap at a woman who was madly in love with another man, Takahara thought. *He could probably find a way to sleep with a woman even if she was calling out my name instead of his. Just like he was licking sap from a tree. Without a single smile. Sadly.*

He was a different breed from Shotaro Matsuo. People flocked to Matsuo. It certainly seemed like people flocked to the leader as well, but it wasn't him they were drawn to. *It's like some viscous liquid is pouring out of him. People are drawn to that liquid. Then their darkest secrets dissolve into that liquid.*

The wet sound grew louder. Was the woman trying so hard

to close her legs because she was embarrassed, or because she was about to come? Takahara's mind went blank as he watched the woman's thin body rise. She grabbed the sheets she had soaked. Her long hair glinted in the white light.

It couldn't have been Ryoko, Takahara thought. *Ryoko certainly noticed something, but she doesn't have evidence.* But no, that's why he'd told her to leave. *If I do the negotiating, she could get out. Probably.*

There's no need for us to be together. For her to be involved in my life. This irreparable life.

Narazaki wound up helping set up for Matsuo's lecture.

The organization had no official registry, but there were plenty of people who left contact information so they could be notified next time there was an event. The people who left their email address were easy, because they could all be sent the same message, but calling everyone who left a phone number took quite a lot of effort.

"Does this flyer look okay?" Mineno asked Matsuo.

"Aren't you going to put a picture of my face on it?"

"Do you want me to?"

"I mean, my face is pretty moving, right?" Matsuo said, and stared at Mineno seriously. A tangerine came flying at him and Matsuo batted it away with his backscratcher. When Matsuo threw the tangerine back at Yoshiko, she caught it, and tossed it again. Matsuo batted it down again

with the backscratcher. Yoshida stepped between them to
get them to stop.

"Get out of the way, baldy," Matsuo told him.

Yoshida got mad. "I'm not bald, I'm a monk."

"Liar! Your hair fell out! Isn't that right? You just became a
monk because you went bald!"

"Are you really going to say that?" Yoshida challenged.
"Are you?"

"Yeah, I said it. You went bald! You can't change the fact
that you lost your hair!"

Narazaki and a woman named Komaki still needed to sort
through the folding chairs they'd line up in the garden and
remove the rusted ones. As he tried to leave the room the
tangerine struck his back.

"Yes?"

"Where are you going with Komaki-chan?" Matsuo asked,
angry.

Narazaki didn't understand the anger. "We're going to sort
out the chairs."

"You're just going to fool around, aren't you?"

"What?"

"You're going to go fool around with Komaki-chan, right?
Cozy up in the corner of the storehouse? You'll whisper
things to each other like, 'Oh, we shouldn't! Everyone's right
outside. Oh no!' Right?"

Narazaki was shocked.

"Is that why you asked me to help?" Komaki asked.

"No, of course not."

"Is that what you've been thinking about me?"

"No. Don't be stupid," Narazaki said to Matsuo. "Please,
give it a rest."

"Well then, answer this honestly," Matsuo said. He pointed his backscratcher straight at Narazaki. "Have you really never, not once, thought about Komaki-chan sexually? Even just for a second? If you lie, you get the candy punishment. I'll put my dentures in your mouth like a piece of candy!"

"Well—"

"I knew it!" Matsuo said.

Komaki let out a yelp and backed away from Narazaki.

"But this is unfair. When you ask that way . . . Yoshida-san, help me here."

"Shut up!"

"Don't tell me to shut up!" Narazaki was suddenly shouting.

"Don't be angry because you lost your hair, Yoshida," Matsuo said. "But if we compare your body to a globe, I bet there's still some hair in Australia."

"What? Why are you talking about continents?"

"Stop," Mineno said. "Yoshida-san's bald head has nothing to do with Narazaki-kun. Yoshida-san lost his hair all on his own. Right?" She had turned on Yoshida as if to start a fight. "You did that all by yourself."

Komaki was staring at Narazaki suspiciously. *What's wrong with these people?* Narazaki tried to edge out of the room, but Tanaka entered, blocking Narazaki's path. Today she was wearing a Che Guevara apron. *Where do they sell these?*

"Sorry to interrupt, but there are reporters here," Tanaka said with an anxious look on her face. "I'll try to get them to leave, but what should I do? There's a little bug spray left in the kitchen . . ."

"That should do it," said Yoshiko.

"You can't do that," Narazaki interrupted.

"Why not?"

"It's fine," Matsuo said. Tanaka nodded and tried to leave, but Narazaki held out a hand to stop her.

"Oh, right, Narazaki-kun," Matsuo said, pointing his backscratcher at him again. "You take care of them. Make them think you're crazy. Go out there without any pants, and say this: 'Are you the dentist? My penis has a pretty bad cavity.'"

"No thank you."

"Okay, Mine-chan, you go."

"No."

In the end, no one stopped the visitors from coming in. They were reporters from a magazine. There was a female interviewer and a male cameraman. Someone had turned down an interview over the phone, so they had come in person. They claimed to be investigating the renewed activity of this religious organization, but their aim was clearly to expose some suspicious cult activity. Narazaki was wary of them.

"While we can't offer much money, we would pay for an interview."

Matsuo's eyes looked strange. "We don't need any money. Instead, will you let me poke your boobs?"

"What?" the interviewer gasped. The cameraman lowered his camera. "Excuse me, but is this a joke?"

"No, I'm not joking. Let me poke your boobs," Matsuo told the interviewer seriously.

Mineno and the others exited the room, abandoning the shocked interviewer. Didn't they care about what would happen? They must know the repercussions of treating the media like that. Narazaki had no reason to, but he stayed in the room.

The interviewer was obviously angry. "I'm sorry, but are you making fun of us?"

"I'm not. I just asked if you would let me poke your boobs. After all, that's how it is, right? In life there are those who poke, and those who get poked. Maybe I'm the one who'll get poked. Maybe you are. Everyone has the potential to be poked. Do you follow me?"

"What?"

"I'm going to begin the incantation. *Mokopen, mokopen, who will be poked, mokopen!* Please, close your eyes."

"No."

"What did you say?" Matsuo suddenly lowered his voice. "Why won't you be poked? Why?"

"What?"

"Be poked, you bitch!" Matsuo stood up. The interviewer screamed, and the cameraman stepped between them to protect her.

"I'm sorry," Narazaki said. "He's possessed now."

"Possessed?"

"Yes. The personalities of all humans reside within the leader. And today . . ."

Narazaki escorted the interviewer and cameraman out of the room, then returned to Matsuo.

"What are you doing?"

Matsuo was sulking. "They came to make fun of us, so I made fun of them."

"No, that's not true. You really wanted to poke her boobs, didn't you?"

Matsuo waved his backscratcher left and right in front of his own face. "Of course not. It was just revenge."

"You're lying. You definitely wanted to poke her boobs, at least a little."

YOSHIKO WATCHED Mineno as they listened to the interviewers leave. With one hand on her stomach, Mineno looked at the flyers she'd printed. *Maybe,* Yoshiko thought. *Maybe she's not pregnant at all. Maybe she just thinks she is. Maybe she is that desperate. Maybe.*

Mineno turned around, so Yoshiko smiled at her. *If that's true, I need to embrace her. I'll have to hold her close and help bring her back. I'll have to make her forget about Takahara-kun.*

When Mineno first joined this group, she had clearly been looking for a home with Matsuo and Yoshiko. She hoped to get what she hadn't had as a child. Yoshiko and the others were aware of this when they took her in. Now, seeing Mineno with her hand on her stomach, Yoshiko thought, *That's why we must take care of her.*

Last night she'd seen a lizard in the mansion. Had it actually been black, or had it just looked that way in the dark?

Something was about to happen. There was a fluttering in her chest. Something she hadn't felt in years.

There was still some time before Matsuo's speech, but over the past three hours many attendees had already shown up.

If they had set up all the folding chairs before people started arriving, things would have been easy, but Matsuo said selfishly that it would look bad if there were more chairs than people, so they had to set up more chairs as people arrived. There was a relatively large number of young people. There were even some who eagerly brought notebooks.

People continued to arrive in droves. Narazaki handed out plastic bottles of tea. Matsuo was watching TV in his room, not practicing his speech or anything. The incident with the interviewer the day before still hadn't made the paper. They'd expected there would be more onlookers, but thankfully the talk came before anything was published.

Narazaki looked for Mineno, but he couldn't find her anywhere. Strange. He was sure she'd been handing out bottles with him until a moment before. He went to get more bottles, but froze. There was a long-haired man in the audience. The man who had led Narazaki to the twenty-first floor of that compound. Narazaki stared at him. *Why is he here?*

"Narazaki-kun," Yoshida called out to him. Narazaki's heart was racing. "See that man with his hair tied up in the back?"

"Yes."

"He's from that cult. He used to come here, and when Sawatari disappeared, he vanished as well. There's no mistaking him."

Narazaki couldn't look Yoshida in the eyes.

"Pretend you don't notice him. We don't want to start a scene before Matsuo's talk. But after it's over, Arayama-kun and Kato-kun will grab him. Don't let Matsuo-san know." Yoshida's voice was quiet as a whisper. "He already knows what I look like. Arayama-kun and Kato-kun are relatively new, so he won't recognize them. He doesn't know you either. So when the speech starts, I want you to sit behind him with Arayama-kun. Once he's out the gate, grab him."

Narazaki couldn't manage a response.

"Don't make a big fuss about it. We can't make a scene. We don't want Matsuo-san to notice. Just talk to him, see if you can get him to go to a café or something with you. We want to find out where their cult is located. We thought about tailing him, but we don't know anything about that kind of stuff, so it probably wouldn't go well. You got it?"

Narazaki nodded ambiguously and Yoshida left. *Do they trust me?* Narazaki wondered. *They must be testing me. If I do anything strange after hearing this, they'll have proof that I'm*

*involved with the cult. Someone is probably already keeping
an eye on me.*

Narazaki exhaled. *The danger is that the man with long
hair might be surprised to see me and give me away. Does he
know that I'm here because Sawatari told me to come?*

There were flyers placed on the three seats behind the
man with long hair. *Someone saved our spots*, Narazaki
thought. *I have no choice but to sit.*

People streamed into the garden. *How many people is this?
About two hundred?* The noise faded, and when Narazaki
looked up, Matsuo had climbed to the edge of the mansion's
deck. It seemed Matsuo was just going to start without any
introduction. Narazaki rushed to his seat, the one diagonally
behind the man with long hair.

"Everyone, thank you so much for coming!" Everyone
clapped. *He's lost weight*, Narazaki thought. *Compared to
what he looked like on the DVDs, he's lost a lot of weight.*

"I didn't announce this ahead of time, but today will be
my last talk." A quiet rustling ran through the crowd "I want
to talk about the first half of my life. Well, I'll probably wind
up telling my whole life story. I want to tell you about my
sins."

MATSUO-SAN'S LECTURES, IV

I was born in Aichi Prefecture. My mother was a housemaid at an inn. My father wasn't a zaibatsu, but he owned an incredible amount of land. Children like me, the products of affairs, are generally kept secret, but I grew up in my father's mansion. My mother lived there as well. I didn't see his legitimate family much, but they provided us with a room in the corner of the mansion. And after my mother died of some illness, I was raised there by a nurse.

If my father's wife hadn't had any children, I would have taken over his business as his successor. At least that's what the arrangement seemed to be. I thought that when they had a child, I'd be chased out or sold off somewhere. I didn't want to stay in that mansion, but I was still a child. I couldn't live on my own. I prayed they wouldn't have any children. I spent my childhood full of twisted thoughts like that.

But they did have a child, and, just as I thought, I had to leave the mansion. Of course, I wasn't sold off. I was sent away as an apprentice. Following my father's wife's wishes, I left Aichi and went all the way to Tokyo. I had no choice. Of course, they were happy to get rid of me. I was an obstruction. Happiness depends on one's disposition. It also requires the exclusion of many other things; it can only exist in a closed space. From my father's wife's perspective, there was nothing else to be done. She was sad as well. I lived and worked at a factory where they made tiles by hand. The owners of the factory were good people. As for school, I only made it through elementary.

Then there came a great war. The Pacific War, or World War II.

When I was twenty, I got my draft card. I was going to war.

The first thing I thought was, shouldn't this draft card have been sent to that kid in that mansion? They are sending me to war so that kid doesn't have to go. Of course, that wasn't the case. I was thinking too much. That's just how twisted I was back then.

I had no interest in war. I didn't want to be a soldier. When Japan was heading toward war, the socialists did a lot of underground organizing. I didn't participate in that, but in exchange for distributing their manifestos, they'd lend me books. I wasn't interested in socialism, but I wanted to get my hands on books however I could. English books were hard to get at the time, but I read many of them and tried to study on my own. I often heard the words "American devil," but I could never understand what was evil about this country that could produce such amazing literature. I wasn't taken in by progressivism or anything. I just hated Japan, or the soldiers that talked about how great Japan was. They made me think of my father. My father was a staunch jingoist. But that was natural for people of his generation. Basically, at the time, my understanding of the world was framed entirely by my personal likes and dislikes.

I was sent to join the army's 357th division. The front line in the north central Philippines. Do you all know that the majority of deaths in the war were caused by starvation and illness? Many Japanese soldiers were sent by their boastful but powerless country to wander in tropical forests, never encounter an enemy soldier, starve, and then die of malaria. After three months of training, I joined those forces as a recruit. We were tasked with guarding the central coast, but a scout found close to a hundred American ships approaching us, and both my small platoon and the whole larger battalion hid in the mountains. More than half of us already had malaria.

There's no way we can win—that's what I thought then. The battalion leader and other higher-ups would never say such a thing, but we lowly recruits were almost all certain we had no hope of winning. The silver of the enemy's steel ships crossed the ocean calmly and surrounded us. The same silver of their war planes was already flying across the sky. That great dull luster seemed to repel everything that tried to touch it. What could we have done, faced with that tremendous force? All we wanted was to hide in the mountains of that southern country, which was so hot it felt like it was on fire, and wait to lose the war. I wasn't simple enough to believe the military's lies that if we lost the war our country would be obliterated.

However, we received notification that reinforcements were coming, one hundred and twenty shock troops. But with just a few machine guns, what could we do even if another hundred and twenty reinforcements came? Were they telling us to fight the Americans' sophisticated long-range fire with single-loader rifles, swords, and the hand grenades they provided us with to commit suicide? They were sending reinforcements just to die. All while the commanders did nothing. They just watched as this key territory in the Philippines got snatched, and sent more living people in as reinforcements so they wouldn't be criticized by the government leaders in Japan. And when the troops all die, our officers will tell the Japanese people that they fought with all their strength, that they fought to uphold the honor of our country. Of course dying is scary, and we soldiers were resistant to the idea of death, so they kept telling us that even after we died we'd live on as heroes in Yasukuni Shrine. People have always egged on soldiers with religion since time immemorial. They were encouraging those in our platoon to go and die.

I didn't yet have malaria, so I was part of the group sent to greet the reinforcements. When the five of us left our shack, the Americans began shooting. It wasn't a battle. All we could do was run. The platoon scattered.

I joined up with a platoon led by a lieutenant with dark eyes. By now I had gotten malaria. I had a high fever, and on the second day, I began tripping on my own legs. By the fourth day, I couldn't really speak. My tongue wouldn't move like I wanted it to. The lieutenant's platoon left me behind. That was just the way things were. I had left behind many people as well. I had sworn to my friends that we'd never abandon each other. Friends who stumbled through the jungle using thick branches as canes, who didn't even notice their hands were bleeding from the bark. Who didn't notice that they were shitting and pissing themselves. Those friends who had grown so thin and collapsed. I, who couldn't even speak properly, had to lie and tell them we'd help each other go on. Countless men who'd fallen knowing that what I told them was a lie. But still they smiled at me sadly, knowing that I, also walking with stick for a cane, could do nothing else but lie. Incontinence. That's one of the signs that death from malaria is coming. This time, it was my turn. I collapsed, and looking up I saw the leaves of the jungle. "That's right, that's right," I remember whispering to myself. The green, green grass stood up as if to rub my cheek. I didn't know what was real.

When the sun rose, the heat pierced through my clothing and burnt my skin. The forest continued on forever, and the branches piled on top of each other, out of control. They stretched out irregularly, indefinitely. I was alone in that foreign forest. Maggots popped in and out of a long wound on my arm. I couldn't remember how I'd gotten it. The maggots seemed to hide whenever I spotted them. As if they were ashamed. They were ashamed of me. It was like they were trying to prove a point. I assume it hurt, but I couldn't feel pain. It felt as though it were someone else's arm these maggots were eating. My vision narrowed. Maybe it was one of those special malaria fever delusions, but I could see all those leaves dimly swirling in my vision. The leaves had begun to feel like countless tiny hands on my body. I thought I wanted to die. I wanted to throw up, but even when I tried to, there was nothing in my stomach. My throat was so dry it burned. I had to end the pain quickly. My stomach hurt from starvation, and for some reason that pain stretched to my chest and throat. My body would sometimes twitch and I would begin to lose consciousness, but then pain from somewhere would return me to consciousness. I tried again to vomit, but nothing would come out.

I had one hand grenade. They were called type 99s. I thought that's how I would die. I had seen one of my comrades try to commit suicide with a gun and fail. His teeth were shattered, and the bullet pierced his chin and cheek, but he lived on for another hour. I was covered in twisted branches, but there was no wind, so the thick leaves didn't move. I placed my grenade on the ground. It was covered in grass so thick it could cut you. As I stared at it, that hexagonal orange metal canister we used to call the pumpkin, I thought about the reasons I had to die. I put my hand to my cheek. It was so sunken that I could feel the position of each one of my teeth. I tried to sum up my life.

I would die in this war. I would die because of my

powerless country and their worthless plan. That was clear. So what was this war? I wondered about it. We were fighting for Japan's victory. What was victory? *What would victory get us?*

If Japan could take control of the Philippines, we would gain control of a route for transporting fuel and other supplies. If we did that, we could continue to send fuel to Japan and fight America much longer. That was all. And if Japan beat America, what would happen? If America and the Allied forces petitioned Japan to end the war, and they agreed to Japan's conditions for surrender, what would happen? We would be able to hold on to our territory in China and the other Southeast Asian countries we had conquered. That's all. Who would be happy about that? The zaibatsu who owned those territories, the business people and politicians, and the top brass in the military who pandered to those with economic power. And what would become of Japan? The people would be a little bit better off, but they'd only be getting the scraps from those deals. That's all. Or instead, if you wanted to be better off, you could just work.

By the way, more than three million Japanese died in the Second World War.

I no longer knew why I had been sent to die. I thought about the opposite scenario—what would happen if we lost? Japan would be forced to agree to unfavorable conditions of surrender and would fall to a low position in the international community. That's all. They told us if we lost, our country would be trampled, women would be raped and children killed. I wasn't simple enough to believe that stupid military propaganda. If we fell to a low position, we could just work our way back up. We could make ourselves great again from the bottom. Japanese people can work.

When the war ended, one way or another, someone would decide the conditions of surrender.

The war would decide who got the better deal.

Is there ever a case when the conditions for ending a war justify the numbers who died in that war? I'm going to repeat myself. Over three million Japanese died in that war.

We went to war because of *good feelings*. We faced death for our country. For the beauty of sacrificing ourselves to destroy our enemy. All this nationalism was about *good feelings*. Why does it feel good? It's not just because of our qualities as social animals — because when we gather together we grow excited and passionate. Is it? When this ill-defined self of mine is swallowed up by a greater purpose, I have a position to fill. Providing us with an enemy gives us somewhere to direct all our dissatisfaction. We get deluded into thinking that we are better people than our enemies. Humans love to believe in superiority and inferiority. Humans also become most violent when they assume there's such a thing as being good. We use goodness and justice as a cloak under which we can let loose our violent tendencies.

And then I was set free from the militarist thinking that claimed things were this way or that way. The war had nothing to do with what was right or wrong. Instead of giving in to military propaganda, I found comfort in giving myself up to my own thoughts. I convinced myself that my philosophizing would transform into something great.

In his novel *The Adolescent*, the literary master Dostoevsky talks about how thought can restrain an entire person's being. People consumed inside and out by a certain way of thinking grow hardheaded because of their feelings, and no matter how much they come into contact with people who disagree with them, they cannot change. It is more or less impossible to change their thinking with logic or reason. If there is anything that can change them, it is another feeling. If they experience something that causes their emotions to shift drastically, then they will finally be freed from their way of thinking. Dostoevsky wrote along those lines, and I think it's completely true. People's thinking their thoughts harden. This is at the root of all the tragedies of human history. The soldiers who felt good shouting *Nippon banzai!* would certainly not be moved by logic. They cut off any other thought before it could enter their minds. Those sorts of single-minded groups still exist. They are psychologically weak and fear really thinking over any possibilities besides the ones they embrace. We could call them ideologues.

Those ideologues seemed to me the pinnacle of childishness. Having been tossed around and used for the sake of other people's happiness, lying on the rain forest floor, staring at my hand grenade, I found that "great principle" to be childish. I thought it was stupid. So incredibly stupid.

Then there were shots.

The spot where I had collapsed was thick with branches. They spread out like they were trying to grab each other. There was a gentle slope. As I tried to climb up that slope, it grew gradually steeper. From the other side of that hill I could hear shots. And it wasn't only the Americans firing. I could also hear the Japanese firing back.

While I criticized the war like some leftist intellectual, right behind me my comrades were fighting.

I was just a recruit, but I was still a soldier, and on reflex, I gripped my pistol. I remember thinking to myself, but you can't move. Yet somehow my body moved. I couldn't run, but I had the strength to pick up my gun, climb to the top of that hill, and show myself to our enemies.

The image of what I would do next floated up in the back of my mind. That image visited me like some sort of revelation. If I climbed this hill, I could get closer to the enemies than my allies could. This Japanese soldier who suddenly appeared at the top of a hill, me, would aim for the Americans and throw his grenade. All that I would be able to do after that would be fire until my life was up. The slope I had hidden behind was a blind spot from the Americans' position. That meant I could at least kill a few Americans, and at least buy time for my allies to escape. Killing just one more American meant saving at least one more Japanese.

And I wasn't going to get very far before dying anyway.

I gripped my pistol and heard more shots. No. I didn't hear them. I felt their vibrations travel through my body.

They shook me so violently I could feel the positions of my organs in my body. I was caught in those vibrations. And then these unexpected words popped into my head: *I don't want to kill.*

I didn't want to kill the American soldiers. They probably read the same books as me. They had people they loved. They spoke a different language, but under the right circumstances, we could have laughed and gotten drunk together. I didn't want to kill them. Thinking that made me feel relieved for some reason. What was I relieved for? What was I thinking?

But then another image visited me like a revelation. There was no need to kill. That image told me so. I would show myself to the Americans and throw my grenade to the edge of the field. The Americans would notice me because of the explosion. They would be distracted by me, and they would fire at me while they looked for others, and my allies could run. I was going to die soon from malaria anyway. I could accomplish what I wanted without killing. My heart raced. Still unsure of why it was racing, I felt myself getting dizzy. I placed my gun on the ground and grabbed my grenade. I felt like I was being watched. I tried to stand.

But my body wouldn't move.

Everyone, I'm sure you already know what I was feeling. I was scared. Even though I was about to die, I was scared of dying. I made up excuses, like not wanting to kill the Americans, but really I was just scared. Those powerful vibrations shook my insides. Would the evil heat of their bullets rip my body apart? If I stayed here I'd be safe. I thought I heard a voice: *Just stay here. Just hide*

here like a bug. Amid all that gunfire, I stared desperately
at the indentation of a footprint, probably mine, in the dirt
in front of me. Shouldn't I just run while the Americans
slaughtered my allies? My thoughts wandered. Isn't this
my chance? Should I crawl from this spot, like an actual
bug, and escape? You work at a tile factory, don't you?
That's right. Didn't you promise the owners that you'd
come home safe? It's not for your sake. You're going to
run away for them. Shouldn't you run, so you don't make
them sad?

This war was wrong. That was obvious. But even
though I hung around socialists who opposed the war,
I hadn't participated in their protests. I'd watched from
the side as they got arrested, and suffered and died in
jail, but I'd done nothing. It was probably natural for
me, who did not die in jail with those socialists, to go
off to war. Of course it was a cruel fate. But I still had
to choose how I lived.

My innards still shaking from the blasts of American guns, I began to crawl. Feeling proud of my
righteousness, saying I didn't want to kill Americans
like I was some leftist intellectual, that was all lies. I
truly didn't want to kill them, but the reason I couldn't
move was fear. Even though I was about to lose my
life to malaria.

Then I heard these words. They seemed to be coming
not from outside, but inside me. No, it felt like something outside me used my body to relay those words.
"Because thou art lukewarm," it seemed to be saying.
That was the enemy's god. The book of Revelation, from
the Bible. The words of the enemy's god. *"Because*

thou art lukewarm, and neither hot nor cold, I will spew thee out of my mouth." I tried to flee, crawling, from the gunshots. "*Because thou art lukewarm.*" As I crawled I felt the vibrations of the gunshots on my back before my ears heard them. And my back, which had become just like an ear, heard those words. "*Neither hot nor cold.*" I was a lukewarm being. I was sent to this war not having accomplished anything. I wanted to savor life a bit longer before dying of malaria. I used my life to crawl away, leaving my allies to die. "*I will spew thee out of my mouth.*" When the gunshots suddenly stopped, I froze on all fours, dazed. Is it over? I wondered. Had the firing stopped before I even made it to safety? They're coming, I thought. "*Because thou art lukewarm.*" They're coming. After the fighting had stopped, some of the Americans must have been dead or wounded. Though it was said that they were an advanced country and did not kill their prisoners of war, would they have the mental composure to treat Japanese soldiers so kindly right after a battle? "*Because thou art lukewarm.*" Still on all fours, I stopped moving. Though I read their words, and was growing close to their god, I was being repelled by him at the same time. But the soldiers never came. War gave me no bullets and no courage. All it left me with before it passed over my head was malaria. All it left me was proof of the ugliness of my existence. After that, there was no more gunfire.

I cried. I don't know if there were any tears, but there was a sharp pain in my throat from sobbing. It was so cruel. Suddenly the thought rose up within me:

life is so cruel. Of course I thought that because I hadn't died a beautiful death, but still I wondered why I had to be shown so cruelly how trifling my own existence was.

Then it began to rain. In the dry season in the tropics it rarely rained. But still, it rained a few times on those islands. I lost consciousness while still on all fours, but just for a short time. I collapsed face down, and water began to puddle around me. I should have suffocated, but not being able to breathe woke me up. My body was disgustingly stubborn. There was no beautiful transience. It was ugly, but I drank the water from that puddle, and my body regained a little strength. Next thing I knew, I was standing up.

I didn't want to be there. That was where I'd betrayed my allies. But wherever I went, I would be there. I lived in my brain, and I would follow myself anywhere I went. My throat hurt from sobbing. I'd left my allies to die, was forsaken by my enemy's god, and had nowhere to go. There was nowhere I could stay. I felt the grenade in my pocket. I had to die. My life had no value. But soon I remembered what had just happened and thought, if that was true, why didn't I die then? I didn't die when I should have, and now I'm going to die pointlessly. I can't be alone, I thought. But there was no one around me. I remembered something, and tried to hold on to it. But I had no one to remember at times like this.

My mother had died when I was young. I couldn't remember what she looked like. I'd never had a lover. So the woman I thought of then was my father's wife. The one who'd chased me out. If only she had been kind, and let me call her mom. When I was young, I had fantasized about her being a kind mother. Crawling on the jungle floor, I remembered that fantasy. I held out my hand as if reaching toward her. My left arm, the one without any maggots. It would be rude of me to use the one with the maggots, I thought. I fell. At the time, I thought if I collapsed again I'd die. My vision narrowed. I couldn't make out anything. An intense pain shot from my stomach to my bowels. I thought I had to say something at the end of my life. Something, before I fell. What could I say? I couldn't find any words. I had no right to speak. I cried and fell, my arm reaching out for something.

But my body didn't fall. Something was propping up my back. Though I thought I had been moving forward, I was in fact leaning on something. Was it holding me up? No, it was more like it had caught me. What was it? My consciousness began to fall apart, but I could feel it against my back. It was a tree. It was a Japanese camphor tree with a big trunk, a sort of tree that shouldn't have been in the northwestern part of the Philippines, on Luzon. The tree was bracing my body. This tree stood in the way of my marching on to death. I broke down sobbing, my back to that tree. The tears leaving my eyes were probably the rainwater I had drunk leaving my body. My life was so trivial. I was forsaken by my enemy's god. I had rejected the gods of my own country, but now was being embraced by that tree. Things can change, I thought. Even in the middle of life, things can always change. I had no knowledge of physics then, but now I know that in this great flow of atoms from the past to the present, the drifting of my atoms was being embraced by the drifting of that tree's atoms. Because they were all atoms. Because we were the same. The tree stretched forward. It took in the light of the southern sun, and grandly embraced my tiny body. It stood there with such overwhelming presence. It stood so, so tall. The light slipped through its leaves and fell on my head.

Apparently when the Americans found me, I was collapsed near the edge of a river. That area was dense with mangroves, but their trunks are thin, not thick like the camphor. There didn't seem to be any big trees at all. So what had I experienced? What was that thing that embraced my tiny body?

I became a prisoner of war. After we lost, I returned to Japan.

MATSUO-SAN'S LECTURES, IV, PART 2

After returning to Japan, I spent my days idle. I had internalized all the lives lost at war, as if they had entered into my own insignificant body. I felt as though they'd continue to suffer inside me forever. Most of my interiority was consumed by the past and the dead. I drank questionable alcohol. I'd go out, choose people at random and follow them. For some reason, when I followed someone it rid me of my loneliness. I felt a connection with a living person. If nothing else, I felt some relation to those strangers. I felt a sort of relief in seeing others living idly or entering a shabby home. But from time to time, I'd remember that great tree. What was it? That towering tree that seemed to have caught me when I was falling forward. That tree that had felt so real.

About fifteen years later I joined a certain religion. At the time you probably couldn't have called it a religion. I became a disciple of the teacher Suzuki.

My teacher was a terribly strange man. He was tall, and though he was getting on in years, he had a muscular build. His nose, mouth, and ears were all strikingly large, but his eyes were strangely narrow. He was well versed in every religion, and also knew a lot about natural science. Our group lived in a commune in the mountains of a certain prefecture. We lived off of what we produced. I confessed my war experiences to my teacher. Many of us in that group had psychological and physical wounds from the war. My teacher had me tell him about that tree in detail. He said he had also seen it.

My teacher had once been so sick he was on the verge of death. Just when he thought he was at the end of his life in that hospital bed, something caught him. It wasn't a big tree, but what seemed like a dirty black bundle of cloth. It fluttered around my teacher's body and held him there. He had never figured out what it was. A bundle of black cloth? Of course I couldn't tell him what it was either. I only figured that out much later.

There were about a hundred members in our group, and we managed to support ourselves. But sometimes our teacher would put on a suit and leave with some of our members to go to Tokyo. They managed the land he owned and also traded stocks. I was surprised the first time I went along. I couldn't believe our teacher was doing something so profane.

But I soon learned why. He used that money to create an orphanage for the many Japanese children left homeless after the war, and to send trained members to Africa and Southeast Asia to help provide medical care to people in need. On our commune, all we got was the food we grew for ourselves. "But we'll all get a turn to eat something delicious in Tokyo," he would say, smiling. We also drank at hostess bars. It was very comfortable, not being totally pious. I trained hard under my teacher.

I trained through meditation. I meditated in the forest, deep in the mountains, and learned to hold on to mental images. For example, I'd look at the grass and flowers in front of me, and then as I meditated with my eyes closed, I'd make myself see those flowers and that grass and work to eliminate the separation between myself and those flowers and that grass until I felt as though those images were actual phenomena. Once I reached that point, when I sat on the ground and meditated, the border between myself and the trees and flowers around me became unclear. I learned to recognize myself as just one part of this great flow. I also trained with other people. Practicing with others, you gradually lose the concept of self.

Encouraged by my master, I went to the city, rented an apartment, and found a job. I went to visit him just on the weekends. He told me that I was better suited to training in the real world. He said I should make myself useful out there. Apply my training. He told me that when my borderlessness reached the size of a whole town, I could go even one step further.

I worked in a factory, and eventually got married. To Yo-chan. At the time, I still thought I was disgusting. All I had was my war experience. But even if I was disgusting, couldn't I destroy myself, and continue living as just a concept or an action? Could I exist only for the purpose of helping others? Did it really matter whether my interiority or the ugliness of my past had any meaning? I had to at least hope for happiness. What changed me was my teacher and Yo-chan. Yo-chan listened to my confessions and told me they meant something. She told me that I had to make use of my experiences to help others. That no matter how ugly or sad my past was, anything could still help others. Even wretchedness and regret have value. It doesn't matter what kind they are, experiences are experiences, and there's no way they couldn't help someone.

But my teacher began growing absent-minded. I thought he was just getting old, but it seemed that wasn't all.

"In this world, because of our brains—in other words, because of those collections of countless particles we call brains—there exist countless consciousnesses," my teacher once told me. "Of those countless conscious-nesses that exist in this world, as many as possible should feel happy. I do not mean that only in a humanist way, but also *scientifically*. As a universe-wide chem-ical response. Don't you think so?"

I think I nodded when he asked. But he looked at me with a troubled expression.

"But what if increasing the number of happy consciousnesses increases the number of sad ones as well?
*What if that is the nature of the chemical arrangement
of our total consciousnesses formed by particles?*
Isn't that terrifying? It is, isn't it? All we'd be doing
is moving happiness from one place to another. To
save some people, we produce sad consciousnesses
somewhere far away. What if that is the nature of the
circulation of particles in this world and we simply
can't grasp it? That's the way society is, isn't it? If
there are more rich people, there are more poor. It's
not quite that simple, but one can generally see it that
way. Society is produced through the grouping of these
beings called humans. Humans are made of particles.
Wouldn't that mean that society is the expression of the
nature of particles? Then wouldn't the particle world
also be that way? If happiness increases, sadness must
as well. This is probably not mathematically accurate,
but generally speaking . . . What would it mean if the
evils of this world were not caused by man, but were
rather some chemical phenomenon caused by particles?
Since men are made of particles, the true origin of evil
must be particles, right? These particles are filled with
the potential to create all types of evil. To put it more
accurately, the humans particles create are filled with
the possibility of creating what they perceive as evil.
That would mean that evil is not created by humans, but
from the moment of the birth of this universe, its existence was *desired* . . . But then what would the world
be? And what would evil be?"

At that time, in the sixties, students were protesting

vehemently. They were fighting against the Joint Security treaty between Japan and the United States. In other words, they were protesting against America. I thought I was uninvolved, living deep in the mountains, but when the authorities learned of our leader's economic activities, we started getting these absurd threats. You're harboring suspected revolutionaries! You're giving them money! Our group, which had been very open, began to close itself off. Personally, I was angry. The war had ended and we had taken due responsibility, but because of the Americans we were being dragged to the front line again. Anyone interested, try searching the term "Reverse Course" online. America was so threatened by the Soviets and the communist sphere that they tried to return Japan to a rightist country. They were attempting to use the island nation of Japan as a breakwater for communism. But I didn't care about that. The lives of those who stood up against that great flow of history were precious. But weren't those who tried to save the weak from becoming sacrifices also precious? For example, there were men who had children, and they would say they believed in this or that and run off, abandoning their women and children, to protest. Were they right to do that? I can't say. But all we did was try to take care of those abandoned children.

My teacher began using the word sacrifice.

"In our constantly changing history, the world may demand regular sacrifices. There are chosen ones in this world . . . And thanks to that fact, we may be able to produce much good."

I couldn't understand what he was saying. Somehow I understood the words, but I didn't know what he based them on. If we'd had some holy book, that would have been different, but we didn't have anything like that. Don't you think it's scary? All religions' scriptures are trusted just because they were written long ago. They are thought to be unchangeable just because they were written long ago. Even if those scriptures were truly produced by gods, I'm certain those gods must have been speaking based on the conditions of the world they saw then. Yet humans insist on being governed by the past. *We will continue to live in the distortions between past and present.* That is the situation humanity lives in now.

My group gradually became more of a formal religion. That was the natural result of closing ourselves off. At the time there were tons of new religions. Amid all that, it was only natural for members to get jealous of other groups, and for some reason, my teacher also actively tried to make things flow that way.

I'm sorry to digress, but if I were asked why there were so many new religions at that time, I'd say it's because it was a period of rapid economic growth. Many of the new religions promised to help you obtain the treasures of this world. In other words, the people who joined simply wanted the pleasures of everyday life. And in periods of rapid growth, people's lives naturally become more comfortable. Thus it's easy for religions to proclaim that they'll help you acquire the treasures of this world, and it's easy for those who have grown wealthy from the changing times to think it was thanks to religion. In Japan now there aren't many new religions being born. In this long period of economic stagnation, it's hard for religions to claim that you'll find happiness if you join their faith. Thus the religious leaders become fortune-tellers. They approach rich individuals and promise them happiness. Maintaining a group requires a lot of money, so by approaching just one person at a time they can cut costs. It's also easier to brainwash an individual. It's highly effective.

Anyway, the student protests grew more and more violent. The longer the revolutionary activities and riots went on, the harder they became to suppress, and the more violent they grew. It was like a chemical reaction.

One day my teacher called for me late at night. He was as old as I am now. I entered one of the rooms in the small hotel where my group—and by this time they were clearly a religious organization—lived. There was one other man there at the time. I believe some of you here know him as well. His name is Sawatari. I didn't know much about him, except that he was young, and a talented doctor. He had been sent somewhere on an errand by my teacher and had only returned the day before.

". . . In the Edo period, farmers had a custom."

My teacher spoke haltingly. He seemed to be scared.

"When it didn't rain and there were famines, they would damage and dirty the statues of Jizo. It wasn't to anger the gods. They believed that if one of the servants of the gods was dirtied, the gods would send rain to make them clean. They used the gods' servants as if they were hostages here on earth. It's a quite interesting bit of folklore . . . I must also be dirtied."

At that time, my teacher had stopped using the name Suzuki and had started calling himself Ilaya. Because I was only going to visit my teacher on the weekends, I didn't fully grasp how drastically he and the group had changed. I pretended not to notice. The members and our teacher were all of one mind, so the change happened very quickly in that isolated space. The time for me to face reality had already passed.

"If I make myself horribly filthy, surely god will show himself . . . We need a sacrifice. Do you understand?"

I didn't understand. My teacher told me over and over that I must not tell anyone what I heard in that room. As I was leaving, a young woman entered through the door in the back of the room. She went up to my teacher.

"Did you see that?" Sawatari asked me as we were leaving the hotel. I nodded. Sawatari continued, "Even though he can't get it up, he's got women like that around him . . . This is just too much. Don't you think?" Sawatari said, laughing.

I scrunched my eyebrows and said, "That's rude. Take it back," even though I didn't really mean it.

"All right, I'll take it back. But I wonder what he's planning . . . I'm kind of excited to see what it is."

He might have been a doctor, and he might have been talented, but why was this man part of our group? I thought it was strange, but I didn't ask.

The next time my teacher summoned me and Sawatari,

he told us strange stories. Finally, he got to the main point.

"I have a list here." He handed us a thick envelope. "Next Wednesday at one. Take this list to Tokyo Station."

His voice had changed. It seemed cloudy.

"You must not look inside . . . They haven't specified a particular place. Walk around outside the station. They'll find you."

I couldn't understand what he was saying. Sawatari lowered his head respectfully and left the room with the envelope. He was also carrying a heavy looking bag. I followed him.

"Let's hide out for a while," Sawatari said suddenly when we were about ten meters from the hotel. "That would be best. We shouldn't see each other until next week."

I couldn't follow what was happening. "Why?" I asked. "What's in this envelope? Do you know something?"

Sawatari smiled. "You had better take your wife with you. I'll get you a hotel room. Please, just do as I say."

Why did I listen to him then? Even though I had no idea what was going on, I didn't trust him, but deep in my heart I trusted my teacher even less. I gave in to this man, Sawatari. I felt something terrifying inside him, though he was still young.

I took Yo-chan and went to the hotel, just as he told me to. He came to our room and threw a bundle of papers on the table. It was the contents of the envelope.

"Just as I thought. It's a list. A list of all the former

students involved in leftist activities. The ones who belong to dangerous groups."

"What? Why does our teacher have that?"

Sawatari ignored my question. "Do I need to say anything else? Our teacher will probably try to kill us soon, to get this back."

I was confused. Why would our teacher come to get something he had handed over to us? But, as some of you may know, Sawatari's voice has a certain hypnotic power. Even though I didn't understand what was happening, I was somehow convinced he was right. His voice goes right past the part of your brain in charge of rational judgment and reaches deep inside. But I didn't just believe everything he said. I asked many questions, but he wouldn't answer them. I had already decided not to take that list the next Wednesday as my teacher had commanded. I couldn't do something I didn't understand the reasons behind. I told Sawatari we should take the list back, but Sawatari wouldn't give it to me. I'd become involved in this strange incident and knew nothing about what was going on. But surprisingly, Yo-chan sneaked behind Sawatari while I stood there. And you won't believe this, but she brought a kitchen knife up to his throat.

"Explain what's going on," she said calmly. Yo-chan is small and nimble, but I never expected her to threaten someone with a knife! Everyone, never think you know everything about your wife! But she did that for me.

"Right now, Shotaro is in trouble. Explain what's happening, or I'll cut you."

But Sawatari didn't show the slightest concern.

Yo-chan with her knife, and me watching, we were already panicked. Sawatari narrowed his eyes and looked at me, then smiled faintly.

"Gnosticism."

"What?"

"You know about Gnosticism, right?" Sawatari spoke as if there was no knife to his throat. "I think you know that in 1945, ancient documents related to this faith were discovered in Egypt. Those documents were deemed apocryphal by Christianity and excluded from the Bible. What they found was just a small portion of the Apocrypha, but it was a tremendous find . . . Now in Europe and America research on Gnosticism is booming. Recently, even the teacher's been thinking of nothing else."

I may need to explain a bit here. It is said Jesus Christ was born on this earth in 4 BC, performed many miracles, and saved lots of people. However, he was betrayed by one of his disciples, Judas. Because of Judas, Jesus was captured by the authorities, was crucified, and died. In Christianity, Judas is synonymous with backstabber.

The Bible was not written by Christ. Those touched by Christ's teachings recorded his words after his death. The church long ago selected some of those writings and compiled them into the Bible. And, of course, there were writings that did not conform with the teachings of the church. Those writings were deemed heretical and dismissed as Apocrypha. But some of them survived, and were later discovered. It's only natural that this caused an uproar. Gnosticism was one form of heretical thought that was prohibited by the church.

We still didn't know it existed at the time, but in 1978 the Gospel of Judas was also found in Egypt. Christ is portrayed as he was seen by Judas. This book was first published in the 21st century, but people have been arguing about this heretical Gnosticism for a very long time.

The definition of Gnosticism is quite broad, and I won't discuss everything here, but I would like to mention one thing.

Gnostics stopped worshiping the god who created this world where they suffered from plagues and starvation. They believed that the god who created this imperfect world could not have been good or omnipotent. They thought that the god who created our world must have been a very low-level deity. It would be strange if that weren't the case. Therefore, there must be other true gods. The Gnostics thought they should worship those true gods who have nothing to do with life on this world. Thus they came to curse the god who created this world, the one who appears in the Bible.

This line of thought gave rise to lots of explanations pertaining to the backstabber, Judas. Some say that Jesus and Judas had actually made a secret pact. Jesus thought that by sacrificing himself he would become a legend, and Christianity would spread and gain strength, so he made Judas betray him. In other words, only Judas knew Jesus's true intentions.

And even if we move away from Gnosticism, there's no one as tragic as Judas. Even in the orthodox books of the Bible, Jesus knew that Judas would betray him.

Either way, Judas was being used. It is written both that Judas later hanged himself and that he ripped open his stomach. But what if what ripped open his stomach was actually demons leaving his body? In the orthodox Bible it says that Satan entered Judas's body before he betrayed Jesus. If that's true, then Judas was possessed. And as such, he did not betray Jesus of his own will, but while being controlled. That would be tragic. It wasn't Judas's fault. And of course god also knew that if his son died nailed to a cross, Christianity would spread explosively. Judas was an important piece in making that happen. They needed a traitor, so they set the devil upon Judas, and even though he loved Jesus, he was manipulated into betraying him. This would mean that the true sacrifice that allowed Christianity to spread as a charitable faith was Judas. Yet in the end he died a violent death. He was used by god, and then squashed like a bug.

Sawatari told me that our teacher was growing obsessed with this sort of Gnostic thought. He also said, "Our teacher was one of the officers of the army's 357th regiment."

I was shocked. That had been my regiment.

"I don't know what he did in that war, but I guess some pretty awful things must have happened."

"Quit talking nonsense," I told him.

"Didn't you ever think that the good he does could be to make up for the bad in his past? Do you think all good people were good all their lives? Are you that simple?"

I shut up.

"I'm sure he was put on trial. Not as a Class A war criminal, but for some lighter crime. But why was he released? I think the Americans were behind that. To use him in the future for something. That time has come. Japan's student protests are a nuisance to America. They're not a real threat, but they're certainly a nuisance. A few years ago, an officer with the Public Security Bureau approached our teacher. It was after that that our teacher started behaving strangely. He must have been told to put together a powerful revolutionary group with his money. And once he got them together, to hand over everything he knew about them. That way the authorities could arrest tons of radicals all at once. Once they'd been betrayed by the person who funded them, they'd begin to grow suspicious of each other as well. The groups would crumble from the inside."

He went on. "But that useless do-gooder, he couldn't do anything like that, right? That's why he's trying to justify his actions. His aging brain has started to develop split personalities. I'm a doctor. I know. He is clearly showing signs of multiple personality disorder. In other words, his brain is gradually trying to produce one personality that will betray the students, and another that knows nothing about it."

"What nonsense," I said.

"You think it's nonsense? You've been watching him quietly fall apart, too. There are some people who develop more than a dozen personalities. His consciousness, or rather his unconscious, is trying to act out the Gnostic faith. Although really, it's not Gnosticism anymore."

By the way, multiple personality disorder has come to be called dissociative identity disorder. Anyway, Sawatari kept talking.

"Our teacher thinks that god wasn't involved in what happened between Jesus and Judas. In other words, he thinks it was a symptom of Jesus's multiple personalities. He thinks Jesus was split into one personality that wanted to be betrayed and die as a bringer of justice and make himself into a legend, and another that wanted to serve the people for as long as possible. When he was under the control of the first personality, he told Judas to betray him. However, once he was on the cross, he returned to his normal self, was stupefied, and yelled those famous words: 'Oh god, oh god, why hast thou forsaken me?' Shall I go on? What if the voice of god Jesus heard was just an auditory hallucination caused by a psychological condition? How tragic! He could hallucinate the voice of god in his mind. His personalities divided, and his fate was handed down to him from a hallucination. He told Judas to betray him, and headed for the cross. And once there, he came back to his senses. He couldn't hear god. Cruelly, his condition was cured by the shock of being on the verge of death. Jesus probably saw Judas from the cross. He had already forgotten that he had told Judas to betray him. All that remained were vague memories of Judas actually betraying him. He would look at Judas with eyes full of hate. What sadness Judas must have felt seeing those eyes! Our teacher's unconscious is trying to convince him to reenact that historic tragedy. *There is no helping it, for this has nothing to do with individual indecency;*

it is a historical, mythical phenomenon. That's what his unconscious mind is trying to make him think. You must have noticed. What he's trying to do now, it's got completely different implications from what Christ did. One tried to become a bringer of justice; the other is simply being used by the Public Security Bureau. But tragically, he's trying to make himself think that his situation looks like Christ's even though it's completely different. He may be destroying his own personality. For someone as incompetent as he is to survive such a difficult situation, his only option is to go mad!"

"And," I asked, "this is why you said he'd come to get these papers? Because he'll return to his senses temporarily?"

"Yes. That's why we hid. You haven't seen Yanagimoto recently, have you?"

Yanagimoto was the second-in-command of our group.

"He may have been killed. He was the first one this list was handed to."

I was amazed. "Why us?" I asked.

"You don't know?" he asked, smiling faintly. "You must at least know that there are members of the group our teacher is unhappy with, right? The only ones he's trusted lately are Yanagimoto, me, and you. We're special, you know? We have *something* that draws people to us. You must be at least vaguely aware."

I didn't think there was anything special about me, but I did know that Yanagimoto and Sawatari had that *something.*

"We are getting in the way of his plans. So he has an

unconscious desire to kill us. Thus when he comes back to his senses and is full of regret for his decision, the chances of that desire mixing into his thoughts are high. His mind is already in shambles."

I probably sat silent for the next thirty minutes, trying to make sense of the situation. Maybe longer. On the table was that thick stack of papers, the list of radicals. At some point Yo-chan also lowered the knife she was holding and began to think.

"That's not all," I muttered suddenly. I didn't mean to say it. "Our teacher is not just copying these myths because of his failing mind. Deep inside, there's still a clearheaded part that has an idea . . . If the traitor is not himself but us, he might be able to find a way to escape."

Sawatari stared at me, and then smiled slightly.

"Of course . . . You think so little of people that you could have that thought. But you're correct. He may be trying to make everything out to be our fault to get through this pinch . . . As if he were the sacrifice. He may be thinking that even though Christ died, he himself could make it out unscathed."

"Are you really planning to hand this list over to the Public Security Bureau? Why? We don't have to play along with any of this."

". . . Because it's fun."

"That's why? Shouldn't we be trying to convince him to rethink what he's doing?"

"Is that possible?" he asked. "Listen. If we hand this to the Public Security Bureau, and the people on the list get arrested, what will happen? Can these student protesters really change the world? Of course they can't. Some of them will try to play revolutionary. They'll brainwash themselves, and when they're feeling good, run off to commit acts of violence, and it will all end with a few sacrifices. The ones who wake up will find work at the big companies that are exploiting them. These protests will make the remaining revolutionaries waiting in the wings lose hope, and an unforgiving attitude toward revolutionaries will spread through the public. It will all end as convenient fodder for the conservatives. Don't you think the protesters will probably live more fulfilling lives afterward if they're arrested now? Those on the list may think extreme things, but they've yet to do anything big. They'll be arrested as a warning to the others, and then set free. They'll have families, and become the sort of idiots who belong to a wealthy nation that exploits poor countries and say things like, 'I was a bit wild then,' and, 'Kids these days are so pathetic.' Wouldn't that be better for them?"

Sawatari smiled. But I didn't agree. I remembered the war. I couldn't let Japan start leaning right again. I couldn't let us go to war again. I couldn't shake the thought that anything that even slightly slowed down our transformation was good. But at the same time, I also imagined that while some of the people on this list were true radicals who would eventually self-destruct, many of them really would just return to everyday life.

"I don't want to." That's what I said. I didn't want to betray anyone, or get caught up in this.

Then Sawatari said, "*Because you are lukewarm.*

You know it, right? That part of the Book of Revelations."

"Why did you say that?"

"What?"

"No, never mind."

It seemed Sawatari said what he had by coincidence. But it wasn't just a coincidence.

In the end, I didn't help Sawatari or try to stop him. I just stayed in that hotel room while my teacher and those around him collapsed. Yo-chan and I watched a whole group of radicals get arrested on TV as if it had nothing to do with us.

Rumors that my teacher was involved with revolutionary groups and that he had betrayed them began to spread in the blink of an eye. But he wasn't punished by the authorities. Maybe they had a secret arrangement. Even though Christ got nailed to a cross.

Maybe he tried to stop the group from falling apart. After the arrests, he had gathered the believers. He was giving his first lecture in a long time. Both Sawatari and I were there. He announced that he had supported the revolutionaries so he could reach "Ideal Sublimity," and then he screamed that he was exposed by his own followers and betrayed. He pointed at me and Sawatari. His face was full of contempt. He had clearly forgotten the orders he'd given us. At the time, he genuinely hated us.

The other followers stood up. Amid the screams and yells, many of them reached out for us. Then suddenly a large voice boomed through the room. It was like the voice of god.

"I have a list here."

The hall gradually grew quiet.

"Next Wednesday at one. Take this list to Tokyo Station . . . Are you listening? You mustn't . . ."

It was the teacher's voice. Everyone went silent from shock. His voice was coming from the speakers in the hall. Sawatari had recorded it. That was when I realized why he was carrying that heavy bag when we met with the teacher. Back then we didn't have portable audio recorders like we do now.

It was a cheap and simple performance using the hall's speakers. But at certain times those sorts of simple tricks work the best.

"Sawatari-san," yelled a tall man. Sawatari had planted him in the crowd. "Sawatari-san loyally followed our teacher's orders. You all see, right? Our teacher is mad!"

Our teacher lost his composure. It was as if the thin old man had gotten caught shoplifting, and wanted to resist arrest with his whole being. But he seemed so full of disappointment he couldn't move from that spot. After making a strange motion with his hand a few times, he seemed stunned and stiffened up. Eventually, he grew so stiff he couldn't move at all. Everyone stared at him, dumbfounded. It felt like such a long time.

After that, our group fell apart. Some left, and some followed Sawatari. I took over the orphanages our teacher had managed. Sawatari told me once, *"I hoped you would turn out like this."*

I saw my teacher once after that. He'd been sent to a sanatorium for old people. Even when he saw me, he didn't know who I was. He had forgotten everything. He had a pinwheel in his left hand. He looked like a child.

But, to put an end to everything, I asked him why he'd chosen me and Sawatari to be his betrayers. He had sat there dreamily that whole time, not producing any distinguishable words. But then suddenly he said quietly:

"Because you're not the kind of person who would let his comrades die at war."

After saying that, he turned back to his pinwheel, completely entranced by the spinning.

I remembered the dirty black bundle of cloth that my teacher had seen, the one that caught him when he was about to die. Had his life been saved just so he could experience being the person he became? Was it telling him he still had things he had to do? If that cloth had had a personality, maybe it would have told him something like, *I want you to do these things in my place. So keep living.*

But . . . what for?

After that, Sawatari came to meet me many times. He brought along fanatical, dangerous followers, and after sucking up their money, he'd send them away. And when he saw those who stayed with me just barely getting by running charities, he whispered this to me?

"You tried to use me to make this group sound again — your unconsciousness has. *By watching silently.* You needed someone like me . . . Isn't that right?"

Eventually, I left someone else in charge of that group. Out of the blue, my father had secretly left me . . .

Matsuo collapsed.

21

I don't want to be left alone.

Mineno felt a chill on her back and shoulders as she stared at the nape of Takahara's neck.

I'm lonely, she thought. Takahara-kun had fallen asleep as soon as they'd finished. *I want him to hold me after we have sex. I get so scared. I feel like I've been abandoned. I feel all alone.*

She felt goose bumps rise on her back and legs. But if she pulled the cover, moved and rattled the mattress springs, Takahara might wake up. Mineno stared at Takahara while feeling the chill in the air. *I'm all alone*, she thought.

Two weeks ago, she'd gotten her period. Even though she'd been positive she was pregnant. Even though she had definitely been pregnant. She still couldn't get her feelings straight. *Someone probably took it from me. Someone probably took the baby from my stomach.*

She shivered. *I want to shake him awake and make him hold me again*, she thought, even though he was right by her side. *I want him to be obsessed with me*, she thought. Three times in the middle of the act, Takahara-kun had checked whether there was anything wrong with the diaphragm. *He's such a coward. He's always been like that.*

She got wet again. They'd just done it so much she could still feel it down there. *Disgusting*, she thought. *I want more*, she thought. *Even though we just did it so much.*

Her mind grew fuzzy. She looked at her cell phone. She'd placed it next to the bed. She'd recorded them with an app on her phone. Her voice, Takahara's voice, the sound of the bed shaking, the dirty words he'd purposefully whispered, trying to be mean, the wet noises of penetration . . . She got wet again. When she closed her eyes and listened to it, she could feel Takahara by her side. She'd masturbate, jealous of her own self being fucked by him.

I have to hurry and stop the recording. I don't need a recording of this lonely time. She didn't care anymore if she woke him up. She stood up and put on her underwear.

When she started dressing, she suddenly wanted to hurry herself up, as if she felt guilty for what they had just done.

She put on the short skirt she wouldn't normally wear. The blouse that exposed one of her shoulders.

Takahara woke up. *I hope he's not upset*, Mineno thought. *I don't want to see that smile he always puts on when he's hiding the fact that he's upset.*

"I'm sorry. I fell asleep."

"Don't worry," Mineno said, smiling.

"But I was the one who called you so suddenly."

"No, don't worry. I wanted . . ."

"What?" Takahara smiled at her.

Mineno made an embarrassed face. "I wanted . . . to do it, too," Mineno said. She leaned down and kissed Takahara. She didn't want him to think she was a burden. *If he thought that, he would stop seeing me.* Takahara wrapped his arm around Mineno. Laughing, Mineno petted his head as he buried his face in her chest. His hand reached into her skirt and tried to pull down her panties.

". . . Can we do it like this?" he asked.

"No."

She didn't want to do it with clothes on. She wanted him to undress her properly. But she tried to accept him. She wanted him to think she was an adult, and that they could meet casually. How stupid. Takahara's tongue was in her mouth. *But I love this man so much I can't stand it. I love him so much I want to kill him.* Takahara searched for the diaphragm with his right hand. Mineno held his arm down gently.

"Leave it alone. It doesn't even matter today."

Did her words sound casual? It did matter today. In the morning, she had taken the test in the bathroom. The line was dark. She was about to ovulate.

"Mm," she whispered in his ear. "It feels good . . . It feels good when you come in me . . ."

Takahara was still smiling, but he reached for the diaphragm again. He only wanted safe fun.

Should I whisper *coward* in his ear? Her body grew hot. How would he react?

Takahara suddenly stopped moving and looked hard at the clock. Mineno kissed him, but he froze completely as if shocked by something.

"What's wrong?"

"I slept too long," he said, still staring at the clock.

"I have to call . . . my leader."

"What? Well, you'd better hurry," Mineno said, even though she didn't mean it. She pulled her body away from his. She looked at him. *He's lying,* she thought. *He's not going to call Sawatari. It must be Rina . . . I mean, Ryoko Tachibana.*

"I'm sorry, but can you step outside for a second? I can't let other people hear my conversations with the leader. It's a rule . . . Or, I can go outside."

"It's fine. I'm the one wearing clothes."

Mineno was already leaving before she finished speaking. She glanced at her cell phone, still sitting next to the bed. She hadn't stopped recording. *I don't want to listen to him talking to Ryoko Tachibana. Or maybe I do. Maybe I do want to listen to it. Even though I know I'll go mad with jealousy, I think I have to hear it.*

She left the room. *What must I look like! A woman standing alone in the hallway of a sleazy hotel like this!*

I SAID I'd call at 4:00 P.M., and I'm already five minutes late. I wonder if it will be okay. Takahara's mind kept racing. "They" were strict about time.

He listened to his phone ring. They weren't picking up. *It's because I'm late. This is bad. If I lose their trust, I have no future. Not even a short one.*

"You're late."

It was a man's voice. Takahara's head began to hurt. "I'm sorry," he said. "It took some time to get away from everyone."

"We don't need your excuses. What about your tail?"

His voice was low and sounded hoarse. Takahara tried to hide his nervousness when he spoke. "I'm not sure, but it seems like you worried too much. There are no traitors among my group. And no one else has noticed. Even the leader hasn't."

He heard the other man heave a short sigh. Where was he? He could hear bustling in the background. He wasn't sure why, but for some reason that sound seemed familiar to him. His head began to hurt again. It felt like he was being strangled. He felt the same pain when he had sex with Mineno.

"These things require extreme caution. I'm sure you know this already, but if you fail . . ."

"I know. We've got the machine guns—fifteen. Once we finish training, we can move."

"You're very fast. Any problems?"

"None. The trade went off without a hitch. Thanks to my men. We've also made arrangements to get explosives. We have eight trailers, and we'll fill them with gunpowder. The trailers themselves serve as bombs. All that's left after that is to do it."

"Let me say this is impressive."

"Of course it is." All traces of nervousness had disappeared from Takahara's voice. "We love destruction."

STANDING IN the hallway beside the door to Takahara's room, Mineno heard a knock from the inside and stepped back into the room. The call had been shorter than she had expected. What did they talk about? Did he whisper stupid nothings to Ryoko Tachibana? *If that's the case, I'll make her listen to me moaning. And the sounds he makes when he's inside me.*

" . . . Sorry. Sending you out of the room in this kind of place."

"It's fine . . . Was that really the leader?"

"Hm?" The pitch of Takahara's voice rose.

Mineno stared hard at him. It must have been Ryoko Tachibana after all.

"It wasn't Tachibana-san, was it?" She meant to say it as a joke, but her voice trembled slightly. *Did he notice? That I'm upset?*

"Why would you think it's her?"

"What? Oh, I heard from Yo-chan-san. That that's who you're dating."

"But why do you know her name?"

That's right, Mineno thought. *She gave us a fake name. It would be strange if we knew her real name. And I don't think they know about Narazaki-kun.*

"I'm not sure. Yo-chan-san just knew it."

". . . We broke up."

"Liar." Mineno made herself smile. As naturally as possible. But just trying that hard already made her seem unnatural.

"It doesn't matter anyway, does it? To you, anyway. If you're just going to make fun of me, can we do it some other day? My head hurts."

"I'm sorry."

"Me, too. Oh, I need to tell you . . . You won't be able to get in touch with me for a while."

Mineno looked straight at Takahara's face. Her pulse quickened.

"We've got this plan at the cult. It's a training period for the officers. We have to block all calls to our phones."

"Why not just turn them off?" Why do they need to block all calls? *Because he can't turn his phone off in case Ryoko*

Tachibana calls. He's just going to block my number. He's going on a trip with her.

"We have to be able to take calls from the leader. But we still have to stop all other communication."

Lies. It's all lies. Mineno's body grew hot.

"So . . . Go see your boyfriend while I'm gone."

"Well, I guess I don't have a choice." Mineno smiled. She didn't have the energy to stop her face from twitching. *I don't have a boyfriend. You're all I have. But if I didn't lie to you, you wouldn't see me. You're actually such a coward, and so cold, but kind in all the wrong, weird ways. If a woman didn't have a partner, you'd think treating her the way you treat me was unforgiveable. A child,* she thought suddenly. *If we have a child. Yes, a child.*

"Hey, then maybe we should finish what we started." Mineno reached a hand out to Takahara. But he didn't take it. He didn't pull her onto the bed.

"I'm sorry. I have to go."

"What?" Mineno just stood there. "Never mind. It's fine. Make up for it later," she said, and put her phone in her bag. *I'll listen to what I recorded at home and shake with jealousy.* But her phone rang suddenly, surprising her. It was Yoshida.

"I'm sorry, my phone."

She pressed a button and answered the call. Yoshida was speaking so quickly she couldn't make out what he meant. The hospital. Matsuo-san. What was he saying? He . . .

The world went dark.

When she came to, someone was holding her. *Takahara-kun. Takahara-kun is holding me up.*

"I have to go," she said. She noticed she was crying. "I have to go. Matsuo-san is going to die."

The moment Matsuo collapsed, Narazaki ran to him. Yoshida called an ambulance. The audience stood and made a bit of a fuss, but when the ambulance got there, they cleared a path and Matsuo made it to the hospital without any trouble.

They managed to save his life, but he was in critical condition. According to the intensive care unit doctor, given the state of his health, the very fact that he was alive was surprising, and though he might regain consciousness, he would only last a few more days.

Even his wife, Yoshiko, was not allowed to see him. She was surprised at how calm she remained, but when she thought about it, she realized she'd been prepared for this. Both she and Shotaro had lived too long already. Considering his age, this would make for a peaceful death.

Yoshiko remembered the first time she met Shotaro Matsuo. She'd lost her parents in the war, and in the confusion that followed, she'd been chased out by her relatives. She sold her body to make ends meet. Just like today, that hadn't been a rare position for a woman to find herself in. She lived in a huge house that served as a restaurant and also had rooms for prostitution.

Her body was small, but she quickly grew used to the garish makeup and kimonos they wore. She had never really liked sex, but she considered herself good at her job. *What was I thinking back then, living like that?* Yoshiko wondered. *I can only remember it vaguely now. But that's thanks to Matsuo.*

He was a war vet and a member of a strange religion who worked in a nearby factory. The second she saw him arrive as a customer, her pulse quickened. He'd looked at Yoshiko vacantly, talked quietly about his life, and then left without sleeping with her. That night Yoshiko realized that there were still things in life that could unsettle her. She hated Matsuo. But if she'd really been so shaken up, she wouldn't have been able to stand the days that followed. The smell of oil from the factory that clung to his clothes lingered faintly in the small room.

When he appeared again the next day, she was shocked. And out of the blue he said, "I've fallen for you." He said, "Please date me, on the condition we eventually get married."

What is this man talking about? Yoshiko had wondered. *Is he playing a trick on me?* But he seemed nervous, as if he were confessing his love to some high-class lady. He kept scratching his head the whole time. He was even sweating.

"I'm sorry, but I work in this sort of establishment . . ."

He looked at her strangely when she said that. "And is there a problem?"

"What?"

"Is there someone else you like?"

They didn't understand each other. Yoshiko had no choice but to say it again.

"I'm telling you, I work at this sort of establishment."

"And?"

"Doesn't that bother you?"

"Bother me? Oh, right. I forgot to mention that. If you date me, please leave this place. I'll support you."

They still didn't understand each other. The small room went quiet. The floor was tatami, and the only furniture was a simple futon and a low table for drinking sake. They could hear the voices of some bureaucrat and a noisy drunk woman from the next room. Yoshiko's heart was racing, she couldn't breathe, and she didn't know what to do.

"That's not it. I mean, I'm . . . this kind of woman. My past . . ."

"Your past? That doesn't matter." Matsuo looked at Yoshiko as he spoke. "Whatever kind of life you've lived, whatever happened in your past, it doesn't matter . . . That is, if what you choose in the end is me."

Yoshiko stared at Matsuo, flabbergasted.

"You may have painful memories . . . But the thing about memories is if you make new ones, those old ones will fade. We'll just have to make more memories together and get rid of the painful ones." He kept speaking. "The cells in your body—they'll all be replaced with new cells. Your memories don't even have a physical form to replace. You can change."

And after that, when Yoshiko found out it would be hard for her to have children, Matsuo did not seem the least bit depressed. "I'm married to you," he said. "I love you. I don't need children."

Remembering all this, Yoshiko cried. What a great life they'd had together! Tears welled up and wouldn't stop. *What Matsuo said was right. The older we grew, the more the memories of before I met him faded. Only the memories I had with him increased.*

They'd lived together in the decades that followed, fighting, leaving the house, thinking about how they wanted the other to die, and making up. It was a long, long time. *I wouldn't trade it for anything.* Yoshiko began to cry again. *What a great life! At this age, even memories of fights make me want to smile.*

Before she knew it, she was telling the other old members, who were sitting with her in the hospital, about first meeting Matsuo. *The only one here who doesn't know I used to work in a brothel is Narazaki, I think. But he came here because he was interested, so of course he's not the least bit surprised.*

"Men," Yoshiko said, smiling. "This may just be the wish of a selfish woman, but men should be like Shotaro. If you can, be like Shotaro."

Yoshiko knew from the sound of hurried footsteps that Mineno had arrived. The second she saw Yoshiko, she collapsed in tears as everyone watched. A man's presence lingered on her body. *Why?* Yoshiko wondered. *Why does this child take everything out on herself?*

Yoshiko held Mineno, stroking her hair. *She's warm,* she thought. *She's just over thirty. Her real life has just begun.*

She smells good. Yoshiko tried to comfort Mineno, but she knew she herself was the one being saved by that lingering warmth.

"Everyone, please go home," Yoshiko said, but none of the old members made any signs of leaving.

"Everyone still at the house is probably worried . . . Narazaki-kun," Yoshiko said, smiling, "at this rate, Mine-chan will collapse, so take her home . . . Tell everyone waiting there the truth. That Matsuo won't live much longer."

Narazaki teared up, and seeing that, Yoshiko almost cried again, too. *This one, too,* Yoshiko thought, looking at Narazaki. *This one also needs saving.*

"Narazaki-kun." He was already supporting Mineno, who couldn't walk properly, when Yoshiko called out. She came up to him and said softly, "If anything happens to me . . . take care of her."

"In other words, you failed."

The man with long hair was standing directly in front of the leader. The room was too quiet. It was so quiet he was careful even to avoid swallowing his own spit. It was dark, and his legs hurt. The leader was lying in bed, facing the ceiling. What was he looking at? He probably wasn't looking at anything.

"He collapsed, so . . . we . . ."

He couldn't say any more. Anything more would just be an excuse. All the leader wanted was to hear that they'd succeeded. He had no interest in the reasons they hadn't.

Bring Shotaro Matsuo to me. That had been his order. The man had been certain Shotaro Matsuo would come on his own—all he'd have to do was hand him a note with the leader's name and address. They could just take him in their car. There was no problem with the plan. The man with long hair knew Matsuo very well. He'd once looked up to him as his teacher. But Matsuo had collapsed without any warning. There was no way he could have brought him.

"Will he die?"

The man with long hair swallowed quietly. "I just spoke with Narazaki. He said they're not sure."

"Mm. In that case, he'll probably die."

Narazaki feels for Matsuo, the man with long hair thought. *The whole time he was here, Matsuo was in his heart. When he took my call, he was clearly unhappy.*

"Leader?" the man with long hair asked. There was no reply. But the man with long hair didn't give up. He wanted to talk about the secret he and the leader shared, just for a moment. "Why did you want me . . . Why did you want me to bring Shotaro Matsuo here?"

His voice began to shake as he spoke. The room suddenly grew cold. He dropped to his knees in a fit.

"I'm sorry! I'm sorry!"

He was shaking. He was scared. Unbelievably scared. If he was kicked out, he'd have nowhere to go. If the leader abandoned him, there'd be no reason for someone as pathetic as himself to go on living. *It's no good. I'm no good. I don't want to go back to the outside world. The world is trash; it fails to recognize my greatness and the possibilities within me. I can't stand to live surrounded by that trash any longer.*

Why? Why did I just do something so pushy? That's right. It's because of Matsuo. Because I heard that story about the leader when he was a young man. He seemed almost like a different person. I can see him. I can imagine when he was young . . . What is this feeling? What is it? Can I say it while I'm kneeling? What? What do I want to say?

"Leader."

What am I saying?

"Leader . . . What did you do?"

He stopped breathing. But his mind was full of words. *Where did you go after leaving Matsuo? What did you do? What did you do to become the way you are now? No, I must ask more clearly.*

How did you become like this?

His vision narrowed. *What am I doing? Am I resisting? Am I an obedient insect? If the leader gets mad at me, I'll die. I'm confused. What should I do? What should I . . .*

"I'm sorry . . . I . . ."

He pressed his forehead to the ground. *Please, end this silence. The silence.* He pushed down with his forehead. The floor was hard. But he had no choice but to press down with his head.

"Don't worry."

The leader's voice was kind. The man with long hair began to cry.

"I'll tell you one day. *Just you* . . . You are my special pupil."

Tears streamed down his cheeks.

"Thank you. I . . ."

"Mm. Go."

The long-haired man left the room. The confusion he had felt until a moment ago, that was certainly because of Matsuo. *I got confused because of the things he talked about. Iron will. That is what I need. Iron will that will not heed any other thought. The harder it is, the more beautiful. The leader has told me that before. I gave myself up to the leader. Everything. My suffering, my sadness, my confusion. I no longer have to think. I no longer have to worry about anything.*

The leader will lead me. All I must do each day is carry out his commands. What beautiful days! So beautiful!

Someone was coming. *At this hour?* He was slightly startled.

". . . Rina-san?"

Rina was standing in front of him.

"Where are you going? I . . ." The man brought his right hand to his chest. "I may become an officer. An officer! Just like you, and Sugimoto-san, and Takahara-san, and Maeda-san. One of the officers who have the coins . . ."

"Really? Is the leader here? I have to see him."

"Oh, yes, he's in."

It was too dark for the man with long hair to make out the expression on her face. However, her voice was trembling. "I have something urgent to report."

When Matsuo woke up, he told Yoshiko he wanted to
move. He didn't want to be hooked up to machines like
this. He wanted to die at home. Yoshiko brought her ear to
his mouth and listened. She had known he would say that
if he came to.

The doctor let him do as he pleased. Matsuo had known
him for a long time, and they had already talked about what
they would do at the end of Matsuo's life. When they heard
that he had woken up, the old members wanted to come
to the hospital, but Yoshiko stopped them. She could just
imagine not only the old members but many others rushing
there and making a scene.

As Yoshiko began preparations to leave the hospital,
Matsuo, staring off absentmindedly, said suddenly that he'd
stay there for the day by himself. Though his voice was thin,

Yoshiko heard him clearly from the doorway. "Why?" she asked.

"I've come to understand a lot of things," he responded vaguely.

No normal wife would have allowed such a thing, leaving her husband who could die at any moment alone in a hospital room. But Yoshiko nodded. Matsuo had his own way of thinking.

"But, Yo-chan . . . I promise," Matsuo said slowly. "I won't die today . . . I'm sure of it. Don't worry."

THAT NIGHT it began to rain.

Matsuo heard another faint sound mixed with the sound of rain. The careful footsteps of someone trying to sneak around. He was lying in bed, but he could have sworn he'd heard those steps the moment they crossed the hospital threshold. The man walking, too, could sense every sound he made being picked up. As though every step were part of something out of his control.

The sound of footsteps finally stopped in front of the door to Matsuo's room. Matsuo was waiting with open eyes. When the door opened, Takahara was standing on the other side.

Takahara saw that Matsuo was awake, and his body instantly went stiff. *This old man was waiting for me.* His pulse quickened.

The room was small and dark. Matsuo was in bed with a blanket spread over him. His body was partially raised, and he leaned back, his head pressed against the wall. *This room is terribly cold,* Takahara thought. *Maybe this old man can't feel the cold anymore.*

"I heard you're about to die."

Takahara roughly placed the shabby bouquet he'd brought

on the windowsill. Through the curtain leaked the lights of the city. Lights that never go out, even at night.

"And now you won't be able to expose us for what we did . . . Even after we took your money, you didn't tell the police. You like people too much. You won't be able to sexually harass anyone anymore, either." Takahara stared at the flowers. "Your talks, they were pretty good. I heard there were lots of people who thought they were boring, but I thought they were good, at least." Takahara was nervous.

"Why are you crying?"

Takahara wiped his cheek with his finger. He had been crying since he arrived at Matsuo's door.

"Who knows. I guess there's some human blood in me too."

From the other side of the wall, they could hear a motor vibrating.

"Do you still have nightmares?"

Takahara couldn't look at Matsuo. "I don't need your help. I don't . . ."

"Probably not. But still," Matsuo said.

Takahara's body grew stiff again. *How can he speak so clearly even though he's half dead?*

"The problems you have now . . . They have no physical form."

Takahara's head suddenly began to hurt. It was so bad he felt dizzy. He thought he was going to vomit, and crouched down right where he stood.

"What do you know?"

"Oh, if I could only move right now . . ."

"What would you do? Kill me?"

"I'd grab you by the shoulder and shake you. I'd take you somewhere, just the two of us, and I'd give you a good shaking."

Takahara finally looked at Matsuo. His body began to

tremble slightly. *Why am I losing my nerve in front of this half-dead man? I feel more pressure than when I'm with Sawatari. This generation,* Takahara thought. *This generation is terrifying. The times they lived through were different.*

"You're too late," Takahara said.

The floor shook slightly. It was a small earthquake. Neither Takahara nor Matsuo paid the shaking any mind.

"I feel like I've come to understand a lot," Matsuo said. "There are these lines . . ."

"Lines?"

"Countless thin lines stretching everywhere . . . They're all tangled together. There are lines for the powerful people who control the world, and lines for those people who don't leave their homes . . . But believe it or not, they're all the same."

Takahara stood there unable to move.

"The lines intersect, and make all these things happen . . . Stories . . . Stories keep overlapping . . . I don't know what will happen, but there will be a great tragedy soon. And I know I can no longer stop it. Even you all may not be able to stop it. Your consciousness . . . Even though you're one of the main characters caught in the whirlpool of this story, you're also just a spectator . . . The particles are making a lot of noise now. They're going to keep going . . . But." Matsuo looked straight at Takahara. "All I can do is ask you to help me. I'll start with the things closest to me."

"I'm not sure I can do what you say."

Matsuo took a shallow breath to steady himself. "First, give back Mine-chan."

"What?"

"Give Mine-chan back to herself."

Takahara stared at Matsuo. He was trying to smile.

"She likes me. She's not such a serious girl . . . And she has another, proper boyfriend."

"You must at least realize she's lying about that." Matsuo exhaled. "You know she's lying, but you stay with her . . . Leave her. And," Matsuo continued. "Make Ryoko-chan happy."

"Ryoko?"

"You're going to destroy yourself, so you don't want to get her involved—that's what you must be thinking. You're siblings, but strangers."

Takahara's father had married Tachibana's mother. On paper, they were siblings, but they weren't related by blood. They'd started having sex when they were thirteen. In that small room, without anyone noticing. Even after their parents got divorced, they'd stayed together.

"If you told Ryoko-chan you wanted to break up, she wouldn't listen or believe you. That's why you started dating Mine-chan. To put distance between the two of you. What a stupid plan. And you pretend that you don't know Mine-chan is seriously in love with you. You're an idiot. It's like you're one big bundle of all men's stupidity." Matsuo's voice dropped. "But even if you go through with this, even if there's some sort of mistake . . . The great flow will swallow it all up and keep going . . . We're powerless in the face of that flow. There is a great tragedy before us . . . But, please just remember this."

Matsuo stared into Takahara's eyes. Takahara was overcome by fear. He had come to Matsuo wanting something. He had wanted to hear hopeful words. But he rejected everything the old man said. It was like he was being sentenced for a crime. *Whatever Matsuo does, whatever I do, that great flow will swallow it up, and keep going?* Matsuo's eyes grew dim. His face and the upper half of his body stiffened.

"Stand up straight, and be strong."

Takahara stood, stunned. His fear grew even greater. Matsuo opened his mouth, as if to say something else. Suddenly, Takahara couldn't understand him. Was that really Matsuo there? Was it something else taking his shape? Who? *No.*

"There is one way."

Takahara's heart was racing. He felt as if it were Matsuo's heartbeat. He could tell that Matsuo—no, that thing taking Matsuo's shape—was growing excited. He opened his mouth. *On/Off switch.* The words sprang to his mind. He was trying to reach for some switch, for something he should not. Matsuo's mouth kept trembling. Words were still falling from his lips. Several seconds passed, but it felt like minutes. Matsuo was still talking. There was a siren blaring somewhere in the distance. Takahara's ears started ringing, and his arms and shoulders felt light. The room grew more relaxed, and he could hear his own breathing. Takahara couldn't understand what had happened. Matsuo's body was losing strength. Matsuo was turning back into himself. Takahara could do nothing but stand there.

"But I can't ask anyone to do that. I can't say it . . . It may make this tragedy even worse . . . *You may be saved, but many others would die* . . . Sawatari is too much for me to understand. What should I do?"

Takahara grabbed the bouquet he had brought and left. He wasn't sure why he was leaving. He walked down the hall. It was as if he were simply watching himself walk away. The hallway was also cold. Just as cold as the room.

His heart was racing. How much time had just passed? For some reason, the flowers he had thought he left Matsuo were in his right hand. *When did I pick these up again?*

Takahara kept walking. *Matsuo will probably die tomorrow,* he thought.

A man lay on the floor of room 1603, on the 16th floor of the nameless cult's compound. No one had found the body yet.

In the room was a bed, a plain black desk, a small table, and two chairs. The man lay on top of the rug. Maybe he had been sitting, for one of the chairs on the side of the bed had toppled over, and a glass had also fallen to the ground.

His name was Yoshioka. He was one of Takahara's secret cell, a former member of the Self-Defense Forces.

The cushion of the chair that hadn't fallen was indented slightly, and was still warm.

Around Yoshioka's neck were vertical red scratches. Maybe he had scratched himself. They were so vivid, as if each was an expression of fear and desperation. Scars of fierce resistance. An attempt to force out of his body something that he couldn't spit up. There was still some translucent liquid in the glass on the ground.

Two believers walked past room 1603, chatting. They passed by the room and continued to their own rooms.

The indented cushion of the chair that hadn't been knocked over began returning to its original shape, little by little, so gradually that one couldn't see it happen.

EVERYTHING HAD been left where it was the moment Matsuo collapsed. Now that news had reached the mansion that Matsuo would return, the members began putting away the chairs in the garden. Some people remained at the mansion, and others left gloomily, saying they would come back the next day. About thirty people in the mansion remained.

Mineno was asleep on a futon in a room on the second floor. She had a dream of when she was young.

"Sit there," her mother said. Mineno, who had just returned home and still had on her dirty backpack, sat on a cushion. Her mother always seemed to be glaring. Mineno couldn't avoid that glare, even by averting her eyes. Mineno forced herself to look down, even though she wasn't the one who had been bad.

"No one will listen to what I say. You're all I have left . . . You understand, right? Your father never came back yesterday."

Just like she did in this dream, Mineno's mother used to tell her in detail about the bad things Mineno's father had done. What her mother had to deal with every day. She told Mineno that he was a pathetic human. He was filthy, made her mother unhappy, and had ruined her future. Telling a child things like that—that must be one of the things one absolutely must not do when raising children.

but Mineno couldn't hear them. Her mind had wandered far away and was only gradually returning. *Yes. This man always looks at me so lustfully . . . Maybe this man can help me have Takahara-kun's child. Yes, this man.*

Narazaki looked at Mineno and his mouth dried up. *Were her eyes always like this? Is she herself right now?* She certainly hadn't been in her right mind when he'd brought her there. For some reason, she had screamed at Komaki, and then, crying, apologized.

Narazaki placed the tea he had brought in front of Mineno. She reached for the buttons on her blouse, and undid one. Narazaki stared, shocked.

Smiling, Mineno watched Narazaki with vacant eyes. Still sitting on the futon, she spread her legs and rolled up her skirt. Her mouth hung open. She undid more buttons until Narazaki could see her white shoulders and her black bra.

"Narazaki-kun . . ." Mineno said quietly. Narazaki was breathless. "Take me."

WHEN HE had finished recording his last DVD in his hospital room, it was already night out.

Matsuo and Yoshiko left the room together. Yoshiko held on to his arm, but Matsuo walked with confidence.

The hospital staff loaded their things into the trunk of a taxi, and Matsuo and Yoshiko sat in the back. The driver asked for directions, and Matsuo answered. "Toyotama in Nerima." His voice was relatively clear. "Yo-chan, let's go see the place where we used to live."

The cab started moving. Thirty years ago they'd found out that Matsuo's father had left him a considerable inheritance. His other relatives had hidden that fact, and Matsuo

Because their hopes will vanish. Their hopes for adulthood. Their hopes to love someone, and start a family.

"That woman is just obscene. Your father keeps going to her. And you know what they're doing, right? I have to tell you, even though you're just a child, so you can understand. Your father takes off all of her clothes. He gets her naked. Then he licks her body all over. He sticks his red tongue right out of that thick beard he can't even shave off and he puts his mouth on that vile woman's body! . . . Isn't it disgusting? And filthy? That's what your father is."

Her mother always said "Your father." That made Mineno feel like she was being blamed, even when she was little. While her mother talked, she scratched her cheek. It was a habit. She was always scratching one of her cheeks. It was like there was something in there, and she was trying to dig it out with her long nails.

But her mother wasn't the only one who upset Mineno. Her grandparents did, too. They were also cold to her mother. When they visited her grandparents' house, Mineno could sense that acutely. Her mother had always been either tortured or neglected. That's why Mineno had to stay by her mother's side.

But gradually Mineno came to see her mother as an obstacle. She'd get irritated listening to her speak, and wanted to scratch her own cheek just like her mother. When she started high school, her grades, which had been really good, suddenly dropped, because she started hanging around boys. She tried to get away from her mother. But her mother clung to her. "You're all I have," she'd say. "It's because I gave birth to you. Because I gave birth to you, I lost my future. I don't have anything. *That's why you can't abandon me.*"

But Mineno continued to run from her mother. Then, once when she spent four days at a man's home, the cell phone her mother had given her rang.

"Come home today. I'm getting in your way, right? Well, I'll give you what you want, then."

When Mineno got home, she found her mother unconscious. She had taken sleeping pills. Mineno called an ambulance.

Maybe her mother had purposely avoided taking enough pills to die. When she woke up in the hospital, she saw Mineno and wept. "You saved me," she said. "I'm so happy. I knew you'd save me."

Mineno felt scared then. Her mother's health declined rapidly, and a few years later, she died of pancreatic cancer. When she was in the hospital, Mineno would visit, and her mother would be happy, but she also noticed Mineno had already lost all love for her. And Mineno noticed that her mother was aware of that.

"You are your father's child," her mother said quietly, as if to get revenge for the suffering she felt from her illness. "Even though I was the one who gave birth to you . . . You're such a cold child . . . My life was so unhappy. There's no god, there's nothing."

When her mother died, Mineno did not feel like she'd been set free. She felt guilty. The roots of this guilt went deep, and no matter how much she scratched her cheek or clenched her jaw, she couldn't get rid of it.

Mineno woke up on the futon. There were tears streaming down her face. She wasn't sure if they were tears from the dream or for Matsuo.

There was a break in her memory. Narazaki had taken her from the hospital, and then what? *I feel like I shouted at someone, crying. And then . . . That's right! The recording.*

Before falling asleep, her mind hazy, she had tried to listen to the recording of herself and Takahara. She wasn't sure why she wanted to listen to it then. But no matter how much she listened, she couldn't understand. Well, she understood. But it wouldn't stick in her mind.

She put on earphones and played it again. She couldn't focus, but her heart beat fast as though it understood everything.

Machine guns? Trailers filled with explosives? . . . What was this? *What does he mean, the leader hasn't found out? . . . We love destruction. What is he saying?*

She picked herself up suddenly. Her heart beat even faster. *There's something wrong with Takahara-kun. Takahara-kun . . . Now is not the time to sleep.* She called him, but he didn't answer. *That's right. I can't contact him . . . If he'd blocked her number, she couldn't send a text message either.*

What should I do? I can't just sit here. Even if I talked to him, would anything change? My head hurts. What should I do? . . . Oh, I'm almost ovulating.

Mineno sat there dumbfounded. *My child. Yes, I was pregnant. Wait, no, I wasn't. I wasn't pregnant? That's right. That's definitely it . . . My head hurts. If I had a child, Takahara-kun would come back to me, wouldn't he? He would. He definitely would. That's how my mother married my father.*

But Takahara-kun was always so careful when they had sex. *He's a coward . . . But diaphragms aren't perfect.*

There was a knock at the door. Mineno almost shrieked in surprise. Narazaki came in. He said some worried words wasn't notified. But one of the honest descendants appeared at Matsuo's home one day and split the fortune with him. Included in it was the mansion he now lived in with yoshiko.

Matsuo thought about donating all of it, but he knew that by managing it he could make larger, regular contributions to charity. That's how Matsuo had become wealthy after he was already quite old.

The taxi got on the highway. Yoshiko's right hand touched Matsuo's left. His left hand shouldn't have been able to move, but Matsuo squeezed her hand back gently. Yoshiko was surprised, but she didn't say anything. If she pointed it out, she might jinx them.

"Oh, the moon!"

At Matsuo's remark, she looked out the cab's window and saw an enormous full moon rising over the city. Its color was deep and its light so strong she thought it would enter deep inside them. Just like her heartbeat, the moonlight twinkled, strong and then weak.

"Driver," Matsuo said. "The moon is beautiful, isn't it?"

The driver took a short glance out the window and said something.

"I want to keep looking at it like this, so can you please stay on this highway till it ends?"

The driver nodded, and slowed down the cab so it ran steadily along the highway.

"Nature is fair . . . The moon will shine even on someone like me at the end of their life."

Yoshiko held his hand tight. She could smell him.

"I . . ."

When Matsuo said that, Yoshiko began to cry.

"I was happy to be with you."

Yoshiko kept crying. Matsuo's hand was just too warm.

"Any man who gets to tell that to his wife . . . He's a winner." Matsuo laughed.

"I was happy, too. Thank you so much." Yoshiko smiled. "There were just two nights that I didn't feel that way."

"What are you talking about?"

"Hee hee hee."

Yoshiko leaned on Matsuo's shoulder. Though he should have grown weak, he supported her firmly. His shoulder had no flesh on it, but its core was strong.

"I can see it . . . I can see it . . . Nature is amazing," Matsuo said, staring out the window. "All the particles. They're shaking . . . They're going to tell stories . . . This world is amazing."

Yoshiko nodded. The large moon shone on them.

"Our story happened in this world, too."

"Yes, yes it did."

The moon shone bright outside their window.

"Take care of them. Everyone at the mansion."

"I will."

"They still need help."

"Yes."

"Yo-chan. Yoshiko," Matsuo said. Her heart beat faster.

"Will you kiss me?"

Yoshiko wrapped her arm around Matsuo's shoulder and kissed him.

"Thank you. I love you."

"I love you, too."

They kissed again. Their second kiss was long.

The longer they kissed, the larger Matsuo's smile grew. Yoshiko sensed his death from the feeling of his lips.

PART 2

The leader was sitting in the dark. At first the woman thought he was sleeping, but then he made a slight movement, as if something small had gotten caught in his throat. His eyes opened briefly.

She examined his face carefully, but the leader closed his eyes again. It was like he had already forgotten the previous moment's discomfort. He kept his eyes closed, even though right in front of him were many naked men and women with only bath towels covering their bodies.

"Today is Monday," Maeda-kun said. His voice carried well. He had good posture. He was kind. And he wasn't the only one—everyone here was kind.

"There is no need to think. The leader will take on all your suffering, your sadness, your doubt. You are free. You have been released from all the shackles of your lives. Become nothing. Today is Monday. The day the leader grants us."

She remembered having sex with Maeda-kun. He had moved patiently, gently, kindly, until she came, completely devoured by sensation . . . she got wet just remembering that.

"So set it free. Set your madness free. And your love. We are one. We are all one being. There are no borders here. There is no need for the indecision you felt in your lives." His voice grew a little louder. "When the god of the West first created man, Adam and Eve were naked and happy. When they ate the forbidden fruit of knowledge and gained reason, they grew embarrassed by their nakedness. As punishment, they were banished from paradise. God wanted us to be naked. Christianity's strict rules about sex fundamentally contradict god's wishes. We must spew back up the fruit of knowledge. Let's forget ourselves!"

Those words served as the signal, and men and women threw themselves together. The woman started kissing the man in front of her. She wanted to call to the leader: *Fuck me. We've started. I—we—want to, too. Leader.*

The room pulsed with movement. Men and women sucking each other's genitals, devouring them. A man offering his finger, and a woman accepting it inside herself. She twisted and moaned, wrapped tenderly in this man's strong muscles . . . The woman watching was jealous. *Leader. Leader.* The leader's finger moved silently. It touched her chest. *He woke for me. The leader.* The particles in front of her were reacting frantically. Her breasts weren't very large. She wanted him to like them, though. As he touched her chest, she squeezed her arms into her sides to create more cleavage, hoping he didn't notice the trick.

"Ah . . ." she cried. The middle finger of her right hand was in his mouth. "Leader . . ."

She was wet. His mouth was moist, and shrunk around her finger. He sucked it forcefully. *This feeling* . . . It was what her finger felt like when she did it by herself . . . Her body suddenly grew hot. She hadn't been able to wait for Monday, and yesterday . . .

"Ah! Ah . . ."

She felt the sensation inside her even though he was just sucking her finger. His mouth was mimicking what the inside of her body feels like. A feeling he knew so well. Next, he sucked on her ring finger. Her body had turned to liquid.

"Go."

"What?"

"Do it with those men."

Countless hands reached for her body. They pulled her away from the leader. They ripped the bath towel from her body. She was naked in front of the leader. Countless hands reached for her and touched her body. They played with her like she was a toy. Who were they? Their faces were beautiful. They kissed her. They smelled sweet. One of their tongues moved in her mouth. She accepted it. She wrapped her arms around the neck of the man kissing her. She was kissing one man, and another was sucking on her breasts feverishly. They were all mad for her body. She cried out. There were fingers inside her. Whose fingers? Why was he so good? They were moving inside her. Gently, but persistently.

"Ah . . . Ah!"

"You're wet," the man playing with her pussy whispered in her ear.

His fingers moved inside her as if he were searching for something. *No, no,* she cried. If he kept going, she was going to squirt in front of the leader. The noises were so embarrassing. Her body was quaking. *Ah . . . Ah!*

"I'm going to come . . . I'm going to come . . ."

"It's all right. Come."

"No! Ah!"

Liquid gushed from her pussy. It wouldn't stop. She felt so ashamed. But she wanted that man to finger her more. The women around her were watching and commented— "Amazing," and "Wow"—in their thin voices. *No!* She didn't want other women to see her pussy. Did she? The more she thought about it, the more she actually wanted to be seen. *Ahh! Ahh!* It was too much. The leader was watching. *I give everything up to you. I offer myself to you as a sacrifice. This pleasure, the squelching coming from my pussy, everything, I give it to you. Ahh, ahh! I want to be embarrassed! I want to feel more!* She whispered to the man gently sucking her nipples, "Do me."

"Hm?"

"Put it in my pussy."

His penis entered her. She gushed liquid again. He moved inside her violently. She couldn't think anymore.

"Ah, ahh, ahh!"

"You're so wet."

"Ahh, this is too much!"

"It's amazing inside you."

"My pussy . . . Do you like it? Do you like my pussy?"

"Oh, I'm going to . . ."

The man humping her closed his eyes. She felt tenderness for this man in the throes of pleasure. She kissed him.

Because their hopes will vanish. Their hopes for adulthood. Their hopes to love someone, and start a family.

"That woman is just obscene. Your father keeps going to her. And you know what they're doing, right? I have to tell you, even though you're just a child, so you can understand. Your father takes off all of her clothes. He gets her naked. Then he licks her body all over. He sticks his red tongue right out of that thick beard he can't even shave off and he puts his mouth on that vile woman's body! . . . Isn't it disgusting? And filthy? That's what your father is."

Her mother always said "Your father." That made Mineno feel like she was being blamed, even when she was little. While her mother talked, she scratched her cheek. It was a habit. She was always scratching one of her cheeks. It was like there was something in there, and she was trying to dig it out with her long nails.

But her mother wasn't the only one who upset Mineno. Her grandparents did, too. They were also cold to her mother. When they visited her grandparents' house, Mineno could sense that acutely. Her mother had always been either tortured or neglected. That's why Mineno had to stay by her mother's side.

But gradually Mineno came to see her mother as an obstacle. She'd get irritated listening to her speak, and wanted to scratch her own cheek just like her mother. When she started high school, her grades, which had been really good, suddenly dropped, because she started hanging around boys. She tried to get away from her mother. But her mother clung to her. "You're all I have," she'd say. "It's because I gave birth to you. Because I gave birth to you, I lost my future. I don't have anything. *That's why you can't abandon me.*"

But Mineno continued to run from her mother. Then, once when she spent four days at a man's home, the cell phone her mother had given her rang.

"Come home today. I'm getting in your way, right? Well, I'll give you what you want, then."

When Mineno got home, she found her mother unconscious. She had taken sleeping pills. Mineno called an ambulance.

Maybe her mother had purposely avoided taking enough pills to die. When she woke up in the hospital, she saw Mineno and wept. "You saved me," she said. "I'm so happy. I knew you'd save me."

Mineno felt scared then. Her mother's health declined rapidly, and a few years later, she died of pancreatic cancer. When she was in the hospital, Mineno would visit, and her mother would be happy, but she also noticed Mineno had already lost all love for her. And Mineno noticed that her mother was aware of that.

"You are your father's child," her mother said quietly, as if to get revenge for the suffering she felt from her illness. "Even though I was the one who gave birth to you . . . You're such a cold child . . . My life was so unhappy. There's no god, there's nothing."

When her mother died, Mineno did not feel like she'd been set free. She felt guilty. The roots of this guilt went deep, and no matter how much she scratched her cheek or clenched her jaw, she couldn't get rid of it.

Mineno woke up on the futon. There were tears streaming down her face. She wasn't sure if they were tears from the dream or for Matsuo.

There was a break in her memory. Narazaki had taken her from the hospital, and then what? *I feel like I shouted at someone, crying. And then . . . That's right! The recording.*

Before falling asleep, her mind hazy, she had tried to listen to the recording of herself and Takahara. She wasn't sure why she wanted to listen to it then. But no matter how much she listened, she couldn't understand. Well, she understood. But it wouldn't stick in her mind.

She put on earphones and played it again. She couldn't focus, but her heart beat fast as though it understood everything.

Machine guns? Trailers filled with explosives? . . . What was this? *What does he mean, the leader hasn't found out? . . .* We love destruction. *What is he saying?*

She picked herself up suddenly. Her heart beat even faster. *There's something wrong with Takahara-kun. Takahara-kun . . . Now is not the time to sleep.* She called him, but he didn't answer. *That's right. I can't contact him . . .* If he'd blocked her number, she couldn't send a text message either.

What should I do? I can't just sit here. Even if I talked to him, would anything change? My head hurts. What should I do? . . . Oh, I'm almost ovulating.

Mineno sat there dumbfounded. *My child. Yes, I was pregnant. Wait, no, I wasn't. I wasn't pregnant? That's right. That's definitely it . . . My head hurts. If I had a child, Takahara-kun would come back to me, wouldn't he? He would. He definitely would. That's how my mother married my father.*

But Takahara-kun was always so careful when they had sex. *He's a coward . . . But diaphragms aren't perfect.*

There was a knock at the door. Mineno almost shrieked in surprise. Narazaki came in. He said some worried words, but Mineno couldn't hear them. Her mind had wandered far away and was only gradually returning. *Yes. This man always looks at me so lustfully . . . Maybe this man can help me have Takahara-kun's child. Yes, this man.*

Narazaki looked at Mineno and his mouth dried up. *Were her eyes always like this? Is she herself right now?* She certainly hadn't been in her right mind when he'd brought her there. For some reason, she had screamed at Komaki, and then, crying, apologized.

Narazaki placed the tea he had brought in front of Mineno. She reached for the buttons on her blouse, and undid one. Narazaki stared, shocked.

Smiling, Mineno watched Narazaki with vacant eyes. Still sitting on the futon, she spread her legs and rolled up her skirt. Her mouth hung open. She undid more buttons until Narazaki could see her white shoulders and her black bra.

"Narazaki-kun . . ." Mineno said quietly. Narazaki was breathless. "Take me."

WHEN HE had finished recording his last DVD in his hospital room, it was already night out.

Matsuo and Yoshiko left the room together. Yoshiko held on to his arm, but Matsuo walked with confidence.

The hospital staff loaded their things into the trunk of a taxi, and Matsuo and Yoshiko sat in the back. The driver asked for directions, and Matsuo answered. "Toyotama in Nerima." His voice was relatively clear. "Yo-chan, let's go see the place where we used to live."

The cab started moving. Thirty years ago they'd found out that Matsuo's father had left him a considerable inheritance. His other relatives had hidden that fact, and Matsuo wasn't notified. But one of the honest descendants appeared at Matsuo's home one day and split the fortune with him. Included in it was the mansion he now lived in with yoshiko.

Matsuo thought about donating all of it, but he knew that by managing it he could make larger, regular contributions to charity. That's how Matsuo had become wealthy after he was already quite old.

The taxi got on the highway. Yoshiko's right hand touched Matsuo's left. His left hand shouldn't have been able to move, but Matsuo squeezed her hand back gently. Yoshiko was surprised, but she didn't say anything. If she pointed it out, she might jinx them.

"Oh, the moon!"

At Matsuo's remark, she looked out the cab's window and saw an enormous full moon rising over the city. Its color was deep and its light so strong she thought it would enter deep inside them. Just like her heartbeat, the moonlight twinkled, strong and then weak.

"Driver," Matsuo said. "The moon is beautiful, isn't it?"

The driver took a short glance out the window and said something.

"I want to keep looking at it like this, so can you please stay on this highway till it ends?"

The driver nodded, and slowed down the cab so it ran steadily along the highway.

"Nature is fair . . . The moon will shine even on someone like me at the end of their life."

Yoshiko held his hand tight. She could smell him.

"I . . ."

When Matsuo said that, Yoshiko began to cry.

"I was happy to be with you."

Yoshiko kept crying. Matsuo's hand was just too warm.

"Any man who gets to tell that to his wife . . . He's a winner." Matsuo laughed.

"I was happy, too. Thank you so much." Yoshiko smiled. "There were just two nights that I didn't feel that way."

"What are you talking about?"

"Hee hee hee."

Yoshiko leaned on Matsuo's shoulder. Though he should have grown weak, he supported her firmly. His shoulder had no flesh on it, but its core was strong.

"I can see it . . . I can see it . . . Nature is amazing," Matsuo said, staring out the window. "All the particles. They're shaking . . . They're going to tell stories . . . This world is amazing."

Yoshiko nodded. The large moon shone on them.

"Our story happened in this world, too."

"Yes, yes it did."

The moon shone bright outside their window.

"Take care of them. Everyone at the mansion."

"I will."

"They still need help."

"Yes."

"Yo-chan. Yoshiko," Matsuo said. Her heart beat faster.

"Will you kiss me?"

Yoshiko wrapped her arm around Matsuo's shoulder and kissed him.

"Thank you. I love you."

"I love you, too."

They kissed again. Their second kiss was long.

The longer they kissed, the larger Matsuo's smile grew. Yoshiko sensed his death from the feeling of his lips.

PART 2

The leader was sitting in the dark. At first the woman thought
he was sleeping, but then he made a slight movement, as if
something small had gotten caught in his throat. His eyes
opened briefly.

She examined his face carefully, but the leader closed his
eyes again. It was like he had already forgotten the previous
moment's discomfort. He kept his eyes closed, even though
right in front of him were many naked men and women with
only bath towels covering their bodies.

"Today is Monday," Maeda-kun said. His voice carried
well. He had good posture. He was kind. And he wasn't the
only one—everyone here was kind.

"There is no need to think. The leader will take on all your
suffering, your sadness, your doubt. You are free. You have
been released from all the shackles of your lives. Become
nothing. Today is Monday. The day the leader grants us."

She remembered having sex with Maeda-kun. He had moved patiently, gently, kindly, until she came, completely devoured by sensation . . . she got wet just remembering that.

"So set it free. Set your madness free. And your love. We are one. We are all one being. There are no borders here. There is no need for the indecision you felt in your lives." His voice grew a little louder. "When the god of the West first created man, Adam and Eve were naked and happy. When they ate the forbidden fruit of knowledge and gained reason, they grew embarrassed by their nakedness. As punishment, they were banished from paradise. God wanted us to be naked. Christianity's strict rules about sex fundamentally contradict god's wishes. We must spew back up the fruit of knowledge. Let's forget ourselves!"

Those words served as the signal, and men and women threw themselves together. The woman started kissing the man in front of her. She wanted to call to the leader: *Fuck me. We've started. I—we—want to, too. Leader.*

The room pulsed with movement. Men and women sucking each other's genitals, devouring them. A man offering his finger, and a woman accepting it inside herself. She twisted and moaned, wrapped tenderly in this man's strong muscles . . . The woman watching was jealous. *Leader. Leader.* The leader's finger moved silently. It touched her chest. *He woke for me. The leader.* The particles in front of her were reacting frantically. Her breasts weren't very large. She wanted him to like them, though. As he touched her chest, she squeezed her arms into her sides to create more cleavage, hoping he didn't notice the trick.

"Ah . . ." she cried. The middle finger of her right hand was in his mouth. "Leader . . ."

She was wet. His mouth was moist, and shrunk around her finger. He sucked it forcefully. *This feeling* . . . It was what her finger felt like when she did it by herself . . . Her body suddenly grew hot. She hadn't been able to wait for Monday, and yesterday . . .

"Ah! Ah . . ."

She felt the sensation inside her even though he was just sucking her finger. His mouth was mimicking what the inside of her body feels like. A feeling he knew so well. Next, he sucked on her ring finger. Her body had turned to liquid.

"Go."

"What?"

"Do it with those men."

Countless hands reached for her body. They pulled her away from the leader. They ripped the bath towel from her body. She was naked in front of the leader. Countless hands reached for her and touched her body. They played with her like she was a toy. Who were they? Their faces were beautiful. They kissed her. They smelled sweet. One of their tongues moved in her mouth. She accepted it. She wrapped her arms around the neck of the man kissing her. She was kissing one man, and another was sucking on her breasts feverishly. They were all mad for her body. She cried out. There were fingers inside her. Whose fingers? Why was he so good? They were moving inside her. Gently, but persistently.

"Ah . . . Ah!"

"You're wet," the man playing with her pussy whispered in her ear.

His fingers moved inside her as if he were searching for something. *No, no,* she cried. If he kept going, she was going to squirt in front of the leader. The noises were so embarrassing. Her body was quaking. *Ah . . . Ah!*

"I'm going to come . . . I'm going to come . . ."

"It's all right. Come."

"No! Ah!"

Liquid gushed from her pussy. It wouldn't stop. She felt so ashamed. But she wanted that man to finger her more. The women around her were watching and commented— "Amazing," and "Wow"—in their thin voices. *No!* She didn't want other women to see her pussy. Did she? The more she thought about it, the more she actually wanted to be seen. *Ahh! Ahh!* It was too much. The leader was watching. *I give everything up to you. I offer myself to you as a sacrifice. This pleasure, the squelching coming from my pussy, everything, I give it to you. Ahh, ahh! I want to be embarrassed! I want to feel more!* She whispered to the man gently sucking her nipples, "Do me."

"Hm?"

"Put it in my pussy."

His penis entered her. She gushed liquid again. He moved inside her violently. She couldn't think anymore.

"Ah, ahh, ahh!"

"You're so wet."

"Ahh, this is too much!"

"It's amazing inside you."

"My pussy . . . Do you like it? Do you like my pussy?"

"Oh, I'm going to . . ."

The man humping her closed his eyes. She felt tenderness for this man in the throes of pleasure. She kissed him.

Until a moment ago he had so much energy, but now he was already going to come. *How cute*, she thought. *This man is so cute.*

"Come. You want to come, right? You want to come inside me, right?"

"Ahh!"

He came inside her—he couldn't help it. Even though he was so strong, his body was shaking. And it was because of her pussy . . . *Leader, I give this to you as well. This pleasure will also be joined to the master through me. The leader's nerves will tremble. Us, our pleasure.* The exhausted man pulled himself from her, and the next man's penis entered her. "Wait, stop," she said, even though she didn't want him to stop. She was smiling. She was glad he started right away. She still hadn't come. He flipped her over and pierced her relentlessly. There was another penis in front of her, which she took tenderly into her mouth. She made loud sucking sounds for him. The man behind her kept going. It felt good. She screamed. She could feel the shape of his penis, that's how tight her pussy was wrapped around him. Her legs went numb. *This man can probably make me come.* Ah, she was going mad. She couldn't think. She'd always been a perverted girl. She remembered realizing how much she liked the climbing poles in elementary school. She'd begun masturbating by rubbing up against furniture. She used to only be able to come when she masturbated. She'd been scared of coming in front of men. *Mm. Mmm. Does the leader feel something? Does some small fraction of his nerves connect to this feeling? Ahh! Ahh! I give this to the leader. This terrible pleasure. I give it all to the leader, and*

we will become one great being, a great being. My sex. I
give him my sex. Ahh!

She was going to come. She vanished.

"HEY, ARE you gonna come again?" she asked the man on
top of her.

Watching another woman squirt, she had begun to feel
it rising inside her again. She might be a little bit of a les-
bian. She was cute, that girl. But now the woman was
looking up at the desperate face of the man above her as
he fucked her.

"Ah! . . . Hey, do you think you're gonna come again?"

". . . I'm sorry!"

". . . You left your job and your family to join this religion,
didn't you?"

"Yes."

"And you must be at least twenty years older than me.
Mm . . . And are you . . . Mm . . . planning to come twice . . .
inside a little girl half your age?"

"I'm sorry. I'm sorry."

He kept humping her. She didn't know why, but suddenly she thought of the girl who had killed herself because
she had stolen her boyfriend. She had showed up at the
girl's funeral like nothing happened. That useless man had
blamed her, made her out to be the bad one, to try and erase
his own feelings of guilt. She hadn't cared about that man,
she just hated that other girl. She'd had no interest in him
after she stole him from her.

The woman thought now that she'd probably actually
been interested in the other girl. She'd probably loved her.
That's probably why she'd done it. But then why wasn't she

sad when the other girl died? She'd lit a cigarette off the incense in her funeral offering. Like she was making fun of her death. What had she been trying to get out of it all? Cruelly killing the person she loved?

"Are you going to come? Inside a little girl?"

"Oh! You're so wet . . . Your pussy is so wet."

"It's you! Mm! You made me this wet. Are you going to come again? Mm. Are you going to come in my pussy?

"Yes! Oh, I—"

Her eyes met the leader's. When she'd first seen him, she'd felt the kind of shock that could change someone's whole being—a complete change of heart. She'd reacted the moment she saw his face. The evil in her could never compare with what was in him. What she'd done, it was just a tiny fraction of what he was capable of. No one here would run from her. There was no one here like her father, who took her virginity and then told her she had to go to school. Did he think it was normal for him to fuck her just because he could? Even though he had a wife and children? His evil was nothing. He was strict with her because he didn't want to think her failure was the result of his own crimes. If his crimes hadn't been so trivial, she might not have killed him. She hated that the men who had ruined her life were all so pathetic.

She had been working in a brothel when she was scouted by the believer who brought her here. Here, she would never be rejected. The murder she had committed was erased by the leader's evil.

Her eyes met the leader's again. That instant, she was on the verge of coming. He was the person who had changed her. She used to hate sex. She was shaking.

"Mm, mm, mm. You're so rough. Do you want to come that badly?"

She started to smile. *My vices will be swallowed up by the leader. They will melt along with the pleasure I feel, and I will give them up to the leader. They will become part of him.* It felt good. She didn't want to think. She didn't want to think about anything. She wanted to be part of the great being.

"Hey, are you going to come? Are you?"

Ahh. I came. Her body quaked. She was reduced to the sensations of her body. *Ah, ah, ah!* Her body was falling . . . Her mind went blank.

There was something on top of her. It was dark, and there were people around her. *Ahh!* She was having sex. Her pussy was tingling, and she was moaning. The motion of the man's hips grew more violent. It felt good. It felt good. Even when she came, he didn't stop. He licked her nipples and kissed her roughly as he moved his hips. Her body was being devoured by him. She felt like she was going to come again. *The smell of this man.* The intervals between orgasms were getting shorter. There was no end. He pierced her again. He squeezed her tight, and thrust his hips roughly. He kept hitting somewhere deep inside her. Over and over and over and over. The tingling heat made it up to her head. *Ah!* She came again. She lost her mind. She vanished.

"Ah! Ah! Ah!"

"I'm going to—"

"No, no! My pussy! Mm. I can't take anymore."

"Ah! Ah!"

She died. Her pussy—her pussy was so happy. It came again. *I'm so vile. I'm so vile. I'm, I'm—*

"Ah! Ahhh!"

"Ah!"

"Are you still coming? Mm. You're still coming. That's amazing. Still coming . . . Mm. I'm going to come again . . . Ah, ah!"

Someone collapsed on top of her. Their body, wet with sweat, moved up and down as they breathed. Her mind was blank. Her body was still trembling.

"Was it good?" she asked, smiling. She could feel the warmth of his cum inside her. When he pulled his dick out, another wave of pleasure ran through her body.

"Mm . . . It's great, right? To do whatever you want."

She petted his head and kissed him gently. Their tongues met. His was soft and warm. Even though they were surrounded by vice—no, because they were surrounded by vice—she wanted to treat someone kindly.

"After we take a little break . . . We can do it again. Let's do it as many times as we can . . . I love you."

WHAT IS this?

Takahara was looking down at Yoshioka's corpse. On his neck were several vertical red lines, as if he'd scratched his throat. There was blood and skin stuck to the tips of his fingernails.

"If this were suicide, why is there a second glass? Someone else was in the room," Sasahara said quietly, looking at the glass left on the table. The glass that Yoshioka seemed to have been drinking from lay on the floor.

"Maybe he tried to make his suicide look like murder. Suicide is forbidden here. But still . . ."

Adachi was in the bathroom throwing up. *Could someone have pressured Yoshioka into suicide?* Takahara wondered. *He*

had an important job. Sasahara was looking at him with confusion and concern. *Maybe I look too calm, standing in front
of a dead body.* He couldn't tell them he was used to it, or
that he'd seen people killed in far more horrible ways. If he
said that, he'd have to explain. His head began to hurt. It
was worse than usual.

"Does anyone else know about this?"

"I don't think so. Today is Monday, so everyone's in the
hall. Adachi and I only came here because we had to talk to
Yoshioka about the trailers—we can't just leave them there
. . . And he was the only one with a license for large vehicles."

"And the door?"

"It was unlocked."

"I see." Takahara felt his heart leap when he looked at
the ashtray. His body reacted faster than his mind could
process things. "These butts are Yoshioka's, right? He
always smokes these." But no, Takahara thought to himself. It was Yoshioka's brand, but there was too much ash
for that number of butts.

Yoshioka always cleaned out his ashtray with water. He
was a meticulous man. He would never just pick out the
butts and leave the ash. But why would an intruder take
the trouble to remove their cigarette butts but leave their
glass on the table?

His head hurt. Yoshioka had obviously been murdered.
But why? And by whom? Was this the doing of the person
who'd caught wind of their plan? Even if that were the
case, why kill Yoshioka?

"I'll report this to the leader," Takahara said, his voice
trembling. "Don't say anything to anyone—and make sure
Adachi knows not to, either."

"But . . . we leave his body here?"

"We have to get it out of here. There must be something in the basement . . . Something we can put it in . . ."

"It?"

"Oh, I'm sorry. I'm upset. Something we can put Yoshioka in."

Corpses are such trouble, Takahara thought. *Living humans are bothersome, and so are their dead bodies. I wonder if there's anything as hard to deal with as a dead body?*

"Is it too dangerous to take him outside?"

"We can't. What would we do if someone noticed? Remember, we're hiding from the Public Security Bureau."

"So . . . There are planters. We can fit him in one. We could cover him in dirt. But . . ."

Takahara's thoughts were swirling. *The leader can't learn about the body. We can't let anyone else find out.* "Right, we can't leave him for long. Let's hurry. We don't even have three hours until the party is over."

". . . And the leader?"

"I said I'd tell him!" Takahara exploded. The situation had gotten to him, even though he had vowed to remain calm no matter what.

This is it, Takahara thought. *This is it. We've used up all the time we had to sit around. We have to go through with the plan. Even if we have to force it to happen.*

"You need to think about your breathing, Narazaki-kun."

Narazaki was sitting on the mansion's veranda, smoking a cigarette and recalling one of the last conversations he'd had with Matsuo. The two of them had been alone, preparing for Matsuo's last talk. He'd been sitting cross-legged on a cushion, poking Narazaki's shoulder with his backscratcher.

"That's the Zen way of thinking, anyway. In Zen Buddhism, breathing plays a very important role. When you feel uneasy or have evil thoughts, you take slow, deep breaths and focus only on your breathing. Imagine you are nothing more than a vessel that inhales and exhales."

Narazaki nodded uncertainly. Matsuo's backscratcher was irritating him.

"The main point is not to suppress your unease or your evil thoughts. Suppressing them means you're taking them too seriously. Don't chase unease or evil thoughts with your mind. Just let them flow away. And then focus on only your breathing. Breathing is a quiet activity. If you do that, your unhappy thoughts will vanish. You'll stop being conscious of them."

Suddenly Matsuo stopped poking his shoulder.

"This is the first step in Zen. From there, you try to reach enlightenment . . . You know how in Zen you sit cross-legged? That's called zazen. You focus hard on that posture, your left and right legs crossed together, focus on the fact that you have one right leg and one left leg, that they make this shape that shows you that you have two legs. That's the first step to enlightenment. You saw the DVD where I talked about the Buddha, right? 'Not one who imagines the world as it is, or imagines the world wrongly, nor one who does not imagine, nor one who has obliterated his imagination. Those who can understand this will obliterate form.' That's what the Buddha said. These words can't be understood just by reading them. They can't be interpreted logically. 'Not one who doesn't imagine, nor one who has obliterated his imagination.' What's that? One is one, and two is two. But you can't understand this sort of thing through our normal thought patterns. It's like saying one is one, and one is also two. Just like your legs when you practice zazen. And I also want you to think of it like the particles in the vacuum at the start of the universe, popping in and out of existence. Speaking in terms of physics, they're 'neither nothing, nor something.' Like how light is a particle and also a wave . . . The further we force ourselves into this micro world, the more things deviate from the logic of words, even if that's the most accurate way to explain them scientifically. The truth of the universe is probably somewhere in this seemingly illogical space . . . Through Zen, humans can distance themselves from the logic of words and melt into the true form of the universe. Enlightenment, or 'nirvana,' is probably the 'peace' we feel at that moment." Matsuo regarded Narazaki for a moment. "Why did I tell you that?"

"I don't know, why?" Narazaki asked, surprised.

"I have no idea. Don't ask me!"

Just as Narazaki wasn't sure why Matsuo had brought up breathing, he had no idea why he thought of it again when Mineno began undressing. He thought she was beautiful. He didn't feel so much romantically attracted to her as he felt a primal, immediate desire to have sex. Whenever Narazaki saw her, he was overcome by feelings of sexual desire. Sometimes he even stole glances at her when he was sure she wouldn't notice.

When she began undressing, Narazaki suddenly found himself taking deep breaths. *Why am I doing this?* Strangely, he felt as though Matsuo were there inside his breathing.

"Mineno-san . . ."

He knew he had already decided not to sleep with her when he said her name. He saw that she was not in her right mind. Men should not have sex with women who will regret it later.

"Mineno-san, you're very attractive, and beautiful, and honestly, I really do want to do this," Narazaki said, pulling her body gently toward his. If he'd been anywhere else he wouldn't have been able to turn down a woman undressing like that. "But what are you doing now? You'll regret this later. You had better go back to sleep."

As he spoke, Mineno crumbled on top of the futon. Startled, Narazaki realized she was asleep. He wasn't sure whether to button up her blouse, and in the end, he just covered her with a blanket.

As he was about to leave Mineno, he heard her say a name: "Takahara-kun." He knew immediately that she was talking in her sleep, but he stood there for a moment and watched her. "Kun"—so Takahara must be a man. Ryoko Tachibana's last name had been Takahara once, he knew from the documents Kobayashi had found. But Takahara was a common name. *Maybe it's just a coincidence?*

Now Narazaki smoked on the veranda, wondering who Takahara was. He began to imagine what would have happened had he slept with Mineno, but immediately stopped himself. *What's wrong with me? Of course, sexual desire is normal. But like this? Was I always the sort of person who could only think about girls? Have I been brainwashed? Does the cult promote excessive sex just to make people easier to brainwash?* He suddenly began to get hard. He had started imagining having sex with Mineno again. He would press his tongue against hers, and undress her, stroking her body, push her over on the futon. Even if she came back to her senses in the middle of things and told him to stop, Narazaki wouldn't. "This is your fault," he'd say. "We're already doing this. We're doing it." He'd suck on her lips. He'd play with her body, enjoying her unwillingness and confusion. It was a terrible fantasy. *But isn't that what everyone is like on the inside? Even if a man acts like a gentleman, he still has fantasies like that.* He didn't feel any guilt over it. But . . .

There was a woman standing in front of him. Komaki. When he tried to speak, she kissed him. Narazaki was surprised, his eyes still wide open. She pulled her lips away and smiled at Narazaki.

"What?" Narazaki finally managed to ask. "Komaki-san?"

"Let's go back. To Sawatari-sama."

Narazaki stared at her in shock.

"You're . . ."

"I was sent here. Just like you. Come on, we're going back. We've been summoned."

The image of her happily setting up for the talk flashed through Narazaki's mind. She was part of Sawatari's cult? She was a spy, just like him? *I had no idea. I can't think straight.*

"Sawatari-sama told me to get you. He asked why no one called you back sooner. He seemed very worried about you."

He's not worried. That's a lie, Narazaki thought. But part of him was happy. No one had ever worried about him. *No.* As soon as his thoughts turned to the people at the mansion, Komaki kissed him again, gently but deeply. Her fingers stroked his ears. She ran her mouth along his neck. Narazaki still could not process that she was a member of the cult. But the situation was progressing.

"Let's go back. To our home."

Narazaki took her hand when she offered it. His hand moved on its own, as if abandoning the confused part of him. He felt his body follow Komaki, trying to convince him. *You could expose the true nature of the cult, and save this mansion.* This wasn't about Komaki's round hips, or any of those other women. *I have no desire to be complimented by Sawatari. Destruction is a temporary thing. I can come back to it at any time.* He kept telling himself that.

When I was with the women at that cult, I was outside of reason. I was outside of logic. A place where I forgot myself. Isn't there a point when sex is piled upon sex where we can move beyond reason? It was peaceful, he thought. It was like being inside someone else's nirvana. That place had seeped into his whole body. *We were like the naked men and women before they ate the fruit of knowledge.*

MINENO WOKE up on a futon. She was crying.

This is the second time I've woken up crying today, she thought. *What kind of cycle am I stuck in?* She noticed her blouse was open, and tried to remember what happened. It was like trying to remember through a hangover.

Did I say something weird to Narazaki-kun? Why don't I feel mortified? It's because I'm not interested in him at all. Whatever I said to him, it doesn't matter. But what would I do if he tried to sleep with me? What did I do? He covered me with this blanket and left. How can I care so little about him when he treats me so kindly?

I'm a terrible woman. That's what I think of myself. I'm a stupid woman who just keeps running back to someone who doesn't care about me. Takahara-kun. But I can't stop. My mind . . .

She remembered her recording, and got up from the futon. Out of habit, she transferred the recording from her smartphone to a USB drive. Once it was there, she felt like it was safe. *But what am I going to do now that I've saved it? This terrifying recording. I have to stop Takahara-kun. But how? I can't contact him. I don't know where he is.*

Suddenly she felt hot, and headed for the window. As she opened it, she noticed herself looking down into the garden. Her mind struggled to process what she was seeing. Komaki was offering her hand to Narazaki. What were they doing? Narazaki took her hand.

Mineno's heart began to race. Yoshida was suspicious of the two of them. He wondered if Komaki was a spy from Sawatari's cult. Had Narazaki-kun been lured in by them? *Has he been to the hideout? If they have,* Mineno thought. *If they have been there . . .*

Mineno hurried out of the room, only taking the time to grab her wallet, cell phone, and the USB drive. *If I follow them,* she thought, *if I follow them, I can get into the cult. I can see Takahara-kun.*

3

In hindsight, it was obvious they would take a car. From the backseat of her taxi, Mineno stared at the station wagon in front of her.

Even if she found out where their base was, Takahara might not be there. He might have already left with Ryoko Tachibana. *But that's fine,* she found herself thinking. *Even if they lock me up, everything will work out. Then Takahara-kun will come back to get me. I don't care if he thinks I'm a nuisance. I want to tell him what I feel. I've taken all I can handle.*

The station wagon slowed down, then came to a sudden stop. Mineno panicked and had the taxi stop, too. Narazaki, Komaki and a man she didn't recognize got out of the car. Mineno paid the driver and hurried to follow.

They went down a narrow alley with few lights. *Could this really be where their hideout is? It seems like a normal residential area.* Mineno felt more and more hopeless. *Will they actually lock me up? Do I have the courage for this?*

At the concrete wall at the end of the alley they turned left, passed a home with garish potted plants in front of it, then turned right at a corner with a telephone pole. Mineno followed them, keeping her distance. *Can I really go through with this?* Mineno kept thinking. *I should stop. I should see where they go and then sneak back.* Walking along those narrow, dark alleys, she grew more and more scared. *What am I doing? These past few days I've been off. But I want to know where they're going. And Yoshida-san has been trying to find their hideout for a long time, too.* She followed as they turned another corner. Narazaki and Komaki were walking side by side. Mineno's lips grew dry. She couldn't keep her thoughts straight. *Haven't I come far enough? I can come back tomorrow with Yoshida-san. But I've come so far already . . . I'm confused.* But she kept walking. *This is dangerous. I'm not ready, I'm confused, I'm just being swept along by the situation.*

When Mineno was young, a big man she didn't know once called out to her. He showed her a flyer. He couldn't speak clearly. He told her that he had a speech impediment, and that he wanted to buy the product on the flyer but he couldn't explain that to the clerks at the shop. He was embarrassed, so he wanted her to go with him and tell them what he wanted. He spoke slowly, with halting words. She'd had the same feeling then. She knew she shouldn't go anywhere with a strange man, but she'd felt bad for him and followed. She'd felt confused, but she just let things happen. When they reached his small blue car, she realized she didn't know what she was doing. Once the doors closed, she wouldn't be able to go back. It was a special trap prepared just for her. He offered her his hand. It was large and rough. His sleeves were worn and his fingernails dirty. She felt like things would start happening quickly the second she touched his hand. She ran away as fast as she could, convinced that if he could really drive that car, he must have lied about his problem with the flyer. In hindsight, that had been silly; speech disorders and motor skills had nothing to do with each other. But she was just a kid and didn't know what was happening, and she knew something didn't add up. It had been the right decision. A few months later she'd seen the same man arguing with someone at a bus stop. He was talking normally.

Her heart was racing, and she made herself breathe deeply. The lights in the alley were blinking. *I keep turning down the alleys they take. Even though I'm not ready. Even though I'm not brave enough. Something's off. I'm so nervous, and I'm confused. I'm missing something.*

A man grabbed her from behind and a towel was thrust in her mouth. It stunk of disinfectant. *Where had he come from? There was no one there—*

"Since you've made it this far, we can't let you go home," he said quietly. He was strong. *This isn't disinfectant.* She couldn't even attempt to run away from him. This man had nothing to do with the man with the speech impediment, but it seemed to her as if her past was telling her *We finally got you.*

"Everything's going to be fine," the man whispered in her ear. "When you wake up, you will be our great leader's woman."

"WHY ARE we walking?" Narazaki asked Komaki. The man who had been walking with them had disappeared. Narazaki didn't know what was going on.

"We can't use the parking lot today."

"The car didn't have any curtains this time. Now I pretty much know where the compound is . . . Which means . . ." Narazaki felt a hint of nervousness. "You won't let me go back?"

Komaki smiled at Narazaki's words. She didn't affirm or deny them.

If I'm going to run, I have to go now, Narazaki thought. *If I don't get back now, I won't ever be able to. The man is gone; if I start running, Komaki-san won't be able to do anything.*

The narrow alley gave way to a wide street.

"Here it is," Komaki said. A tall apartment complex rose against the night sky. *This is where I was*, Narazaki thought. It was hard to believe. *Right in this residential area, in this clump of apartment buildings, there's a secret cult hideout.* But that didn't matter. *If I'm going to run, I have to go now.*

The man was back. He was carrying an unconscious woman. Narazaki's heart beat fast as he recognized her clothes. *Isn't that Mineno-san? Why is she here? Why is that man carrying her?*

"Mineno-san!" Narazaki shouted. But the man ignored him and continued through the open back door of the apartment building. Narazaki ran after him, but several other men were waiting. They grabbed him.

"What's going on? What's going on?"

The men held Narazaki back, but they seemed uncertain. Narazaki struggled, but he couldn't break free. "Wait! She has nothing to do with this! Let her go!"

"Her? Her who?"

"Let go! Come on!"

"What's the matter? We're your friends. What happened?"

"I'm sorry, this was our mistake," Komaki said, stepping through the door. She wasn't out of breath. She did not appear flustered at all. "She followed us, so we had no choice but to take her in . . . But she'll be fine. She does have a connection to our group. And the leader is interested in her. She's not my type, but she's beautiful."

"Let me go!"

"What should we do? He seems to be quite excited."

"We have no choice. We'd better put him to sleep." They held a towel up to his face.

I can't inhale. If I inhale, I won't be able to move.

"You know, it's very strange," Komaki whispered into Narazaki's ear as he struggled. "At the last minute, you got scared and wanted to run away. I couldn't have stopped you; you could have escaped. But in the end, you didn't run. It's the sort of phenomenon that can't be explained logically, with words . . . *Because Mineno-san followed us, you had a chance to escape. But because Mineno-san followed us, you couldn't run away.*"

Narazaki was still struggling, but his mind had begun to cloud.

"This, too, must be part of Sawatari-sama's power . . . How interesting. I wonder what will happen?"

HER HEAD hurt. Her back as well.

The floor was bare concrete. It felt rough. Sleeping there would shred your clothes, she thought.

Mineno's heart began to race. When she'd last been conscious she'd been standing in the middle of a street. *Where am I? Is this their hideout?* She panicked, and checked her clothes. Nothing had been removed.

The door opened and a man came in. Mineno tried to get up, but she still didn't have the strength.

"You're awake?"

She looked up at the large man, and grew scared. His face was beautiful, but also disgusting. She didn't want to be fucked by this man.

I . . . I . . .

"We have to pat you down."

Mineno tried to move away, but she couldn't even make herself stand up. She held down her skirt.

"Someone!" Mineno cried out. But her throat felt hoarse, and she couldn't raise her voice. The room was small. There was nowhere to run. She flailed her arms, but there was nothing to grab onto. There was no one to save her.

The ceiling was low. The dim light cast her and the man's shadows on the wall. She screamed and tried to push herself away, her clothing scraping against the rough floor.

"Look," the man said. His voice seemed to leak out joyfully, without his willing it. "Don't get the wrong idea. I wouldn't force myself on a woman."

Mineno looked up at him standing there. He looked concerned.

"Do I look like that sort of man to you? I'm shocked." He spoke as though he were genuinely hurt. "But we have to pat you down. No, wait a second. Let me get a woman to search you." He smiled awkwardly.

Finally a woman came in. Her shadow stretched across the wall. Her hair was long.

"I'll wait outside." The man stepped out of the room. The woman stared at Mineno, sizing her up.

"Hah, you."

"What?"

"Are you really Takahara-sama's woman, like Komaki-san says?"

Mineno looked at her. Takahara-sama. From the sound of those words, and the way she was looking at her, Mineno knew this woman was after Takahara.

The woman approached her. She grabbed Mineno's breast.

"Stop!"

"Ha! You!"

Her hand went up Mineno's skirt. She ran her hand over Mineno's underwear, over her privates. Mineno tried to struggle, but her body wouldn't move. The woman ran her eyes over Mineno's breasts and hips, her eyes full of hate.

"So this is the kind of woman he likes. Wow."

Groping, she took Mineno's wallet and phone from her jacket. She noticed the USB last.

"I need that."

"Is this something special?" The woman studied the USB.

"It's not important to you. Give it back."

"How interesting. I think I'll keep this."

Mineno's throat went dry. On the recording, Takahara spoke of making sure the leader didn't find out. Would Mineno's USB get him killed? She'd heard that many members of this cult had been killed.

"Wait!" Mineno said. "Please!"

But she couldn't move. The woman left the room, smiling.

4

"You're up sooner than I expected," Komaki told Narazaki when he came to. "Don't worry, everything's fine."

"Wait!"

"For what?"

"Mineno-san has nothing to do with this," Narazaki finally managed to say. When he tried to get up, he realized that he was on a bed. His head hurt, but the pain wasn't unbearable.

"I said don't worry. Didn't I?" Komaki turned around and unbuttoned her blouse. "She's Takahara-sama's woman."

"Takahara?"

"Yeah. He's one of the officers here. Practically speaking, he's number two."

Narazaki stared at Komaki blankly. "She's part of this cult?"

"Oh, no . . . She's not a believer. But since she's his woman, it's not that strange she wound up here."

"But . . ."

"Yeah, she'll have to meet with the leader. He might make her his."

Narazaki tried to leave, but Komaki held him back by the arm. Her blouse was open and he could see her bra.

"You were looking for Rina-sama, right?"

"Rina?"

"Ryoko Tachibana." Komaki smiled. "She's also an officer. And Takahara-sama's sister. And lover."

"What?"

"They're step-siblings. They're not related by blood. And they've always been lovers. *For ever and ever.* They're a strange pair."

Narazaki thought about his time with Ryoko Tachibana. *Why did she approach me? Why did she come to me if she had someone like that? An officer? What was she after?* His thoughts were mixed up.

Smiling, Komaki unhooked her skirt. "You don't have to worry about what will happen to Mineno-san. She's already someone's woman. Her, and Rina-sama, and Takahara-sama . . . You're not part of their little affair."

"But . . ." Narazaki finally said. "You just said she might become the leader's."

"Don't worry about that. The leader doesn't sleep with anyone who isn't obsessed with him. If he does fuck her, it will be of her own will. She will have just moved on from Takahara-sama."

"But isn't that brainwashing?"

Komaki smiled at Narazaki's words. "You say such funny things." She brought her body to his. "Brainwashing, romance . . . How are they different?"

Her neck gave off a sweet smell. Her body was thin but

sexy. She wrapped her arms around Narazaki's back. "Why worry about other people's women?" She kissed him, and pushed him onto the bed. "You can do what you want to me. I know how you looked at me at the mansion . . . Do what you imagined then. You can do whatever you want. Whatever you want."

WHAT SHOULD I do? I'm running out of time.

Ryoko Tachibana stood up from her chair, then lay down in bed. She had been moving between the chair and bed for a while now. *I can't handle this*, she thought. *I can't handle him, or myself.*

It was Monday. She couldn't make herself relax. *If I listen hard, I can probably hear those other women's voices.* On Mondays the building always felt like it was shaking. Like the air were infected with what they were doing. *This is the leader's place. This space appeared in the world just for him.*

I can't go there and have sex with some man I don't love, she thought. *Does it make them feel free? Don't they feel like they'll never be able to take it back? I've imagined having sex with a strange man. But I could never actually do it in real life.*

But . . . What was real life?

Her mind went to places she didn't want it to. How were her feelings different from normal ideas of chastity? Wasn't she just scared? Tachibana closed her eyes. This was a gift, being so connected to him, even before they had discovered sex. "It feels good. It feels good." They had been whispering that to each other since they were children. When they were thirteen, Takahara put his penis inside her for the first time. Takahara and Tachibana lived in their own private state of happiness. But that happiness came too early, and was probably the sort of thing one should not experience. It had bred a hatred in them for the rest of the world. They wanted to prove together that they were removed from everyone else by doing something they shouldn't. Because hatred and pleasure were so closely tied together.

The greater the pleasure they felt, the more they felt they were arriving at something. Something great and black, that stared down on their insignificance.

Even as they got closer, they knew that great black thing would take no responsibility for what became of them. It would use them up and abandon them.

There was a knock at the door, and a woman came in. A Cupro girl. *Even though today's Monday. Did she take the day off?*

"Rina-sama. I have something to tell you."

Ha, Rina, Tachibana thought. *As if we could keep on running from it.* It had been his suggestion she use a fake name.

"It's about Takahara-sama."

Tachibana stared at the woman. *That's right. She came on to him. But I thought she was sent to counseling. She should be on the 21st floor. She has a strange air about her.*

She was holding a tape recorder.

"Today is Monday. Should you be here?"

"Yes. I took the day off."

"And what about the twenty-first floor?"

When Tachibana asked, the woman glared at her. "The leader wouldn't sleep with me. I just sat there in his room . . . I think that's why he forgave my desire for Takahara-sama."

"I wonder."

"Please, listen to this."

She hit the switch on the recorder. She had recorded it off Mineno's USB. Takahara's voice rang out. He talked of his plan to fool the leader and incite the believers. Tachibana's heart began to race.

This was proof. The proof that Tachibana had been searching for. *With this,* she thought. *With this, I can stop him. But he's already gone so far.*

"What is this?"

"I know that you and Takahara-sama are dating. And that you have permission," the woman said. "But I don't think he loves you anymore. He stays by your side because you want him."

"What are you trying to say?"

"Please, give up on Takahara-sama. If you do that, I'll destroy this, and I won't tell the leader."

Tachibana looked at the woman, who showed no signs of faltering.

"If the leader learns about this, Takahara-sama will probably be killed. You understand, right? If you leave him, you can save him. So—please, don't come any closer."

She's crazy for him, Tachibana thought. *She isn't making sound decisions. He always acts so nice if he's even a tiny bit interested in a girl. And then he causes these kinds of problems.*

"Please, calm down. Can I get you a drink?"

"No thank you."

"Give me some time to think. This is too much."

Tachibana stood up, hit the switch on her electric kettle, and made some black tea. Black tea helped her calm down. She made a cup for the girl as well. She couldn't let herself be carried away by the girl's frenzy. She needed to act like her normal, everyday self.

The woman was glaring at Tachibana, but when she finally took a sip of tea, she let out a short sigh. It didn't show in her expression or her voice, but Tachibana knew she was nervous. *She seems rather brave*, Tachibana thought. *But she's also truly stupid. I can't stand this kind of woman.*

"All right. Please stay calm and listen to me. What you just heard, that was a hallucination."

"What?"

"I didn't hear anything. You played me the sounds of trains."

"What are you saying?"

". . . Have you been thinking about suicide? We may have to send you to counseling again."

"I've had enough of this."

The woman grabbed the recorder from Tachibana and stood up. She was tall. If they fought, Tachibana would lose.

"I'll play this for Takahara-sama. He'll know that I have control of his life. He's mine. As long as I have this . . ."

She collapsed onto the carpet. Tachibana gingerly picked up the recorder from beside her. The drug had worked more slowly than she'd hoped.

Tachibana undressed, then prepared herself to go out. Seeing the clothes she'd taken off lying next to the woman on the floor made Tachibana feel disgusting, so she picked them up. Next to her, she now saw, was a USB drive. Could the original recording be on this? Tachibana picked that up as well.

This idiot, Tachibana thought, as she looked at the shadows of the breasts and hips of the defenseless woman. *I wonder if he slept with this idiot.*

"Rina-sama!" Her door was flung open and men entered. They were crying.

"What? What is it?"

"Rina-sama. We have to take you."

"What?"

"We're sorry."

They seized her arms. She tried to shake them off, but they were strong.

"What happened? What's wrong?"

"We can't say. We're sorry."

Tachibana quickly slid the recorder and the USB drive into her pocket. The men were crying, but that did not stop them from taking her. They didn't pay any attention to the woman on the floor.

"Wait! Please, calm down . . . I was just drinking some tea."

"We're sorry."

"Who told you to do this? At least tell me that much!"

"We can't say. We can't say!"

They hauled her out of the room. They were crying, but wouldn't answer any of her questions. Maybe they were taking her to the down room, where they put believers who start scenes. Yes, just as she thought, they led her down a long hall, and opened the down room door.

"This is only temporary. Just stay here a little while!"

They left. She didn't know what was happening. The only way an officer could be treated like this was at the command of the leader, or by the decision of the officers' council. But why? Who? They had waited until a Monday, when almost everyone was busy elsewhere.

Tachibana felt short of breath, but she tried to get up.

Then she finally realized she was not alone.

Yoshiko took Matsuo's body back to the mansion in a cab.

The old members came to meet her and they laid his body out on a futon. It was the middle of the night, but many had rushed over when they heard of Matsuo's death. They looked at Matsuo's body, which seemed to have gotten much smaller, and cried quietly.

"But," one of the members said. "But—he's making a kind of strange face."

Someone let out a quiet laugh. Everyone had already vaguely noticed.

"He's grinning . . . He must have died thinking something dirty."

Everyone laughed. They laughed while still crying. Yoshiko laughed too, but there was a warmth lingering on her cheek. *I can't tell them he was kissing me when he died*, she thought. *That precious memory is mine alone.*

Matsuo had said they didn't need to have a funeral for him. He claimed that dying was becoming one with noth-ingness, that living was existing alienated from that great nothingness. Dying was just going back to where you came from. It was completely natural.

"Think about before you were born," Yoshiko had heard Matsuo say long ago. "There was nothing, right? But that's somehow comforting. Or think about when you're sleeping. If you die asleep, you won't even notice that you've died. Death is a natural thing. Living is being alienated from that peace. It's weirder than death."

This is probably some sort of Zen thinking, Yoshiko thought. But we still have to bury him.

"Yoshida-kun," she called, although he was already at Yoshiko's side. Yoshiko always addressed him with -kun. He was forty-four, but to Yoshiko he was still a youth.

"Mineno's gone," Yoshida said decisively. His eyes were wet, but he was trying to focus on the things he'd have to do. "And not just her. Narazaki-kun, too. And Komaki-san."

Yoshiko was struck dumb.

"This is what I think. Narazaki-kun and Komaki-san were summoned back to the cult. Mineno noticed and followed them, or they noticed her and took her with them . . . None of them will answer their phones."

Yoshiko felt her mind wandering, but then suddenly returned to her senses. Now wasn't the time to be shocked. Yoshiko stood. She had faith in her legs. They could still move smoothly.

"Everyone, listen. Mine-chan is gone. So are Narazaki-kun and Komaki-san. There is a chance they were taken to Sawatari-san's cult."

A rustling ran through the hall.

"I will go to the police. Everyone else, please split up and look for them. I know we don't have any clues, but we can't sit here and do nothing."

Everyone knew of Sawatari's cult. They began discussing how to look for their friends.

Matsuo had said it was possible that no one would be able to stop what was going to happen. *But even if that's the case, we have to resist. Right*, Yoshiko whispered in her head, looking at Matsuo. *We have to resist. If Shotaro were still here, it's what he would do.*

"Yoshida-kun, can you take care of Shotaro's burial at your temple?"

"Of course." He nodded. "Matsuo-san was always a little resistant to normal religion . . . And going to another world after death." Unease lingered in Yoshida's face, but he made himself smile. He turned to Matsuo. "But I'll say a prayer just in case."

MINENO WAS shocked to realize that the woman the men thrust through the door was Ryoko Tachibana. But Mineno saw the surprise in Tachibana's eyes as well, and knew she, too, had not expected this meeting. Overcome by jealousy, Mineno forgot about her own situation. *Why this woman? Sure, her face is beautiful, but there's nothing appealing about her.* Her hair was too long. And her make-up wasn't right.

The only thing you've got on me is that you used to be Takahara-kun's sister. You just met him first.

But Mineno didn't say anything. She kept her intense feelings bottled up. She always hesitated to argue with others. She'd hated herself for hiding her true feelings from those she disliked.

"You? Why?" Ryoko Tachibana asked first.

Mineno worried about what to say. She didn't want to say anything she'd regret later. "I was brought here."

"Brought? This is your first time here, right?"

"Yes."

"If that's true . . . If that's true, you'll have to meet the leader."

"What?"

"Do you know what he'll do?"

Their eyes met. It lasted just a few seconds, but to Tachibana it felt like close to a minute, and to Mineno several.

Tachibana seemed to be thinking about terrible things, to see a dark future for Mineno. But Mineno couldn't help but feel that she was also confused about something.

Eventually, Tachibana heaved a small sigh. "It's been a long time. I'm sure you have a lot you want to say . . . But now—now there's something we must do, before you tell me what you think of me. Let me warn you—when you meet the leader, he will have sex with you."

"Why?"

"Yes, it's insane. But there's nothing we can do about that. The inner workings of any cult are far removed from the normal workings of the world. Cults produce a sort of fictional world within themselves in order to keep themselves running."

"So he'll rape me?"

"Not necessarily . . . Even if he forces you at first . . . I don't know quite how to put it, but the leader has this disgusting power. You'll understand when you meet him. *He's special* . . . I never did it with him, though. I had a special induction."

Because you joined as Takahara-kun's woman, Mineno thought.

"But there is one way you can avoid that. And it may lead to exactly what you're trying to accomplish. We want the same things right now."

"What do you mean?"

"You're the one who brought this here, right?"

Ryoko Tachibana took out the recorder and then the USB drive. Mineno was shocked.

"How did you—?"

"These wound up in my possession. I believe we want the same things . . . Make the leader listen to this."

Above them in the great hall, many men and women were devouring each other, their lust let loose. It all tangled together, spewed forth, a tremendous uproar surpassing both logic and emotion.

"But if I do that, Takahara-kun will be killed."

"Don't worry. He won't be killed. Trust me. He's number two here. There are many believers who worship him as well. The leader won't hand down that kind of judgment— or at the very least, not right away. If you show him this, he'll have more important things to take care of than raping you. This whole cult will be shaken up. And all that man wants is to maintain this cult. This hell."

"And you?"

"I'm not a believer. I'm an officer, but I just . . ."

Tachibana swallowed her words. But Mineno knew what she was going to say next. She'd come to save Takahara-kun. That must have been it.

"I can't believe Takahara-kun won't be punished."

"He'll probably be punished. And eventually he may be killed. We'll go to the police before then. *You are being held captive here.* Once the police know where this place is, they'll have no trouble getting a warrant."

"Tachibana-san . . ."

"The only one who can stop Takahara-kun is the leader. The only way to stop him is to lock him up somewhere. You listened to this, didn't you? You know what sort of situation he's got himself into!" Tachibana's voice grew louder. "He will really go through with it. It may be a few days from now. It may be tomorrow. We don't have time. If he does do this, he really will be killed. The Japanese police don't just arrest terror suspects. You know how conservative the government is now? They'll shoot to kill—make him an example. Maybe some people will criticize that, but now, in this political climate, the mass media won't criticize the police or the government for violating international laws and successfully shooting down a terrorist. The media will just be dragged along, rejoicing. Even on the Internet, everyone will side with the police. They'll make Takahara out to be the brains behind a terrorist plot. His whole life will be destroyed . . . There's no time. The only one who can show this to the leader is you. No matter how important the matter, the leader won't meet with any of us unless we're called. That rule is absolute. I tried to meet him earlier, but I couldn't get in. But he'll probably call for you in the next couple of hours. You're the only one who can show this to him."

"And what about letting the police know?"

"Of course that would be the best thing for us to do. But that's not an option. We're both locked up. We'd likely never get out of this building. But if there's some sort of panic, we might have a chance."

The ceiling was low, and the room was small. Mineno thought of the other idea that must have occurred to Tachibana—an idea she had rejected. She could have not told Mineno about the USB and just let her be raped by the leader. She could have let Mineno get brainwashed, and become the leader's woman. Then one of the people standing between her and Takahara would be out of the picture. It was a terrible thought. Because if she hadn't handed over the USB drive and let Mineno get raped, it would have meant giving up this precious opportunity to stop Takahara. *She must have thought about it, imagined a way to destroy me even though it would put Takahara-kun's life in danger—she might have hated me that much.*

Maybe she's also thought that if Takahara-kun dies, she won't have to worry about him anymore. Thought he should just die, along with the woman he cheated on her with. Has she spent so much time worrying about Takahara-kun that she could even consider letting him die? Has she been whittling away her own life? To love someone, to sacrifice years of your life, and then consider his death when you can't do anything about it. His death would destroy her as well. Could she feel she's been dragged so low that she wouldn't mind being destroyed on the inside if that meant it was all over? Mineno felt as though she somehow understood that feeling.

"But even if there is some sort of panic, how will we tell the police about this place? There's no guarantee anyone will let you out of this room."

"Yeah, that's the only problem we have left. It's against the rules to have a cell phone here. The only ones who do are the leader and Takahara-kun . . . And none of the believers will let us tell the police about this place."

Mineno thought of something. She spoke quietly. "Narazaki-kun is here."

"What?"

"Narazaki-kun is here somewhere. He could . . ."

"Narazaki-kun?" Tachibana's eyes were wide with surprise.

Mineno didn't understand. "What's wrong?"

"Narazaki-kun?"

"Yeah. He's here. Didn't you lure him here?"

"Me?"

"What? Tachibana-san?"

Tachibana's body had gone limp. There was something wrong. *Narazaki-kun first came to our group to look for her. Did they have some kind of relationship? If that's the case, if I can get her and Narazaki-kun together . . .* Mineno's thoughts wandered. *If I just say the right thing, maybe everything will work out.* Tachibana was staring blankly off into the distance. *Maybe if I tell her Narazaki's put everything he has into searching for her—that he was so dedicated to finding her that he even came to this cult. That wouldn't be a lie. I don't know the details, but it wouldn't be a lie.*

But that won't work, Mineno thought. *I don't have the courage to say that. I never do what I should and I regret it later. Why? Why do I always do this?*

"I don't know much . . . But I'm sure he's here," Mineno said. She was sick of hearing her own noncommittal words.

"Yeah. You're right . . . Maybe he can get out of here if we start a scene over Takahara-kun . . . Maybe he could get out. Maybe he could." Even as she spoke, Tachibana's expression remained blank.

The door opened suddenly. It was the same large man as before.

"Mineno-san, the leader has summoned you."

Ryoko Tachibana stealthily passed the recorder to Mineno, who took it in her hand behind her back. There was a moment of contact, when Mineno's index finger touched the tip of Tachibana's. It was warm. Hate ran through her body. *Takahara-kun slept with this woman. This woman made him happy . . .*

"Please. This is the only way left," Tachibana said quietly. Mineno nodded. But she hated Tachibana even more than before.

Maybe if she had taken advantage of me as if I were a child, I wouldn't hate her so much. Even if I resented her, I wouldn't hate her like this.

Out of the room, she glanced at the face of her escort. He looked weak-willed and obedient. *It will probably work.* She waited for the door behind her to close heavily, and spoke sweetly.

"I'm sorry, but—can I see Takahara-kun before we go?"

She felt as though something had passed through her body. "What? That's impossible."

"Please! Before I meet the leader. Just for a second." Mineno's voice shook as she spoke. It was actually shaking, so there was no need to act.

"I know that you have been seeing Takahara-sama," he said kindly. "And I adore him. So maybe we can make something up to buy a little time. Yeah, we'll say you went to the bathroom."

"All right."

"Takahara-sama was just taking something to the basement," he continued, innocently. "He seemed to be in a rush, so I didn't talk to him, but if we head there now, we can probably catch him."

Mineno felt her body stiffen as the elevator descended. Even though she had asked to meet Takahara, it seemed like the small elevator was carrying her along against her will.

The door opened. The dimness spread out before her was unbroken by even a single light.

"Oh, where's the switch?" whispered the tall man. Mineno caught sight of it on the wall to her right, but she was afraid to light up the room. She wasn't sure what sort of face to make when she saw him. And she knew her face was hideous now.

Ryoko Tachibana's plan wasn't the only way to solve this problem.

I can meet with Takahara-kun directly. Even if Tachibana-san couldn't convince him, I can.

Mineno repeated what she would do again and again in her head. *I'll get him alone. I'll play him this recording. I'll confess that I recorded it. Then I'll lie. I'll tell him the leader listened to it. And that the police already know. If I tell him that, he'll only have one choice.*

Run away with me. I'll tell him to run away with me. We'll run away together, not just from this cult and the police. We'll run from the whole world. And our lives. Together.

After that, she would tell the police how to find the cult. She'd tell them that Narazaki had been kidnapped. She wasn't sure why, but she felt guilty. *It's like I'm leaving in Narazaki-kun's place.* But he would be free soon.

When Takahara-kun finds out the truth, will he leave me? He may want to kill me. That's fine. If I can just have him to myself for a moment. She didn't want to think about what would come after that confrontation.

I'm sorry, Yo-chan-san, Mineno thought. *But please, understand. There are women in this world who can't be like you. There are many women who, unlike you, don't get to meet a man like Matsuo-san.*

"Oh, they're here . . . I wonder what they're doing," the man whispered. In the distance she could see three men. They were working on something.

"What are they doing? It looks interesting. Let's be quiet and surprise them."

Mineno stared at the man's back as he approached the group cheerfully. She was too nervous to move forward. There was a scream—Mineno's escort—then lots of voices, but Mineno couldn't make them out. Someone had grabbed the tall man's shoulder, and was asking him something. "Who's there?" Then came an even louder voice. "Someone's here!" One of the men came running for her. Mineno thought about running for a second, but her body was frozen

and she couldn't move. Takahara was there. Right in front
of her.

"Mineno?" Takahara was panting. When he saw Mineno,
he went stiff.

"I'm sorry."

Why am I apologizing? Mineno wondered. But those were
the only words she could get out.

"I'm sorry . . . I . . ."

"What happened? Why are you here?"

"Takahara-san!" someone shouted from the dark.

"I'm fine. You take care of him," Takahara yelled back.

Something crawled up Mineno's throat. This was the first
time she'd seen Takahara like that. *It's no good. I don't know
what happened, but this is no good.*

Mineno took a deep breath. *But now's my only chance. I
have to do it.*

"I was brought here . . . I was careless."

Takahara couldn't fully grasp Mineno's words. He had not
yet recovered from the surprise of seeing her.

"Who? Why you?"

"I don't know . . . But that doesn't matter."

Mineno grabbed the recorder in her pocket. But she
wasn't brave enough.

"You're planning something scary, aren't you?"

"What?"

"They know. They know already. What you were trying to
do in secret from the leader."

Takahara stared at her.

"The police know, too. So . . . So . . ."

Mineno's hand moved suddenly.

"Let's run away together."

Mineno reached tentatively out into the darkness. She offered her hand to a man who could see nothing but destruction in his future. A man who could see nothing but this hell, closed off from the rest of the world.

Takahara's head hurt. That familiar pain suddenly overcame him.

"What are you saying? Start from the beginning."

"There's no time . . . There's no time."

"What do you know? What are you saying? I don't know what you're talking about!"

Takahara was yelling. His usual kindness was gone. Mineno was scared. But it had to be now.

"I recorded you. Your phone call. I recorded it by accident, and now they all know."

"Recorded? . . . You mean—when?"

"Here!" Mineno took out her tape recorder and showed him. He stared at it. Mineno had expected Takahara to be upset, but for some reason, he looked calm. *Is this Takahara-kun? Is this really the same Takahara-kun?*

"You're lying," Takahara said quietly.

Mineno shook her head. "You're wrong. I really did!"

"You couldn't have. Maybe you really recorded it, but you couldn't have gotten it to the police or to the leader."

Takahara looked straight at Mineno. There was no love in his eyes, only the determination to prove Mineno wrong.

"If the leader listened to this, why are you holding that recording now? I'm sure he would hold on to it as evidence. There's no way the police could know. You wouldn't give this to the police without talking to me first."

"I . . ."

"And why are you acting so desperate now? You've just been playing with me, right? What are you trying to prove?"

Mineno felt dizzy.

"Stop joking around."

She couldn't stop herself anymore. She spoke quietly, without control of what she was saying.

"You know. You know what kind of woman I am. You just pretended not to. I don't have any other man. Of course I lied, but I do have the recording. I love you. Let's run away together. Come on. Let's run away together!"

I hate hysterical women, Mineno thought. *But that's what I've become now. I had to do this. My only saving grace is that I have a soft voice.*

"I love you," Mineno said again, even though she knew her words wouldn't reach him.

"Let's end this," Takahara whispered. He spoke with all the force of a man who didn't have the courage to hurt his lover. "That is, if you think we've been dating . . . No, that's a cowardly way of putting it. This is all my fault. I'm no good. Leave me."

Mineno began to grow angry. "Your fault? What are you saying?"

"Let's end this. That recording . . . Do what you want with it."

Mineno wanted to hit him. But she felt herself hesitating.

"If you were brought here, that means you'll have to meet the leader." Takahara smiled. It was clearly forced. "You'll become his woman . . . He must be much better than me."

Mineno stared at Takahara as though she had lost all her strength. She was tired. "It's fine . . . You don't have to say that," she said. She couldn't find any energy in her body.

"I don't know what's happening anymore . . . But hold me. Just for a moment. Everything feels terrible right now, and I'm lonely. I'm so lonely I could die, and I have nowhere to go."

Takahara took one step toward her. But then he looked at his own hands. They were covered in dirt. They had touched a corpse.

"You won't even hold me?" Mineno asked. It seemed strange to her that she could still stand on her two legs. "Really? You won't even hold me?"

Takahara was just looking at his own hands.

Mineno must have blacked out. She didn't fall over. She was still standing. But she lost a fragment of her memory. The next thing she knew, she was with the tall man from before, leaving the basement. The tall man was unsettled. He was saying something to her. Mineno tried to listen.

"Takahara-sama said to hide you in my room. And then, this will be really hard, but to find some way to get you out . . . It's against the rules, and we really aren't supposed to do it, but I believe in Takahara-sama. And what I saw there . . . I believe in him. He said he would take all the responsibility. I . . ."

Mineno smiled. Takahara-kun wouldn't give up on his half-assed kindness until the bitter end. Everything would work the way he wanted it to. He would stop her from meeting the leader, so the leader wouldn't hear the recording. And this way, too, he wouldn't have to feel guilty imagining her getting fucked by the leader.

If I play this for the leader, I can stop his terror attack, and in the end, save his life. Ryoko Tachibana may be right. To save his life I have no choice but to show this to the leader.

Mineno began to cry. She threw the recorder on the ground.

I won't save him. He can go through with his stupid attack and die in shame. He can suffer the guilt of imagining me sleeping with the leader.

The man walking next to her was flustered. He didn't seem to notice that she'd tossed the recorder.

"Keep going. Take me there," Mineno told him. She was smiling lifelessly. "To the leader. He can do whatever he wants to me."

"Not yet," the man said, gripping his cell phone.

"The paperwork . . . It's not done yet. You know what that means, right?"

He appeared to be in his fifties. The suit he was wearing wasn't cheap, but it wasn't particularly expensive either. His shoes and watch weren't tacky, but one couldn't say they were particularly refined. His face was not particularly ugly, but it wasn't the sort that would attract women.

He snapped his phone shut, and looked lazily to one side. Next to him was a man in his thirties. He wore a nice suit and was staring at a computer screen. His eyes were large and his eyebrows neatly plucked. Women would find him attractive.

"Do you know why the judge will give him the death penalty?" the man in his fifties asked.

The man in his thirties looked up from his computer to show that he was listening.

"Because he's all about precedent. When most judges give the death penalty, they're thinking about the precedents. Judges just follow the examples set for them in the past when they give their verdict. It lessens their own inner burden. One judge doesn't have any right to make exceptions. If nothing else, he can tell himself that."

He took a sip from his tea. He did not seem to enjoy it.

"Recently, that practice has been criticized. People have been saying judges should stop blindly following precedents. They should think about each case on its own and give each its own unique sentence . . . They're right. But at the same time, that would increase the psychological burden on judges. Who's happy to give out the death penalty? No one really wants to."

"Why are you telling me this?"

"Of course, there are also people who say that if you're going to choose to work as a judge, you must take on that responsibility. Just like they hope that the prison guards who must force a crying prisoner's neck into the noose will take responsibility for those deaths. Just as they hope that our soldiers will do their jobs and kill . . . Our lay judge system was designed to avoid that sort of dissatisfaction. We citizens divide up the responsibility for the administration of justice. No one will complain about sentencing. Japan and a few states in the US are the only places in developed countries with the death penalty that force their own citizens to decide the sentence. Most people don't even know that. For a country to force its citizens to take on that responsibility—it seems like insanity if you're looking at it from the EU. But still, this system continues. The government needs the death penalty. The death penalty, in other words state murder, allows the government to enforce the rule of law. It's also connected with our right to go to war. The number of jurors suffering from psychological trauma is increasing. But if anyone complains, the government can just use the media to manipulate public opinion. Rather than discussing the psychological injury caused to a juror, the media can just talk about the importance of taking care of your own mental health. It's so obvious. This country is heaven for bureaucrats!"

"Why are you telling me this?" the younger man repeated. The older man never really listened to others. Normally, the younger man didn't butt in much, but he wanted to say something.

"We don't need a name," said the older man. The younger man wasn't sure if that was an answer to his question or not. "We focus on the product. The conveyor belts in factories that deliver products to where they're supposed to go, they don't need names . . . We're just working based on precedent."

The younger man gave up on saying anything. But he couldn't turn his eyes back to the screen.

"Humans can generally be divided into two categories regarding their response to trauma. There are those who can savor it. They use it to change themselves and can enjoy that experience. The others just shut down. They protect themselves by not thinking deeply about it. Being shaken to your core is stressful, either way. Which type do you think you are?"

The younger man pretended to think. He held off on answering because he knew the older man would speak first.

"You want to think you're the first type, don't you? But

you're the second type. I'm the second type as well. You could say we're stubborn."

The older man made a strange face. He wouldn't normally call himself stubborn. But the look of chagrin soon vanished. He never doubted himself.

"So you had best stop acting like you're working for justice. Those who work earnestly for this organization, and those who do the same work with misgivings—in the end, they're the same. You're only different on the inside. You're easing your emotional burden slightly by telling yourself that you question what you do. But if you consider the outcome, it's exactly the same."

The younger man tried to respond. But he couldn't find the words. This man knew everything about him.

"And, unlike me, you have a family, right? Sometimes I read your tweets. I enjoy them, even though they're so boring. It's a good example of how childish people can become on the Internet. Your Twitter name is great. What was it again? Oh, right! 'Child-rearing samurai'!"

The younger man's body tensed. He felt embarrassment and rage well up within him. But he quieted those feelings. *Why does he know that?* But he didn't ask. The man knew everything.

The older man laughed quietly. "Ha ha ha . . . *Happy boy.*"

He laughed even louder. But the younger man knew it wasn't real laughter. It was a performance. A performance that no one would enjoy. It was just to make him uncomfortable. The older man always put on these kinds of shows as if it were part of his job. The younger man had wondered before if it was just his twisted personality.

"In a certain sense, the number of crimes committed is a

numerical representation of the degree of dissatisfaction in our society."

As if to prove his point, the older man stopped laughing. The topic of conversation had changed.

"Do you know why there hasn't been a dramatic increase in crime even though class division in this country is wider than ever before? There are plenty of reasons, but one is the Internet. It serves as a place for people to vent their dissatisfaction. What a great invention! It's a pressure valve for some of the growing unhappiness in our society. I'm genuinely grateful. Aren't you? We can maintain people's dissatisfaction without forcing them to commit crimes. Or to put it another way, we can maintain the level of dissatisfaction that we need. To make this country lean right we need that dissatisfaction from the class divide. We produce dissatisfaction, turn it toward another country, and militarize. Very few people realize that hate for other countries is just an expression of dissatisfaction with ourselves. Don't you think it's pathetic that people fail to realize that this logic has been used over and over to control people for centuries? And yet they are still so easily turned violent. It's sad, right? Oh, that's right, I had something to tell you."

He's in a good mood today, the younger man thought, watching the other continue to talk. The younger man was unfortunate to have such a boss. The older man had a bad reputation. His education was the best one could get in Japan, and everyone said he was quite intelligent. But the gap between the brightness of his mind and the plainness of his face was unnerving, and there was nothing worse than his personality. It was so bad, supposedly, that all his subordinates eventually wound up ill.

But the younger man had already regained his composure. He knew that in a few minutes his boss's story would be over and he would be able to get back to his own work. He was smart, just like his boss. And he also had a way of maintaining his mental balance.

At five o'clock, when he'd finished with work, he would leave this all behind. He would transform from his work self into a good husband and a good father. When he was at home, he didn't think about work at all. He hugged his wife and child close to him, smiling.

"YOU'RE LATE," Komaki told the woman, panting. She was on top of Narazaki, raising and lowering her hips. When the other woman entered the room, Narazaki hadn't tried to stop Komaki.

"You were late, so I've already started . . . Mm. He's almost finished a second time."

"I'm sorry. That woman—I forgot her name. I was told to look for her," she said, placing a tape recorder on the table.

"What's that?"

"I'm not sure. That woman dropped it."

Komaki pulled Narazaki's head toward her. Her hips continued to rise and fall. She pressed Narazaki's face into her breasts.

"Are you going to come? Are you going to come like this?"

The room was dark. Sawatari lay in bed looking at her.

Mineno stared back blankly. The impression he gave off hadn't changed much since the time she'd seen him at one of Matsuo's talks. His eyes were sharp, and his face was disgustingly handsome. She couldn't tell how old he was.

"What a great expression."

Sawatari didn't move, just lazed on his side, looking at her. Mineno's chest grew taut. What was this pressure?

"Did you give up hope? That's not bad. But you still haven't hit rock bottom."

Sawatari's limp body looked as if it were gradually sinking deeper into the bed.

"When I give the signal, several men will come. They will tie you up. You will be raped by me. Then, when it's over, you will be at the very bottom."

Sawatari touched his left eyelid and pulled it gently with

his finger. Something was moving in his mouth. That movement wouldn't stop. Mineno couldn't take her eyes off him. It felt like pressure was rising up around her, and she couldn't breath.

"I can say one word and completely change the rest of your life . . . Mm. I always think . . . in moments like this . . . There's this strange sensation . . . You . . . you attended Matsuo's talks, so you probably know. The connection between the brain and consciousness. And the universe and fate."

There were light and dark spots in the gloom of the room. Mineno thought it must be an illusion, but the room seemed darker at its furthest points.

"I'm thinking about whether or not I will fuck you . . . Or, properly speaking, the countless particles that make up my brain, and several of the billions of nerves made up of those particles are . . . are sending countless electrical signals . . . They're trying to decide what to do to the woman in front of me. And I, my consciousness, is watching all of that."

Sawatari removed his finger from his eyelid and shut his eyes. It was as if he had fallen asleep inspite of what he was saying. When he reopened his eyes, he shot Mineno a strange, brief look. He started talking again in a whisper.

"If the movements of all the particles were decided by the Big Bang . . . What will happen to you has also been decided. But if they move randomly, your fate has not yet been set."

Sawatari's eyes moved as if to reconfirm Mineno's shape. It was as though he had forgotten who he was talking to, and had finally returned to the conversation.

"I wonder which it is. I always think about this—is everything decided, or is it not? In moments like this when I make decisions . . . Of course, there are many factors involved. For instance, today is Monday, and I've already had too many women. You came on Monday. Or rather, the particles that compose you at the moment appeared in front of the particles that compose me at this moment on a Monday. Does your appearance here mean anything or not? Or does it just seem to have no meaning to us humans—does it mean something important to the particles?"

"Do you think you're in control?" Mineno asked. She began to smile. "You are nothing but a tool to make me give up hope."

Sawatari looked at Mineno questioningly. He appeared to be smiling, but it was too dark to see.

"When I saw you at Matsuo's talk, you would never have said anything like that. You were just a little girl . . . How wonderful."

Men appeared out of the darkness. They grasped Mineno's body. She didn't resist. She was about to face off against the darkness. Against something that could destroy every part of her being. She felt scared. But not as scared as she'd expected. She was taken over by a strange sensation—as if the darkness were a kindness. *Why do I feel this way? Why do I feel this way about the darkness even though it's trying to destroy me?*

"Don't misunderstand. We won't hurt you," said one of the men.

There were doors. Many doors.

"You're lucky. You get to see it all unfold."

HER HEAD hurt. She couldn't believe Rina would do that to her.

She walked down the hall pressing on her temple.

But why would they take Rina? Who had ordered such a thing? The only person who could seize an officer was the leader, or the officer's counsel. But that didn't matter. Rina had taken the recorder. The recorder wasn't that important. But Rina had taken the USB drive, too. That was awful. She must still have it. *But I can't go look for it.*

I thought I'd be allowed to become Takahara-sama's woman. But now I'll have to keep sleeping with strange men. I don't want to anymore. I don't want to have sex with anyone besides Takahara-sama. She'd managed to get out of the Monday activities, but her head still hurt. *I want to run away. If I can't be with Takahara-sama, I want to leave this world. There are still a few days left. I can get out. What happened to me all of a sudden? Not wanting to sleep with any other men. Is the brainwashing wearing off? Was I brainwashed? My head hurts. What will I do when I leave? I'll just wind up clinging to another good-for-nothing man . . . Try to stop thinking.* How many years ago had she realized that she didn't have to think? A few days after she'd started working for that call girl service. She'd stopped thinking about what kind of man she was waiting for and just went to the hotel. There was less stress when she made it a kind of mechanical task.

All of a sudden she remembered one man she'd had to sleep with because she couldn't give him his money back. He'd been on top of her and asked, "Should I come inside you, or on your face?" She'd thought it would be absolutely horrible if he came on her face. Even though it was so much safer for him to come on her face than inside her. But she couldn't let him. Her face was too close to the real her. Her insides were further away. Back then, she'd tried to think her insides weren't part of her.

She opened the door. Komaki was getting dressed. Another woman was petting the man's hair. Who was he? Why did this man get three women?

"You're late. I'm leaving," Komaki said.

I have to make some excuse. "I'm sorry. They asked me to pat someone down."

"You're too late for that to be all."

Her heart started racing. The recorder was on the table.

She snatched it and hurried outside. The other women were saying something behind her, but it didn't matter. She pressed the button for the elevator. *I'll go to the 21st floor. I will make the leader listen to this. I'll have him lock up Takahara-sama. I'll have him make me Takahara-sama's caretaker—my reward for showing him this. Takahara-sama won't be killed. They'll lock him up, but they won't kill him.* The elevator arrived and the door opened. No one was following her. She got in, and pressed the button for the 20th floor. *It will be fine. They won't kill Takahara-sama. They probably won't kill him. I'll become his nurse. But if they kill him . . . Now's not the time to think about that.*

As soon as the elevator door opened she ran up the stairs to the 21st floor. It was the first time she had run like that since she was in school. *I don't want to remember the past. I don't need the past. I'm fine without it. I can't think about anything besides getting my hands on Takahara-sama. That's all I have. I don't want to sleep with other men. I don't want to leave here.*

"Hey! Wait!"

There was a man in the hallway—the watchman. She ignored him and ran by.

"Hey, what are you doing? You don't have permission! You can't get in anyway! The door won't open!"

She halted in front of the gigantic door. She was scared. But this was an emergency. *The leader will forgive me. If it won't open, I'll scream.*

When she put her hand on the lever, it opened.

"Leader!" she screamed, out of breath. He was lying down. He looked tired. Someone else must have just been there with him. *I wonder who? It doesn't matter.*

"Leader!"

He didn't answer. It was as if he didn't see or hear her.

"Leader. Please! Please, listen to this."

She pressed the button on the tape recorder. Takahara-sama's voice rang through the silent room. His terror plot—he was organizing believers secretly. He was trying to take over the cult. She felt like something was breaking— like everything was crumbling away silently. Her body grew hot.

". . . Wow," the leader finally said.

She spoke desperately. "Leader, did you hear? He's trying to do something terrifying. He's trying to betray you. Please, catch him! Make me his caretaker! I'll change him! I'll, I'll . . ."

"Let me hear it again."

The leader stood up slowly, as if he were chasing away his sleepiness. She held out the recorder. *Please make me Takahara-sama's caretaker. I want Takahara-sama. I would do anything to have him. Whatever it takes.*

"Your reward."

The leader put his hands around her neck. She couldn't breathe.

What? What is this? I was helping him— Their eyes met.

He stared into her face as he strangled her. The recorder fell to the floor.

"Lea . . . Leader . . ."

She gasped for breath. Her body rose up. *Air. If I didn't . . .*

"I guess you're going to die."

The leader's voice grew distant.

"Since you've heard that, you must die."

Takahara sank deep into his chair. He was so tired he didn't want to stand back up.

"Tomorrow we'll begin."

Sasahara and Adachi sat sunk into their own chairs. They had all washed their hands over and over. And not just because they were covered in dirt. They had just handled a corpse.

"Roger," Sasahara replied. Though he was tired, his voice was resolute.

"You two will leave now. I've gotten permission from the leader. Rest up in a hotel somewhere. You need to get as much sleep as possible. Tomorrow at eleven. We'll meet where we discussed."

The two stood up. But Sasahara turned to Takahara.

"And the others?"

"They've already gone. The machinery and materials are ready, so all that's left is to meet tomorrow. You two, hurry."

"And you?"

"I still have a few things to take care of. I have a meeting with the leader."

"Understood."

The two left the room. Takahara got up from his chair. He unlocked the drawer of his desk and took out the pistol.

The moment he touched it, the sensation sent a shiver through the nerves of his arm. *Something greater than me*, he thought. *This machine is far greater than me—far crueler.*

He put the pistol in his pocket, got in the elevator, and pressed the button for the 20th floor. His legs grew weak. *I have to go beyond myself.* He took several deep breaths. *I will have to be the gear that sets the machine in motion.*

He got out of the elevator and quietly climbed the stairs. The watchman was standing in front of the leader's door, looking troubled.

"Takahara-sama," he said. He seemed relieved. "A woman, one of the Cupro girls, forced her way into the leader's room. I can't touch the door. It's a sin. I don't know what's happening inside. I . . ."

Takahara silenced him with a gesture. The gun in his pocket felt horribly heavy.

"I see. Leave it to me."

"But Takahara-sama—"

"I've been summoned."

"I . . ."

"You haven't heard?"

"Yes."

"How strange . . . But I've been summoned . . . You don't believe me?"

"No, of course I do, but . . ."

His mind grew hazy. Suddenly everything seemed like such a burden. *Should I kill him? I'll certainly feel much better the moment I throw my whole future into this.* A feeling like dense, coarse mud rose up within him. He thought about the gun in his pocket.

But Takahara smiled. *I must do what's required of me as an agent.*

"This is an emergency. A woman entered this room without the leader's permission. Isn't that right? I, an officer, must resolve this. I'll take all responsibility."

"Roger." The man had relented.

"Stand back."

The man looked at Takahara uncertainly, but took a step back. Takahara continued to stare at him, and he took another.

"Return to your regular position! Do you want the leader to see you all flustered?"

The man left, surprised. Takahara laid his hand on the door. It was unlocked. How convenient.

The leader was sitting on the ground in the dark facing Takahara. His legs were crossed, and he was hunched forward. He was sucking on some woman's lips as if he were eating them. Takahara froze in shock. She lay there lifeless and fully dressed, her head supported by one of the leader's arms, while his other hand pinched her chin and pulled it up. The leader was devouring her lips like he was sucking the seeds from a slice of watermelon.

"Mm . . . What is it?" the leader asked when he noticed Takahara. He immediately returned to the woman's lips.

"Who is that woman?'

"Hm? . . . She seems to be unconscious . . . Or maybe dead . . . I don't know."

The leader continued to suck on her lips. *This insect,* Takahara thought. *This disgusting insect.*

Takahara gripped his pistol with trembling fingers. *It's a perfect shot,* Takahara thought. *The leader's posture is perfect. The position of his head is perfect.*

Takahara wasn't ready. But he took out his gun. Humans can act, even when they aren't ready. He breathed in deeply. His vision narrowed, and he tried to force the stiffening joints of his arm to move. He was too tense, but he didn't know how to relax. He inhaled deeply again. His fingers and palm gripping the pistol were soaked with sweat. In his mind he thought, *I want to stop.* Even now he was searching for a way to justify his actions. *I heard a woman burst into your room, so I came to protect you.* If he said that now, he could still turn around. But he moved his body. He felt like throwing up. *I should do it. If I do this, everything else will fall into place on its own.* The leader was still crouched on the ground. Takahara pressed the muzzle of the gun to the back of his head. His heart was beating loud, and the strength suddenly left his legs. But it was too late. There was nothing left but for him to do it. He couldn't go back.

"Please do what I say."

The leader looked up at Takahara as if the gun weren't even there. Then he returned to sucking on the woman's lips.

"I will record you. I have a script here. You will read it. We are going to carry out an attack. You will be our figurehead. I am in charge now. I took over this cult while you were drowning in women."

Takahara was sweating copiously. He had never been this close to the leader. He was so close that he noticed the smell coming from the leader's skin. His breathing was heavy. He felt a pressure bearing down on him. *What is this pressure?*

". . . Oh."

"Do you understand? You can do what I say, or I can kill you. Either way is fine with me. Will you call your helpers from the other room? If you do, I'll just kill you. You have no choice."

"Takahara . . ."

The leader moved his face. Takahara knew he couldn't shoot the leader in the back of the head.

"Don't move. I'll shoot."

"Takahara."

He didn't pull the gun away from the leader's head. But the leader's head moved. And the muzzle grazed the back of his head, his ear, his cheek. Takahara's heart beat so fast it hurt. The gun was pressed into the leader's cheek, twisting the flesh. But the leader acted as if it weren't there at all.

"I'll shoot."

"Takahara. *Have you ever seen the true shape of god?*"

The space around the leader grew cold.

"What? No. How could I?"

"Oh . . . *I have.*"

The leader looked at Takahara blankly. The muzzle of the gun dug into his cheek.

"Under the right circumstances, at the right time, god will appear . . . And after you see god, even when the particles inside you are replaced, god will stay with you for a certain amount of time."

"What are you talking about?"

"Watch . . . *I will give you strength.*"

He felt a shock to the heart. Matsuo had told him the same thing. His heart felt like it would burst.

"And what should I say?" the leader asked.

"What?"

"Your script. Did you give up on that already?"

His hands shaking, Takahara took out the script. In that moment, the gun strayed from the leader, but Takahara didn't notice.

"Ah, I see."

The leader looked at Takahara. Takahara panicked, but turned on the recorder. The leader began to read.

"You have all worked hard to secretly carry out my will. Now it will all begin. Go! Spread my will around the world. My friends! You are all part of me, and I am part of you. You who rush to battle, you are my pride. We will soon follow you!"

The leader put down the script, and began sucking the woman's lips again, hollowly. The lips of that woman who might just be dead. It was then that Takahara realized somewhere in the corner of his mind that she was the Cupro woman who had come on to him. He noticed, but Takahara did not have the energy to feel anything.

"Leader . . . What . . ."

"Hm?"

"What are you?" Takahara found himself asking, as he gripped the recorder. He himself didn't understand what he was asking. He had completely forgotten about his gun. *"What are you?"*

"If you're finished, get out of here," the leader said lazily.

Takahara left the room. He had no memory of getting in the car, but there he was, gripping the steering wheel, out of breath. He stepped on the accelerator and left the building's parking lot.

It will begin tomorrow.

Ryoko Tachibana woke up on the concrete floor.

At some point, she had fallen asleep. She wasn't sure if it was light or dark outside. Was it almost tomorrow?

What's happening outside this room? Is he locked up? I have to get out of here fast. I have to let the police know where this place is.

But she had no way out. It didn't seem like anyone was coming. *I thought they'd at least bring me food.*

"If friendly aliens ever come to the earth, I'm sure they'll be surprised by how good humans are at creating poverty," Takahara always used to say. He really cared about the world's poor.

But his compassion did not come from virtuousness. He cared most for the starving, and that was because of his personal experiences.

Before they'd become siblings, he had starved. He hadn't

just experienced the psychological pain of feeling hungry while staring up at the lights of wealthy people's houses—he had been completely starved, locked up in a tiny room with no food at all for a long time. He hadn't spoken often with Tachibana about that. When they finally found him and he was taken to the hospital, he was in critical condition. He had digested all of his own muscle; he was on the verge of death. It was a miracle the doctors were able to save him, that he hadn't lost his eyesight or suffered from brain damage.

Sometimes he would throw up when pictures of famines were broadcast on the news. It wasn't because of his passion for others so much as from the pain that came when he was reminded of the terror he had actually experienced.

"Why do poor countries exist? Why do countries full of starving people exist? It's because rich countries want them to be poor."

When she listened to him speak, it became clear to her that the world was carefully producing poverty as part of its system. She'd heard him talk about it so many times she remembered most of it verbatim now.

"First imagine that some natural resource—say, crude oil—is discovered in a country in Africa. If the king of that country grants the right to extract that oil to a rich country, then their relations will continue as usual. But if they refuse, then we, the rich countries, will gather up all that country's poor people and get them to form a rebel group. They'll arm them and start a rebellion. The media will call it a 'popular uprising' against 'dictatorial oppression.' Many people will die in the rebellion and many children will become orphans. That country will become even poorer. The rebels we support will eventually defeat the king, and

make one of their own the new king and start a new government. And then we get the oil. And it's more helpful if the
new king and government are full of corruption instead of
truly concerned about their own country's poor. You want a
king you can bribe, so you can get his oil easily.

"Let's say, for example, the king of a certain poor African
country is worth five trillion yen. That's an absurd amount
of money. Let's say the total population of that country is
around sixty-six million people. And backing that king is a
powerful Western country. If that country has oil, it could
be rich, you'd think. But that's only if the country's government and government agencies function properly. Once that
country finds crude oil, it will run headlong to dependence
on that oil. The country's currency will drastically rise in
value, and all its exports aside from oil will receive a death
blow. When they extract the oil, they have to pressure it
to the surface. They'll run it through pipelines and attach
valves, but that will cause a lot of damage to the surrounding
environment, and many fields will be ruined. Countless
farmers will be left without a livelihood. And the increase
in jobs that comes from harvesting crude oil is actually far
lower than that created by manufacturing. Only those who
work with refined oil will suddenly start making money.
The rich countries just want to get their hands on oil for
a slightly better price. They'll drown the government and
agencies that own that crude oil in bribes.

"But eventually the country's poverty will become a global
issue, and there will come support. It's called Official Devel-
opment Assistance. ODA money comes from rich countries'
taxes. Of course businessmen in those rich countries work
behind the scenes with these ODAs. To give a simple

example, let's say an international organization gives an enormous public donation to a poor country. It's not uncommon for that donation to become pocket money for the country's top officials and the people who work in the agencies below them, and never make it to the pockets of the poor. There's data on this. Of the money a certain country's finance ministry earmarked for medical clinics for farmers, less than one percent of that expenditure actually got to the clinics. There are also cases where those large donations conveniently wind up in the banks of rich countries. The poor country has to withdraw the money from them. And of course, those banks turn a profit.

"As long as poor countries keep existing, it's easy for rich ones to create ODAs. Often they are public businesses. I wish I could believe even half of these ODAs actually do their job, but that's often not the case. For example, Company A uses money from an ODA to do something in a poor country. Poor people will get the leftovers, but Company A will take at least half the profit. That's what these public businesses called ODAs are about. The system guarantees that some percentage of the money winds up in the hands of wealthy private businesses. One could say that just by existing, these poor countries allow ODAs to make a profit.

"Let's look at farming. It's actually a lie that we don't have enough food. If we distributed the present amount of food we produce to everyone in the world, we'd still have too much. Rich countries pay their own farmers huge subsidies. Because of these subsidies, wealthy countries can easily export the food they produce at low prices. And that food winds up in Africa. African farmers can't compete in terms of prices with these cheap products produced by wealthy countries. Why do rich countries protect their farmers with subsidies? The reason is simple. It's a vote-getting machine in election time. All countries want to raise their own food production rate in case of war. But they also know that exporting this cheap food they subsidize to Africa hurts African farmers. There's a trick here, too. Those African farmers will start growing other crops instead. The rich countries want to make poor Africans grow things that are useful for them. Like coffee. Or chocolate. They'll get them to produce vast quantities, which lowers the prices, so their own industries can import those products cheaply. The cheap things we get in our own country come from the unfair wage systems in these poor countries. People starve in Africa because they can no longer farm to sustain themselves. African farmers should have the power to grow their own food. But instead they get buried under manufactured poverty.

"Poverty is produced deliberately by wealthy countries. But in the past few years, things have changed. In some African countries, a middle class has gradually begun to emerge. Instead of just using Africans as cheap manpower, wealthy countries have been looking for another world market, and they've tried to force Africa into being a consumer society as well. We've yet to see if it works, if it will help with the eradication of poverty. If they want Africa to become another world market, then Africans will have to become wealthy. But if businesses run off to drain them of all they're worth, Africa will be forever impoverished. Now's their chance to change."

Takahara grew passionate once he started speaking.

"The main problem is businesses in wealthy countries. If we can control their reckless behavior, then, theoretically, starvation will vanish from the face of the earth. It's fine for these companies to try to develop poor countries to make a profit. Not all businesses can be charities. But it's no good if they don't imagine success for the poor countries as well. That's why we must send watchdog agencies to oversee these multinational businesses. NGOs are too weak to monitor them on their own. If a country wants to use an ODA, then they should also send another agency to watch them. Then we'll have them report the results in the mass media, and also to the Diet every year. What is that business doing over there? Are its activities hurting the local people? Businesses will have to pay attention to their image. The businesses can appeal to the public as trying to end poverty. If the economy that provides their profit is also tied to work to end poverty, things will move quickly.

"Of course, it's unrealistic to ask rich countries to stop subsidizing their own farmers. If they did, African farmers would be able to compete in international markets. But at least we should stop exporting our subsidized foods to African countries. Then African farmers could eventually start rebuilding the industry to feed themselves. Africa's food self-sufficiency rate would increase.

"We should create an international law that when rebellions occur, both rebels and government must make public where they got the weapons and funds they're using. If we do that we'll find out which wealthy nations instigated the uprising and are controlling it. We'll see who's really behind that fight.

"It's a lie that the Internet will connect the whole world. In the poor villages where they really have important things to say, there's no Internet. So we have to create a system in which people everywhere can say when and where problems are occurring. Those who say that providing the infrastructure for such a system will take too long, that it's unrealistic—they don't know anything. After all, guerrillas in the mountains already use the Internet and satellite cell phones. If we tried to do it, we could. We need sites like Wikipedia—proper, detailed public pages, for everyone in the world, so everyone can hear everyone else's voice.

"We must introduce an international tax. We can use the money from taxing the profits of the global economy outside national borders to solve the world's problems. This already started in part of the EU with their carbon tax on airlines. If we could tax financial institutions just a tiny, tiny bit, we would have a huge amount of money to spend on the poor.

"Total fair trade. Fair trade certifies that products weren't produced under inhumane conditions by over-worked employees. That they were produced fairly, and that employees were properly paid. It helps reduce poverty, but the system still has to be perfected, and it hasn't spread very far. Instead of leaving it up to small, local grassroots movements, we should use our taxes and require television commercials. It may be difficult for local television stations to demand commercials from international corporations, so the government will have to make it mandatory. In Japan's case, NHK should be broken into two. NHK is run on money collected from the public, and even though it's supposedly independent from politics, it tends to lean in favor of whoever's in charge. Of course, that's because that bent is also the bent of the people who elected that government. Since NHK is unlikely, then, to broadcast attacks on the government, I want it split in two. One half would be the NHK we have now that plays safe, public programs. Of course, there's great value in that. And the other one would be like a more progressive BBC, a radical public broadcast that picks up the provocative scoops. It would cover the crimes of businesses—their criminal pursuit of profit. I want a powerful media agency that has nothing to do with business advertising."

When Tachibana had listened to him talk, she'd thought it was all just the beautiful fantasies of a young man who wanted to end poverty. But she also doubted herself. People died—they starved to death, were worked to death by rich countries, died by gunfire. And in this world, we call the actions of those who try to stop that death cycle fantasies.

He used to say he wanted to be a writer. But at some point he stopped writing. "I gave up on writing stories," he said. "Instead, I'm going to write my own life. I'm going to act. I'm going for the root of it all. I'm going to change the world."

He worked for many NGOs, and expanded his network. He had a way of looking down on people, and he was very proud, but he was also genuinely smart. He gradually grew famous in the world of NGOs.

Of course, there were many problems with his theories. For example, sending agencies to monitor multinationals in Africa. Since those agencies acted on moral and ethical principles, they had no strength to fight. They'd lose to the companies with no morals or ethics, who just wanted to consume the resources of those countries.

Let's say a well-intentioned company tried to begin developing some resource in Africa. They'd sign contracts with local businesses. They wouldn't bribe government agencies or those in top positions at local companies. They'd improve working conditions and work to help improve the local infrastructure. But if the local businesses and governments weren't also well-intentioned, they'd find all that a waste of time. They'd simply hand those resources over to someone else who didn't pester them. In Africa, there are actually many cases of this occurring.

When Tachibana had told Takahara that, he just smiled. "I simply have a vision," he said. "Executing the system—that's a job for the people who can create something so detailed."

It was true, most of the world's problems were created by businesses. And they were behind all the world's conflicts.

But gradually Takahara had changed. He stuck to his principles, but he started searching for radical ways to make things happen. He took a long trip, and when he returned he didn't talk about it much, but Tachibana saw his passport and knew he'd passed through several African countries.

He didn't tell her why, but he had suddenly gotten interested in this religion. Unlike many of the believers, who were sucked into the cult by Sawatari's charisma, Takahara had sought out Sawatari deliberately, only pretending to adore the man.

Tachibana heard the pounding of feet down the hall outside. What had happened? Had Takahara been captured?

YOSHIKO AND Yoshida were at the police station.

They were already familiar with the officer in charge of the Cult X case. Matsuo had opposed telling the police about Sawatari's scam, so they never had, but the police had approached Matsuo for information about Sawatari many times. Matsuo and Yoshiko would try to help, but they didn't know where the cult was located, and they couldn't tell the police anything useful.

"If they kidnapped someone, that would be quite serious," the detective said. "We investigated them seven years ago for an incident involving the murder of one of their members, but we couldn't locate them. We tracked them down once, five years ago. But then they vanished. We'd thought they'd broken up." The detective sighed. "But it seems like they're still at it. We're not sure what they're up to now, but we will do all we can. If we just knew where they were."

"Come quick!" A young officer burst through the door. He was clearly panicking. "Oh, this is perfect. Yoshiko-san and Yoshida-san, come too . . . The news. I don't know what's happening."

TAKAHARA AND his men were assembled in a hotel suite in the city. There were thirty of them. Today they moved. They were doing a last check of their positions when the news broke. They all stared lifelessly at the TV. Takahara tried to calm himself down, but he couldn't.

"Why?" he whispered. "Why?"

THE BELIEVERS rushed to the twenty-first floor, screaming, "Leader! Leader!"

The watchman tried to stop them, but they pushed past him.

"Leader!" one man shrieked, sounding as though he was on the verge of tears. "Leader! The building is surrounded by the riot police!"

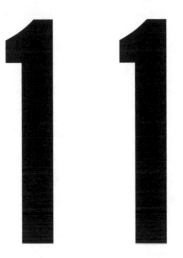

The door opened and the leader came out.

He was tall when he stood up straight. He was wearing a brand new, plain white robe.

"Explain the situation." The leader stopped the believers who were trying to kneel with a wave of his hand.

Officer Maeda spoke. His voice was quivering. "Someone pressed the interphone. Room 1001. Of course, the believer in the room ignored it, but whoever it was kept pestering him. He thought it was someone trying to sell something. And when he looked at the screen, it was two men wearing suits. When I received the notification and went to check from the observation room, I saw the riot squad."

"Have you started preparations?"

"Yes. Following emergency measure two, we've cut power to the automatic door in the front and have begun setting up a barricade. The back door has also been blocked."

"The other officers?"

"They are directing the reinforcement of the windows. All of the windows are already reinforced with steel shutters, but we are attaching iron bars to further reinforce them. As instructed."

"Mm . . . Gather all the believers in the hall. And the officers."

"About that . . ." Maeda faltered. "Takahara is gone. And not just him . . . Some twenty believers have also vanished."

YOSHIDA STARED transfixed at the TV in the police station.

Yoshiko turned toward it and her face went pale.

There's too much happening all at once, Yoshida thought.

"Why did this happen?" the police officer interjected. "Aren't we the ones in charge of this case? Why didn't they let us know about this? And how did they find the cult?"

The Tokyo Metropolitan Police Department's Public Security Bureau—they operated on a different philosophy than the police. They hadn't contacted the officers who could properly claim this jurisdiction because they didn't trust them. Who could say there wasn't a mole from the cult in the police?

In 1995, when another cult spread deadly sarin gas through the subways, there was an informant working for the police who leaked information from their investigations back to the cult. To prevent that sort of leak now, probably only a few of the top brass had been told this raid was coming.

In front of the rope that cordoned off the press a suited reporter was shouting his broadcast, his voice hoarse.

"What are they under investigation for?" the female newscaster back at the studio asked.

"We still do not have precise information about that. However, we did get a report claiming that a man and a woman have been abducted and imprisoned."

A man and a woman. There was a rustling in Yoshida's chest. It must be Mineno and Narazaki.

"And why have the riot police been mobilized?"

"It seems there are also reports that this cult possesses a large number of weapons."

"We were the ones who got that report," the young officer said. "How do they know?"

On the TV screen was a tall, stylish apartment building. Not a place one would imagine to house a cult. Through the automatic glass doors of the front entrance, a sturdy barricade was visible. The people on the surrounding block had been ordered to evacuate.

The reporter continued, "We believe that this assault is the result of a long-term secret investigation by the Public Security Bureau."

Yoshiko's lips were trembling. The shock was too much for her, Yoshida thought. When he tried to move her away from the TV, she spoke up suddenly. "This is very dangerous."

"Yes," Yoshida said, nodding. "Mineno and Narazaki-kun are caught up in all this trouble."

"That's true, too, but it's much worse than that."

"Yoshiko-san?" The officers and Yoshida turned to Yoshiko.

She said, "If anything happens to Sawatari, they . . . They'll all kill themselves. That's one of the rules there . . . The moment the riot police break down that barricade and get in . . ."

On the TV, the riot police were readying their riot shields. "They'll all die."

THE BELIEVERS were all gathered in the hall.

There were about one hundred and twenty men and fifty women. Maeda grew nervous heading to the stage with the leader.

I have to calm their unease. Can I do it? Can I manage this kind of speech? If only Takahara were here, he thought. *He would be able to. His appearance, his voice draws people in.*

When he climbed onto the stage and looked out over the believers, he was dumbstruck by their frenzy

That's right, Maeda thought. *They are not weak sheep. They are not powerless people who simply flock behind a leader. They have all been alienated from society. They all look at society as their enemy.*

With those believers before him, filled with hope, gazes full of encouragement, Maeda felt tears well up in his eyes. *That's right. We are one. We will accept the hostility of society, and turn back with hostility of our own.*

"Everyone, listen." Maeda began to feel elated. "Society has found us, and they are trying to persecute us. As you all know, those outside are all trash. They have no refinement. They are just trying to get rid of anyone who gets in their way so they can protect their own trifling profit." He raised his voice even louder. "Are we going to give in to them quietly? Are we going to let ourselves be buried by this worthless society? Absolutely not. We absolutely will not. Look at this!"

The officers removed a vinyl sheet covering the stage. Guns. A cheer rose from the audience.

"We will fight. We will show them now, we will show those people who chased us out that they—*they!*—are the trash!"

The cheers became shouts. The hall was electrified.

"The leader is on our side. God is on our side. Justice is on our side!"

"Leader!"

Shouts of joy rose up from the crowd.

"Leader!"

"Leader!"

"Men, take your weapons," Maeda screamed. "Women, you will be the men's support. From here on out all forms of personal interaction and sexual acts are allowed. The thirty-five Cupro girls, those who are here under contract, need not take part in any of this. A safe spot has been prepared for them in the basement if they choose."

But none of the Cupro girls tried to leave. They looked with passionate eyes up at Maeda and the leader.

"We are one! We are one!" The shouts of joy grew to a roar. The air in the hall rose like a tornado.

"Several of our members have already left this building, and now they are working to launch an all-out attack on society. They have over fifty tons of explosives. They will shake this worthless society to its very core. We have food for two months. We can fight as long as we need."

Maeda did not know exactly why Takahara was gone. But he didn't need to. The leader had told him what to say.

"Be the spark! This is the most beautiful moment of our lives. This is the most beautiful point of our lives!"

Maeda couldn't hear his own voice over the gyrating roar of the believers' screams. His body was shaking. He was quivering with excitement. *Is this the first time?* Maeda wondered. *Is this the first time I've ever experienced this sort of excitement? It feels like my own existence is becoming something larger than me. It's like by becoming one with the leader I can become something enormous.*

The leader suddenly stood up. The believers began to cry, still screaming.

"My talented disciples!" he said. The believers shouted in response. "We will fight. I will hold on to your lives!"

The believers screamed at the top of their lungs. The hall roiled with shouts of joy. Tears fell from Maeda's eyes. *How great*, he thought. *How great that I followed the leader. My life doesn't matter. We will shake up this society. We will give those worthless pieces of trash a real shock.*

The officers Sugimoto, Rina, and Unabara began handing out weapons and assigning the believers positions. When Maeda saw Rina, he froze. Why did she have such a tragic expression on her face?

She was probably worried about her lover, Maeda realized. That would make sense. He didn't know much, but it seemed Takahara had received a very important order from the leader.

Why had she been locked up until a moment ago? he wondered. But Maeda quickly stopped thinking. Thinking was a waste, and it didn't matter. *Even if it costs me my life*, Maeda thought, full of conviction, *I will protect my leader.* He felt proud of himself for thinking that. *I want to be a sacrifice. For this great thing. For this great thing.*

Takahara stared at the TV screen, rapt.

The riot police were sent in because a man and woman were believed to be imprisoned? *There's no way. Did my plan leak out? But if that were the case, why did they surround that building? Weren't they following me?*

But this is convenient for me. We'll move while they're distracted. He had just had the others check around the hotel and there was no one suspicious there.

This is just the last push for us, to actually carry through our plan. Takahara faced the thirty comrades gathered in the hotel suite.

"As you see, what we are trying to do must have gotten out."

They all looked at Takahara. He thought they'd be nervous, but they were all in high spirits.

"But they're too late. We're already here. They can't stop us anymore."

As he spoke, he began to believe the situation was actually as he described it.

"Listen. The leader has recorded an important message for us."

Takahara turned on the tape recorder.

"You have all worked to carry out my will secretly. Now it will all begin. Go! Spread my will across the world. My friends! You are all part of me, and I am part of you. You who rush to battle, you are my pride. We will soon follow you!"

They cheered. Listening to the leader's voice, Takahara was seized by a strange sensation. It was as if those words had predicted exactly what would happen.

Even though I was the one who wrote them.

"Let's go. The leader is with us!" Takahara shouted, shaking off his unease. They cheered again, and left the room in single file. It was as if everything were moving along smoothly of its own accord. Even though he was the agent making it happen.

Takahara left after them, rode the elevator with Sasahara, exited the lobby and got in a car. A golf bag next to him contained a PPSh-41 automatic rifle.

"Takahara-sama . . ."

"Hm?"

"Actually . . . Some of the weapons have disappeared."

Takahara stared at Sasahara. His face began to go pale, but he continued speaking. "Um, of course, we have enough. But the extra guns we prepared have vanished."

"Why?" Takahara's heart began to race. They moved into the passing lane on the highway. "What do you mean they've vanished? Just the extras? The twenty Colts?"

"Yes."

"Well then, there's no problem . . . Let's just say there's no problem. It's a huge problem . . . But we have to proceed."

Takahara focused on not letting concern show on his face. He couldn't make his subordinates uneasy at this point. But why? If they had all vanished, he would understand. That would mean someone had caught on to his plan and tried to stop it. But why just some of them?

They had to go. Everything was in motion.

A carefully crafted terrorist plot that would leave no one dead, Takahara thought. The more people die, the more attention an attack gets, but that decreases the righteousness of the group carrying out the plot. They do not gain support for their beliefs, and they become mere criminals.

That's why we won't kill anyone. Takahara was the only one holding a gun with the power to actually kill. The rest of the guns his subordinates carried had been altered. If someone were shot with their fake bullets, they'd bleed, but the bullets should not go deep enough to penetrate organs. Unfortunately, they couldn't totally avoid the possibility of seriously injuring someone.

They changed lanes and turned left. In the distance they could see the JBA broadcasting station.

He had ordered his subordinates strictly to shoot no humans. If they did, there was a chance they would find out their guns couldn't kill. *I am the only one who will shoot anyone. I have practice. I can make sure they don't die.*

He looked at his watch. 2:50 P.M. Ten more minutes.

There were no guards with guns at the broadcasting center. Unarmed security could do nothing.

All they needed was an hour.

If we can succeed in an hour, I can complete my mission.

They approached the JBA studio building where the nightly national news was broadcast. They stopped the car in the road. Seven more minutes. His heart began pounding.

He took the PPSh-41 from the golf bag. It was already assembled. He unlocked the safety. Maybe because it was a motion he had repeated many times, his fingers moved automatically, without shaking. He took a deep breath. He could hear his heart beating. Five more minutes.

Sasahara was also nervous, but he was smiling. *That's right. I'm excited, too. My heart is racing, and I'm nervous. I want to run away. But I'm also excited.*

"Two more minutes."

"Yes."

They got out of the car holding their guns. They headed toward the back entrance of JBA's parking lot.

"One more minute."

"All right. Let's go."

The moment he spoke, Takahara's heart beat even harder. A security guard in the parking lot was looking at them—two men approaching with automatic weapons. The guard was thin, and didn't look like he'd be able to fulfill his guard duty. He stared at them blankly, like he thought they were part of the film crew for some TV show. But part of him doubted that, and he was growing more and more nervous.

"Hey, you there!"

"It's three."

"Let's go."

Takahara raised his gun and shot a car nearby. The recoil sent a shock through his shoulder, and a dry noise rang out. The windshield of the car shattered. He trained the muzzle of the gun on the stunned security guard.

"Walk. To the door."

As they walked, a woman exited and saw the security guard with the gun pointed at him, but because the whole scene lacked any sense of reality she couldn't even scream. She just looked on, stupefied, as they passed her and walked through the automatic door. Inside, there was a gate that required an entry card. Takahara kicked the security guard through. Several people were looking at them, but they still couldn't register this scene as real. Takahara pointed his gun at the ceiling and shot wildly. There was a terrifying noise. Several lights shattered and broken glass fell to the ground. People screamed and dove to the ground; one man tried to run and tripped. The security guard also tried to run. Of course he did. He didn't even have a gun.

"Everyone, get on the ground. I want to kill as few people as possible. Don't move. If you hold still, I won't kill you."

The sound of glass shattering and multiple screams sounded in the distance. The same thing was happening at every entrance to the building.

"You, too. Don't move."

Takahara pointed his gun at a security guard in a booth.

"You want me to kill you? You want me to kill you? Then move. I'll shoot."

The security guard put his hands in the air and crouched down.

"All right. Everyone, get up. Put your hands in the air and walk."

But no one moved. They stayed on the ground. Takahara shot again at the wall. They screamed.

"Get up! Go through that door!"

They stood up, watching Takahara in terror. They began moving slowly.

"That way. Go through that door."

There was a loud noise. A young security guard rushed in from outside and tried to grab Sasahara. *How stupid*, Takahara thought. *At times like this it's best to just listen calmly. Such an idiot.*

Sasahara knocked the security guard over and pointed his gun at him as he sat up. A smile began to spread across Sasahara's face.

"Wait! Don't shoot!"

Sasahara let loose. The security guard's body jumped, and a terrifying amount of blood sprayed out. Takahara was stunned. What was happening? The bullets were passing through the man's body and making holes in the wall on the opposite side. Though the gun was supposed to have been altered. The security guard fell back, covered in blood. He didn't move. *Why? Why?*

"Sasahara!"

". . . Takahara-san."

Sasahara pulled a pistol from his left pocket. He pointed it at Takahara.

". . . Sasahara?"

"Thank you for everything."

Sasahara was smiling.

"It's over. Your mission is over. We'll take it from here."

Sasahara pulled the trigger.

There was a dry sound.

Amid the peal of screams, Takahara's body collapsed.

TAKAHARA'S CHRONICLE

I'm going to write about what happened.

Why I'll write it, and who I'll write it for, I don't know. I will try to write down everything that's happened to me. Is it because I can't give up on writing a novel? This is how it always is. Before I write, I question myself. Who cares about the reasons. I don't need a reason. I will just listen to the desires inside me. These may be my last words.

Six years ago, I was abducted from the hotel I was staying at in the middle of the night. A sheet was pulled over my head, my arms were tied, and I was thrown into the back seat of a car. I guessed we were traveling down an unpaved dirt road, because the car bumped wildly as it went. The rough sheet covering my head smelled like some sort of farm animal. Maybe chickens or donkeys. I won't say what country I was in. I can't. It was a small one in central Africa. I worked for an NGO that dug wells. The hotel I was staying in was really just an iron container with a wooden door attached, a quiet, square space that smelled of rust and an unidentifiable sweet odor. Someone knocked, and when I opened the door, there were long guns pointed at me. The kidnappers prodded my back with the ends of those long barrels. They didn't seem to have any plan.

"Where are we going?" I asked in English, but they didn't say anything, just threw me in the car. They had no interest in me, and seemed to think the whole thing was a bother. They didn't understand English, so trying to negotiate would be meaningless. The first thing I thought when they covered my head with that cloth was that I mustn't resist. If they were covering my head, they were taking me to a place they didn't want me to see. Which meant they were still considering sending me back.

Blind, surrounded by the smell of farm animals, bumping up and down along with the car, I felt myself being worn away. They were probably holding me hostage because I was a foreigner. Would my NGO pay them off? Would the government? What if their negotiations failed? I considered what would happen. They'd kill me right away. Here, human life had little value. Death was nothing rare. People died from starvation, from illness, from civil wars, in riots. People were raped and murdered. Lynched. I had seen the torso of a dead woman wearing a T-shirt in the town. That was all that was left of her. They wouldn't hesitate to kill me, and within a few hours, they wouldn't even remember doing it. If after they killed me the hostage negotiations turned in their favor, they'd just think, "We messed up." Like they'd lost a game of cards in a dingy café.

Both of my arms were tied behind my back, and on either side of me was a large man holding a gun. I had no hope of running away. Humans live according to their own will. But I was alienated from my will, from the flow of my life, and I was alienated from my proper destiny. All the work I had done up to now, my skills, my character, the better aspects of my nature, none of that mattered. Nothing that made me human mattered to my kidnappers.

The car stopped. The men grabbed my arms, and took me to some sort of room. I couldn't tell anything about the room except that the floor was hard like concrete. I sensed some sort of bug with many thin legs crawling up the fourth toe of my bare right foot. I thought about my life. I cried, and only then did I realize that I'd been crying the whole time in the car as well. It will be fine, I told myself. I'm a hostage, so they won't kill me. But something inside me was struggling, crying, and screaming. I had to stay calm. In the distance there was some sort of warm, dim light. I didn't actually see it—my head was covered. It felt as though the light filled my vision from within. That light seemed to be my life. My trivial life—the most precious and warm thing. So far, I thought. I'm so far away from that now. That warmth must have been everything I had experienced up till now, but I was so far from it. Suddenly I could see the door to an apartment in front of me. I felt like vomiting, but I swallowed it down. It was a memory from when I was small and starving. Was I going to starve to death like this? I was scared and tried to scream again. The memory probably surfaced to protect me. The fear of starving to death already existed within me. That memory seemed to have a will of its own. It was writhing inside me. By being guided to that fear I always have, I may have been able to push the death approaching right before my eyes out of my consciousness. Just a few seconds was all I needed. My emotions surged like they were trying to force me awake. I remembered the words "lose consciousness." I couldn't lose consciousness. Someone slapped my cheek and I knew I was awake. Despite that, I was caught up in a battle to not lose consciousness. My perception of the world was lagging. It kept trying to stop a few seconds before the present, as if to reject the passage of time. But time flowed on regardless of my will. At some point, there was a man in the room. He smelled like grime and animals, and, for some reason, milk.

"Oh, no."

It was the man's voice. He was speaking in English. I called out from the darkness of the cloth over my head, like I was clinging to some connected memory.

"Save me." I didn't have the time for niceties.

"You're Japanese, right? That's too bad. We made a mistake."

"What?"

"We were planning on kidnapping an employee of the CUUA. Not you. We have no need for you. We'll have to kill you."

CUUA isn't their real name, but this company had made a successful bid for the rights to a small oil field. A tremendous number of farmers' fields were destroyed for this company's sake. The farmers whose fields had been destroyed all flowed into the withered towns looking for income. The women sold their bodies, and the men their children. The NGO I worked for objected to their business. We were trying to inform people of their profiteering.

"I work for CUUA."

I didn't know what I was saying.

"No, you don't. You're Japanese. I saw your passport."

His voice rang through the darkness. I didn't think about how I had promised to devote my life to fighting starvation. Nor did I think about how my friends had laughed at me in a bar when I tried to talk about living life to its fullest. If only we had exposed CUUA's profiteering. But here I was, trying to pass myself off as one of their employees. Someone who would be valuable as a hostage. I wished I worked for CUUA, was jealous of people who did.

"I work for them. Really!"

"Don't lie. You work for an NGO, don't you? We made a mistake."

"You're wrong. Please! Please!"

I struggled toward the man, both my arms still tied behind my back. I probably looked like a wingless yellow insect. But I could never get any closer.

"I haven't seen anything. I don't know anything about you. There's no reason to kill me. Just leave me somewhere, and I'll find my own way home."

"Impossible. You may find our hideout."

"So leave me somewhere far off."

"What?" He sounded surprised. "Are you telling me to waste gas on you?"

I noticed that my crotch was wet, but I wasn't sure when I had started to piss myself.

"It will all be over soon. Yes . . . Oh, I'll take off this hood for you at least."

He snatched the cloth off roughly. The room was smaller than I expected. There were light spots in the darkness. I found myself trying to get up, my hands still tied, to run toward him. But the next thing I remember was being on the floor. The darkness was tinged red. That red eventually mixed with green, and before I was sure if those colors were real, or just an afterimage stained on my eyelids, they were lost in the darkness of the room.

I cried. I screamed. I struggled to untie the ropes on my arms. I wasn't sure if one hour had passed or three. I found myself looking for that bug, the one that had touched my foot earlier. I wasn't sure why—maybe I was trying to help my kidnappers by killing that bug? Look, I killed this bug. I did it for you. I did it for you. I wondered if I was going mad. Even as I wondered, I continued to look for the bug. Maybe it will show up if I pretend I've given up, I thought. If I stick out my foot like this, maybe it will come here looking for warmth. No, I have to act as though I'm not looking for it—even in my thoughts. I'm good at that. But I could never find the bug. It was as if it had vanished. As if to reject my insanity. As if to alienate even me from that insanity.

There were no windows in that room. If there were

a window to give me perspective on the outside world,
would I notice how incredibly small my life was, and
grow embarrassed? But I chewed over the fact that I was
alive. I was tied up, but I could move my hands. My legs
too. One second passed. And now another. My eyes grew
used to the darkness. I couldn't take my eyes off the tiny
cracks in the walls. The cracks in the lower part of the
wall, right at my eye level as I lay there, collapsed. There
are cracks, I thought. Cracks exist. I thought about how
in an instant I would stop existing. I would be forever
cut off from what does exist. They were so heartless. The
walls, and the cracks, and the bug that would never let
me catch it, and time with its seconds just passing by
without me, they were all so heartless. That can't be true,
I thought again. There's no way the world is like this.
The cold, hard stone floor remained cold and hard. I
remembered starving again. I don't know if I was trying
to protect myself. The world was certainly heartless back
then. Because of my body weakening from starvation, the
door, and the television that no longer worked because
the power had been cut, and the metal in the shape of a
heater, and the wood in the shape of a chair, they were
all heartless. I moved toward the wall, and pressed my
cheek against it. I could feel a slight chill. The wall is
giving me its coldness now. Which means that the wall
isn't being heartless. No, but, it is. The wall doesn't care
if I die. I'm the only one who thinks it matters whether I
die or not. The world, this wall, to them this is normal.
The people who are trying to kill me think so, too. I must
also make myself feel that my death is something normal.
But I can't. I can't make myself fit with the essence of the

world. The world and I are totally different things. And maybe I'm the one that's wrong.

The door opened. I shouted something, and a gun was thrust toward me. It looked like a machine gun, but I wasn't really sure. "Let's go. We'll get the room bloody if we shoot you in here." I didn't understand what they were saying.

"I won't get you bloody," I said. "I won't get your clothes dirty. So let me live." My words were failing. They tried to stand me up, but I tensed my body as best I could and resisted. If I leave this floor, I'll really die, I thought. Why aren't I a floor or a wall? I wondered. If I were a floor or a wall, I'd never be killed. They couldn't stand me up, so they dragged me. Like a heavy bundle of grass tied up with rope. Is this a lie? I wondered. It can't be real, can it? I'm Japanese and I have always followed the rules, and I came here out of good intentions, so it can't be real. This can't be life's answer to my good intentions, can it? Even if they're going to kill me, isn't it too sudden? Shouldn't they do something to solemnize my death? When I was taken outside, I felt an oppressive chill. It's cold, I thought. I hate the cold, I thought. I thought it was funny that even though I was going to die, I could think about how I hated the cold, and I wanted to tell them that. Did I tell them, "It's cold," like I was flattering them? Like we were friends or something, and I was trying to confirm the fact that it was cold out? "It's cold. Strange, isn't it? Don't you think so? Even though I'm going to die, it's cold." But regardless of my will, I was pushed down, and a gun was pressed up to the back of my head. The skin where the muzzle touched me twitched in

resistance. I cried. I started to piss myself again. It was like the water in me was trying to run away from the body that would die in a few seconds. "What," I asked, "What are you?"

I didn't ask because I wanted to know who those people really were. I was speaking to the thing that was trying to crush me, that heedless force that would go on to crush so many others.

But they laughed and said, "YG." It was a name I hadn't heard at the time.

Then I heard a car. Based on their response to that sound, I gathered they were expecting someone. The car stopped, and someone got out. He was still far away. I thought that, if nothing else, I'd at least get to live until he made it to us. One second. I can live one second more. One second. This one second. My field of vision kept shrinking, and I couldn't see anything but his shoes. "This is the teacher," the man I had spoken to in English whispered to me. "You've got good luck, getting to meet the teacher before you die. He'll pray for you."

This being called the teacher crouched in front of me. He had black skin and big white eyes. He was a thin, beautiful old man. I tried to speak, to spit up some words to beg for my life. But I couldn't say anything. More tears streamed down my already damp face. I was about to lose my final chance. But that being they called the teacher nodded slightly as though he understood everything I was trying to say.

Words in a language I didn't understand flew over my head. For some reason, the tears I was crying were different from before. A warmth spread through me, and my body *wouldn't stop shaking violently. Why did I know then, that I, on all fours, had been saved? Even though that being hadn't said anything to me.*

That being crouched in front of me once again. I looked at his beautiful black face, crying.

"Help us," he told me, and stood up. I hadn't responded, but it was as if he knew what I would say. Just like the heartless walls and cracks, he didn't care about me. But he wasn't heartless. He was something else entirely.

"The teacher has saved you. You're Japanese; that's rare around here. Since no one will expect you to be a terrorist, we can use you."

But that wasn't why, I thought. That being and I, we just made a deal the others don't know about. I didn't know what the deal was, but I couldn't escape that thought.

This armed organization, "YG," was founded by the adherents of a small folk religion.

They had been persecuted for centuries, but the religion was passed on in secret. Religions have always fought to acquire believers. And they didn't just fight with physical power. The more easily their teachings spread among the people, the more powerful and effective their religion became. In other words, they tried to give the people what they wanted. There's research that claims the reason Christianity included teachings about healing the sick was to attract believers. Actually, when one considers religions not as faiths but as history, you can see that most religious texts show the influence of their various historical contexts and cultural interests.

This folk belief lost out to Judaism, Christianity, and Islam in the battle to get believers. I won't write its proper name, which is forbidden, but it is commonly referred to as "R." R contains a pantheistic element that existed everywhere in the world at that time. Their religious texts, their songs, were passed down orally from about 600 BC. That means that their founding texts are older than those of Christianity, Islam, and even Judaism. In their religion, sex was a religious rite. It was a kindness given from the gods to humans, who are all fated to die, and to make sure that humans experience that gift, the gods were said to descend when people had sex. However, the gods hope that humans are so caught up in the act that they can't sense them. Because of that, the only people who can sense the gods are those who are watching others have sex. And thus, in this religion, there is a custom of watching others have sex. While they watch, those people thank the gods for the kindness granted them in this world. On days of worship, they spread a sheet outside, and people gather around to watch men and women having sex. The young men and women go mad by the light of bonfires. The spectators are allowed to masturbate.

It is an unsophisticated religion. Some may even say it's barbaric. This religion even lacks the essential concept of a division between good and evil. There is only one standard by which things are judged: starvation is forbidden.

Starvation is forbidden. This is both a standard of judgment in their religion, and a religious precept. It's a simple precept, taken straight from the villagers' desire to not starve. Thus if, for example, someone were to kill someone, take their money, and distribute it to the poor, that would be approved of. A rich man would not be considered a good person as long as there were any poor people who lived nearby.

One wouldn't expect such a religion to spread. It's radical, and there are many lapses in its teachings. It's primitive and sloppy and at the same time rejects the rights of those with *power. Religions spread through the powerful. Of course such a religion was suppressed.*

I became a member of YG, and was given a basic lesson on how to use a gun. I had been possessed by a fear of death, but once I knew I was saved, all I could think of was running away. Though the teacher had spared my life, I didn't become one of his disciples. In my desperation I'd thought I would do whatever they wanted if they just spared my life, but once it was spared, it turned out I couldn't keep a promise like that. I was not simple enough to be brainwashed that way. The reason I didn't flee immediately was that my life wasn't in pressing danger, and I thought it would be better to wait for a safe opportunity.

They kidnapped someone who worked for the oil drilling company CUUA, and I played a major role in procuring his ransom. Among the members of the group were many farmers who had been chased from their villages. By kidnapping this man, they got the profit they had expected to earn farming. While it was an empty way to earn money, if you considered those people's livelihood, getting that money was urgent.

Kejaf, as I will call the man who had spoken to me in English, seemed to have a strong body and the willpower not to budge under any circumstances, but he was only nineteen. He hadn't been born there. He had once belonged to another armed group in a distant country. When he was young, that other armed group had attacked his village and kidnapped him. To prevent him from trying to run, they forced young Kejaf to sin.

"They pointed a gun at me and told me to attack a girl from my village. They said if I didn't attack her, they'd kill me. She was my childhood friend. My village was burning. I raped that

fourteen-year-old girl, with a gun pointed at my back. Many men held her down and stripped her. They had already taken her virginity, and there was blood dripping from between her legs. The scars from having her clitoris removed opened up . . . I was crying the whole time. They made it so I couldn't go back to my village. 'If you keep doing this,' their leader told me, 'if you keep doing this, it will become easy. This, your first sin, eventually you won't even be able to think it a sin.' I've killed many people. And the more I kill, the more my past sins feel like nothing."

"Evil" there was not the same as the "evil" in delicate, developed countries. It was more extreme, and uncaring. It existed in that space where the only temporary solace was to be found in the leaves of coca and khat.

But that armed group was destroyed by an American air raid, and Kejaf was left alone. That, he told me, was when he met the teacher. "We don't rape women. We don't mutilate their genitals. Sex is a gift from the gods. It can't be forced. I thought I was saved. If I believed in the teacher, and the gods, I could go to another world. A world without suffering. What should I call it in English? Maybe heaven, I guess?"

Was Kejaf at peace with these horrible experiences in this country where too many people died? No. The people here were all easily hurt, and suffered under the burden of their pasts. If he were diagnosed by a delicate Japanese psychiatrist, the doctor would probably say he suffered from multiple psychological disorders. But the reality of his world wouldn't allow that. Though he sat right next to death, though he endured much suffering, he had to constantly think about living. And Kejaf had completely lost his sense of empathy. He might have given it up on his own. If he hadn't, he wouldn't have been able to go on living. "I'm going to die soon anyway," he often said. As if that were the only thing that would save him from his sins. "But I really wanted to be a tour guide. To show the weak and delicate Westerners the greatness of nature in Africa."

Kejaf was very intelligent. He seemed to have picked up English quickly from the teacher's lessons. But even that sort of knowledge didn't make him indispensable.

I became a member of that group, but I never participated in the kidnappings. They probably decided that a yellow person like myself, with none of the strength of these local ex-farmers, wouldn't be helpful. "When the time comes," the teacher said, "when the time comes, you will work for me, Starved One."

The teacher called me Starved One. When I heard those words, I knew the meaning of the connection I'd felt between us when he saved my life. I hadn't told anyone there about my experience starving. But the teacher must have sensed it somehow. He hadn't saved me because I was Japanese. He hadn't seen me as Yusuke Takahara, like it said on my passport. To him, I was the Starved One. A person who had experienced starvation. He didn't look at my outer layers, but my roots. I, the Starved One, was tied to the teacher. No, not to the teacher, but to his rebellion against starvation. My roots, my very being, were tied to these actions in this flow of history.

I spent every day in the village where their hideout was. One could call it house arrest. Sometimes I was sent to what they called "town" to go shopping. It was a dried-out road with a collection of stalls for trading. I was often surprised at the freedom they gave me. Just in case, Kejaf would remind me not to run away. "If you try to run, you'll be shot in the back, even in town." I didn't believe that; there was no one in the group skilled enough with a gun to shoot me down. If I was going to *run, this was the moment. There were even dirty taxis passing right before my eyes. If I got in one and went to the city, I could get home. I could get back to the NGO. But I watched the taxis pass by. Why? Was it because I thought there would be other, better opportunities? Was that really the only reason I didn't run?*

It came to be my turn for the villagers to watch me have sex. That day, the teacher was in the village. It was a rite of passage to have him observe me having sex. That said, not everyone from the village came. There were fewer than twenty people, and the whole thing had the roughness of a spectator sport about it, like they were watching a fight. Next to the bonfire was an enormous woman. I undressed, surrounded on all sides by villagers, and faced her. The men all laughed at my ridiculous naked body, my top half tanned, and my lower half pale and weak. I had only ever slept with Japanese women before. The sex I'd had was all so delicate. We'd whisper to each other on a clean bed, exchange gentle caresses, and I'd slowly remove her bra and panties. Outdoors, with my first foreign woman, being watched by all these villagers, I couldn't get it up. The villagers never laughed at my impotence. They just saw me as a foreigner who, sadly, hadn't been blessed with the gods' graces. Smiling, the teacher comforted me. "The day he works together with us," he said, "this delicate Japanese man will transform into one of us."

AND THEN *that day was decided. We would carry out a terrible attack.*

We'd go to a neighboring country and plant car bombs we'd detonate remotely with cell phones. That was our mission.

As a Japanese man, no one would expect me to be involved with an attack like that. The teacher thought that even if something unexpected happened, I would be able to get away.

"Even though you Japanese have those kamikazes in your past, you're thought to be the safest people in the world. Starved One, your passport will serve us well."

But I didn't understand the purpose of our attack. There was an international military force stationed in that neighboring country. "It's an act of resistance against them," said the teacher. "As long as they refuse to leave, we will keep attacking. They're here to extract resources from the poor."

I still didn't understand. "But civilians will die."

The teacher looked at me with a strange expression on his beautiful face, then finally gave me a slight nod. "They do not believe in R."

I still didn't understand. "Maybe not now. But they could become believers through your teachings. What about that? Will the gods grant us the right to kill possible future believers?"

The teacher examined me as if I were some rare, foreign hamster. "The civilians will certainly make a noble sacrifice," he said. "After their death, they will travel to that other world in the name of R. They will be elevated to the level of believers. They'll go to what you call heaven."

I had nothing to say in response.

"Starved One," he said, "if you die in this holy war, you will become a war hero in heaven. You can become exactly the person you want to be. You will fulfill all the desires you couldn't in this world."

The teacher didn't just say I could be a hero of war. He also used the metaphor of Yasukuni. He probably didn't know much about Yasukuni, the imperial Shinto shrine that commemorates the souls of all who have fallen in the service of Japan. It was erected in Tokyo in 1869 as Shokon Shrine, and since 1879, when it received official recognition from the state and its name was changed to Yasukuni, "Pacifying the Nation," it was caught up in all of the wars our government started. During the Second World War, Japanese soldiers were told that if they died, they would be enshrined at Yasukuni as heroes. Their spirits would become deities, kami. It was part of a *religion that worshipped the country and the emperor, a god in human form. One could call it a superreligion that sucked in all the nation's citizens. During the war, special festivals were regularly held at Yasukuni Shrine. The relatives of dead soldiers were invited to Tokyo, and were overcome by the spectacle of their sons becoming gods. They were moved as they witnessed the solemn act of the emperor worshipping their own child or husband, and after returning home, they were celebrated as "Honorable Relatives." Declaring dead soldiers as not just heroes but as gods not only served to give conscripted soldiers courage, but also helped recruit new soldiers. Yasukuni Shrine did more than its part for the religion that made war possible. But that was long ago. Japanese people now may outwardly swear their loyalty to the country, but inside they're not at all moved by that sort of system.*

Did I start researching the strange origins of R because of my fear of being involved in an act of terrorism? A few days earlier another armed organization, with a hideout in a village about fifty kilometers from our own, was slaughtered by the government's military—really just citizens hired by the government, mercenaries. Those soldiers tracked down other armed resistance groups and killed them with their highly efficient weapons and raped the women in the villages that hid them. I had witnessed it. There was none of the violence you'd see in manga, the sort of things a Japanese person would immediately think up, like plucking out eyes, or ripping flesh with pliers, or skinning alive. It was much sloppier. They cut off heads. It was considered manly to be able to get the head off in one blow, so they never brought the sword down on the

*neck more than once. When they failed, it was horrible
for the victim. However, they showed no mercy. They
would blame the victim for flinching, and they'd watch
hatefully, full of rage as blood poured forth from mouths
and slashed necks. The bodies, sitting, looked like electric teapots with lids that pop open with the press of a
button.*

*I imagined having my neck slashed. That moment
where my whole life would end so savagely. I thought of
my life, saved by the teacher. And the people who would
die from our bombs. And also, heaven.*

*The basis of R's teachings was a single collection of
songs that had been passed down orally. Because of religious suppression, the original book had been lost. Three
hundred years ago, someone made another attempt to put
the traditions down in writing. However, no one could
verify whether the contents of that second book were
accurate.*

*So what was known for certain about the religion's
founding tenets? Had it always contained a concept of
heaven? Who could possibly say that the heaven the
teacher described wasn't just the invention of some contemporary scribe, or a manipulating leader? What if a
tribal leader told his villagers they'd go to heaven if they
died so he could recruit them to be soldiers? What if
this religion was started to fit the needs of those ancient
villages—to make war possible, to make soldiers not fear
death? And does being old make a doctrine the truth?
Where is the proof of this faith? The believers who had
passed it down were moved by the songs. What if that just
meant the text was an ancient literary masterpiece?*

I cautiously voiced my doubts to Kejaf. He looked at
me with eyes full of rage. "You dare profane the gods? This
is an ancient text of this land!" His anger was natural.
People believe in religion because they want to.

I had a dream about the world being flipped upside
down. A vast stretch of sand became an unfortunate sky,
and dry, brittle trees stretched downward. My neck was
slashed, and my head hung down my back. A thin bit of
skin held it there. I tried to cry out, but nothing would
leave my mouth, since my head was no longer connected
to my body. I looked out over the earth, now an empty
sky with trees growing upside down. When I woke up,
I had lost my sense of balance. I was full of fear. Was I
lying down, or hanging from something? Besides my loss
of balance, my heart was also beating terribly fast.

I was growing weaker. I found the word "invocation"
scratched into the wall in English. I thought Kejaf had
tried to cast a spell for me, to save me. But Kejaf told me
he didn't know what I was talking about. "It's probably a
miracle from god," he said. He was trying to encourage
me. The next day, those letters were carved even deeper
into the wall. I tried to be thankful and to hold on to
Kejaf's kindness, but I also thought this might have been
a plot of the teacher's. Maybe he was trying to show me a
childish miracle, to encourage the Japanese man scared of
the holy war, to send me words directly from god. Could I
fall for such a stupid miracle? I was mad. But ultimately
my anger wasn't over this childish ruse, but rather over
the teacher's demand that I participate in his holy war.
It resembled a child's anger toward the father who abandoned him. The letters grew deeper, and I felt my anger

was about to reach its limit. I didn't have the courage to tell the teacher, so I talked to Kejaf again. Kejaf looked at me with fearful eyes. "You're the one writing on the wall," he said. "You get up in the middle of the night. You always look oddly calm."

I thought I finally understood what was happening to me.

On the day of our final meeting before carrying out our attack, there was a dirty white car parked outside. It was the car that carried me to this village. I felt it was a cruel coincidence of fate that it was a Japanese-made car. "When we end this holy war, you will stop being a delicate Japanese man," the teacher said. "You will become like us. You will change from the Starved One to an agent. You will no longer be disturbed by all the phenomena life shows you."

The holy war would be carried out by two units. The first unit was in charge of planting car bombs. We would detonate them throughout the city to show our resistance to the multinational armies stationed there. The second unit would attack the town's police department. How crude, I thought. This was too ill-planned and reckless to risk my life for. But YG didn't have the power to attack the army directly. The teacher called it resistance. "We are not aiming for victory. We are just setting the stage for future generations." The teacher's words had grown more and more trite.

I tried to tell Kejaf what I thought. I was in the first group with the relatively easier task, and he was in the second. He was going to take a gun and attack the police station. He would probably be shot within a few seconds when the state military came charging in. At first I thought it was strange that the teacher would waste a talented man like Kejaf, who could speak English, that way. But a few days before the plan was announced, I learned that there was another man who could speak English who was close to the teacher. That also worried me. Was there any meaning to this holy war?

"I'm happy," Kejaf said. "Someone as useless as me can become a hero in the name of the great R. I can go to heaven a hero. I, who raped my childhood friend, will be purified. My dead mother will rejoice!"

"Don't you want to be a tour guide? Can you really die for this?"

Kejaf looked at me strangely. His face was so innocent. I remembered then that he was only nineteen.

"What are you saying? I will be a tour guide in heaven."

To begin from the ending, I ran away. Two days before the attack I walked out of the village. I entered a barren forest, got lost, and tried to cross some mountains. In the mountains I saw countless dead bodies. I wasn't sure if those people had been attacked by bandits or armed fighters, but I imagined myself among them in the near future. Some had collapsed, hanging their heads in shame, and others were splayed out as if they were dancing. The rotting women, naked, their hair hanging, had certainly been raped. I wondered if they had been raped before they rotted and became so ugly. Would I see more corpses once I was out of the mountains? I thought no matter how far I traveled, no matter where I was, there'd be corpses in all shapes. The world turned upside down. The dried-out earth became the sky, and from there the smell of the bodies, stacked like a sort of supple feast, rose up. Luckily, those who found me after I collapsed were kind farmers. They carried me to some sort of hospital, then something like a police station, and finally a white man wearing a suit appeared. I learned then that dozens of people had died from car bombs in that neighboring country, and that the armed fighters who attacked the police station had all been shot down in a matter of minutes. This man, who must have been an international aid worker, didn't try to ask me where their hideout was, as if he didn't want to get involved with me. But that was strange. They were an armed resistance. Why didn't he try to locate their hideout?

What I learned afterward was depressing. The teacher had said our attack would be a resistance to force the international military out, but the military had already planned to leave in two weeks. The teacher was involved with a munitions company and a certain government, and had been asked by both organizations to carry out the attack.

For that munitions company, the withdrawal would mean they'd lose work, and their company's profits would drop. But what would happen if there was a terrorist attack? The military wouldn't be able to leave. However, they tried to paint a more humanitarian picture of their motives, saying that if the military force left, the area would grow more violent. "Now is not the time for us to pull out," the people working for the nearly bankrupt munitions company told themselves. "If we sacrifice a few soldiers by pushing back the withdrawal, we can save even more lives."

The foreign government that asked the teacher to carry out this attack thought they'd be able to increase its influence. By throwing this other country into confusion, these politicians could create an opportunity for their own country to intervene and negotiate with the armed groups. In which case, they would simply negotiate with the teacher, who they had hired to carry out the attack in the first place. This foreign government acted indignant that other developed countries were taking advantage of this country. Its leaders talked about ideals in the name of their religion. And that country was, for the big munitions companies, an important place to sell weapons. The longer the confusion continued, the more profit they'd make. And that profit would also spread to their affiliated businesses.

I returned to my NGO. I had gone missing, but I never made the news in Japan. The media had no desire to reveal that a large Japanese company was working behind the scenes of all the unrest and civil war, or that the government was involved.

A call came the day after I returned to the NGO. The timing was too perfect. It made me think they had an informant inside the company. Someone asked me to get the phone. When I picked up the receiver, I heard the teacher's cold voice.

"I won't forget your betrayal."

I wasn't sure why, but I was holding back tears. I told the teacher what I had learned about his lies. But his voice remained composed.

"What does it matter if that's the truth? We need money for our projects. Sometimes we take that money

from our enemies. It's all to spread the holy teachings of R." His words grew harsher, and firmer.

"You're the leader of a religion, aren't you? Or are you just a professional terrorist? Isn't that your real job? Terrorism? And because of your plan, your comrades . . ."

"They're in heaven."

"And the civilians?"

"They are in heaven, too."

None of my words reached him.

"Are you saying that I'm not sad about their deaths? I cried long for all of them."

"Do you know how they died? Their flesh was ripped off by bullets. They were full of pain."

"You didn't watch either, did you?"

"If you had watched, you wouldn't be able to say those things."

The teacher paused for a second. But even I knew that wasn't because of my words.

"The Japanese say strange things," he said quietly. "How many hundreds of dead bodies do you think I've seen?"

I remembered Kejaf's face. The man who said he wanted to be a tour guide, but who had lost all empathy. That talented man torn apart by bullets. His life snuffed out in the name of armed resistance.

"Just because I haven't seen the bodies doesn't mean I'm not sad. I prayed so long. For those heroes. So they could be happy in heaven."

Where does evil come from? Who takes it on? How will it end?

Where does evil come from?

But the teacher didn't call me to debate philosophical questions. He had another intention.

"I won't forget your betrayal," he repeated. "I am always watching you. I am watching everything you do. Do you think we don't have members in Japan? Starved One, I saw your face when you were a child starving in that apartment. With my own two eyes. By the power of the gods."

Why couldn't I say anything then? His words sank into me. My vision narrowed, and I saw someone's feet in front of me. The teacher's feet. The beautiful feet that approached me just as my life was about to end.

"Remember this. Every person around you will die a cruel death. Their heads will be cut off. They'll be torn apart by bullets. They'll be raped mercilessly. In the name of R, which has been passed down from ancient times. Your delicate society will be invaded by us and our violence. There is one way to escape. That is to remember that you are nothing but the tip of my finger. I will contact you again."

I returned to Japan and contacted the teacher. The day after I got in touch with him, I found the word "invocation" on my wall. When I found that

[The diary ends here]

16

Tachibana finished reading Takahara's diary. *What is this? Is this real?* She couldn't get up from her chair for a moment while her thoughts wandered.

Once the assembly in the hall was over, Tachibana headed for his room. She didn't know what had happened to the recording she had given Mineno, or how Takahara had left the building. She didn't know anything. She'd thought Takahara had been working in secret from the leader, but the leader had spoken to the believers as if he knew everything. What was happening? Tachibana searched for any sort of clue.

Takahara's room was spare as always. There was no human touch. It felt as though no one lived there, like the furniture refused to interact with humans, and just sat silent and cold.

She searched desperately for any clue. She looked inside

the bag on the floor, opened all the files lined up on the shelf. Thinking it wouldn't open, she pulled his desk drawer. But it was unlocked. Inside she found the journal.

YG. She had heard that name before. But, certainly . . . Tachibana opened the drawer again, and her heart began to race. This time she noticed the hidden compartment. When she removed the board, she found a laptop computer.

It was forbidden to have a computer in the cult. There was a wireless LAN connection, so it could probably connect to the Internet. She turned it on, but it was locked. The password. Thinking there was no way it would work, she typed Takahara's birthday. It didn't work. Her heart beat faster. Her fingers shook as she typed. INVOCATION. Her throat went dry. The screen unlocked.

Her heart continued to race disgustingly fast as she got online. She began researching YG.

YG. A small armed organization practicing the Rarseshir faith. She continued to search, looking for further details. Somehow she found an article in English. The name of their leader was Nigel A. Alroy. She couldn't breathe. Six years ago, when Takahara was in Africa, this man had carried out a terrorist attack. He detonated six cars filled with explosives and attacked a police department. Fifty-six people had died.

One year ago, an air raid wiped out the entire village housing YG. Nigel Alroy, who was 72 at the time, had been killed. She searched his background. According to the articles, he'd been born in America, moved to Saudi Arabia, then began forming militias in Afghanistan, Lebanon and Central Africa. *Born in America?*

Takahara had said on the phone recording that Sawatari

had had no knowledge of his plan. Could he have been working with this organization?

But they had been wiped out.

Could there be a remaining faction? But he'd been speaking in Japanese on the phone. Was there anyone who could speak Japanese in an African militia? *I don't think so. That'd be absurd.*

She had to hide the computer. It might be her only connection to the outside world at this point. Tachibana kept thinking. She hadn't expected this. She'd assumed someone would stop Takahara before he did anything if not the leader then the police. At this point, it was too late.

Why hadn't the police tried to go for the back door, or carry out a surprise attack? They could have captured whoever they wanted easily amid the believers' confusion. But making such a big gesture and surrounding them with the riot police, and even letting the cult arm themselves—now there was nothing to be done. The second the riot police entered the building, there would be a shootout. It would be quite easy for all the believers to commit mass suicide.

And why had she been locked up? She couldn't ask the other officers. Even their eyes were glittering with excitement. Just like the other believers, they were caught up in this experience so outside the realm of normal life, in their mysterious greater purpose.

What's happening to Takahara-kun now? What is he . . . Tachibana noticed that there were many balled-up pieces of paper shoved in the back of the drawer. White printer paper. When she unfolded them, she saw the word "invocation." It was hand-written, and traced over again and again. *Invocation.*

Tachibana couldn't take her eyes off those letters.

Someone. I need someone, Tachibana found herself whispering. Her heart beat so fast it hurt. *I don't want to think about this by myself. This is beyond reason. I don't want to be alone. I can't bear to be in this place, alone like this. Someone . . .* Tachibana left Takahara's room. Narazaki floated up in the back of her mind.

A loud voice rang out, "Please remain calm." Unsettling—a woman's voice.

The riot police braced themselves. The TV cameras tried to capture who it was, but the speaker was hidden behind a curtain and couldn't be seen. No one aside from the believers knew that it was officer Sugimoto.

"I will say this once again. Please remain calm. What is your goal?"

A murmur ran through the riot police. Remain calm? Normally that's what the police would be saying to the criminals.

A reply came from a megaphone by one of the Metropolitan Police's armored vans. "We have an arrest warrant for anyone connected with the abduction and detainment of two citizens. You will release your hostages immediately, and cooperate with our investigation."

"Hostages?" the woman asked, sounding terribly surprised. "We don't have any hostages. Are you talking about our two new members? They still have not completed their initiation ritual. They are not yet believers. We will release them immediately."

A rustling spread through the riot police. Every television crew was broadcasting the scene from behind the cordoned-off area.

"May we please request that you stop trying to enter? In our faith, we cannot allow those not approved by the leader into this building. This is our sacred land. If you force your way inside, we will commit group suicide. These are our rules. We beg of you: Do not force your way in. We will release the two initiates. Please. Please, let us be. We are simply practicing our faith quietly."

The situation had taken an odd turn. The man holding the megaphone was asking for his commander's decision on a walkie-talkie. He relayed the will of the police headquarter's main office.

"In that case, release your hostages immediately. It is also apparent that you possess a large number of weapons. We have a search warrant for that as well. Abandon your weapons and open the building."

"We don't have any weapons."

"Open the building."

"We don't have any weapons. Just like there were no weapons of mass destruction in Iraq. Just like bin Laden was not in Afghanistan."

"We will provide you with a cell phone. We will then listen to your demands by phone."

"We have no demands. We will release the two you speak

of, and then we would like you to leave. We do not need your phone. You just don't want this conversation to be broadcast by the mass media."

The riot police had come to a standstill. The woman continued to speak.

"This doesn't have anything to do with the upcoming election, does it? You aren't doing this because you don't want to hand over political control of the enormous, tremendous public works projects already in progress to another party, is it? America, too, has offered many concessions to our government, so they're pressuring you to keep the current party in power, aren't they? Are you just trying to make it look like Japan is strong to give yourselves a boost, since elections are coming up? Since internal politics have frozen in place, you're trying to avert the people's gaze to something external and provide them with a sense of unity. That's always been the typical practice. But it doesn't look like it will go well this time. Unfortunately, it doesn't look like any threatening missiles will come flying out of North Korea, like they did before the last election. And Korea and China haven't been criticizing Japan much. Are you trying to win the election by acting like the ruling party is actually powerful? Do you think that this event will be helpful to remilitarize the country? Those who would criticize the government for forcibly suppressing terrorists have dwindled. No, the people would praise such an action. This may also be connected to your desire to extend policing power and increase police armaments. It's strange that the riot police were sent out just because you suspect us of a crime. We can't help but think that there's some ulterior motive. To you it's probably just a bit of a performance, resolving a hostage situation. But we don't want to be involved in such a trivial matter."

Her words bubbled through the crowd. On the other side of the rope cordoning off the area, television crews and reporters from newspapers and magazines gathered, watching the situation.

The police finally responded: "Stop these desperate comments. There's no point in repeating this trash."

"Do you think we haven't noticed the Special Assault Team hiding on the other side of this building? Please, remain calm."

The riot police did not move. An order was given. The TV cameras tried to capture the Special Assault Team, but they couldn't.

"Oh, oh, we're going to be attacked. We asked for calm, and now we'll be killed violently. Even though we said we'd release our so-called hostages. Even though we've done nothing wrong. And after we die, nothing but the lie that we were a dangerous group will be told about us, to try to convince the public that it was the right thing to do. And since this has to do with national security, maybe—I can't believe it, but maybe—the forceful tactics you used will be covered up by the State Secrecy Law. You wouldn't do that, would you? You wouldn't do that, would you? Oh, oh, we're going to be attacked. Even though if we are attacked we have no choice but to die."

All members of the riot police prepared their shields. The area grew tense. *Will they do it? Can they really force their way into a situation like this?* The reporters traded comments with each other. *Really? In this situation?* Though it wasn't caught on film, the maneuvers of the Special Assault

Team had stopped. The riot police were speechless at the information they had been sent via radio. The TV reporters broadcasting the scene grew frantic. One by one, every channel changed what they were showing, and the broadcasters for every network began to read the same report. Armed forces had infiltrated a broadcasting studio. But those who had been watching JBA saw something else. A young man holding an automatic rifle suddenly appeared on the screen. He seemed sad to be pointing a gun at a male newscaster.

The man pointing the gun at the newscaster was Sasahara. His mournful face suddenly burst into tears. As he cried, he faced the camera and spoke. "I beg you. Please remain calm." He continued to cry. "We . . . We have no other choice. If our facilities are infiltrated, we, because of our beliefs, will have no choice but to commit group suicide . . . I beg you. Please leave them be."

The newscaster shed tears as he watched Sasahara, stunned. Several employees of the station had been gathered in the studio, and surrounding them were more than ten men pointing guns.

"The moment this broadcast is stopped, we will kill them. This is not just being broadcast on TV. We have already connected to the Internet and spread this message to the whole world," Sasahara continued. "We broke away from our main organization one year ago, and our group is not affiliated with them. However, we did not leave because we harbor any ill-will toward that group. We still intend to care for them. We want to save them. We want to save them from killing themselves. We have weapons, but there is not a single one in the facility. Those people pose no threat . . . Meanwhile, we have already broken into this news station. It was something that we had to do. But crimes are crimes. We shot a security guard who resisted. We didn't kill him and have called an ambulance. But that does not change the fact that we shot him. We will take responsibility for our crimes. We are all prepared to abandon our weapons, release our hostages, and surrender to the police. All we ask, all we ask, is that you please stop attempting to enter that facility. We beg you. Please remain calm. Let's discuss this."

The newscaster with the gun pointed at him couldn't speak.

"We have one demand. That the government leave our facility alone entirely. Ignore it, as they have up until now. However, we cannot trust a simple verbal promise. We want the land our facility stands on to be recognized as an independent nation. If that is not possible, we would like it to be recognized as a special independent ward. There is precedent for this. If we cannot receive at least that, we will not put faith in any promises made. After all, the authorities promised the people of Japan for decades that nuclear power was completely safe—since Fukushima we have all seen what those promises were worth. No, we cannot put any faith in your words. So we would like official approval from the Cabinet to be recognized as an independent ward. If you cannot do that, it will put us in a difficult situation. We would also like acknowledgment that our leader is unrelated to these activities. The proper individuals will leave that facility and will undergo questioning. If necessary, they will be arrested. But we would like our leader alone to be left in peace. I believe this can be done. I believe you can do this for us. This has happened in the past, at the Tokyo War Crimes Trials. After Japan lost World War II, those guilty of war crimes were judged by the victorious nations. Some voiced opinions that the emperor who ruled Japan at the time should take responsibility for the war. But he was not tried. This was a matter of course. It was the government that had fought the war, and when it began, the emperor was against it. His rule was a total formality. In reality it was the government that handled all political matters. We do not see our leader and the emperor as being on the same level. There's no way one could think that. We respect the great deity, the descendant of Amaterasu Ōkami. And as we are asking to be made an independent ward, we would happily join in this government. We are simply saying that we would like this precedent from the Tokyo War Crimes Trials, and this precedent alone, to be applied in our case as well. We would like you to refrain from laying a hand on our leader. We would like this to end with our surrender."

HIRAI STARED blankly at the man on the monitor in the meeting room. He never imagined he'd be in a situation like this. It was his second year as Chief of Security Division Two. He sneaked a sideways glance at the face of the Deputy Superintendent General and the Director of Security. The Chief of Detectives, Chief of Public Security, Chief of International Affairs Division Three, Security Division One, and Organized Crime

Division Five were also there. They were all stunned. An independent ward? What nonsense were they talking about? No, more importantly, what had become of this whole situation? Criminals commanding the police to remain calm?

First of all, the information they had been provided and the actual situation were too different. The cult they called by code name X was armed, and was going to carry out a terror attack. They had also abducted two civilians. Among them was a man affiliated with an armed African group. This cult was believed to be a branch of an international terror organization. To crush them in one fell swoop would be common sense in the current international situation. But if they were terrorists, why were they talking about group suicide? There was no way to control this situation. How had their information been so wrong? Was it a mistake, or sabotage? Had someone higher up intended this? Come to think of it, where was the chief of Division Four of Public Security? He'd been there a minute ago.

This situation was incredibly troublesome. There was not just one group to negotiate with, but two. And the group that had occupied the television station and the cult itself seemed only loosely connected. There was also the possibility that their intentions did not line up. Hirai thought the chances of resolving this situation were close to zero. *An independent ward? Do they really think we can answer that demand?*

Is this reality? As he watched the crying men occupying the TV station, he remembered the case from 1995, when another cult spread sarin gas through the subways. Back then, something he imagined impossible unfolded right before his eyes. What were they doing releasing sarin in the subways? At the time, Hirai, who had been working at the detective department of the Regional Legal Affairs Bureau, wasn't sure. This cult existed cut off from the rest of the world. The longer they stayed apart from that reality, the further they slipped away from common sense. Then suddenly they appeared in this world as something "unreal." Back then, he thought it seemed exactly like fiction. On 9/11, when New York was attacked, who could immediately recognize that scene as reality? But that terrible event had really occurred. Reality, everyday life, is fragile in the face of these sudden fictions. An independent ward? The Tokyo War Crimes Trials? What were they talking about?

But he had a premonition.

We had better not let them talk anymore.

The Parliamentary secretary entered the room. He was an envoy to the government. The Superintendent General and Chief of Police followed. The Parliamentary secretary whispered something to the Defense Chief, who shook his head. "There are too many inconsistencies in our information. If we forced our way in now and there were many casualties, what would we do? Don't try to simplify things."

"They're armed."

"That's true. That's true, but there's such a thing as timing. And when we begin is up to us. Can you explain our decision to those down the chain who will be shot to death?"

"It would be an order."

"And who would take responsibility for that? Who? I could. But who else?"

Everyone in the meeting room focused on the TV screen, where Sasahara was beginning to speak again. "We also want you to know that we are not alone . . . It has just begun . . . It should be on the news soon."

It made no sense. Everyone simply stared at the screen. Silence lingered. But on one network's broadcast, white text ran along the bottom of the screen. Then the phone rang. There had been a massive explosion in Aichi Prefecture. It was not yet known if anyone had died or was injured.

". . . You'll all see the videos soon." Sasahara continued, crying. "I expect there was a blast radius of thirty meters. But don't worry. No one died or was injured. Our colleagues are on the lookout. We will send you the video of the blast. How we did it. The bomb was detonated by calling a cell phone. This blast was a warning. These types of explosives have been placed throughout the country. What would happen if I lined up all those phone numbers on this screen? . . . Someone watching TV might dial one of those numbers. In other words, the detonators are in the hands of our countless citizens. Everyone has a cell phone."

The meeting room was wrapped in silence.

"But please don't worry. I won't do that. However, the moment the police set foot in either this place or that facility, or the moment this broadcast is cut off by the government, my colleagues on the outside will dial all of those numbers. And we don't just have bombs. There is also a system in place to release vast amounts of sarin gas. Several thousand people will likely die. If you enter here, we'll die anyway, and according to our beliefs, we will all go to heaven as heroes. We no longer need resolve or courage. There is one way to stop this. For all of Japan's cell phone companies to work together and block all service . . . That could work. But it wouldn't change much, would it? We could still set off the bombs without those networks."

Hirai couldn't do anything but stare at the screen. Terror attacks in unspecified locations.

"Let's see if this country, Japan, is the sort of country that would allow so many deaths just to save face."

The meeting room was still silent. The Parliamentary secretary called someone on the phone. Everyone in the room watched him. But there was no longer any other choice. Hirai felt it. Everyone in the room felt it.

"Wait to move in," the Parliamentary secretary said in a whisper. "Negotiate. Since it's come to this, based on the 1998 decision, we'll have to assemble an Emergency Operations Center in the Cabinet. And send the message to all police departments. Immediately detain all people known to have any connection to the cult . . . Search everywhere. Anywhere there may seem to be explosives . . . I know it's impossible. But we must check every corner of this country . . ."

"They're probably listening to us," the white-haired commentator on the JMN Network special program said. The giant monitor in the middle of the JMN studio was playing the JBA broadcast of Sasahara holding the gun. Every channel was airing their broadcast the same way. The JMN commentator turned and spoke directly to the filming camera. "Hey! Cult members, are you watching this broadcast? If you're watching, tell us who you are."

A newscaster tried to cut off the white-haired commentator—they didn't want to be guilty of instigating anything.

But JBA had a live feed of all the other networks' programming, just like every other studio, and Sasahara heard the question and responded. "It doesn't matter who we are. I thought you would understand that." He spoke to the camera as if it were a televideo call. Sasahara and his men didn't know enough about the studio equipment to set up anything more sophisticated.

"We'd understand?"

"Yes. You have your own god, right?"

"God? Well, we have a variety of beliefs here."

"A variety? Don't you all worship at Yasukuni Shrine? When the head of the country, the prime minister, went to worship at Yasukuni Shrine, the media proclaimed it the top religion of the country. Shinto's our state religion, isn't it?"

"What? No. Japan doesn't have a state religion. I'm opposed to the prime minister worshiping at Yasukuni Shrine. But if I had to defend his behavior, I'd say he was paying his respects to those who died in the war. He was mourning, not proclaiming his religion."

"Mourning? Yasukuni Shrine is for mourning those lost in war?" Sasahara asked. He took a single breath. "Yasukuni Shrine was erected after the start of the Meiji Period. It's a relatively new shrine. Those who died fighting to protect the country, mostly soldiers, are enshrined there as deities. However, for example, the members of the Kamakura Shogunate, who died defending us when the Mongols were expanding their hegemony, are not enshrined there. While most of the world fell to the invading Mongols, Japan defeated them. The Kamakura Shogunate actually beat them twice, protecting our country. However, they are not enshrined at Yasukuni. When the Meiji government was established, those who fought on the government's side in the civil war were enshrined, but not those on the enemy side. In other words, the old shogunate and other antigovernment elements were excluded. The many Japanese who died in air raids and from nuclear bombs are not enshrined.

Despite that, those who led us into the Second World War, those Class A war criminals, are enshrined there. What does this mean? The standards are simple, and follow a specific ideology. That shrine draws the line at those who fought for the emperor. Most of Japan's wars were civil wars. There was once even a custom of enshrining the enemies we killed, out of guilt. But Yasukuni Shrine is not like that. Your god is Amaterasu Ōkami, right? Her great-great-great-grandchild Jimmu was the first emperor of Japan. And the imperial line continued from him. The emperor today is his descendant, right? Japanese legends are like Greek legends. We're polytheistic. But the big difference here is that our emperor exists as a descendant of those gods. Even during World War II many of our country's people praised this land as one united under the descendant of Amaterasu Okami, didn't they? When we die, we'll meet at Yasukuni. Soldiers went off to die saying that to each other, didn't they? Many probably died shouting *tennou banzai*, Long live the Emperor, didn't they? The Americans and the English feared the unnatural bravery of the Japanese soldiers, didn't they? And that's not just something from our past, is it? The main purpose of Yasukuni Shrine is not to serve as a place to mourn those who have sacrificed themselves in war. Isn't it a place where we honor them as heroes? To honor them means to let the public know of their contributions, and to commend them for that work, right? That fundamental premise of the Yasukuni Shrine has not changed. When we were occupied by America in 1946, they began to change that stance of ours, and there was an idyllic moment in our history following Japanese independence, but since 1978, things have returned to how they were before. Total conservatism.

Unified thought. That is what the people in charge of this country worship. Aren't you a democrat? Doesn't that make your faith the one of Yasukuni Shrine?"

At the JMN studio, the white-haired commentator's featured guest, a man in glasses, yelled, "Quit this nonsense!" He was known as a conservative pundit. "Are you making fun of our war heroes?"

"I am not."

"What are you saying, then?"

"Those in charge should worship at the shrine with confidence. And they should say they're confident. And they should say, like you pundits do, that Japan wasn't wrong when they went into World War II. They should say that the veterans in Yasukuni Shrine are heroes, and they should be praised as such. They're not sacrifices of a mistaken war; they're heroes who fought righteously in a just war. Japan was right. We just lost. They should say that the Tokyo War Crimes Trials carried out by the international community were also a fraud. Air raids and nuclear bombs went unpunished, but Japan was prosecuted one-sidedly because we lost. Instead of cowardly hiding their true thoughts, those in charge should bravely declare they don't care about the opinion of the international community and they should openly worship at that shrine. That's the fundamental ideology behind Yasukuni Shrine, isn't it? And if anyone complains, we should just pull out of the United Nations, like we pulled out of the League of Nations before."

"Listen," shouted the man in glasses again. "The Pacific War was a war of self-defense. We were being crushed under America's extreme economic sanctions and had no choice but to fight. Those heroes died fighting for our country."

"Pundits like you always say things like that. But will you answer just two questions for me?"

The Metropolitan Police Department's headquarters had already called the JMN studio, ordering them to quiet the pundit so as not to agitate the criminals; the Cabinet had dispatched personnel to manage the crisis in person. But meanwhile the program continued.

Sasahara spoke again. "You say that we had no choice but to go into Word War II. And that after the Hull Note, Japan had no choice but to fight. If that's the case, let me ask this. If that sort of thing happened now, would you do it again?"

"Listen. America tried to get Japan to attack first. We know now that America already wanted to go to war. That was written in American documents from the time."

"Please, for now, forget about the other countries. If a similar situation were to occur now, would you make the same decision?"

"It's wrong to judge past people's judgments by our own values. And the international situations were different."

"That's why I'm asking what you'd do if the situation were the same, and the same things occurred. Shall I change the question? If you returned to that period now, and you were powerful enough to control everything that happened in the country, would you have stopped the war?"

"I would not. We needed to fight."

"I see. If someone like you were to become a politician, the people would probably be quite nervous. I'll ask one more question. Do you and your colleagues worship the emperor?"

"Of course."

"Then let me ask this. Didn't the politicians of the time

expose the emperor to great danger by starting the war? What do you think of their responsibility for that?"

"I said there was no choice, didn't I? That's why the people of Japan risked their lives to protect the emperor."

"You say there was no choice. You say America made ridiculous demands that sent Japan to war. But those negotiations were mostly over China. If we had withdrawn our troops from China, we could have avoided war. Because Japan had expanded its forces too far, our interests clashed with America's. Isn't that right? Wars are born out of clashes between interests. So, would you put the emperor in danger for those concessions in China?"

"You're wrong. If we had let go of China at the time, we would have lost power and been occupied anyway."

"Wasn't it absolutely idiotic to go to war with China when we knew America supported China? America, the country that supplied almost half of the oil we needed just to meet internal demand? What a foolish decision. Even an idiot could have predicted that we'd be put under embargo. The Japanese aren't so weak that we couldn't have given up our concessions in China. We wanted to fight proper wars when our colonies were put in undue danger. That is the true Japanese way. Concessions are profits, and if our national profits decline, that's just money in the end. Does that mean that money is more important than our great emperor, or our soldiers, or the lives of our citizens?"

"No. We fought that war to create the Greater East Asia Co-Prosperity Sphere. We were trying to free the various Western colonies in Asia from the rule of racist white men."

"By joining forces with the Nazis? You must understand that when we joined forces with the Nazis, we did something we could not justify to the world. I'll say it once more. We joined forces with the Nazis. If we hadn't joined the Triple Alliance with Germany and Italy, would America have really gotten so mad at Japan? And if we were really so incredibly powerful, then the Nazis would have won!"

"That's a matter of war strategy. Japan at the time didn't completely understand the Nazis. We were simply petitioning, as the leaders of Asia, for Asian freedom."

"It's best not to make stupid excuses to the international community about not knowing the full extent of what the Nazis were doing. And Asian freedom? We had to send about three-point-two million condoms to troops in our occupied territories in 1942 to fight a war of Asian freedom? That war where we occupied foreign territories and turned them into so-called comfort stations—that was a war for freedom? Don't be so indulgent!"

Sasahara continued. "Your leaders all talk about ideals. Among the soldiers who fought in that war, there were ones so noble and proud that we can't even imagine. I can't read the diaries of the kamikazes, the Special Attack Units, without shedding tears. But isn't it disrespectful to use the purity of the souls of the deceased to try and make others feel that war was just? Those souls have been used not only to manipulate public opinion, but also to make money. And further, not all Japanese soldiers were heroes. I'm sure even you can't say that all of the millions of soldiers stationed abroad obeyed the military's rules. You talk about ideals. But we didn't have the national strength or ability to follow through on those ideals. Ideals are a bunch of self-gratifying nonsense. The more awful the war became, the longer these ridiculous and cruel battles continued. For too long we exposed our soldiers to the stress of thinking they might die tomorrow, or even in a matter of seconds. We didn't allow them to surrender or be taken as POWs. We forced them to see so many corpses. Leaders, friends died in tremendous numbers. In that sort of hopeless situation, isn't it just foolish and ignorant of the reality of war to tell soldiers to go on living as men of virtue? We transformed kind and gentle, delicate Japanese men into madmen. Would you say that no one was responsible? If you count both civilians and soldiers, millions of Japanese died in that war. We were a ruined country. For a politician to say that we couldn't help going to war, that it wasn't wrong, that if it ever happened again, we'd fight bravely—that would be completely unacceptable. World War II was a war of aggression against the rest of Asia. War is not beautiful. There exists no country without any dark spots on its past. The cruelties of war have existed since the start of human history, and they continue, they still continue today. Can you call a pundit who does not try to reexamine each one of the dark parts of our history, who doesn't try to improve the world for the next generation, who says that war was right, and we couldn't help it—can you call that pundit great? What right does someone like you have to tell us how things are?"

The white-haired commentator, who had been silent, tried to speak up. "What you're saying is—"

But Sasahara cut him off. "I've read your writing. You say that Japan should abandon its military force to maintain peace in Asia. But let me ask you this. Is the world a kind place? The true nature of the world is evil. Should one remain defenseless in an evil world? If there are invasions or genocides in other countries, does that have nothing to do with us? In all of Japan's history, we have only lost one war with another country. The only country that has genuinely defeated Japan in all of history is America. And they had an embargo against us, which gave them a huge handicap. Should such a strong country just sit there, not giving anything back? You liberals worry about the country remilitarizing, but can't even work together. Why do you send in so many candidates to the elections, splitting all the votes and letting the conservatives benefit? Later generations will laugh at you! I want to ask you one thing. Say we did live in this play world where your logic worked, a world that was not evil, but good. What would you do if aliens attacked?"

"What? Aliens?"

"Are you going to just say it's impossible? Just like the useless politicians said about possible incidents with nuclear reactors?"

"If aliens did come to Earth, we couldn't fight them. We'd lose no matter what."

"So if that time came, you'd just take the position that we can't win anyway. So when the humans are fighting desperately against the aliens, you'll just suck on your thumb and watch? Is that right? Do you think you can convince the aliens to leave us alone with your great negotiating skills? Will you organize demonstrations against them?"

A sudden laugh rose up in the studio. The main anchor said, "This isn't the time for you to be arguing about politics, is it?"

"I think this is an important issue," Sasahara said, cutting off the anchor. "I don't want to hear grand pronouncements coming out of the mouths of people who can't even get straight what they think of that war seventy years ago where so many people died."

"But this is no longer just a Japanese issue. The world is watching you, and the world won't forgive your terrorism."

"Then I'll ask the whole world. Can you absolutely condemn our actions?"

Then Sasahara began a long, long lecture. A lecture on the problems of poverty and starvation that Takahara had cared so deeply about. But Sasahara named names. On national television he revealed the economic crimes of specific interest groups and politicians. After a few minutes, the Japanese branches of implicated organizations began calling to protest the program, but it didn't end.

The crisis in Japan began to spread to international news. In countries around the world, the broadcast was streamed online and subtitled in one language after another, and even more people began to watch.

In a small room, the fifty-something man was watching the events unfold on television.

"Isn't this brilliant? Ha ha ha. Look. It's great."

His voice was strangely high. His thirty-something companion found him disgusting. Of course, he did not let that show on his face.

"Don't you think there's going to be a big question of responsibility? We have . . ."

"What are you talking about? You're still so green," the fifty-something man said, smiling. "I thought I told you. We don't need a name. All we need is a purpose."

On the screen, Sasahara continued to speak. "Let's just think of the Tokyo War Crimes Trials he mentioned . . . Those trials covered the period from 1928 until Japan lost the war in 1945. Do you know how many times political power shifted hands in those years?"

"Not in detail . . ."

"Prepare yourself for this, now. Seventeen times. Seventeen times in seventeen years. That's why at those trials the international commission had a very difficult job. It wasn't like with the Nazis. In Japan there wasn't one obvious villain who could take responsibility for all the evil done. Every single leader propagated ridiculous domestic and foreign policies, and then when things didn't go well, they just ran from the job. Meanwhile, vast numbers of civilians and soldiers were dying."

Suddenly, the fifty-something man wasn't smiling anymore. "Where is the security guard they shot?" he asked.

"The Shindaiwa Hospital. It seems he's in stable condition."

The fifty-something man clicked his tongue. The thirty-something man was surprised by that sound, but also felt that his own surprise was forced. He already had a faint idea of what he was going to have to do.

"There was another person hospitalized, right? Do you know anything about him?"

"I'm not sure what his name is, but he seems to be a member of that cult. I'm not sure if he broke off from the main group, or what, though . . ."

"What was he wearing?"

"What?"

"I asked what he was wearing." All traces of his earlier mirth had vanished, and he wore his usual languid expression.

"He was wearing a black parka and jeans. He was in critical condition after being shot in the shoulder."

"And where was he hospitalized?"

"Sasagaoka Hospital."

"Great. We can get to him there. Let's go."

The fifty-something man put on a coat that was neither new nor old. The thirty-something man put on a new coat that certainly did not look cheap, even if one could not tell the brand name at a glance.

The younger man picked up his bag to go, but the older man turned the TV on again. He narrowed his eyes at the screen, his expression neither happy nor upset.

"Are we going?" the thirty-something man said, but the older man ignored him.

"Of course he would," he whispered to the television. Finally he grabbed his bag and turned off the TV.

ON HER way down the narrow hallway, Ryoko Tachibana passed several excited believers. They all greeted Tachibana, but she didn't have the time to acknowledge them. *Narazaki-kun*, she kept whispering, her mind blank. *Room 1023. He's here. At least I'm not alone.*

She took the elevator, and then walked down another narrow hall. Room 1023. *He's here.* Tachibana took a small breath and knocked on the door. No one answered. She willed herself to take another breath, knocked again, and finally opened the door.

She was hit by a waft of women's perfume. The naked woman was bathed in red light—it was Komaki, moaning as she moved on top of some man. Her heart raced. The man was Narazaki.

Tachibana stood there dazed. *Of course. What was I hoping for?* As she watched, she felt her heart beat hard. *This is the cult. Of course this is what would happen.*

Though the door had burst open, Narazaki paid no attention. He assumed it was just the next woman, even though he didn't need one yet. He pushed his torso up and buried his face in Komaki's chest, thinking, *I'm still busy with Komaki. I want to devour her body.* When he finally looked toward the door, he froze. Ryoko Tachibana was standing there.

Narazaki tried to pull his body away from Komaki. Komaki turned to look and her expression became one of surprise. Then faintly—so faintly Narazaki barely spotted it—she smiled. She began moving more ostentatiously, as if making a show of it for Tachibana.

"Get off me," Narazaki said. Komaki brought her face toward him.

"Are you sure? If we don't keep going, we'll never do it again—you know that, right?"

Narazaki pushed Komaki out of the way. He grabbed the sheets in front of him and covered the lower half of his body. Tachibana was still staring at him. Komaki left without dressing, her clothes in her arms—without bowing to or greeting Officer Tachibana.

"I heard you were here," Tachibana said softly. "I . . . uh . . ." She couldn't think of the words she wanted. *Should I start over? No, what would starting over do?* Her breathing grew difficult. "Why are you here?" she finally managed to ask.

But Narazaki just kept staring at her, speechless. When he thought about it, it was natural that Ryoko Tachibana was here. He had started all this trying to find her. *But that's not right*, he thought. *Why am I really here?*

A ten-square-meter room with red lighting. Soaked sheets. The sweat on his back suddenly went cold.

I came here to see you, Narazaki thought. But that had only been one of the reasons. He'd also wanted to get wrapped up in something occult. Why had he wanted that? Because he hated the world.

When he was a child, he'd cover up the sounds of his parents yelling at each other with music, and he'd recreate passages from novels in his mind, and live in those stories, in those other worlds. Whenever something bad happened in the world, whenever he felt he didn't belong there, he would choose just the pieces he liked, and live cautiously among them. His days at that awful, exasperating company were the same. He would cover up the voice of his screaming boss with Herbie Hancock's piano; obscure his alienation by reading Meursault's soliloquies from *The Stranger*; and he covered up his own personality, which he'd developed playing go-between for his parents—his desire to be helpful, which always led to his own exhaustion—with Fellini's carnivalesque images. He'd always lived his life that way. But it had stopped working. Reality kept breaking into his fantasies, and he'd grown more fatigued year after year. When reality ultimately punctured one corner of his consciousness, the violence of his desires had come gushing out. *That's why I came here,* Narazaki thought. *To make my own real life seem like a fantasy. Out of contempt for my life . . . No, contempt for the real world.* But Narazaki couldn't say that to Tachibana. He still had an erection. It was an ugly erection from some other woman. *Why does she have to see me like this? And why, now, in this important moment with my old lover right in front of me, is Komaki still lingering in the back of my mind?* "Are you sure? If we don't keep going, you know we'll never do it again?" Komaki's words were frightening. He wanted to fuck her again. *Why am I like this? Why is my body like this?* Narazaki's eyes began to tear up—tears no one could sympathize with. Anger rose up to replace his embarrassment—ugly, inappropriate anger.

Narazaki began to speak—everything he'd been too careful to say before. Now, in this reality that seemed like an illusion, the words just came out.

"Why did you approach me?"

I can't say this, he was thinking. He felt hate in the words leaving him, but he couldn't resist his filthier desires.

"You scammed Matsuo-san—you're a criminal, aren't you? And you had a lover named Takahara, right? So why did you approach me? Did you have fun playing with me? Acting like you'd die, and making me all worried, while you had a real lover the whole time? You were just making fun of me. I can't believe you. Are you going to criticize me for what I've been doing here? Try to make me out to be the bad guy?"

His words were nothing special, not particularly mean, but to such a simple man, they seemed unbelievably cruel. The cruelest he could muster. He thought he would never be able to recover from this embarrassment. But Tachibana remained calm. She had already regained her focus.

"I didn't approach you. Actually . . . I was approaching Kobayashi."

Narazaki was surprised. Kobayashi? The private detective?

"It was an order from the cult. We needed a talented private eye. Kobayashi was chosen as the target. He was still training at his office, but he was incredibly talented. We needed to get him to join us before his company realized how good he was."

Tachibana's voice remained calm.

"To pull one person in requires getting a feel for those

around them. You must obtain all the information you can while you're preparing for the invitation. That's where you came in. That's why I approached you before Kobayashi . . . And then . . ."

Tachibana stared at Narazaki's face. In her voice was neither the sweetness of love nor the conflict that came with any other special emotional attachment.

"I fell in love with you."

Narazaki was frozen on the bed. He couldn't move. The smell of Komaki's perfume still filled the air.

"As you said, I have a lover named Takahara. My mother and his father got married, we became siblings, and we have been lovers ever since. We're tied together in a complex and far too powerful way. He's trying to destroy himself. He's stuck in a state of nothingness and has no interest in his own life. He's trying to do terrifying things to change the world. I keep sacrificing myself to get him to stop. I thought our path would destroy both of us. That's when I met you. Even though I was supposed to be working on luring in Kobayashi, I just kept coming back to you. Our relationship felt so precious to me, but at the same time, I felt like I had already lost your love. Like I had always been fated to lose it. I wasn't brave enough to have sex with you. I have never had sex with any man besides Takahara. I was scared. I was scared I'd change if I did it with you."

Tachibana burst into tears. Narazaki could still do nothing but look at her.

"That's why I left you. That's why I returned. I returned to the bog of my own life. To share a fate with this man heading toward destruction. It seems I'm going to sacrifice the remaining pleasures of my life for him. That's why . . ."

Tachibana put her hand on the door. She felt she couldn't stay in that room for even a few more seconds.

"You were the other fate that I couldn't hold on to."

Tachibana left the room. She noticed that she was crying, but in a few seconds, when she was alone, the tears would dry. And then, as resilient and determined as a junior high school class president, she would rush into the maelstrom, make sure that not a single believer died.

The lights in the hallway were faint. Just like the lives of women.

Tachibana walked down the narrow hallway. Her tears continued longer than she had expected, but finally, they dried.

21

"Let us go to the bathroom," a man in a sweater begged the believer. Next to him crouched a young woman, her head hanging. The believer could tell the man was speaking up on her behalf; he didn't have the courage to challenge the gunmen on his own account. Maybe he was thinking about what would happen after the studio raid was over, was hoping he could impress her with his kindness.

The believer looked at Sasahara, and he nodded slightly. Bracing his gun, the believer stood the woman up and walked her to the bathroom. She was wearing tight beige pants. The believer could see her white bra through her white blouse. The blouse was tight, too, and he could clearly make out the shape of her chest. That sweater man had definitely wanted to sleep with her.

As the woman stepped into the women's room, the believer wondered where he should wait. At the door to the bathroom? But if she escaped through the window, Sasahara would question his responsibility. He'd have failed to satisfy the leader's desires. Instead he stood right in front of the stall door.

He could hear her unfasten her belt, and then the sound of her tight pants rubbing against her thighs as she pulled them down. He felt as if he were seeing all her hidden parts on the other side of the door. He heard her sit on the plastic toilet seat, and turn on the tap so water splashed into the sink. *She's running water to hide the sounds she's making.* He stepped closer to the door.

He remembered his mother. His mother, who had satisfied so many men. She would do it for 20,000 yen. He'd watched her through the hole he'd made with a drill as she accepted the violent thrusts of those men's hips, smiling. Those men, crazy for her body. She'd moan and make them come with her pussy. Those muscular men would tremble and his mother took it all inside her. Even when there were many men, his mother took the lead. She was always ready for more, and they could never wear her out. The believer used to listen to his mother's beautiful moans swallowing up those men. He saw her shine softly, as though she were illuminated from above. He could imagine this woman in the bathroom doing what his mother did. This woman in the bathroom, she could certainly satisfy many men.

The believer suddenly grew jealous of women. Of the fact that they could let go so completely, and reach deeper realms of pleasure than men. He was filled by a growing sense of awe at the woman on the other side of the door. When he noticed he was hard, he felt as though someone were standing next to him—another tall man, with a large presence, although there was no one there. As he got harder, he wondered why the presence felt so familiar. *Is it Christ? Someone like Christ? Is he trying to show me my true self?*

He wanted to make her feel it. Put her in an embarrassing position, make her cry, and make her feel so good she forgot herself. He wanted to be one with that sensation. He'd never wanted to leave the cult's facility in the first place, but now that he was here he would show his loyalty. The water was still running in the stall sink. She must have been taking a long piss. She had been holding it for a long time. She was probably embarrassed about her long piss. To show her that he was listening, he pressed himself against the door so that the toes of his shoes stuck into the stall. Something was egging him on. He was looking forward to her coming out. He wished he could make a hole in the door with a drill and watch her, but he also just wanted to be in there with her on the other side of the door. He heard her pull up her pants. The door opened. That woman's sealed-off world became one with his. He pointed his gun at the woman.

"Take off your clothes."

Her face contorted with fear. *I'm jealous*, he thought. *I'm jealous of the woman I'm about to rape.* He was jealous of her hopelessness. *After I have her pussy a few times, why not put it in her ass? There are women who feel it even more in the ass. I'll never know what it feels like to be fucked in the pussy, but if I try, I can find out what it's like in the ass. Once I know what she's feeling, if I just use my imagination, I can become one with her.* It felt like they were in a perfect closed-off space where no one could intrude. *We can stay here moaning together forever, never leaving for all eternity.* Someone screamed. What was happening? *Why would she scream?* His world began to peel away from this world. Their worlds began to separate; he was being pushed away. Some sort of invisible wall appeared in front of him. His comrades arrived; they were yelling at him. The wall grew thicker. What were they saying? He had just been trying to fit his own world into this one. His comrades shoved him. He fell back into the stall and landed on his ass. His comrades were comforting the woman, telling her they'd had no idea anything like that would happen. *We'll keep a close eye on him*—they were talking about him—*and never let him do anything like this again.* The believer was left there, on his ass, in the stall. With an erection, on the dirty floor of the bathroom. He felt pitiful, even though he was hard.

He had a cell phone. He knew the numbers for all the explosives. He felt himself grow tense. *Even if I dialed them, it wouldn't be my fault, would it?* It was the fault of his comrades who had knocked him over without even listening to what he had to say, wasn't it? His consciousness began to grow thin with rage. He was already holding the cell phone, and everything seemed like a white haze. The leader would understand. He would understand the believer's humiliation. Again. In the distance he could hear his own breathing. *I have to tell someone. I'm being repelled from this world.* He pressed the buttons. *I won't let anyone humiliate my mother.* No one should interfere with his creating his own world. *I need to be rewarded.* His finger hit the dial button. Something inside him began to plummet.

His throat was dry and his heart was racing. What was he doing? What was he? Had he just done something he wouldn't be able to take back? But hadn't he already known that's what it would be when he did it? So many thoughts swirled in his head, he didn't know how to take them all. But then he realized the phone in his hand was ringing. It shouldn't be ringing. It should connect immediately.

The believer stood up and returned to the studio. Sasa-hara strode toward him, his eyes dark with anger. *Where was Takahara-sama?* The believer didn't like Sasahara. He was scary—he'd probably hit him. The believer didn't like get-ting hit. *Calm down—that's right. I have information for him. Information he'll need.*

Full of rage, Sasahara approached the believer.

Trying to attack a woman in this situation? Was there no limit to his depravity? Sasahara couldn't control his anger. *But what should I do? What should I?* he worried. *We're already surrounded by the media and the riot police. If I press him too hard, it could cause problems later. But if I'm not careful, it will set a bad precedent.*

What would Takahara do? he wondered. *I never liked that guy, but he'd probably know what to do at a time like this.* Sasahara took the man into a corner.

"Listen—"

"The number didn't work," the man interrupted, keeping his voice low. "I called. The number. I messed up, and, I messed up and I called."

"What are you talking about?"

"But it didn't go through."

Sasahara was stunned. "What?" He snatched the cell phone and looked at the screen. He couldn't get his thoughts together. The believer really had called one of the numbers. What had he been thinking? But also, why hadn't it worked?

"If you look at the screen, you'll see. I called that number. But it just kept ringing. That shouldn't happen. It shouldn't ring at all. The moment you dial, it should connect and detonate."

Sasahara's neck and shoulders went cold. Staring at the screen, he dialed the number again with trembling fingers. It was true. He put the phone to his ear and listened to the ringing. His legs grew weak.

"Shit. Takahara," Sasahara whispered without thinking. He wanted to hit the frightened man in front of him. Takahara had given them fake numbers.

There was a quiet knock on the hospital door.

It was too early to be the guard change. The officer in uniform rose from his chair and asked who was there through the closed door. But there was no answer. *Who could it be?* the officer wondered. He wasn't the only guard. There were others stationed in front of the elevator, the fire escape, and all entrances to the hospital. No one would have gotten by all those guards; there couldn't be a problem. Nevertheless he was still somewhat nervous as he opened the door. Two men he didn't recognize stood there. One man looked to be in his fifties, the other in his thirties.

"We'll take over," the fifty-something man said listlessly, passing his gaze over the dark room. The thirty-something man said nothing.

"Who are you?"

The men showed their badges. They were from the Metropolitan Police's Public Security Bureau. Something wasn't right; the officer wondered if they were real badges. He reached for the cell phone in his pocket.

"I can't leave here without permission."

"From who?"

"My superiors."

The fifty-something man put his hand lightly on the officer's right arm—the arm reaching for the phone.

"You're careful. That's great. But some very strange things are happening, and they will continue to happen regardless of whether you follow protocol." The man continued listlessly. "You can check for yourself. All of the guards who were out there have vanished. We're going to take over your position, too. You will not mention this at all, and no one will ask you about it. Not you, but another officer will make a mistake and release the person in that bed right now. Of course, that officer doesn't exist, and no one will try to figure out who he was. If things go well, no one will even know that this criminal escaped, and it won't make it on the news. All you have to do is not mention it. And one year from now, all you'll have to do to pass the exam for the promotion you've always wanted is write your name down. You'll be a full detective, and after working for the Metropolitan Police for two years, there will suddenly be talk of personnel changes. Changes that make those around you jealous. And the man who will appear before you as your boss at your new position"—the fifty-something man pointed to the thirty-something man—"will be him."

The officer stared at them blankly.

"As for why you'll have to wait a total of three years, that's to test whether you can keep the secret. If you tell anyone about this, you'll have to take a psychiatric evaluation. And you know what comes after that. Everything's already over once you have to take a psychiatric evaluation."

The officer's right hand went limp. *This is my chance*, he thought. *I don't know what's happening, but my chance is now. A chance others won't get.* The officer saluted the men. The pleasure that comes from obeying an unopposable force seized control of him.

"Good job. You have a bright future ahead of you. Just as I thought," the fifty-something man said quietly. "The order that stationed you in this room in the first place— that order came from us, as well."

—A few years ago there was a civil war here, and there were piles of bodies. The town was filled with this awful stink. Eventually, salesmen started coming by with carts selling strange meat. They'd cut up the bodies, seasoned them, and were selling them. We were starving so we ate it. It was delicious, although some parts were tougher than others. Yeah, they didn't do it out of cruelty. They were high out of their minds. Why did they do drugs? They were scared. Can you stay sane when you're in constant fear of death? Can you stay normal when there are bullets flying all around you? We need drugs. They're absolutely necessary. Another civil war is coming soon.

—One hundred dollars. Yeah, just one hundred dollars is fine. I'll ride you like a rodeo bull. What? More expensive than you thought? Why? Ha ha ha. You're Japanese? What's yen? Money? How much will you give me? How much is that worth?

—*All the weapons here, they're made by the super-powers, you know?*

—*She's asking if you've been to Africa . . . Yeah, she seems to be interested in other countries . . . Her caste? They're called Madiga . . . You've never heard of them? I'll tell you for her. They're even lower than the castes you know. Properly speaking, they're outside the whole caste system. She's an untouchable . . . You came here without knowing about that? Other people won't touch people of her status. Or look at them. They'll get contaminated if they do. When they buy things, too, shopkeepers will just toss the stuff at them. It's against the law according to the constitution, but especially in rural areas it's not rare . . . You want to ask if it's hard being a prostitute? What does she think of the men who sleep with her even though they say she's untouchable? It's not hard for her. Hm? You don't need to ask that. She's a prostitute who's given her life up to the goddess Yellamma. You don't know about Yellamma? What? Caste is hereditary. It's fate. What, you're already done? Go home. You're going back to Africa, aren't you? How old is she? All right, I'll ask. She says she's fourteen.*

—*We killed the kids, cut out their hearts and ate them. Of course we cooked them. You can't eat them raw. What? Of course we don't like eating that sort of thing. Don't lump us together with the characters in your stupid movies. Why? It's like a magic spell. They say that if you eat them, the bullets won't hit you. To do magic requires transcending your humanity. Without that, it's not magic. I guess we do it because eating kids' hearts feels like the worst thing we could possibly do. How'd it taste?*

It's like liver. Well, sort of. When you kill someone, when you're filled with the violence required to kill someone, you can look at them and think, I'm better off than this person, right? I'll die eventually, but at least not right now. Maybe that's why we do it, to feel like we're a little better off than someone else. And what? You dig wells? Well, thanks for that, but do you have any opium? Or alcohol? What? Hey, don't just start talking about money. If anyone hears you say that, you're finished . . . There are outsiders here. To a Japanese person like you we may all look the same, but we can tell ourselves apart just by looking. They have accents, too . . . We have to get out of here. Hurry up. What are you doing? Hurry.

WHEN TAKAHARA woke up in his hospital bed, two men were looking down at him. One appeared to be in his fifties, the other in his thirties.

"What are you doing?" the older man asked. "Hurry and set them off."

Takahara's heart began to race. "Who are you?"

"Don't play dumb," the older man said. "We are messengers of R."

Takahara tried to sit up. Pain shot through his bandaged right shoulder and he grimaced involuntarily. His left arm was hooked to an IV. He could see the call button. *Even if I press it no one will come,* he thought. Sasahara had shot him. His thoughts grew disordered.

"You don't need me anymore."

"We're not done with you yet." The older man drew a quiet breath. "Are you saying you don't care what happens to Ryoko Tachibana?"

"I—"

"Set them off. Blow up all those buildings. Kill. You have to kill. The gods won't be appeased without death. Bring it here, to Japan—the death and destruction that floods the rest of the world. They don't matter to you, do they—normal people? You've always looked down on them."

They handed Takahara a simple prepaid cell phone.

"You're going to dial those numbers at ten P.M. and set off the bombs."

Takahara's head began to hurt. The man's voice sounded faint. "You can set off the bombs and many ordinary people will die. Or Ryoko Tachibana gets gang-raped, has her genitals carved off, and is killed." His voice grew even fainter. "One or the other."

THEY WALKED down the hospital's empty hallway. The younger man decided that it was best not to ask the other anything here. He got in a car, gripped the steering wheel, and stepped on the gas. He carefully chose small roads with no license plate scanners. Quietly, he asked, "What is R?"

"Hm? Oh, it's a religion. It doesn't exist anymore, though," the older man answered. "It's a fundamentalist religion, and he was one of the idiots who joined. Some say that this Cult X is also one branch of the faith, but that doesn't seem to be the case. But that man is certainly a believer."

They took an even smaller road.

"I mentioned its name so he'd set off the bombs."

The car they were in wasn't particularly nice. Nice cars draw attention.

"Our job is to make the cult look bad. Originally I thought that would be taken care of once we sent the riot police in. They'd make a show of infiltrating their compound and subduing the threat. The media coverage should have been great—people would praise the police for preemptively stopping a terrorist attack. We'd take the election easily; there would be no resistance to drastically increasing funding for defense and the police. Everyone would be filled with national pride and we could march forward with militarization. But once they took over that TV station and started spouting all that nonsense about the state of the world, we needed a new plan. You understand what's happening without my spelling it out, right? This is how history is made. We're just following the precedents. The government will issue an order to stay indoors. The police will detain everyone with any connection to the cult. They'll show the people that they're trying. And then suddenly the cult—or properly speaking, that radical Takahara—will blow up those buildings when no one expects it. Even though the government responded in earnest, the cult broke their promise. Innocent people will probably die. The cult's public image will be unsalvageable. At that moment we'll invade both the cult facility and the TV station. We'll kill about half of them and take control. Even if some of the hostages are killed in the process, the public won't criticize us because it was the cult that moved first. We will have prevented further deaths."

The man spoke with his characteristic listlessness.

"History has ironclad rules. Get them to attack first. Wars must be started by the opponent. All through history, America always let the enemy attack first. Before they went to war with Japan, America ordered decoy vessels to sail by the Indochina coast and Cape Cà Mau between Hainan

Island and Hue to get Japan to attack first. And in fact, they were attacked first—at Pearl Harbor. There are lots of stories that claim Roosevelt, the president at the time, knew the attack on Pearl Harbor was coming. Whether or not that's true, it is clear looking at American documents that he tried to provoke Japan to be the aggressor. Think of the soldiers he sacrificed. America broke that "make the opponent attack" tradition when they invaded Iraq, but they insisted they were going after weapons of mass destruction. Japan is the same. We blew up our own railways in Manchuria, claimed it was a Chinese attack, and launched our invasion. It's a childish approach, but all through history people have continued to be fooled by it."

"Can I ask one thing?"

"What?"

"What if . . . I think you know everything, but . . ."

"No, you're right. I don't know everything. I simply recognize the scenarios proposed by politicians' think tanks. I don't know who is behind what's going on today. I just guess. The think tanks aren't the only black curtain hiding who's behind it all. No single industry is manipulating these events. Stock prices are one hint for guessing who's benefiting from these events. Whoever is behind all this, they're just *using* the system of nation states. Countries don't exist except as abstractions these days. Whoever's really in charge, they just employ the concept of statehood for their own purposes. They can do whatever they want to the citizens. If they want to militarize them, they can do it easily. Thankfully, there are always people who want to stay under the control of the conservative government, to keep power in the hands of the people already in power. Look at the Internet, at WikiLeaks. In other countries, people use technology to fight for freedom of speech and expression. Here they just use it to bash the Chinese and Koreans. No matter how horribly we treat the poor, those online conservatives will defend us. If we export the weapons we make, and those guns find their way into the hands of terrorists and are used to shoot schoolgirls, they will defend us. If weapons with the rising sun on them are used to slaughter children, they will defend us. They will even say that the war in which millions of our forebears died was righteous. No matter what we do, as long as we give them 'enemies' they will defend us. They position themselves on the side of the powerful, and, wrapped up in their own ideology, they take pleasure in attacking others. It makes them feel superior. They will never reject our brand of conservatism. Once they believe, no matter what they hear or read they will never turn against us. There aren't many people who can doubt something once they've believed in it; it would mean doubting themselves. Finding the courage to be reborn is incredibly painful. They don't want to think for themselves. They are happy to consider our set pieces their own. They want to be part of something great. They'll come to our rescue this time as well. No matter how much information gets leaked online, they'll monitor it all, better than if they were an official agency we sponsored, and they'll crush it. They do it for their country. When they're given a cause to hide behind, they unleash all the hideousness inside them. By convincing them they need to protect their own country from a foreign menace, we can increase our own gains. We're deliberately enlarging the gap between the rich and the poor, but they don't even notice that's our goal. For the sake of large corporations, we'll take in more immigrants who will work cheaply. Because of the immigrants, there will be workers who can't find jobs. Then we just make them hate immigrants. The country will begin to militarize and the weapons industry will make money. This is the historically standard way of creating a conservative country. Of course, in the end there will have been mistakes in our information. But if our plan succeeds, no one in the country will have a problem with it. If someone high up must be punished, it will all end with just a verbal reprimand. No one needs to get fired; there are cases where 'disciplinary action' doesn't even involve a cut in wages. What convenient words. Their title may change, but their salary and status remain the same. While the grime of the earth struggle down here, those at the top just change positions. If things don't go well, we just quit. Politicians all have money, so they can quit whenever they want."

The car entered the dark. The thirty-something man was not convinced by what he heard. Yet the fifty-something man kept speaking.

"Of course, I don't have the whole picture. I don't know what this Cult X's plan is."

"Their enemy is Japan. They're just trying to get attention," the younger man said automatically. When he spoke, he felt a strange sense of satisfaction.

"How green." The older man smiled faintly. "You don't know Sawatari."

TAKAHARA WAS sitting up in his hospital bed, staring at the cell phone he'd been given.

What they'd said was wrong. No, maybe his expectations were wrong.

YG had ordered him to carry out a terror attack. He was to draw attention to the problems of deprivation around the world in the name of the gods. *Take over a TV station, kill some of those wealthy Japanese, and spread our name around the globe.* If he refused, they would kill everyone in the cult. *That woman, your lover, will be gang-raped and killed.* There was no way Takahara could stop them. The police wouldn't protect the cult even if he asked for help. As long as Ryoko was connected to him, she would always be in danger. Even if he ended their relationship, he couldn't stop YG from coming after her five, ten years from now.

Takahara had originally approached Sawatari because he wanted to change the world. But all Sawatari did was have sex with women. He never tried to do any good for anyone. When Takahara was contacted again by YG, it had felt as though the goals they propounded were the same as his, even if their methods were quite different. They would never plan a terror attack where no one would die. Takahara was done with doing things their way.

He had tried to shape YG's demands into something that would fit with his desires. To carry out a terror attack without killing anyone. He'd tried to fail on purpose. He'd planned to forcibly defend his opinion on TV, start a movement, and purposely fail to kill anyone. YG would not forgive betrayal, but they would not blame him for failing. If he carried out one attack, his actions would make up for his previous failure, and if he died, he thought, they wouldn't punish anyone else. He felt bad for his co-conspirators, who would probably be arrested, but that was better than being killed by YG.

But something had gone wrong. *Why did Sasahara shoot me?*

Was the terrorist attack really organized by YG? Is Sasahara a member?

He had a headache. He also felt slightly nauseated.

I have to get out of here. He removed the IV and got out of bed. His belongings were under the bed. His phone was gone—he had only the prepaid one—but his wallet was there. And a large bottle of pills. Were they painkillers?

Takahara dressed, left the room, and walked down the dark hallway. The silver door that led to the fire escape stood open, like an unhappy greeting. Were they telling him to leave through there? No one was guarding the stairs.

Takahara had to update himself on the situation before he did anything else. He caught a cab and rented a small room in a run-down Western-style business hotel nearby. Intense pain ran through his right shoulder, so he turned on the TV with his left hand. JBA was running footage of cult members pointing guns at the hostages. He flipped the channels, seeing more and more of the same.

This is not an attack by YG, he thought. *This is an attack by the cult. By the leader.*

Had Sawatari known everything he was doing? Was he just using Takahara to plan his own attack? His face always looked so blank. Had he planned this all—made Takahara do it? There must have been other members involved. But why would Sawatari do something so complicated?

Yoshioka, who had been in charge of preparing the guns, had been killed in his room. That wasn't a coincidence. Sasahara's gun hadn't been altered as Yoshioka was supposed to alter it.

But why was Sasahara demanding they become an

independent ward? Why was the facility being surrounded? *It's so suspicious.*

What was Sawatari's true aim?

One thing is clear, Takahara thought. *Those two men were messengers from YG, and YG is upset at this situation. They are mad that their terror attack, my terror attack, was taken over.*

Takahara looked at the phone in his hand. *I'm the only one who knows the numbers. All these terror plots have gotten mixed together, but there's only one thing for me to do. Ryoko's life, or normal people's lives. The answer is easy.*

I've never approved of this world.

I don't care about normal people.

23

"Welcome."

Matsuo looked thin, sitting cross-legged on top of a hospital bed, facing the camera.

"Now I'm going to tell you all what I've always wanted to say.

"These are the words I was meant to tell you from the moment you were born. Welcome to this world. You have been given life. From the universe of nothingness, you have received a brief something. Please indulge in it. Enjoy this world with your whole body. Just like a teenager in the fever of first love, take pleasure in this world with everything you have."

At Matsuo's mansion, many members had assembled to hear his last lecture. Yoshiko, who already knew the contents of the talk, stood in the back watching everyone watch the video. This was Matsuo's will.

"Our universe started with the Big Bang, and eventually living things came to be. Living things are less stable than things that aren't alive. It's possible that the reason they must die is because by doing so they produce diversity. Why are we alive? I'll try to explain that in my own way. We are alive to give birth to stories. The story of having lived as a salaryman. The story of having spent twenty years hiding in a room, then finally mustering the courage to leave. We live to give birth to stories. We live to live through stories. We continue to birth new stories into this world. There's no such thing as a good or bad story.

"Our existence is built on our brains, made from tens of millions of neurons, and the countless synapses connecting them—an astounding feat, the joining together of innumerable particles. Atoms, and the protons, neutrons, and electrons that compose them. For this world to be the way it is required an astonishing combination of microparticles, a very particular value of the elementary charge that determines the strength of magnetism and the miraculous value of the coupling constant that determines the strength of the atomic bonds that hold together protons and neutrons. The collection of tiny particles that would become our world was born in the Big Bang. In .01 seconds, the temperature rose to ten trillion degrees, and in the following three minutes the nuclei of our helium atoms were born. For about 1.37 trillion years this astounding universe has continued to be everything, and now it is the stage for your stories. Our lives are supported by this astounding system. Or we could put it this way. Every piece of this astounding system has been given to us.

"So, why are our stories needed? That I don't know. But

this world wants stories. Because atoms are full of the potential to produce life, they are also full of the potential to produce stories. I don't know what purpose is served by the various stories our unstable lives produce. The world is probably just built that way. Judging from the way the world is constructed, and the fact that atoms are full of the potential to produce life, we should probably just accept that we live to produce stories. God is probably the full form of this world, the universe. So we can probably call the structure of this world 'god.' All the great, ancient religions of this world simply saw god differently because of their different cultures.

"Pray to god. By that I mean pray to everything. Everything outside yourself. You, you don't really exist. Our bodies are always changing at the atomic level, always trading parts. So we could also put it this way: praying to god means praying to everything, which includes yourself.

"While we are the agents of our stories, our consciousnesses are also the audience watching those stories. So let's watch until the very end. As long as we have consciousness, we must watch our own stories.

"I'm going to die soon. I think it may be tomorrow. When you watch this, I will already be gone. But this isn't anything to be scared of. I'm just returning to nothingness. We are all really nothing, and after we enjoy our brief lives, we humbly return to nothing. My body will be cremated, broken down to the atomic level, and will become part of this system of particles that supports your stories, I imagine. We are all one, and each of us is just part of this great world.

"We live to produce stories, and no one has the right to erase another's story. The structure of this world—in other words, god—created us. We do not have the right to kill anyone produced by this world, by god. Aside from eating— aside from consuming life to support life—we have no right to take the life of any living thing. God does not tell us to kill. The only people who say god tells us to kill are scam artists using god's name—false prophets. What right do they have to speak the word of god? How do they know what god wants? What evidence is there? Who is their witness? With what certainty can they speak? Human beings, as simple as we are, cannot understand the truth of god. That is why we must speak carefully, only in postulations. Maybe this is what god thinks. We cannot say anything as absolute as *Go to war*, or *Kill him*. Even if they praise god, we must not listen to false prophets who demand war and death. They are nothing more than ordinary humans who shit and fuck just like us. Please remember that by praising false prophets you risk turning your back on the real god. Consider your- self as being tested by god—you must not be fooled. True prophets remain humble. Humans must not make absolute decisions. Such conclusive actions as war exceed human authority in the face of the god who created us.

"During the Second World War, Japan tried to placate its people by convincing them to worship the nation, not the self. There was a certain pleasure to be found in throwing one's own body into that mad frenzy. People could forget how trivial their lives were, devote themselves to a larger 'cause.' They were set free from the 'burden' of freedom, of having to think for themselves. In Japan now, a group of people is trying to recreate that nationalist war machine.

"It certainly does feel good to be so committed to a cause that you would give your life for it. You feel pride in being

Japanese. However, given the slightest opportunity, that sort of pleasure can give way to a rampage. For humans it is a terribly dangerous state. There were many people in Nazi Germany who took comfort in raising their right hands in the Nazi salute and shouting 'Heil Hitler!' We must not fall into that trap again. This is not just a matter of concern for Japan. Since time immemorial, societies have returned to this sort of pleasure over and over again. We must reject both those who demand murder in the name of god and the pleasures born out of totalitarianism. Only by doing that can humans move on to their next stage.

"From the beginning of the Pacific War until we lost, political power shifted hands seventeen times in Japan. But the war followed a single filthy path. Once the system was put in place, we couldn't stop it. The government that set this pleasure-engine of nationalist fervor in motion couldn't stop the people. The officers who had been mobilized couldn't imagine surrendering and giving up that glorious feeling of pride and purpose. They continued to order their sub ordinates to carry out ridiculous attacks. Think about the berserk actions of the Kwantung Army, which brought down the wrath of the rest of the world during that war. Even level-headed politicians could not stop them. In the midst of such a state of pleasure, it's impossible to maintain balance. Do you believe our current politicians have the capacity to maintain that perfect balance under the totalitarian rule of 120 million people? We will just run wild again. If that particular pleasure-state is restored, Japan will find itself in a dangerous situation. We will drown in that pleasure and leave another dark spot on our history, just as we did in World War II. We must mourn those who died in that war not as heroes, but as sacrifices. Of course it's an ugly point to make, to say after the war that those we sent to battle were not heroes. However, if we don't get past this ugliness, we will never advance. Those in charge of the country should certainly, as our representatives, bow their heads to those soldiers who died. Weeping, they should tell them, We hope for peace. We will not allow the pleasure-state to be revived. So from now on we will treat you as sacrifices. We will always remember that we called you heroes and sent you to battlefields. And we will always mourn you. Your sacrifice was part of a far too heavy lesson we had to learn. And in exchange, in atonement, we will bring peace to this world. If we continue to call them heroes, more humans will go to die in the hope of becoming heroes, too. The more we call soldiers heroes, the closer we get to war. If we worship the fallen, people will long to be like them. And when our country turns to war, people will not resist.

"Dostoevsky said that once someone is seized by a way of thinking, they rarely change. Even if evidence contradicts their beliefs, it is rare for people to change their mind. Dostoevsky said people only change because of their emotions. And so it's not enough to reject one way of thinking. Without finding another way of thinking instead, a person will never change.

"I believe he was right. That's why I must also offer an alternative. However, unfortunately, I have no solution to offer that can compete with the simple search for pleasure that is totalitarianism. I don't have that kind of power.

"What I say will probably sound harsh. I am going to die soon, and I will keep saying harsh things until the very end.

"Japan should become a country that speaks out for

peace. We should be hated by all the countries that long to go to war. So, you'll ask, if another country starts a conflict, do we just ignore it, even if people are suffering? What an extreme opinion! However, have you ever thought about what's behind such a conflict? The calculations of many large governments are tied up in the interests of the over-sized weapons industry. We should oppose not only the forces initiating the dispute but also the corporations behind it. We should keep working to stop those disputes before they happen. We should stop businesses from trying to profit off of war. We must continue to hold peace up as an ideal. If a conflict occurs in another country, let's bravely tell the whole world why we oppose it. Let's name names. This country and these businesses are behind this conflict, and that country and these businesses are trying to profit from that war. If we stop them, war will cease. On the other hand, as long as they're profiting behind the scenes, war will never end. We should put all our energy into pro-ducing a system that makes war unrealistic. We must not let munitions companies just do what they want. The more weapons we have in this world, the more likely we are to go to war. I don't suggest anything as purely irresponsible as Japan's giving up its military—we should maintain the defense forces befitting a developed country. In our recent history we have been not only blatant aggressors, but also victims who experienced the atomic bomb and the air raids on civilians. We've had the special experience of being both aggressors and victims. Can we give up our unique-ness? If Switzerland can remain eternally neutral, Japan should become a country that eternally pursues peace. If we give up our uniqueness, wouldn't the many lives lost in the Second World War be wasted? We absolutely cannot let their lives be wasted. When I think of those who died, I desperately want Japan to devote itself to fighting for the end of war. Some of the leaders of other wealthy countries will furrow their brows at us, as will many international corporations. But the people of the world will support us generously. It is always the common people who suffer in wartime. I believe those who died at war also hoped for peace. I believe they were too noble to demand to be revered as heroes. The world . . ."

The doors were flung open and a member burst in.

"The police are outside," the member panted. "Everyone—"

Police officers flooded the room.

"The world is built on a balance of great powers. If Japan cut the rudder that allowed for war, that balance would be lost."

"Everyone remain calm," shouted one of the officers. "I have a warrant to arrest all of you. We're going to take you into custody."

"Why?" asked Yoshiko. "We have nothing to do with that cult."

"We'll give you the details at the station. Let's go."

"In the end, I never figured out whether or not everything was decided at the moment of the Big Bang. But I did learn one thing. I don't know if it controls everything, but fate is real. I don't mean to say your fate is decided the moment you're born. I'm speaking more broadly. Picture a giant stone pillar—it's being worn away on all sides, pushed by one force or another in one direction or another. Once it begins to fall in a certain direction, no one can stop it. Then that becomes its fate."

"Please stop!" Yoshiko yelled. "We're not involved!" An officer was restraining her as the members were handcuffed one by one.

"Stop!" Yoshida shouted at a member who was resisting arrest. "Don't resist. Don't lay a hand on them. You can't become like one of them."

"That's interfering with arrest."

"He hasn't done anything!"

"It's 7:05 P.M. You are under arrest. You have the right to remain silent—"

"Stop!"

"Let go!"

"Surely someone will object violently to what I'm saying. They'll call me a starry-eyed idealist. But I want to tell those people that they are caught up in a different idealism, one that beautifies war. The world is just that kind of cruel and heartless place, they'll say. But against this tide of popular opinion, I will continue to raise my weak voice. If voices like mine vanish, the world will speed off in the wrong direction. I will continue to say that no one has the right to erase our stories. I will continue to tell the world to open its eyes, even after I die. I will continue to say that we can't allow people to die for profits. I will continue to say that this world is here for us to enjoy."

"Hurry and take them."

"Stop it! Look what you're doing to that old woman. Why? Why are you being so rough?"

"Stop!"

"Stop it! No one's resisting. Are you really so insecure you have to be that rough? Do you have to be violent because you know what you're doing is nonsense?"

"Take them. They're terrorists. They're terrorists!" the police screamed.

"We don't know if they're armed. If they resist, shoot."

"Stop it!"

"Our nation should devote itself to peace. And when our way of thinking has spread throughout the world, when that giant stone pillar has fallen in the other direction . . . Then no one will be able to stop this world from flowing in the direction of peace. I want to believe that is possible."

"Stop resisting!" Yoshiko shouted. "And stop being so violent!"

One by one the members were dragged off. The ground was speckled with blood. The TV had been knocked over. Matsuo's voice continued to ring out, but there was no one there to hear it.

"We cannot let our precious lives be swallowed up by totalitarianism. We must not let our stories be worn away . . . Our bodies are constantly changing, and are eventually replaced entirely. All of you watching—if we go back far enough, we all have just one ancestor. If we go back hundreds of millions of years, the fishes far off in the tropics also share a common ancestor with us. Some amoeba drifting through the water. In other words, we and that fish somewhere were once one.

"Everyone born of that astounding system is precious. When you think you're about to be done in by your daily routine, please try to open your mind, even if it seems impossible. Let's live with great pride in this astounding universe and system of particles. Laugh and cry with all your heart, live with all your might. Please, live actively.

You were given something from nothing. And finally, I want to tell you all . . ."

Someone shouted. Yoshiko was crying as she looked at the bleeding members.

"Thank you for everything. I don't care what anyone says. I love you all. I love all the diversity of this world."

In the Cabinet's Emergency Operations Center, a phone rang.

"Fighter jets." The voice was shaking. "Two fighter jets running drills have vanished from our radar . . . They are heading toward China."

24

The automatic doors were locked and iron barricades were propped in front of them. How hard would the riot police have to work to break through this sullen wall? Ryoko Tachibana had never imagined that the day they'd use those barricades would actually come.

In front of the barricades forty believers waited, armed. The guns looked wrong in their hands. When they saw Tachibana, they lowered their guns and bowed slightly. Everyone was excited. They could never experience this sort of excitement in everyday life. Their excitement might eventually reach their fingertips and pull those triggers.

"Everything is secured," said one of the believers, in a strangely formal tone. Was he enjoying the pageantry? Their faces were all flushed. Not a single person felt depressed by what was happening. There was no way she could convince them. They were in too deep. *The only person in their right*

mind here, who hasn't been affected by the turbulent atmos-
phere, is Narazaki-kun. No, I'm not even sure if he's in his
right mind. I'm not even sure about myself.

She retreated to the hallway. She could hear a woman's
moans coming from one room. Did the people need each
other that way now, in this time so full of unnatural exhila-
ration?

Tachibana stopped a woman who passed her in the
hallway. "Where are you going?"

"To comfort those guarding the entrance."

She was a Cupro girl, not a believer. But her cheeks, too,
were flushed.

"I see."

What else should I say? Tachibana wasn't sure. But the elevator door opened, and Sugimoto, a female officer the leader
was particularly fond of, stepped out. Tachibana knew Sugimoto judged her for never trying to sleep with the leader, even
if she never let on.

"Rina-san, the leader has summoned you."

She was excited, too. The believers had praised her for
her speech to the riot police.

Tachibana nodded slightly and didn't ask why she was
being summoned. If she had, Sugimoto wouldn't have
answered.

She took the elevator to the twentieth floor, then the
stairs to the twenty-first. There were two believers in front
of the door. They bowed to her.

"The leader is waiting for you."

The door opened, and as soon as Tachibana walked
through, it closed again behind her. It had been a long time
since she had seen Sawatari. She tried to contact him when

she returned to the facility because she learned the Public Security Bureau was investigating the cult, but even then, he wouldn't meet with her.

"You'll leave," Sawatari said quietly. He sat in his chair lifelessly and stared blankly at the space in front of Tachibana.

Whenever she was in front of him, she couldn't help but get nervous. "Leave?"

"We said we'd release one of the two hostages they say we have . . . Mm. We will release you."

"Why?"

"Pretend you were a hostage . . . Tell them that we never harmed you . . . Give them proof."

Tachibana realized that her mouth was open, but she was too nervous to speak. Rage bubbled up inside her. *This man*, she thought. *This man must have planned it all.* She opened her mouth again.

"Why are you getting rid of me? What are you planning?"

Sawatari seemed to be smiling slightly. Tachibana was never sure what kind of feelings he actually had.

"You never change . . ." he said listlessly. But his interest seemed to have been faintly aroused. "You take life so seriously. So seriously that you suffer. That's your way of living."

"I pledge my allegiance to you."

"You don't need to lie."

Tachibana felt her body stiffen.

"I don't care about that at all. Mm. Just leave . . . Sugi . . . Sugimoto will negotiate over the megaphone."

"What!" Tachibana screamed. She didn't even know what she was trying to say. "What should I do?" Her eyes filled with tears. "I don't want to let them die. I don't know why I care. I'm probably just pretending to be a good person. But I don't want to let them die. No. I don't know. Takahara-kun."

What am I saying?

"I just wanted to be with Takahara-kun. That's all. But why am I in this position? Why am I standing here paralyzed with a monster like you in front of me?"

Sawatari raised his right arm slightly and Tachibana fell silent. "Is that all?"

"What?"

"You want to suffer," he said in his empty voice. "That is your wish for this life. You just want to suffer. You want to be dragged around by some man, and face his problems with all of your own seriousness. All that suffering will comfort you. That's what you are. That's your only desire in this life."

Tachibana's mind was blank.

"I've met your mother before."

"What?"

"You look quite alike. You and that mother you hate."

The door opened, and men ushered Tachibana out. Her mind was still blank.

When she came to, she was in a different room and Sugimoto was speaking to her. *They're trying to kick me out,* Tachibana realized faintly. *I won't be able to save anyone.* Sugimoto was giving her a concerned smile. *That woman hates me. She's making a worried face, but she's happy that I'm being kicked out.* Tachibana noticed that Sugimoto's face was carefully made up.

Tachibana excused herself and went to the bathroom. She didn't really have to go; it was like her body was resisting something. *I am me. I won't be just carried along at that man's pace. I am me. I am . . .*

In the hallway, she passed a believer. He was holding a small gun.

"Hey. Let me borrow that."

"What? Oh, here."

The believer passed the gun to Tachibana politely. She slipped it into her pocket.

"It's going to be very dangerous," Sugimoto was saying when Tachibana returned. "You will exit the building with both your arms raised. At that moment, they may try to force their way in."

But Tachibana wasn't listening.

I'm going to leave here. Tachibana tried to remain aware of what was happening. *I'm going to leave here and find Takahara-kun.* Tachibana's eyes slipped down, and she stared at the gray floor. *I used to think we could do anything. Even when he was suffering from his bad memories, we held each other in that small bed and made it through. No matter how cruel the world was, no matter what it did to hurt us, we'd be fine together, we could bear it together. We thought we could do anything.* Tachibana quietly stroked the pistol in her pocket.

I must free him from the spell of his god. If he's set free, we can change the ending.

Tachibana held on to those thoughts.

IN THE Cabinet room, a man was screaming, but his face was vacant. "What are you talking about? Self-Defense Force planes in training? How could that happen?"

"But it's true. We must take care of this right away." The face of the man who answered was also vacant.

"Judging from the direction they're heading, it looks like

they're going to Beijing . . . There has also been a report that this may be connected to the current terror attack," said yet another man with a vacant face.

A rustling ran through the office.

"In other words?"

"It is possible that a certain radical group within the country took in two members of the Special Defense Forces, brainwashed them, and they are now trying to attack China."

There was a silence. But eventually yet another man with a vacant face began to speak. "If that's the case, if Japanese planes attack Beijing . . . We'll be forced to go to war . . ."

"Shoot them down," said another man. "Scramble the Defense Forces, and shoot those planes down as soon as we find them."

". . . That's our only choice. But can we really do it? I'll say this just to confirm: We incited them. We encouraged them to see our neighbors as enemies. To make this country work the way we wanted, we turned our neighbors into the enemies of our people. They felt anger, just as we told them to, and attacked on their own. And we old men are going to shoot those boys down?"

The meeting room was filled with silence. Eventually another man opened his mouth. "That's right," he said quietly. "That's what we're going to do."

Takahara was in bed, staring at the clock.

The clock's wooden frame was large and square. *Time flows on without paying any regard to us.* Takahara felt the intense pressure of the situation bearing down on him. In two more hours, he would become one of the most prolific murderers of the century.

He felt himself wanting to smoke. He got up, and a sharp pain ran through his right shoulder. He had just taken what looked like painkillers, but they didn't really seem to work.

He got in the elevator and left the hotel. The lights of a convenience store, those common, everyday lights, struck his eyes forcefully. Takahara sat on the ground in the busy part of town and watched people pass as he smoked a cigarette. Countless legs passed before him. With his eyes at that level, he got a sense of déjà vu. He remembered running away from home.

When he was five, Takahara had left the apartment he lived in to get away from the father who would hit him when he was drunk. On the street, all the big strangers would walk right by him. Takahara didn't cry; he just watched them pass. But he'd felt fear then. Maybe he could have saved himself by asking the police for help, or won someone's sympathy by crying. But at the time Takahara didn't know that. So he just continued to feel scared watching all those strangers pass in front of him, just moving through their lives. The world didn't care that he was alive. This memory overlapped with memories of his mother leaving him. People who looked like his mother walked past him without looking, one after another. One after another.

After running away, Takahara was locked up. His father vanished, and he starved. Back then Takahara was even scared of the TV that was always left on. He couldn't help but fear the people on TV who laughed and cried without any regard to him. It was Tachibana's mother who'd saved him. She came into the apartment one day and opened the door to the room Takahara was locked up in. But she didn't do it out of love. She came because she was worried that if Takahara died, her boyfriend, Takahara's father, would be arrested.

Even when Takahara's father and Tachibana's mother married, his father almost never came home. Tachibana's mother raised them, but not because she loved them. She seemed to think that by raising them and working herself to the bone she could get revenge on Takahara's father. She always acted like a pitiful woman, tormented by life. Sometimes she would demand thanks from Takahara and Tachibana. When anything bad happened to her, she seemed to feel strangely happy, as though she had received some proof of the fact

that her life was unhappy. After she officially divorced Takahara's father, she never bought new clothes. When Takahara
and Tachibana were sixteen, Tachibana's mother died of a
heart attack from overwork. Ryoko found her body in the
narrow hallway in front of the bathroom. Her eyes were full
of hatred for the world, and yet, she seemed as though she
was about to smile.

Takahara stared at the people passing as he smoked. He
recalled one of the poems he read long ago in a holy book.

Master, show me the way.

Please give me a pure heart so I may worship all people.

Takahara always carried this poem inside him. He could
never respect anyone around him, but he tried to make
himself respect them. Eventually he learned that he had
misread the poem. The word he thought was "all people"
actually meant "holy name." What the poem praised was the
name of god. For Takahara, that didn't change the meaning
much. To believe in the god that everyone believes in, one
must be modest.

Master, show me the way.

Please give me a pure heart so I may worship all people.

People walked by. Takahara certainly didn't feel like
blessing those who passed. He could never get rid of his
feelings of condescension. Even though he didn't consider
himself particularly talented, he could never abandon his
bad habit of immediately judging everyone around him as
useless. But when he looked at humans suffering, a desire
to save them welled up inside him. He thought he saw his
old self in them. It was as if the more people he saved, the
further back in time he could go, the more likely it was that
eventually he'd be able to save himself.

But he was trying to put his past behind him. *I have to blow up this city and die. Be despised as a criminal by all those I've looked down on.*

What was my life? Takahara kept wondering.

RYOKO TACHIBANA approached Kurita quietly. He was a tall man, the one who'd first carried Mineno to the "down room." Tachibana knew the Cupro girl had taken Mineno's flash drive, but she imagined that wasn't all Mineno had brought with her. She'd probably had at least a wallet and a cell phone.

When she asked Kurita, he said he had them. "I thought I had better give them to the leader right away, but I forgot because of all of this commotion."

Ryoko Tachibana took the wallet and phone from the confused man.

Back in her room, Tachibana told Sugimoto, "We should call an ambulance."

"Why?"

"That way I'll seem more like a hostage. And for the leader I'm just a smoke screen. He doesn't care about me at all. It's also less dangerous for medics to come here than the police."

Sugimoto stared at Ryoko Tachibana.

"Come to think of it, that's certainly true. But . . . No, that's true. And getting the hostage medical care looks better than giving in to the police."

Hostage negotiations were carried out over megaphone. Many TV cameras were waiting to get footage of the hostage leaving. The ambulance arrived, and everyone inside the facility grew tense. But the police didn't move. It would be bad for their image if they broke in when a sick hostage was being released humanely.

The faces of the paramedics were cramped with tension when they arrived in front of the barricades. Whatever they didn't know about this organization, they knew that they were still terrorists.

"Thank you. She's in a lot of pain," Sugimoto said to the medics, a false expression of concern on her face. Tachibana held her stomach as the medics laid her down on a stretcher.

The believers took down one barricade so the stretcher could pass through, replaced that barricade, then removed the second. When she was finally outside, Tachibana covered her face with a cloth. She was loaded into the ambulance. The riot police made a path and let them through.

Two police cars followed the ambulance. Tachibana leapt up suddenly and pressed the barrel of her gun to the temple of one of her medic guards.

"Speed up. Lose the cops."

The medic was too startled to speak. This wasn't a hostage; it was a terrorist. There was a terrorist pointing a gun at his head.

The driver slammed on the brakes. "If you stop this car, I'll shoot," Tachibana screamed. "I've already killed many people, so I won't think anything of it. If you want to die, stop this car right now. But do what I say and we all walk away from this."

Sirens on, they blew through the stop lights. There was nothing strange about the speeding ambulance. The police took no notice.

The ambulance, Tachibana thought, had been a clever idea. No vehicle could be better for escaping the cops.

"Stop next to that department store."

The ambulance stopped. Tachibana got out of the ambulance as two police cars pulled in behind it. She ran into the store, stripping off her white robe as she wove between product displays. She had put on an ordinary blouse and skirt underneath before leaving. The police didn't know what Tachibana's face looked like; without her cult robe she was just another shopper. As Tachibana exited from the other side of the department store, the police were shouting her fake name at the crowds of confused shoppers.

Tachibana got into a taxi parked nearby. As calmly as a regular shopper would, she told the driver where to go, and he set off. There was no way the police could catch her; they didn't even know who they were looking for. She was safe.

Tachibana turned on Mineno's phone. Takahara might not answer if he thought Mineno was calling, so Tachibana blocked the number before she dialed.

THE PHONE the fifty-something man was holding in his hand was ringing. A blocked number. When he answered, a woman spoke.

Narazaki stood in front of the door.

There were no guards, and the door was standing open. On the other side there seemed to be only deeper layers of dense darkness. Narazaki suddenly remembered the first time he'd stood in front of the gate at Matsuo's mansion. But this time it was Sawatari he had to face.

When he entered the room, the door closed quietly behind him. Sawatari was looking at him. His legs were crossed and his head was hanging slightly. He started to speak, but then stopped as if he were too much trouble. Finally, as though merely exhaling, he said, "Sit there."

Across from Sawatari was an empty chair. Narazaki felt like a figure being fixed into a tableau.

"Why did you call me?"

"Mm." Narazaki thought he saw a slight change in Sawatari's expression. " . . . You really do look like him."

Narazaki raised his lowered head.

"You remind me of someone I knew a long time ago."

The fleeting expression had vanished from his face.

■■■■

SAWATARI'S PAST

Long ago I tried to believe in the god of Christianity —
not out of faith, but rather because it seemed necessary.
The world was bleak and dreary, and I was the sort of
person who thought that it would be hard to bear that
if there was no god. My faith was born of arrogance.
I tried to learn the secrets of god. I studied medicine,
but I also researched the history of traditional religions.
In each religious text you can see the influence of its
precursors. What claims to be the word of god actually reveals the evolution of local folktales. This is easy
information to find if you look. The more I considered
religion as history, the more I researched it, the more
distant god grew. I couldn't help but see the traces of
ancient peoples' different environments. There was no
god. That made the world even bleaker. And if there
was no god, that meant there was no reason for me to
rein in my lust.

When I began working as a doctor, I was taken over
by a particular lust. It always happened when I pierced
a woman's white flesh with my silver scalpel. With that
woman anesthetized in front of me, my throat would
always grow dry, and my mind would go blank, as if I
were intoxicated by that experience . . . What would I
do to this woman in front of me? By moving the scalpel
just an inch more, I could cut an artery, and her blood,

her life, would pour out. I'd open her body and watch the hidden parts inside her working with my own eyes. My will controlled her life, her fate — by letting her live, I controlled everything that would become of her after this. When I felt all that, the tip of my scalpel would always tremble slightly . . . And I would get hard. What a gloomy sight. A sickly pale youth with a scalpel and a hard-on. But I always gave myself over to that lust, even when my coworkers occasionally looked at my eyes peeking out over my surgical mask with concern. When I finished surgery, I would feel relieved for having embraced that lust, and to quiet my excitement I would go to a brothel. The women in brothels were beautiful, but they were nothing more than a way to control my desires. During those days I searched for god, and the more I searched, the more distant he grew.

I was curious about this feeling of pleasure that visited my body when I did good. But I was also interested in the feeling of pleasure that visited my body when I did evil. My mind was wild. I was curious about how far a human could go. When I was a child I often heartlessly killed bugs. I wanted to know how I would feel when I killed them . . . I felt sorry for them, but at the same time, I felt there was something funny about seeing those bugs crushed so pitifully. There are examples in literature, like Goethe's Faust and Dostoevsky's Stavrogin, of those who thirst for both good and evil. The Greek word for cross is *stavros*. You can see from just his name that for the character Stavrogin, Christianity was always in the background . . . I read those books and was comforted, but I also felt that there was a big difference between those characters and me. The nucleus of my feelings was sexual. My desire to hurt others was sexual, and I was far removed from those who suffered for the sake of religion and intellectualism. My mind was closer to sex than theirs. It was more concrete, and darker. Their delicate suffering, born of their ideas of essential good and evil, was quite foreign to me. In the end, I was too different from them.

My search for god went in a strange direction. Like Matsuo, I became a disciple of a teacher named Suzuki. I was very interested in watching this man who I thought was quite close to god grow old and senile. I managed to ruin him quite easily. That, too, excited me sexually. But at the same time, I desired to do good. I traveled to the islands of the South Pacific. I traveled through poor villages, distributed medicines and performed basic surgeries. When I saved someone, I felt myself enveloped by this warm sensation, a pleasure that resembled success seeping through my body.

In southern Malaysia, I met a fifteen-year-old girl named Nayirah. She was beautiful and tanned. She had tuberculosis. She was forced to live isolated from her poor village, and the only medical care she received was chants and prayers. I gave her streptomycin, which anyone could get in Japan at the time, and she recovered. I was happy that she recovered, yet I felt the opposite emotion stir within me as well. My happiness gradually faded.

When Nayirah recovered from tuberculosis, her

beauty was cut in half. The lust I felt when I looked at her at the nadir of her suffering, so thin, death right before her eyes, faded. When she thanked me in her high young voice, warm feelings did rise up inside me, but at the same time, I wished for her to get sick again.

That soon happened. Her immune system was weak, and she suffered from many ailments. Her most pressing chronic ailment was heart disease. But she also got a case of peritonitis so bad that it put her life in jeopardy.

I laid her on one of the village's simple beds, anesthetized and undressed her. My scalpel in hand, I felt my mind draw into itself. My throat grew dry. This girl's life was in my control. I stared hard at her to savor the moment the scalpel split her beautiful skin. If I moved the scalpel in a slightly different direction, she would bleed out and die. There were so many possibilities in that scalpel as it entered her body. Her vital organs seemed to twitch with desire at those possibilities. I was breathless. That scalpel parting her flesh—that silver scalpel was the eye of a hurricane. The rest of the world spun around that eye, loose and wide. I imagined my scalpel slicing open one of her vital organs, and that hurricane spinning wild while Nayirah writhed in pain. I felt so bad for her, I grieved, and I continued moving my scalpel. Though there was no physical stimulation, I felt as though my scalpel were an extension of my penis, and my life force poured out through it. The delusion was complete.

If something had gone wrong during that surgery— some medical accident—no one would have noticed.

On the contrary, I had earned the villagers' trust with the streptomycin. But I finished the surgery without any complications.

When she woke up on top of that bed, she began to cry and thanked me. I felt something warm spread through my body. I had given this innocent girl a future. Not just anyone knows what it feels like to save a life. However, at the same moment those warm feelings appeared inside me, I became unable to escape from this single thought. This curiosity. What if I, the kind man who saved her life, suddenly changed into someone cold and cruel . . . ?

Compared with my curiosity, any conflict between good and evil grew so small and faded so completely that I couldn't feel it. But my heart beat furiously, furtively.

"Take off your clothes."

Did she think this was part of the medical treatment? She undressed. Embarrassed, she hid her breasts, which were just beginning to develop. I got close to her.

"Take off everything and spread your legs. You cannot resist. If you do, I won't help you anymore."

I savored every sound, every sentence as I spoke. For some reason, I was filled with the same warmth as when I did something good. I was belittling this fifteen-year-old girl, holding her life hostage. That hideousness raised the level of my desire. But then something strange happened. The girl, who I thought would hesitate, calmly revealed her breasts.

She took off her underwear, faced me, and spread her legs. When I saw her body trembling, I climbed on top of her. Even though we were in the tropics, the room was cold. Her face twisted in pain from her stitches. I felt sympathy for her, and while I tried to be careful of her wounds, I made them hurt more. I sympathized with her pain, and the harder I worked my imagination, the closer I came to that pain. I managed to feel close to her suffering. My ability to sense others' pain was highly refined. And the more she suffered, the greater my lust. As I moved on top of her, my shadow spread over the cracking gray walls. I felt bad for her, being raped by someone like me, but that feeling of pity drove me on. While I gently wiped away her tears, I made her cry more. I was wrapped up in this powerful pleasure. When I came inside her, I felt a dull remorse. For the first time, I had realized only *one part* of my desire. After ejaculating, these sorts of languid thoughts rise up in men. However, she smiled at me with tears in her eyes. I didn't understand why. Nayirah looked at me and said, *Save me again. Save me again. Then you can do this again*, she said.

"Do you hate your life?"

"Not at all."

"Then why?"

She just cried, and didn't answer my question. I gave her sleeping pills and left. I felt as though I had touched something mysterious, and was now running away.

Her peritonitis healed, but then she developed a fever. It was just a cold, but I was worried it would develop into pneumonia. Watching her suffer, I felt that violent lust again. I administered cold medicine, but I diluted it. I wanted her to suffer forever. As long as she suffered, she would always be close to perfection. The act of secretly giving her diluted medicine increased my lust. She grew slightly healthier, and regained the power of speech. I made her denigrate her body again. Though she was suffering from a fever, she moaned. Though she was emaciated, she held me tight with her thin arms.

"Why are you enjoying this?" I asked from on top of her. "I'm only using you."

"Yes."

"Then why?"

"You can do whatever you want to me," she said. Her face was flushed. Her vagina clenched like an adult woman's. It was dripping wet. "My life is in your hands . . . That makes me happy. I am entirely yours. I don't need a will of my own. I can leave everything up to you. You make me suffer, but you give me life and pleasure. I am a dog. I will follow you no matter what. Please, keep toying with me. Keep fucking me. I, I . . ."

She leaned back blissfully, her body quaking.

"You are my god."

I came violently inside her. But I wasn't done. I kept moving, and came again, and then started again, and came again.

"Treat me badly. Kill me. Kill me, bring me back to life, and kill me again. Do whatever you want to me. I love you."

Was she mad from her fever? I wondered. Even her voice sounded strange. But she stared at me with knowing eyes. I had to tell her about my doubts.

"How can you love someone like me? What would others think if they saw this?"

"What are you saying?" she asked. "If you hadn't come, I'd already be dead from tuberculosis. To me, the people who don't do anything for us might as well not exist. I don't need to listen to their morals."

While watching Nayirah moan in pain and suffering and hopelessness, my vision grew cloudy. I ran my tongue over her body, and I thought about Buddhism. In stories, the Buddha takes the shape of ordinary people, like beggars, or poor young boys. Gods occasionally descend to this world and take the form of humans to test us. What if Nayirah was the Buddha? Wondering about that made me laugh. If that was the case, I'd raped the Buddha. But what if I was being tested? For what? Should I abandon my ideas about good and evil and love Nayirah? What was the point of acting out that sort of idiotic Buddhist fable? What if I fell into terrible regret at Nayirah's death, and then I was reborn as a good person? I raped Nayirah every day, and was overcome by a strange sensation. As I held her, I felt the same clarity I had when I'd killed bugs as a child. I could observe my emotions in great detail, without letting anything escape. And then I understood one thing clearly. I felt more lust when Nayirah screamed in pain than when she moaned in joy.

Nayirah noticed, too. She demanded that I treat her more roughly. She knew that her pleasure would not make me happy, and that only her suffering could bring me joy. She had me change positions, take her in the most humiliating ways possible. She reveled in the pain. I raped her more often when she was weak from illness. I was repelled by the sex; I could only feel pleasure in others' pain. I was far removed from the beautiful sex that came with mutual love. If sex was the richest form of communication between individuals, I was an aberration, for I could only be satisfied by my partner's rejection and misery. Was god trying to show that to me? To shove the truth about me in my face?

But I wasn't the type to shrink away. I wasn't constrained by Christian morality, like Faust or Stavrogin. To me, Christianity was just history; it had nothing to do with flesh and blood. I was free from its rules. And since I was free, I was boundless. Nayirah told me that there were moments when she was no longer herself. Something else was using her body, but she could feel its emotions and sensations. This is not Buddhism, I thought. Fundamentally, Buddhism preaches nothingness. It teaches that everything will vanish eventually. This, though . . . This was something else.

I remembered how I had pretended to train under Suzuki. We would meditate on the grass. As you imagined the grass and trees around you on the inside, the border between yourself and that grass and those trees would gradually grow indistinct. Just once, while doing that, I experienced something strange. I felt the earth's sexual appetite. I felt the grass and trees, the earth and stones feeling lust. Everything wanted to connect to everything else, and even if those things around them rejected them, they tried to connect; when they did connect, they trembled with pleasure. My mental image stretched to encompass the town. In that moment, I felt as though I could see with my own eyes all the lust of the men and women in that town. Men and women howled and moaned and the world trembled. Atoms, I thought. Atoms are filled with the possibility of bringing humans to life, and at the same time, they are filled with the possibility of bringing about carnal desire. They flow and change places and stretch out like a hurricane, and through their constant generation, they also generate lust. That image surged through my inner vision. The particles trembled, flew in all directions, tasted the pleasures of lust, then came to want more and more. The particles that made up Nayirah's brain were connected to the particles that made up her body, and constantly longed for pleasure and pain and ecstasy. The earth's lust, the world's lust, my lust— none of those things were either good or evil. They were nothing more than one violent vibration, like a grinding of teeth, that brought this world into being. And I, I was just caught up in all of that. I continued to spend my days with Nayirah, traveling to surrounding villages practicing medicine. Because of my skills, I could feel the pleasure of saving many lives. I could smile at a child running about innocently, and then, when she paused to look down over a low cliff, sneak up behind her and gently push her over. I felt I had to. That fallen child's face twisted in pain—it was horrible. I liked the feeling of thinking things were horrible. My right hand still tingled with the warmth of having pushed her small back. I ran over to where she had fallen, asking if she was all right, and treated her minor wounds. That child thanked me, completely oblivious to what I had done.

I felt something funny about that innocent child. Her mother visited my medical office to thank me. When I pulled her body toward mine, she looked at me with a rapt expression, as though she were worshipping me. I fucked that woman, and as I mocked her, she just took it. When I saw her so happy to be used, I felt lust. I felt no regret or conflict. My pleasure spiraled out of control. It would never end. It wasn't a spiral that led to the foot of god. It was a spiral that led endlessly away from god.

There were only temporary reprieves, all coming from the outside world. People in distant villages who heard rumors of me came to beg for medical treatment. Nayirah realized that if I stayed in her village that would mean there would be other lives I wouldn't be able to save. Nayirah already had a fiancé. He was a drunk widower over fifty, and it had been decided that when she turned eighteen she'd become his wife and take care of his house like a maid. Even if the world were to somehow become just, there would still be places like this, holes in the net where justice would never reach. Nayirah asked me to kill her and leave the village. *Without you here, I'll die of some illness anyway*, she said. She couldn't run away with me; her family would be ostracized.

I didn't agree to do it. I still longed for her body. But Nayirah's heart was failing, and she had to have surgery or she wouldn't live. She begged me to kill her, but she also begged me to save her. Even though she wanted to die, she didn't want to be separated from me for a minute. She was so young. I made my preparations, and a few days later I anesthetized her, laid her on the operating table, and undressed her. I cut her open with my scalpel.

When I opened her body and saw her defenseless heart, my pulse began to race. I took deep breaths to help me concentrate, but my own heartbeat wouldn't settle. Though she should have been subdued by the anesthetic, her heart was racing as well, as if it were responding to my heart. I was overcome by lust. I wanted to do irreparable damage to this vital part of her, her heart. For some reason I forgot that I couldn't let her die. Her fate was in my hands. My hand, holding that silver scalpel, began to tremble.

I'll just try, I thought. I'll just cut her heart a little. I'll just stop myself before I actually damage it. I don't have to do it for real. But I'll see what it feels like to almost do it. First, I sighed deeply while my assistant watched. *This is horrible. This is no good*, I said. The assistant who helped me in the village didn't have any deep knowledge of medicine; I would not be blamed even if something went wrong. *I have to cut here*, I whispered, pointing with my scalpel to an entirely different part of her heart than the one I had to operate on. As I spoke, my heart began to race again. Nayirah's heart, as if nervous in the face of my intentions, or maybe inviting me to proceed, also began to race. I brought my scalpel closer to her heart. If I moved it just a bit more, her life would end. I was straddling the line between life and death. My breathing grew labored. I felt drunk, and as I grew aroused, my body went limp. Nayirah's heart wouldn't slow down. It was still going. Even though I stopped my hand, the choice remained.

Should I try? I felt my body growing wet with sweat. This is what I'd always wanted. To take a life and in doing so destroy all the possibilities it had. I brought my scalpel up against her heart again. I was a bit surprised to realize that my fingers had stopped shaking. I was so close. Could I stop myself, so close? Happiness spread through my body. The light above the operating table pulsed, and for a moment I looked directly into it. I realized the room had lost all color. Under my hand, Nayirah's insides were black and white. At some point, I had stopped seeing colors—perhaps my brain had removed all color to ease my sense of cruelty. But now Nayirah's red insides were spread out before me. Her bright red heart shone in my eyes. *I'll get past this*, I thought. I plunged my scalpel into that bright red heart. I expected it to open right up, but for some reason its elasticity resisted. That thin membrane was the border separating me from another world. My heart beat so fast it hurt. My heart seized, as if it were being closed in on by the scalpel. The scalpel entered, and then cut. At that moment a sharp sensation pierced my heart. Blood began to spurt. Human bodies are beautifully built. They are also beautiful when they crumble. All those organs struggle and resist death violently. But my scalpel wouldn't stop. I cut through that life, all its resistance. No matter how much it resisted, I cut through it, enraptured. My life force poured out. It was a pleasure that made all existence tremble.

Her blood pressure fell, and her pulse suddenly began to quicken. The electrocardiogram continued to beep. Before I'd anesthetized her, she had been staring at me. Did she know she would never wake up? I thought she looked at me with a certain determination, an innocent expression on her face. But even if she did know, what did that mean? The EKG began to beep faster. My assistant panicked, but since I had whispered to him that the surgery would fail when I first opened her body, he just started crying and didn't interfere further.

After my lust had been satisfied, I waited to feel something else. Maybe a sense of regret would come over me. I looked at her innocent face, thinking it would cause me emotional pain. She looked like she was sleeping. Five seconds passed, then thirty. I thought I would collapse in tears, but nothing happened. The EKG alarm went off, and the beeping grew irregular. I felt surprised at my own calm. All I felt was a quiet satisfaction. The beeping grew even more erratic. It should have already stopped. *It's still going?* I thought. *It's still going?* It went on longer than I'd expected. I thought maybe I should try to cry even though I didn't feel sad on the inside. Perhaps that thought only crossed my mind because I had time for it. To try and make myself cry, I thought about her beauty, and how pathetic she was. Eventually I grew sad and tears began to fall. Then I thought about how I had used her beautiful body however I wanted, and in the end, I'd even done what I wanted with her life. I thought about penetrating that final border. The sides of my mouth rose into a smile. Good and evil intermingled, and my feelings trembled. My consciousness became something I could control without any resistance. The sound of the EKG grew distant and then finally stopped. *Repelled.* That word floated up in the corner of my mind. Stavrogin, who constantly worried about god, had suffered from a guilty conscience. Faust, in the end, embraced the good. I was being repelled from guilt over good and evil. Soon after she died, I raped Nayirah one last time. I felt thrilled doing it, and I also felt the pleasure of being able to come. Later, in front of her parents, I felt truly sad and cried. When I left the village, I felt cheerful. I caught myself naturally making small talk about the heat to the driver taking me to the next distant city.

In the next city, and the city after that, I did the same thing. I didn't meet any girls as young as Nayirah, but I saved lives only to play with them, and my feelings transformed rapidly. I never lost my color vision again. The emptiness of my days vanished as my lust grew. Or to put it in the opposite way, what sort of life lacks emptiness? Life eventually ends. Good and evil are ultimately nothing more than crutches for people who will eventually cease to exist, and even if a great tragedy like the Second World War occurs, days will march on, and nothing is special about any of it. I thought it funny that anyone who knew about the world's tragedies but did nothing about them would criticize my morals. Humans want to think themselves good, but the world is made of heartless evil. My ancestors had protected our useless bloodline just for a monster like me to be born.

But these are just the things that I would whisper listlessly to others. On the inside, I truly didn't think them. I felt satisfied at saving the lives of those suffering from poverty, and I also felt satisfied in humiliating women in horrible ways. The nothingness that Stavrogin fretted over so much was the major premise of life to me, not something to fear. On that point, I may just have a complicated connection to Buddhism.

My interest was in whether or not there was a god. If there was, my way of living might be rejected. From time to time I watched happily as people prayed. For example, athletes praying before sports competitions. There is no way a god who continues to ignore starving children cares about the success of some athlete. A god who leaves sinless children to die in natural disasters and of sickness has no right to censure us. If nothing else, within the limits of human reason, no one can say that god is as good a being as I am. Maybe god will punish me after I die, but even then, that would depend on god having more power than we do, and thus there'd be nothing we could do about it. We would look on this god who only controlled us by force with contempt. It's convenient for us to say we can never understand the will of god. For if we can never understand the will of god, that means there is always a possibility we will be accepted by him.

I built a new hospital in Indonesia. One day I had hooked an IV up to a girl on the verge of death from malnutrition, and had received heartfelt thanks from her parents. As they stood thanking me, I tried to drink some clear water from a clear glass. But there was an uncanny feeling in my fingers, and I put the glass down.

I stared at that glass. It looked slightly cloudy now for some reason. I grabbed the glass again. But the feeling of closing my fingers around it seemed different from before. I realized that the mother who had just been there a moment ago was gone. I looked around the hospital room. The operating table, the medical instruments, the chairs, even the walls—everything was slightly different. I drank from the glass, filled with that sense of uncanniness. I felt the warmth of the water, tasted the slightly rusty flavor. I returned the glass to my desk. I heard clearly the hard sound of the glass touching the desk. But none of it was natural.

The world had somehow lost its naturalness. When I touched something, I felt the sensation of touching it, and when I moved something, that object moved. But all of it felt awkward. It was as if I were trying to forcibly change the way things existed in the world. Then I remembered that word again. *Repelled.* I got the feeling that I didn't fit in this world.

I went outside. The tropical trees were shaking, and the warm wind hit my cheeks. Dust rose up. But all of that felt distant, and it seemed as though it only appeared in front of me because I was watching it. I noticed my body temperature drop suddenly.

From that day on, the feeling would come to me haphazardly, randomly. But I didn't feel lonely when I experienced these occasional changes. Loneliness was natural to me, and not something I worried about anymore. Viewing the world as someone repelled from it—that was something I could bear. I had not been born this way. When I felt my temperature drop and the things around me grow distant, I often thought this. When Nayirah's heart was in front of me, I overcame my mind, my mind that made me see in black

and white. I created a world of vivid color, and I surpassed myself. I had become this way of my own will,
I thought.

I returned to Japan, sought out women who were doing
sex work and created a harem. I left the hospitals my
father used to run in the hands of other doctors, and sat
back and lived off the profits. I thought that by playing
the role of a fake god I might actually come to be called
god. Would god leave someone like me alone? For
me, god had to exist. My arrogance wouldn't allow me
to do something as stupid as live in a world without god. I
continued to act like a god, half in jest. But no real god
appeared, and my believers increased. It seemed that the
empty space inside me attracted people. I, who had been
repelled from everything, attracted others. I felt as if I
were peeling away part of the world and pulling it toward
me. Though I was repelled by everything, I could go on
living, feeling no sadness or emptiness, only pleasure.

But this led to one problem. To do either good or evil
requires energy. And the energy within me was fading.

I thought that my desires would only grow fainter,
and that I would gradually shrivel and die. I thought that
I had reached the limit of human achievement, that I was
headed toward oblivion. But it turned out that wasn't
the case.

I went abroad once more, this time, to India.

I took a few believers with me, and we did medical
work in poor areas. The disparity between the wealthy
and the poor in that country was very interesting to me.
Right beside someone who might as well have been a

billionaire was a child with only one arm, begging. His parents had cut off one of his arms in a bid for sympathy. I was curious what I would feel saving the lives of weak children now that I was losing energy myself. But the satisfaction was quite weak. My temperature continued to decline despite the strong sunlight shining down on me. Huts made of scraps of cloth, the clouds of dust cars kicked up—it all seemed somehow unnatural.

I walked along a road a little outside of the center of town. I suddenly felt sexual desire. I wasn't sure why. There was nothing there to arouse me. I noticed a dirty ball rolling right in front of me. That ball stood out strangely from its surroundings—it seemed to overflow with its own presence. I looked past that ball and saw a girl and her mother. The girl was balancing awkwardly on top of a tall wall while her young mother was talking to someone on one of the pay phones that had just started appearing in the area. She wasn't watching her daughter. Judging from their appearance, they were well-off. The ball rolled toward the girl. She finally noticed. My throat grew dry and my heart began to race.

She'll fall, I thought. She'll be distracted because of the ball I kicked, and she'll fall. I wasn't sure why, but I had a feeling she wouldn't survive the fall. The road wasn't paved, but the ball rolled straight along it. It was as if that ball were drawing a beautiful line, a straight line that would cause the girl to fall. I hadn't planned it. My leg had kicked that ball reflexively, its motion never passing through my consciousness. I noticed the rest after. The slowness of consciousness, and the motion of the mind . . . It was as though my mind had moved my body so as to invite me to action, because I was losing strength and doing nothing. She'll fall, I thought. The ball drew closer. Not yet? Will it take a little longer? No one could stop that ball rolling any longer. The ball arrived right below the girl. The girl jumped toward the ball as if she were trying to get the attention of her mother. I was breathless. The moment her small body hit the stony ground below she appeared an adult in my eyes. I thought about that body jarred by that impact, and I lusted intensely for it.

Her mother screamed and ran to her. But they no longer looked like people to me. There was one collection of particles that because of a violent impact had begun to lose its life, and another collection of particles running toward it, and a collection of particles that was me. Human identity had been lost. My lust quickly subsided, and it seemed that all that was in front of me was the movement of those particles. That straight line the ball had followed, the line that had caused such a stir in the particles, was perfectly clear. I approached them without any feelings of good or evil or lust. It was as though there were two collections of particles in front of me that both did a good job imitating humans. But actually, humans really are just collections of particles, so they weren't imitating anything. I stopped my consciousness. I could do it. I heard my own voice.

"You have a beautiful face."

And then I strangled that mother. *Can I do this?* I wondered the whole time. I wondered if I was going to kill her because the girl who had lost her life so violently a moment ago looked like her mother. No one was around. In this area where there was so much crime, what would anyone think of a woman's brief screaming? The wall in front of me and the two abandoned cars would shield me from view. Though I was surrounded by humans, I was in a space visually separated from them entirely. The mother's eyes were full of confusion—why was she being strangled? That was only natural. I didn't know why either. My body grew cold, and everything became awkward. I tore at her clothes, pushed her down, and licked her body. As I strangled her, I began moving my hips, imagining I was raping the girl who had just died. I felt that if that girl had lived, this would have been her. I felt as if I could see time. The past, the future that should have come, and the future that would actually arrive were all mixed together. But I wasn't aroused—I did what I did as though it were my duty. I had felt that sense of duty several times before. That sense of duty separated me from physical sensations. I was moving away from reality, leaving a shell of particles behind me. I was in a dangerous place of knowledge. The world was changing. I had peeked inside the world—I had seen past its surface particles. I was crushing that woman for the me behind the real me, the me who was still human, still looking at the surface of that world, feeling carnal pleasure—for those particles that made up the me behind me. I wasn't sure if she was dead yet, but I humped her. Pleasure formed behind me. The straight line that had led me here had finished its job; it began to waver, to loosen, and eventually eddied out of existence. That line had probably marked the moment a human lost his humanity. The scene I saw when I raped that woman was different from everything before. There was no warmth, no meaning, no sensation. The thing I had previously recognized as a woman grew blurry. It was as if the laws of perspective had vanished. It seemed everything was cloudy, but also clear. The pleasure of humiliating this woman continued to build within my body. But I had slipped beneath the surface of this world. There was no happiness, or loneliness, or pleasure. Just particles joining together and drifting around. Everything was there, and nothing. Particles were born and then vanished, vanished and then were born again. And the organ I was could do nothing more than stare as though that had some sort of meaning. For a moment, I felt terribly scared. A cold shiver spread inside me. I was terrified because I had always existed in this sort of system. The cold I felt inside myself and the cold of the scene may have actually been one and the same. But that fear was momentary. I became accustomed to it, and became part of the scene. I came inside the woman. I didn't feel anything, but unbelievable pleasure exploded around me. After coming, the scene around me restabilized. I returned to myself, and my energy began to deplete rapidly again. I thought I had learned the secrets of god, the secret of this system that allows him to fool humans. From then on I'd occasionally see the world that way, and then return from that world to the human one, and be able to experience pleasure as I used to. I didn't fear it anymore.

. . . My final curiosity was to see what would happen to someone like me in the end. If there was a god, what sort of end would he give me? It would be fitting if I were destroyed. But nothing bad happened to my body. After decades, an abnormality appeared. Cancer. When I learned of it, I was slightly surprised at its ordinariness. I had lived so long and now had cancer. I, who tortured women, and sometimes even killed them, would die of cancer in the end. I wanted to ask god, is this enough of a punishment? Wouldn't something much more extreme have been appropriate? Won't this destroy the order of this world? I had drugs that would kill me before I felt any pain from that cancer. And since I had no attachment to this life, even that didn't make me unhappy. My cancer progressed normally, and I faced death normally. But because of my arrogance, I wanted my life to end with me facing off against god. I didn't care whether he existed or not. I couldn't be moved by anything that wasn't greater than me. If god didn't exist, I just needed to create him. If I did that, I could realize my own destruction. In other words—

Sawatari had fallen silent.

"Why are you telling me this?" Narazaki asked in a whisper. He was sitting in front of a monster, but he couldn't help but ask.

"You look like him."

"Who?"

"My assistant," Sawatari said vaguely. He seemed to have lost interest in what he had been talking about. "My assistant who watched me kill Nayirah. He was simple, but passionate. A hilariously incompetent man.

Back then he bothered me just very slightly. He couldn't do anything, and he didn't have the courage to criticize me publicly, but he always seemed like he wanted to say something."

"What are you talking about?"

"When Ryoko Tachibana set her eyes on not that detective, but you, I saw your photo in her papers, and thought it would be kind of interesting to see that soft-hearted assistant ultimately begin to devour women, too. And now we will be engulfed in flames."

"What?"

"You still don't understand?" Sawatari spoke as though even speaking was a burden to him. "This has all been arranged for my destruction. I don't have any beliefs to prove. This is nothing more than a terribly selfish act to celebrate the final moments of my life."

"That's . . ."

"That's all. There's nothing else."

Narazaki stared blankly at Sawatari. His mind raced through everything he had heard was happening—the riot-police raid, the terror attack on the television station, the unexploded bombs, the two Self-Defense Force planes that had gone missing. "You set this all up?"

"That's right."

"How many people—"

"They never expected that I'd attack China. Isn't it spectacular? I found some Self-Defense Force officers who were interested in certain kinds of radical thought. I encouraged them for a long time, fermented their anger at the government. I don't have any political beliefs. I don't care about politics at all . . . The riot police will be here soon. They will probably open up holes in the bottom of this building and enter through the sewers."

Sawatari leaned back in his chair.

"When the riot police enter, I will kill myself amid the raging flames. That will be my last moment. Fitting. I can't have Matsuo at my side, but I thought I should at least have you, the assistant who assisted me in taking my first life, Nayirah's. The good, pure man I ruined with women. You're here as a little art piece, part of my tired performance. Just like these flames . . . This is all being recorded."

Narazaki couldn't move.

"By now this live recording should have been brought to the attention of Sasahara and the others who have taken over JBA . . . To those who thought I was going to send my final orders."

Smoke began to rise from behind Sawatari's furniture.

"Those men who have been abandoned by the world will be abandoned again—by me . . . That's a bit amusing."

"I . . ."

"Won't let me? You, who devoured my women?"

Sawatari was watching Narazaki. Narazaki couldn't say anything. Flames rose higher. Sawatari stood.

"All the believers here should be sleeping by now. They took drugs as part of the ceremony . . . What will become of those people abandoned by the world, and then abandoned by me? It would be interesting if they go on to do even more evil. I think they could probably use a bit of a shock. But it doesn't really matter. The weapons downstairs are all toys, anyway. They couldn't kill anyone with them if they tried. If you want them to live, let them live. Do what you want. I don't care about that sort of thing anymore . . . Go."

The flames rising behind Sawatari grew larger. Smoke billowed, and Narazaki tried to speak. "I . . ."

"Didn't you hear me?" Sawatari said idly, as if he were brushing away a bug. "I don't care about you."

The world was crumbling away. Narazaki realized he had exited Sawatari's room. What didn't crumble away was the fact that he had tried to believe in this man's power, that he was surprised by how hurt he was, and that he had lost Tachibana by losing himself to the women this man had provided him with.

Narazaki's legs were carrying him toward the stairs, but his uncertainty overwhelmed him and he froze. *What should I do? What? What should someone as pathetic as me to do at a time like this?*

Sawatari stood among the flames and smoke. He showed no sign of discomfort.

The color of the fire shone faintly on his white clothes. He took a gun from his pocket. Even that action seemed like a chore to him. He was slightly disappointed by how slowly the fire was spreading; he'd hoped to be more thoroughly engulfed by the flames. He stared at the gun. He pulled back the hammer. He paused, seemed to remember something, then pointed the gun at his genitals.

Sawatari put his finger on the trigger.

But he didn't move. He stared blankly at his crotch and then at the muzzle of the gun.

He moved the gun suddenly up to his temple and pulled the trigger. There was a dry noise, and then he collapsed.

The door behind him opened. Mineno approached Sawatari. He was on the ground, surrounded by flames, with the gun in his hand. His hand had slipped, and the bullet had passed only partially through his skull. He was dying, but not dead. Mineno crouched down next to Sawatari and tugged him into her arms.

"Aren't you surprised I'm still here?" she whispered. Sawatari looked up at her strangely. "I was listening the whole time, although I only heard about half of what you said. Does it hurt? But that pain won't give you the destruction you desired, will it?"

Mineno smiled. She stared into Sawatari's face and kissed him.

Sawatari looked shocked. The flames rose behind them.

"You've been repelled by everything, and now you're a little pathetic . . ." Mineno smiled. "What if your whole plan was arranged by god?"

The furniture of the room began to collapse into the fire. "If this was the will of god, it might be wrong for me to interfere . . . Goodbye."

Mineno kissed Sawatari again. It was a long kiss. He didn't move. Mineno wasn't sure when he died, since his eyes never stopped staring up blankly.

". . . Mineno-san."

Narazaki wasn't sure why he'd returned, but the moment he heard the gun fire, he was back in the room. The flames and smoke were growing more intense. Sawatari was already dead.

"It's dangerous. Let's get out of here." Narazaki pulled on Mineno's arm. She was just sitting there.

"Why?" Mineno whispered. "Why do we have to live? Why do we need life?"

Narazaki couldn't answer. He was just overcome with rage. Rage at this world. Rage at his own insignificance.

Narazaki pulled Mineno away, leaving her question unanswered. Behind them, Sawatari's body was engulfed by flames. Sawatari burned just like the floor and chairs around him. There was nothing at all special about the fire that consumed him.

This isn't Takahara-kun, Tachibana realized.

It wasn't just the voice that was wrong. She also sensed an odd energy emanating from the other end of the line. Someone had taken Takahara's phone.

Her fingers grew damp with sweat. "Where is Takahara?" She spoke impulsively—later she would wonder how the words escaped her mouth. "I speak in the name of R."

It was risky—whoever was on the other end might be related to R, or impersonating members of R. There was also a chance that they were with the police. It might also have been someone from the cult.

The fifty-something man also had to think. Were there really members of R out there? If this person was connected to R, would it be expedient to just tell her where Takahara was? Briefly, the man ran through all the possibilities. Takahara still seemed to be a long way from making a decision.

He might get scared. In which case, R might give him a final push.

He could not ignore the possibility that this person had nothing to do with R. Yet that was just what he decided to do. He smiled weakly. He felt as though he were part of some great flow. Why not just move along with the current? Sawatari's image floated up momentarily in the back of his mind.

When he'd first seen Sawatari, this man was still in his twenties and had just joined the Public Security Bureau. He was investigating a new cult that was fomenting public unrest. The man impersonated a member and followed along on a supposed charity trip Sawatari took to the Philippines. He trailed Sawatari as he walked lazily through Manila. Sawatari hadn't turned and looked at him even once. But suddenly, he changed directions and approached him. The man was uneasy. Had he been made?

Sawatari closed in on him in the open-air market, noisy with locals. It would be dangerous to run now. The man waited. Maybe a path would open up. He still hoped Sawatari might not suspect him.

Sawatari walked right up to him, then suddenly grabbed his chin. It felt as if his body were floating in the air. He couldn't speak. He was more than surprised. He was genuinely scared.

"You've got some time, I see," Sawatari said. "To come all this way."

His cover was blown. It was over. Would he be killed? He had heard that several people close to Sawatari had died mysteriously.

But Sawatari didn't move. He looked straight into the

man's eyes. He stared so long that the man thought he had stop breathing.

"Mm . . . I see," Sawatari whispered. "You're a monster yourself."

Sawatari turned his back and walked away as though he'd already forgotten him. The man sat there, his heart still racing, his breathing wild, unable to move. Sawatari had seen through him. He couldn't stop sweating. *Is that the sort of person it takes to found a religion? Or is this man just special?* The man felt as though his own hopes and his dark passions had been stripped bare. Sawatari had reached inside him and seen the filth buried so deep that to acknowledge it would be to acknowledge that nothing could save him.

There was nothing else that had ever reached so deep inside him.

"I'm sorry. I am holding on to this phone for Takahara-sama," the man said.

"Where is he?" the woman on the line asked.

The fifty-something man let out a silent sigh. *This can't be right*, he thought. *If she were impersonating a member of R to find Takahara's location, she would have asked who we are, and why we have his cell phone.* Was this Ryoko Tachibana? Regardless, he admired her intuition and bravery.

"According to the GPS in the phone he's carrying now, he is in downtown Nishigamori-chō. Under the clock tower."

The fifty-something man was telling the truth. He was smiling. He didn't know how this would end, but he genuinely wanted her to know that much.

"I see. I'll head there now."

She hung up too fast, the man thought. *She forgot to feel out the situation.* The man leaned back deep into the sofa, still smiling. He placed the cell phone on the table and reached for his tea.

"Who was that?" the thirty-something man asked.

All the older man said was, "It's almost ten. Time for the explosions."

The room was dark. The thirty-something man stood up. "I'm going to pay him a visit. If he gets cold feet, I'll exert some pressure. I'll get the numbers from him and dial them myself if it comes to that."

"He won't tell you anything," the older man whispered. He didn't seem to enjoy his tea, but he drank it anyway.

"In any case . . . He's seen our faces."

The fifty-something man looked at him closely as the younger man gathered his things. "Do you know who Karl Eichmann is?"

"Not in detail."

The hands of the clock moved steadily.

"He was a Nazi official, integrally involved in the Holocaust. He's remembered as cold-blooded, but sometimes he would pull a flask of liquor out of his breast pocket and drink. It took liquor for Eichmann to be able to do that kind of killing. But for you . . ." The fifty-something man put his cup back on the table. "You don't need anything."

The younger man didn't understand. He headed toward the door.

"I've decided to retire," the older man said, stopping the younger in his tracks. "You take care of the rest, Child-Rearing Samurai."

NARAZAKI AND Mineno walked down the stairs and got in the elevator.

Narazaki had always thought the top of the building was set up strangely. The 21st floor where Sawatari lived was only connected to the lower floors by stairs. Was that by design, so that the flames wouldn't spread to the rest of the building? If that were the case, Sawatari had already thought about this ending when he moved the cult here.

They got out of the elevator and headed to the great hall. It was just as Sawatari had said: believers collapsed, empty cups scattered among them.

In the middle of them was a giant vat and the charred remains of a small fire. Maybe it had all been part of the ceremony.

"They're not dead. Then why knock them all out?" Maybe Sawatari hadn't wanted them to interfere with his suicide. But he could have killed them. "Was he trying to save them?"

"There's no way," Mineno whispered.

"Maybe he felt bad for getting them so riled up."

"Even though he made them that way?" Narazaki and Mineno looked down on the sleeping believers. When they woke up, they would have to face the truth. "I don't think anything mattered to that man. Even killing himself seemed like a chore to him . . . He didn't have any use for them anymore, and they'd started to annoy him, so he put them to sleep. If he'd had poison, he probably would have killed them instead. That's just the kind of person he was."

Narazaki picked up a gun from the ground. It looked like the real thing, but what if what Sawatari had said was true? Narazaki thought through the possibilities.

"The whole country freaking out about a cult of passed-out idiots with toy guns . . . What a nightmare for Japan." He picked up a fallen megaphone. "Let's tell the riot police that everyone is asleep. We can let in one camera so the police don't go wild. There are probably some idiots out there dying to cut loose in the name of national defense."

Lying on the floor by Mineno was the Cupro girl who had taken her USB drive. But Mineno didn't notice her. Narazaki looked at the bodies spread around them, thought of all the lives to be saved. His eyes paused on Komaki, lying still. He thought about her body. Sexual thoughts tried to take him over again, but he chased them away. Ryoko Tachibana was not lying in the great hall. *She must have escaped*, Narazaki thought. He'd worry about her later. "First we have to save these lives," he said out loud. Even if there was nothing he could do to save their spirits.

"They all wanted to die together with their leader," Mineno said. "Once they learn of his true intentions, will they be able to go on living? What's the point in trying to save them?"

The believers looked like babies lying asleep there. Children, each wounded in their own way. Maybe they were only safe in their dreams. On the top floor, Sawatari was burning.

"I don't know," Narazaki answered honestly.

Matsuo would do this, Narazaki thought. Matsuo would do whatever he could to stop these people from leaving this world, even if it was against their will, even if they shouted him down for getting in the way. Narazaki would follow the voice of Matsuo inside him. He believed that was his calling.

Narazaki picked up the megaphone. Outside was the vast expanse of reality. He had to calm their rage. He fought to steady his ragged breathing and faced the window.

"That can't be," Sasahara finally managed to whisper. He stared at the video playing on the computer. All the color had drained from his face. He had expected the video would be his final orders from the leader. If the leader had said to kill all the hostages, Sasahara would have. If the leader said to attack the riot police, Sasahara would have fired his gun with wild rapture. And when he was shot down, his last thought would have been of the leader, and he would have died happy. But Sasahara was just part of the leader's plan to destroy himself? Was that man on the video even really the leader? That man who'd shot himself? Sasahara felt a primal scream bubbling up inside him. If he didn't let it out, he'd go mad. The members and hostages were staring at him. Why? He realized he was already screaming. His consciousness stuttered. The image of the leader collapsing lingered in his mind. The shocked, staring members knew nothing. He took the headphones from his ears. He was still screaming. *The leader. The leader. No.* Tears were streaming from his eyes.

The leader he had adored.

The leader had ordered him to let Takahara plan the attack. He said that Takahara was very talented when it came to those sorts of things. When the time comes, take over, the leader said. It had been good advice. Takahara had even scripted what Sasahara should say on TV. When Yoshioka, who was in charge of weapons, suddenly got scared and said he wanted out, Sasahara had killed him without a second thought. The leader had not so much as batted an eye. *The leader is not attached to anything,* Sasahara realized. *That's right. That's the leader. The leader manipulates everyone around him like they're children.*

Sasahara had joined this cult because he was curious about the leader. He was interested in this man who was so different. Sasahara constantly fretted over everything. He wanted the leader's strength.

Before Sashara joined the cult, everything he did was half-assed. He'd considered himself talented, until he failed college entrance exams. That led to him not being able to find work, and he thought if he couldn't get the kind of job he deserved, there was no reason for him to work. Companies were a waste of time—groups of talentless humans who gathered together just because they were good at communicating. The people who always got in his way. But he couldn't find a way to beat them. Even though Sasahara deserved to be in a position of power in society, when he finally tried to straighten his life out, he couldn't find a job. His pride gradually eroded. He needed to convince himself of his own worth. Any sort of achievement would have been fine. But time passed and society gave him nothing, and gradually he felt his core beginning to twist out of shape. He wanted revenge on society, but he couldn't execute it. He didn't want to do anything petty, like becoming a random murderer. He just sat in his dark room, cursing the world.

There, in the darkness, he'd felt something calling him. Whatever it was, it must have carried him to the leader.

Of course the leader would do this. He betrayed us. Who besides the leader could care so little about the people around him? But Sasahara didn't even feel betrayed. *If I confronted him, the leader would probably just give me a funny look. And then he'd whisper to me, Yes, that's right, I betrayed you.*

Tears flowed from Sasahara's eyes. *But, but, but what should I do? Now that I've been abandoned by the leader, what should I do?* His cracking consciousness grew distant. He was going to pass out. Sasahara brought his fist down on his leg as hard as he could, trying to maintain his grip on reality. *I'm still here. So are the members, and the hostages. But it won't last. It's going to break. What should I do? What should I do?*

His vision was narrowing, but he saw a man approach him. The pervert who had tried to attack a woman in the bathroom. He was trying to say something.

"Tell me who." *What am I saying?* "Tell me who the leader is now. Give me someone to replace the leader. This is no good. It won't last. It's going to break. Tell me who! Tell me who!"

"I saw it," the man in front of him said. His face was pale. "I was watching. The leader is dead."

He saw! Sasahara's mind focused on that one single thought. *If he saw, I can't let him live.* A gun appeared in his field of vision. *I'll kill him first. That's all I can do. I don't know why, but it's my only choice. I'll kill the people here, and then myself. That's the only option left. No. Instead of suicide, after I kill them, I'll attack the riot police. I'll kill all of them, too.*

Sasahara pointed the gun at the man.

Just as he was about the pull the trigger, the man yelped, "There is no one to replace him!"

Suddenly, Sasahara found himself storming over to the hostages. He was screaming, "All of you, get up! Stand! One at a time. I'm going to shoot you."

The faces of the members changed. They still didn't know the truth; they thought it was an order from the leader.

"You can't. Please stop."

A man stood between Sasahara and the hostages. Through his hazy vision, he realized it was the pervert.

"Get out of the way."

"No."

"Why? Why are you stopping me?"

"Because," the man whispered. "Because my mother's here."

Sasahara stared at the man blankly. Then he stared at the terrified hostages behind him.

"There's no way she's here."

"Yes, she is. Well, women like my mother."

Sasahara didn't understand.

"What are you saying? I know all about you. You're just a thug who joined the faith so you could fuck all day long. I've hated believers like you from the very beginning. You're trash. Get out of here. If you don't, I'll shoot you first."

"I'm not going anywhere."

The man was shaking violently, but he stared at Sasahara's gun. He should have raised his arms to resist, but they were still hanging at his sides.

"Why? Why are you protecting them?"

"Because I love this world."

"This world? The world that abandoned you? That tormented you for being a pervert?"

"That's right." The man was crying. "I was abandoned by the world. I was always looked at with scorn by women. But I love women." He kept crying. "I'm a pervert, and I suffered for that, but sex is my core, and I love myself. Sex is the only thing I've ever believed in. I don't want to kill these women. I want to have sex with them. Even if I can't have sex with them, I want them to have sex, because sex is great. When I get angry, I forget about myself and try to do bad things. That's why I was really relieved from the bottom of my heart when the bombs didn't explode after I called the cell phone number. It was a good thing the numbers were wrong."

Sasahara stared, dazed, at the crying man.

"This religion is over. We're going to be thrown back into society. I'll probably live alone and jerk off all the time. Maybe I'll be able to go to brothels sometimes. But that's fine. Sex is amazing . . . And I really don't want to kill anyone. Killing people would mean rejecting sex. I can't let you kill these women. Or men. All sex is beautiful, men with women, men with men, women with women . . ." The man took a step toward Sasahara. "I learned how beautiful sex is from this faith. The women never rejected me. They accepted me, even though I was an outcast. That was the first time I was accepted by anyone in this world. They taught me . . . Isn't that right?"

Sasahara wasn't listening. He raised his gun. But the man tackled Sasahara and wrestled him to the ground. The hostages screamed. The other members didn't know what to do. They tried to pull the men apart. But the pervert had managed to steal the gun. He pointed it at Sasahara.

"Don't move. Don't even try to threaten me with your weapons—none of them are real. I'm holding the only real gun." The man was crying. He was shaking but held the gun steady. "Don't make me mad. Don't come any closer. If you come any closer, I don't know what I'll do. You should all watch the video. The video of the leader that Sasahara just watched. It's open right over there." He pointed to the computer Sasahara had just been using. "You should all watch it . . . Let's tell them on TV . . . That we surrender. And then . . ."

The man collapsed. Sasahara stood behind him, holding the pistol he used to shoot Takahara. He was close enough to take back the machine gun, but he couldn't move. One of the members was walking over to the computer. The others followed.

Takahara was still sitting on the ground watching the legs pass him by.

He thought about unrelated things, like how it might rain. *Three minutes until 10 p.m.* His mind was trying to avoid that thought. He wondered about his own lingering attachment to this world.

He lit yet another cigarette, and realized a pair of legs had stopped right next to him. When he looked up, his heart began to race. Ryoko? Why? Her head was silhouetted by the town's neon lights, and her eyes, locked on Takahara, looked damp.

"I finally found you," she whispered. *Found.* He wasn't sure why, but for some reason that word echoed inside him.

"Why are you here?"

"It's already over."

Pedestrians continued to pass them by. Stuck in traffic on

the way here, Ryoko Tachibana had caught up with the news on the car radio and the smartphone she'd stolen. Sawatari was dead. The cult's compound had been opened up. The members in the TV station had given themselves up. The two planes heading for China had been shot down by Japanese forces before they could engage with the Chinese military. The pilots had ejected themselves mid-flight, and it was yet to be confirmed whether they'd survived, but that wouldn't change the fact that Japanese soldiers had been shot down by Japanese soldiers.

Tachibana relayed that information to Takahara simply, one piece at a time. Takahara listened silently. Something about him was off. Aside from the news of Sawatari's death, he didn't appear to have heard any of it.

"So it's all over," she said again. "Now there's something you must do. No, something that we both must do." Despite her conflicted feelings, she said, "Let's turn ourselves in. And then testify that the leader brainwashed everyone, and the other believers were all essentially innocent . . . We're the only ones with the power to help right now. We need to make the others' punishment as light as possible."

"You're wrong."

"What?"

"It's not over yet."

Takahara stood up slowly. He looked at Tachibana. *She's beautiful*, he thought. He also thought unnecessary things like, *She could do something with her hair*. He couldn't touch her anymore. It seemed to him that his attachment to this world was all concentrated within her.

"Their attack may be over. But ours is not."

Invocation. Tachibana clung to the word. "Calm down and listen. I read your diary."

Takahara didn't react. He seemed to be distracted by something else.

"YG has been destroyed. There was an air raid—they're all wiped out. And their leader, Nigel, he's dead, too. Your nightmare—it's already over."

"I know that."

Tachibana was shocked at his words.

"But there are survivors."

"What do you mean?"

"They contacted me. They told me to carry out an attack in Japan."

"What if you're being tricked?"

"What?"

"Even if you were really approached by survivors—what authority do they have over you? It can't be what it used to be. And . . . they contacted you in Japanese, right?"

"How did you know that?"

"Remember. According to your diary, none of them could speak Japanese. You're being tricked. Sawatari, or some other group, was using you to carry out this attack."

"That can't be," Takahara whispered. "They tracked me down at the hospital—"

Tachibana cut him off. "What are you saying? The hospital where the police were holding you? Come on. Wake up! If the police were guarding you, how could anyone from YG have gotten to you?" Tachibana had an epiphany. "Was it two men, one older, and one relatively young?"

"How did you know that?"

"They're from the Public Security Bureau. I learned about

the two of them when I was working as a scout. They've been investigating us." Tachibana grabbed Takahara's shoulder. "Listen, you're not thinking straight. If you were your normal self, you would have realized something was off right away."

"Even if that is true." Takahara sounded like he was begging. "Even if things are as you say. Even if everything's been destroyed, and YG doesn't have the kind of power they used to. Even if somewhere along the way I was tricked by Sawatari and the Public Security Bureau, *can you say that there is zero possibility that was done by the will of Rarseshir, by the will of R?*"

"What?"

"What if . . . what if there really is a god? What if that god is Rarseshir, and he chose me to act in place of those organizations that were destroyed?"

"What are you saying?" Tachibana began to cry. She shook Takahara. "God would never ask for something like that!"

"You don't know. You don't know them."

"Takahara-kun!"

"I'll convince you . . . Not here. Let's go somewhere else."

Convince me? I'm the one who should be convincing him.

Takahara began to walk away. He seemed frightened. She followed him down a quiet street. There were fewer and fewer people. They entered a parking lot without a single car.

"Listen. YG is—"

"I don't care about YG." Tachibana didn't want to hear anything else. She pulled a gun out of her pocket.

"What are you doing?"

"I know what you're thinking. You're trying to protect me. They threatened you and told you to go through with this in exchange for my safety. So if that's it, if that's why . . ." Tachibana pointed the gun at her temple. "I'll just die."

"Hey!"

"Don't move." Tachibana began to cry, pressing the barrel of the gun to her own temple. "You plan on carrying out this attack and then dying, right? There's no meaning in a world without you. I've known that since long ago. If you die doing something horrible to protect me, I'm going to die anyway. We both lose either way."

"What are you saying?"

"No, what are you saying?"

Takahara couldn't move. Ryoko Tachibana did not make idle threats. *If I excite her, she might actually shoot.*

"Listen. Why did you get sucked into R? Fear—terror. They imprisoned you. But, when you look deeper . . . You were also drawn to them because of their teachings, their desire to rid the world of starvation, right? You were a victim of your own past. I don't know if it was a conscious or unconscious choice, but part of you wanted to be brainwashed . . . And there's one other thing. You look down on others," Tachibana continued. "You were trying to reject the life that was passing you by, right? Becoming a terrorist and dying young—some part inside of you wanted that, right?"

"That may be true," Takahara admitted. He had realized that a long time ago. "But how can you respect any of this world's organizations? Let's say we turn ourselves in to the police, like you want. If we did that, my life would be over. I'd just be giving in to my past, and be mocked by all the people I hate. I don't want to lead that kind of pathetic life."

"Of course," Tachibana screamed. "That's why a part of you wanted things to end up like this. You're trying to make

yourself into an idiot legend through terrorism. But that's
not true power. Even if you're unhappy, even if you think
you're suffering, live until the end. That's true power."
Tachibana's voice dropped. "I feel like I've finally understood what Matsuo-san meant when he said life isn't about
comparisons. That you have to live following your path,
your own path. It's fine to get ideas from others. To be influ-
enced by them. But it's no good to compare too much. Are
you listening? Hear me out. *It doesn't matter how you compare to others.* What's important is to walk the path of your
own life as it appears before you. There's no meaning in
comparing yourself to others. Every life has the same value.
The problem is—no matter what kind of life you have—the
problem is how you live it. Each life is independent. You
must spend your unique, individual time all the way to its
end. No matter what kind of life you live, even if it's one that
doesn't fulfill you, isn't it a great thing to see it through? The
more difficult your life is, the more you struggle to make it
better, the greater you are when you've lived it through. So
please, stop this stupid bullshit. Let's go to the police. Help
me make the other members' punishments just a little bit
lighter. It doesn't matter if people laugh at us. I don't care.
We should live our lives proudly. How about it?"

"But R . . ."

"Idiot." Tachibana pounded his chest with her fist. That
was all she could do. "You're brainwashed. What matters to
you more? Me or god?"

Takahara stared at Tachibana blankly. He felt like his world
was crumbling. But in the corner of his peripheral vision he
noticed a single man. Takahara's heart began to race.

"That man's here."

"What?"

"Don't look." The warmth of her body spread through his. "I'll believe what you say for now. Honestly, I'm still not sure myself, but I'll make myself believe you. They're not part of R. But if they're members of the Public Security Bureau . . . we have to outsmart them. I have an idea."

"What?"

"You've got a smartphone, right? Leave me here, find somewhere he won't be able to see you, and record what he does."

"But—"

"Catch him on video, an investigator approaching a terrorist. If there's video, he won't be able to make any excuses."

"Takahara-kun."

"I'll get rid of him. I'll be fine. This is to help the other members, right?"

Tachibana let go of Takahara. She let go solemnly. She turned and went around the corner, pretending she hadn't noticed the man. *For the other members,* she thought. *But really . . .*

But really, none of this matters. Really, I should have said what I wanted to.

Let's run away together.

It's fine if we're mocked by the world. Just the two of us, together forever.

But Tachibana began to film. *When this is done, I'll tell Takahara-kun,* she thought. She felt something inside her beginning to loosen, to crumble. *I don't want to go to prison. If things don't go well, I may never be able to leave. We'll give this video to Yoshiko-san. It's selfish of me, but I want to set myself free.*

Tachibana was warm from Takahara's touch for the first time in a long while, and tears began streaming down her face again.

She watched through the screen of the smartphone as the man approached Takahara. It was one of the Public Security Bureau men. The young one.

THE THIRTY-SOMETHING man was irritated.

The cult members had surrendered just as orders to invade were issued. The heavily armed riot police had been facing down a bunch of insurgents with mostly fake guns. The nation was already losing face. Panic had spread through the people and the media when the two Self-Defense planes deserted—not because they were afraid of terrorists, but because they were afraid of the government. Of militarization. On TV, terrorists talked about the problems of poverty, and criticized the government and allied corporations extensively. The force of that message was also already spreading through the world. This was the worst possible situation.

But there was still one possible solution. He had to get this man, Takahara, to set off those explosives. The Public Security Bureau could say that the cult had pretended to surrender and then set off the bombs. And that they weren't done yet. That they'd just gone underground. Everyone would support the government in fighting the imaginary enemy. Everything would go the way they wanted.

But what if he got scared?

Was it just in his head? Takahara's face looked a little different than before. It was probably just in his head.

"Do you know what time it is?" the thirty-something man asked quietly. Takahara nodded. "Really?" He looked at his watch. "You have two more minutes."

The man did not miss the look of misgiving that crossed Takahara's face. Of course. He still wasn't prepared. He had been right to come.

"Do it already. No need to wait two minutes."

"No." There was hesitation in Takahara's voice. The man could hear it, even if Takahara tried to hide it. "I'll do it on the hour."

"Don't tell me you're not ready?"

"Of course I'm ready!"

"Tell me the numbers. I'll do it for you."

Takahara's eyes met the man's. They were the same age, although Takahara didn't know it.

He slowly pulled the cell phone from his pocket. He dialed numbers with his thumb. The moment stretched between them.

"Let's end these games. You're not part of R. You're from the Public Security Bureau. Isn't that right?"

The thirty-something man met Takahara's gaze. "Yes, let's come clean. That's right. I work for Public Security."

"Whether I press the buttons or not, you'll kill me. Isn't that right?"

"That's right." Of course they couldn't let him live. He had seen their faces.

"Even if I run now," Takahara said after taking a deep breath. "You'll use every agency in this country to track me down. Right?"

"That's right."

It was past ten. "I have a request," Takahara said. His own

voice sounded meeker than he had ever heard. Defenseless. "Please, let me go."

The thirty-something man said nothing. He just stared at Takahara.

"Politics, religion. I don't care about any of it anymore. I'll never tell a soul about you. I . . ." Takahara spoke in an unimaginably childish voice. "I want to live."

The thirty-something man took out a gun and shot him in the head.

I have to move, Takahara thought, but his body didn't move. A terrible heat ran through his body, like it was begging for more time. He felt himself falling to the ground, but his vision was locked on that image of the man lifting his gun. The moment he wondered if he was still conscious, he felt his eyelids closing. He felt himself being forcibly ended. It was completely different from the feeling of falling asleep. A dark shadow enveloped his vision.

That was his final moment.

When Tachibana saw the man take out a gun through the smartphone screen, her mind could no longer keep up with what was happening. She knew she gasped. But by that time, Takahara's body had already fallen.

No, she thought. *This can't be true. Takahara-kun said he'd be fine. This is some kind of mistake.*

She thought she was going to scream—she was forcing herself to stifle that scream. The smartphone slipped out of her hand.

What am I doing? Shouldn't I scream, run to Takahara, get myself shot by that man? Why am I still hiding here and fighting back my screams? Why? The moment she thought it, she realized she was worried about the video. *If I'm killed here, he'll take this video. Takahara-kun's death will become meaningless. I have to hold back my screams now.* Tachibana's eyes were filled with tears. *How can I make such calm judgments? How can I be so silent at a time like this?* You look like your mother. *Am I like her? Am I suppressing my sadness at Takahara-kun's death? Am I trying to present myself to them as the heroine of some tragedy? Am I demanding thanks? No. No, Takahara-kun is dead. No, he's not. He can't be dead.* You look like your mother. *I don't. And he's not dead. I . . . I . . .*

Tachibana realized she had screamed. The moment she heard her voice, she felt something inside her drop. She felt set free. Her tears flowed. *This is fine. I'll die here with Takahara-kun.* The man was coming toward her. *I'll die here. It's fine. It's fine now. I'll go with Takahara-kun . . .* Suddenly, the man froze. He had heard something. A scream from another direction. There was another witness.

The thirty-something man took off at a run.

Tachibana ran toward Takahara. Tears were dripping down her face. She held her mouth. His head—he'd been shot in the head. Of all places, that man shot him in the head.

"Hey . . ."

She heard that word come from his mouth. But Takahara was no longer conscious. He was probably not aware of his voice.

"Am I forgiven for my sins?"

"Sins?" she asked, holding his arm and crying. "You've never sinned. There's no way you could have. You were hurt when you were a little boy, and just tried your best to live in your own clumsy way. You don't have any sins."

Takahara lay still. Tachibana couldn't speak.

"Takahara-kun," she tried to say, crying. But she couldn't. Her words vanished halfway through.

"Let's run away togeth . . ."

THE THIRTY-SOMETHING man got in his car and drove away from the scene.

He turned the steering wheel gently and thought about the witnesses. Who was that woman? And there was another woman behind me. *But they are harmless. They don't know who I am.*

The police in that jurisdiction were under their control. There was no problem.

He noticed there was blood on his sleeve. The man clicked his tongue. *I just took this shirt to the cleaners. If I keep taking it in, the fabric will wear thin.*

He was forgetting something. *That's right. I need to sympathize with that man, Takahara. Because that's what proper humans do.*

How sad, the man in his thirties made himself think. He's another sacrifice. Another sacrifice for this system called the country. I don't want to do these things either. He was a noble sacrifice. There's no helping it. He had no luck. The man thought about all of the things he should think at a time like this. He was the sort of person who could instantly come up with a reason for his actions. And once people have a good enough reason, they can do anything. He did think it was a bit of a bother to justify everything he did, but it also made him feel safe inside. *Why do I have to do this instead of someone else? And get my sleeve dirty too? He should have just killed himself. If he had, I wouldn't have to go through all this trouble.*

The man went home. He lived in a rather nice apartment.

It was owned by the government and used to house government employees. He only paid a small rent, but he was unhappy to have to pay rent at all.

When he opened the front door, his wife came to greet him. Normally she'd take his bag, but for some reason she was excited today.

"What is it?"

"He stood up."

"Huh?"

"Kai-kun stood up!"

The man rushed inside. His son, Kaito, was standing. He was standing on his own two unstable legs.

"Kai-kun!" the man yelled. This wasn't a performance. It was a moment acknowledged to be beautiful in every culture around the globe. "You're standing! You're amazing!"

His wife smiled and watched her overjoyed husband hug their child. She had already noticed the spots of blood on his sleeve. But she didn't show any reaction. She didn't care what her husband did to whom outside of this apartment. If her family was happy—and more important than anything, if everyone thought her family was happy—that's all that mattered. If her husband was a gangster or something, of course that blood would bother her. But her husband worked for the government. That made him a just, honorable man.

A speck of blood clung to Kaito, and a little gunpowder residue.

After getting out of the bath, the man checked Twitter on his smartphone. His handle was Child-Rearing Samurai.

I'VE GOT A BIG ANNOUNCEMENT! he typed. FOR THE FIRST TIME EVER, KAI-KUN STOOD UP!

The man wasn't sure which emoji to put at the end. A crying one, or a happy one? The man's face showed far less expression than any emoji. He chose a crying one, and tweeted his message. Responses came from his followers, one after another. The man smiled faintly. He wasn't satisfied unless he could tell others about every happy part of his life.

But those responses were slightly strange. Many of them seemed excited about some news.

HOW GREAT! REMEMBERING MY CHILDHOOD MAKES ME CRY, TOO. THE WORLD IS SO SCARY, WE HAVE TO HANG ON TO THESE HAPPY MOMENTS.

There was a photo attached. It was him standing in front of Takahara's body.

CONGRATULATIONS, KAI-KUN! GOOD JOB! I GUESS YOU DON'T KNOW, BUT EVERYONE'S RILED UP OVER THE BIG NEWS. THIS MAN SHOT A TERRORIST. HOW SCARY! CHECK IT OUT ON YOUTUBE! THEY STARTED SHOWING IT ON TV, TOO! SO SHOCKING!

Everything was there in that video. His conversation with Takahara. His face.

30

Many members had gathered at Matsuo's mansion.

People talked happily in the garden and the sitting rooms. The police had busted into the mansion and arrested many of them, but they were all released right away. They resumed the regular meetings Matsuo had held on the second Tuesday of every month.

Yoshiko removed herself from the group and walked quietly to the front gate. A woman in a hat and a blue coat was waiting there. It was Tachibana.

"I'm sorry . . . Making you come out here." Tachibana had been one of Sawatari's group that had scammed Matsuo. She couldn't enter the mansion.

"Don't worry . . . I'm sure you were innocent. An unintentional accomplice. Isn't that right?"

That was true. But still Tachibana felt responsible.

Yoshiko read Tachibana's mind. "Please, don't worry about it. Come in."

"I . . . I can't." Tachibana looked into Yoshiko's eyes. "I'm going to the police now."

The aftermath of the events was still a hot topic on the news.

A body had been found in the basement of the cult's facility; the specific cause of death was unknown. The explosives Takahara and his gang had set up had been located, thanks to the confessions of several of the believers, and had all been safely disposed of. All in all, no ordinary civilians had died. In fact, the only person who died was the leader, who committed suicide (and the gun found in the burned wreckage had been empty— he'd had only a single bullet). Takahara, a leading insurgent, had been shot by an investigator for the Public Security Bureau, but miraculously lived. The Public Security Bureau's shady behind-the-scenes work had come to light. It would be strange if people didn't get riled up over such a story.

The believers were currently being held in prison. How they would be tried and sentenced was also getting a lot of attention. No one was sure what kind of crimes they could be charged with. They had fake guns—that was all. Those who occupied the TV station—especially Sasahara, who also shot a security guard—were expected to receive heavy sentences, but the other believers? They had all turned themselves in.

Because of the video showing Takahara's exchange with that man from Public Security, a feeling of distrust spread through the country. People speculated that the person who took that video was the woman who escaped from the cult's facility in an ambulance, disguised as a hostage. So of course Tachibana, who really did release that video, was wanted.

"I have to testify for their sake."

Yoshiko's eyes filled with tears. Tachibana was so earnest. This child. Life must be hard on her.

"I see. That's the way you live, isn't it?"

"That's right."

Yoshiko hugged Tachibana. *She's warm*, Tachibana thought. Tears began to well up in her eyes as well.

"We are all on your side. No matter what happens, we'll protect you. Trust us."

Tachibana nodded. She wiped tears from her eyes, still wrapped up in Yoshiko's small arms.

"How is Takahara-kun?" Yoshiko asked.

Tachibana shook her head. "He'll probably never regain consciousness . . . But."

"Yes."

"They're still not sure. There may be a miracle."

"You don't have to fight so hard," Yoshiko said. She looked straight into Tachibana's eyes. "You never did anything wrong. We will support you. When you get out, please come back here."

"Yes."

"I'll go with you to the police."

"No. I'll go alone."

Yoshiko noticed Narazaki standing off to the side. Yoshiko looked at him, then at Tachibana, hugged her once again, and walked away.

Tachibana had noticed Narazaki long ago. A warm wind flowed from the mansion through the gate.

"I . . . said some horrible things to you." Narazaki spoke in a whisper.

"It's fine," Tachibana said, smiling. "It's all fine. Don't worry about it."

They shared a silence. They both knew they would never be together again.

"What are you going to do now?"

"I'm going to the police."

"I see. I, I really . . . Tachibana-san, I . . ." Narazaki's voice was growing fainter, but he somehow managed to put some strength into it. "I'm glad I met you."

Tachibana looked at Narazaki's face. She could have chosen to be with him.

"Thank you. I'm glad, too."

"Take care."

"You, too."

Yoshiko watched them from afar, and let out a faint sigh.

"They would have made such a great couple," she found herself muttering. "But even they couldn't stick together."

UNREST CREPT over Yoshiko as she walked back into the mansion. She remembered what Matsuo had said after filming his final message.

Only killing Sawatari will end this tragedy. But if he dies, many believers will commit suicide.

Sawatari was dead, and so far no one had committed suicide. It seemed like nothing had gone as Matsuo had prophesied. But what if it wasn't over yet?

Yoshiko shook her head, willed her thoughts to clear. *We just have to get through this.*

Yoshiko tried to smile. *If Shotaro were here, that's what he'd tell me. We just have to get through this.*

TACHIBANA TRIED to hail a cab.

She needed courage to go to the police. She couldn't be

sure what sorts of crimes she'd be charged with, but her testimony would certainly be problematic for the courts.

They'll crucify me in the media. All my faults, my darkest secrets, will be in every paper.

No taxis passed by. When she began walking, thinking it best to try another road, she saw Mineno. The other woman had a shopping bag in her hand.

"Tachibana-san! You're not going to the mansion?"

"I'm going to the police."

"Oh . . ." Mineno looked at the ground. She thought of many things she could say, but eventually decided to be frank. "We'll never be friends, will we?"

"I guess not."

The two smiled faintly at each other.

"It's fine, though. I'm not particularly unhappy," Tachibana said. She wasn't just putting on a strong face. "Takahara-kun won't wake up, so I doubt I'll be able to stay entirely faithful to him."

Mineno caught herself smiling at Tachibana's words.

A taxi came by, and Tachibana hailed it.

"Tachibana-san," Mineno said as Tachibana was about to get in the cab. "I hated you, but . . . I was just jealous."

"Yeah?" Tachibana stepped into the cab. "I probably felt the same. I wanted to be like you."

THE MEMBERS gathered around Yoshiko. Yoshiko's voice still carried well, and she didn't need a mic. In the middle of the sitting room was Matsuo's picture.

"Everyone, thank you for coming today."

Today was the forty-ninth day after Matsuo's death. While it varies from sect to sect, in Buddhism it is thought that on the forty-ninth day, the soul of the deceased finally leaves this world. In other words, where it will go in the next life had been decided. There's a customary service, and close friends and relatives gather.

"Yoshida-san was supposed to chant a sutra for us, but he's ill and has lost his voice. He's called a monk to serve in his place. Everyone, please boo Yoshida-san."

The crowd booed Yoshida. He tried to reply, but he couldn't speak. Everyone laughed.

"For Matsuo, pacifism was the ultimate ideal. But if we just call it an ideal and make excuses about reality, it's easy to fall into the pattern of not acting to make reality better. If we abandon our ideals, humanity will move backward. What's important is to hold up our ideals proudly, and work hard to try and make them real. Let's be proud as Japanese people striving for peace. As we follow in Shotaro Matsuo's footsteps, we will not simply follow him lock-step, our heads lowered. Let's also add our own ideas to his!"

Yoshiko took a deep breath.

"We will affirm this world. It doesn't have to be the whole world. Let's affirm parts of it. There are certainly good things in this world, and there are good parts of each of us, even though we have our faults. Matsuo had his faults." Yoshiko paused. "Long ago when I was poor and working in a brothel, I went for a walk outside in the snow. I was hungry, and I found a small cart selling steamed potatoes on a dark road. I had almost no money, but I bought one. When I took a bite, I thought, Wow, this is delicious. Suddenly, I found myself crying. I thought, *even someone like me can find happiness in food*. There are parts of this world that are kind even to the lowliest of us . . . Even if you have no sense of taste, there must be something else you can appreciate. Maybe beautiful scenery. If you can't see, maybe you can appreciate beautiful sounds. If you can't hear, maybe you can appreciate warm touches. Even if you can't feel the touch of another . . ."

An image of Takahara appeared in the back of Yoshiko's mind.

"Maybe you can dream. If you're alive, you must have a dream, even if it's something very small. Something you can affirm in the world. Even if we ourselves are the only change we can make in the world—just adding that one positive attitude—that's something. Let's just do simple good things. If everyone in Japan chipped in one hundred yen, we'd have twelve billion yen. It would be enough to change the world. In our day-to-day lives, let's all do just a little bit. Care about something; be a gear in the machine that will turn this world toward good."

There was a burst of applause. But that applause was not for Yoshiko's words. It was for all of humanity. It was an act of encouragement. Humans are imperfect and unstable, but somehow keep on living. *Shotaro.* Yoshiko whispered his name in her head. Amid all the applause, she looked at his photo. *I will not go to you yet. There's still a lot I have to do. I have to help those in front of me. I also have to help those cult members who have been imprisoned. They may say I'm a nuisance, but I will live like you did.*

Yoshiko was already old, but there was still a passion burning inside her.

Life is strange. Yoshiko smiled. *I never had children, but I wound up surrounded by all these kids.*

"Everyone, I am a human. I'm unstable, but I am human."

The applause continued, and cheers rang out.

"Let's go on living together!"

THE RAIN suddenly stopped.

I'm still not used to this weather, Narazaki thought. *You always have to have an umbrella. The people here don't seem to mind getting wet. Maybe since rain is part of nature, getting wet is natural.*

There was some money set aside in Matsuo's will to create teams to do volunteer work overseas. The various groups split up the money and started different organizations. Narazaki's group was using the money to buy freedom for young prostitutes. They set up a facility where those girls could live and attend school.

Meanwhile, Tachibana was still fighting the courts. Mineno was living with Yoshiko in the mansion.

Narazaki didn't feel entirely settled. He worried about an attack on their school, that an armed organization might try to kidnap the girls studying there. The anxious voices in his head never quieted. And their plan was still not on track. The local police and military wanted bribes in exchange for cooperation. Not all of them were trustworthy.

There was nothing to interrupt Narazaki's view. He'd climbed a small hill and sat on the gravel at the top. *I've come far,* he thought. Narazaki still wasn't sure what he wanted to do with his life. When he closed his eyes, he saw the bodies of women from the cult. He'd escaped nothing. But still, he had decided to move forward.

Narazaki was already quite tan.

"What are you doing?" a girl called out to him. School had ended. Maybe she'd followed Narazaki from the office.

She was a thirteen-year-old they'd taken into their care three months ago. At first she hadn't talked at all, but then she gradually began to open up.

"I'm looking far away," Narazaki told her in English. He had begun learning English. He was shocked at how slowly he improved, but he also got the feeling that learning another language would let him be born anew.

Language was at the root of every person, after all.

"You look sad," the girl said.

Narazaki smiled bitterly. He couldn't let this girl worry about him. He forced a smile. "I was thinking about things from a long time ago."

"A long time ago?"

"Yes." Narazaki nodded. "About a country far away."

The girl ran down a path, stopped, and called Narazaki. He stood up. The path the girl had taken was muddy and seemed dangerous. Narazaki tried to stop her.

"It's harder that way."

The girl turned around. A ray of light struck her as she stood atop the vast earth.

"It's fine."

She seemed to be smiling slightly. If it was truly a smile, it was the first time she'd done that since Narazaki met her.

Narazaki ran after her. *She's right*, he thought. *Even though it's a bit muddy, you'll be fine.*

"Wait," Narazaki said. He chased after her. The sun had begun to sink past the horizon. "Let's go together."

Narazaki offered his hand to the girl. She gripped it lightly.

References

Vēda no shisō, from *Nakamura Hajime senshū [ketteiban]*, 8, Nakamura Hajime, Shunjūsha, 1989.

Buddha no kotoba, Suttanipāta, translated into Japanese by Nakamura Hajime, Iwanami Shoten, 1984.

Hokekyō (Gendaigoyaku daijyō butten 2), Nakamura Hajime, Tokyo Shoseki, 2003.

Hanyashinkyō Ta (Gendaigoyaku daijyō butten 6), Nakamura Hajime, Tokyo Shoseki, 2004.

Shakason no shōgai, Nakamura Hajime, Heibonsha, 2003.

Zen maindo begināzu maindo, Suzuki Shinryū, Sanga, 2012.

Zōho shinban shūkyo tagen shugi (Problems of Religious Pluralism), John Hick, translated into Japanese by Mase Hiromasa, Hōzōkan, 2008.

Magudara no Maria ni yoru fukuonsho (The Gospel of Mary of Magdala: Jesus and the First Woman Apostle), Karen L. King, translated into Japanese by Takao Yamagata and Mitsugu Shinmen, Kawade Shobō Shinsha, 2006.

Genten Yuda no fukuonsho (The Gospel of Judas), translated into English by Rodolphe Kasser and others, translated into Japanese by Fujii Rumi and others, National Geographic Japan, 2006.

Nō wa sora yori hiroi ka (Wider than the Sky: The Phenomenal Gift of Consciousness), Gerald M. Edelman, translated into Japanese by Fuyuki Junko, Sōshisha, 2006.

Nō wa naze kokoro wo tsukutta no ka, Maeno Takashi, Chikuma Shobō, 2010.

Ishiki to wa nandarōka, Shimojō Shinsuke, Kodansha, 1999.

Noma Hiroshi no kai kaihō 15 gō, Fujiwara Shoten, 2008.
Seibutsu to museibutsu no aida, Fukuoka Shinichi, Kodansha, 2007.

Seimei to kioku no paradokusu, Fukuoka Shinichi, Bungei Shunjū, 2012.

Nemurenakunaru uchū wa nashi, Sato Katsuhiko, Takarajimasha, 2008.
Uchū wa hontō ni hitotsu na no ka, Murayama Hitoshi, Kodansha, 2011.

Uchū ga hajimaru mae ni wa nani ga atta no ka? (A Universe from Nothing), Lawrence Krauss, translated into Japanese by Aoki Kaoru, Bungei Shunjū, 2013.
Shinsōban fukakuteisei genri, Tsuzuki Takuji, Kodansha, 2002.

Ryōshiryokugaku no tetsugaku, Morita Kunihisa, Kodansha, 2011.

Higgusu (The Particle at the End of the Universe: How the Hunt for the Higgs Boson Leads Us to the Edge of a New World), Sean Carroll, translated into Japanese by Tanimoto Masayuki, Kodansha, 2013.

Yasukuni mondai, Takahashi Tetsuya, Chikuma Shobō, 2005.

Yasukuni jinja, Ōe Shinobu, Iwanami Shoten, 1984.

Sensō wo shiranai hito no tame no Yasukuni mondai, Kamisaka Fuyuko, Bungei Shunjū, 2006.

Yasukuni sengo hishi, Mainichi Shinbun Yasukuni Reporting Group, Mainichi Shinbunsha, 2007.

Yasukuni jinja jinja honchō hen, PHP Kenkyūjo, 2012.

Kokka Shinto to nihonjin, Shimazono Susumu, Iwanami Shoten, 2010.
Tokyo saiban, Higurashi Yoshinobu, Kodansha, 2008.

Jūgun ianfu, Yoshimi Yoshiaki, Iwanami Shoten, 1995.

Nihongun "ianfu" seido to wa nanika, Yoshimi Yoshiaki, Iwanami Shoten, 2010.
[Shinjūwan] no hi, Handō Kazutoshi, Bungei Shunjū, 2003.

Furyoki, Ōoka Shōhei, Shinchōsha, 1967.

Taitero sensō kabushikigaisha (War on Terror, Inc.), Solomon Hughes, translated into Japanese by Matsumoto Tsuyoshi, Kawade Shobō Shinsha, 2008.

Sensō ukeoi kaisha (Corporate Warriors: The Rise of the Privatized Military Industry), P.W. Singer, translated into Japanese by Yamazaki Jun, Nippon Hōsō Shuppan Kyōkai, 2004.

Amerika no kyodai gunju sangyō, Hirose Takashi, Shūeisha, 2001.

Saiteihen no jūokunin (The Bottom Billion), Paul Collier, translated into Japanese by Nakatani Kazuo, Nikkei BPsha, 2008.

Enjo ja Afurika wa hatten shinai (Why Aid Is Not Working and How There Is Another Way for Africa), Dambisa Moyo, translated into Japanese under supervision of Kohama Hirohisa, Tōyō Keizai Shinpōsha, 2010.

Shokuryō terorizumu (Stolen Harvest: The Hijacking of the Global Food Supply), Vandana Shiva, translated into Japanese under supervision of Uramoto Masanori, with Takeuchi Seiya and Kanaizuka Tsutomu, Akashi Shoten, 2006.

Sekai no hanbun ga ueru no wa naze? Jean Ziegler, translated into Japanese by Takao Mayumi, Gōdō Shuppan, 2003.

Kokusai kōken no uso, Isezaki Kenji, Chikuma Shobō, 2010.

Rupo shigen tairiku Afurika, Shirato Keiichi, Asahi Shinbun Shuppan, 2012.

VICE Japan: *The Cannibal Warlords of Liberia, Prostitutes of God,* http://www.youtube.com/user/VICEjpch (URL cited 9/20/2014).

Fuminori Nakamura

was born in 1977 and graduated from Fukushima University in 2000.

He has won numerous prizes for his writing, including the Ōe Prize, Japan's largest literary award; the David L. Goodis Award for Noir Fiction; and the prestigious Akutagawa Prize. The *Thief*, his first novel to be translated into English, was a finalist for the *Los Angeles Times* Book Prize. His other novels include *The Gun*, *The Kingdom*, *Evil and the Mask*, *Last Winter, We Parted* and *The Boy in the Earth*.